MYSTERY
IN THE
SUNSHINE STATE

Florida short stories by
Florida's mystery writers

STUART KAMINSKY
Editor

PINEAPPLE PRESS, INC.

Inquiries should be addressed to:

Pineapple Press, Inc.
P.O. Box 3899
Sarasota, Florida 34230
www.pineapplepress.com.

Library of Congress Cataloging in Publication Data

Mystery in the sunshine state / [edited] by Stuart Kaminsky.
p. cm.
ISBN 1-56164-185-5 (pb : alk. paper)
1. Detective and mystery stories, American—Florida. 2. Crime—Florida Fiction. 3. Florida Fiction. I. Kaminsky, Stuart M.
PS648.D4M92   1999
813'.08720832759—dc21   99-33326
                                                CIP

First Edition
10 9 8 7 6 5 4 3 2 1

Design by Osprey Design Systems
Typesetting by Shé Sicks
Printed and bound by The Maple Press, York, Pennsylvania

To the memory of
JOHN D. MACDONALD

Contents

Introduction
ix

The Blue Highway
David Ash   1

The Handyman
E. C. Ayres   14

Good Night, Mrs. Chisholm
Wayne Barcomb   41

Sierra Reveals All
Nancy Bartholomew   52

Ghosts
David Beaty   65

The English Tourist
Edna Buchanan   89

The Great Persuader
Stanley Ellin   96

Flora Africana
DeLoris Stanton Forbes   114

Death by Pliers
Carolina Garcia-Aguilera   127

The Full Marty: A John Francis Cuddy Story
Jeremiah Healy   153

Reliable Witness
Stuart Kaminsky   189

The Case of Johnny Walker Black
David A. Kaufelt   195

Document of the Keys
Peter King   206

Machete
John Lutz   220

The Works
T. J. MacGregor   236

Framed for Murder
Harold Q. Masur   245

Instant Replay
Stuart McIver   264

Heartbreak Avenue
Billie Sue Mosiman   277

Midnight Pass: A House-Sitting Detective Story
Robert J. Randisi   289

Tahiti Junk Shop
Les Standiford   307

Heart Throb
Robert W. Walker   329

Hole in the Boat
Eric Wiklund   345

Author Biographies
355

Acknowledgments

The editors gratefully acknowledge the permission to reprint the following copyrighted materials.

"The Blue Highway" by David Ash. Copyright 1996 by David Ash. Reprinted by permission of the author.

"The Handyman" by E. C. Ayres. Copyright 1999 by E. C. Ayres. Reprinted by permission of the author.

"Good Night, Mrs. Chisholm" by Wayne Barcomb. Copyright 1999 by Wayne Barcomb. Reprinted by permission of the author.

"Sierra Reveals All" by Nancy Bartholomew. Copyright 1999 by Nancy Bartholomew. Reprinted by permission of the author.

"Ghosts" by David Beaty. Copyright 1999 by David Beaty. Reprinted by permission of the author.

"The English Tourist" by Edna Buchanan. Copyright 1997 by Edna Buchanan. Reprinted by permission of Don Congdon Associates, Inc.

"The Great Persuader" by Stanley Ellin. Copyright by Stanley Ellin. Reprinted by permission of Curtis Brown, Ltd.

"Flora Africana" by DeLoris Stanton Forbes. Copyright 1962 by DeLoris Stanton Forbes. Reprinted by permission of *Alfred Hitchcock's Mystery Magazine*.

"Death by Pliers" by Carolina Garcia-Aguilera. Copyright 1998 by Carolina Garcia-Aguilera. Reprinted by permission of the author.

"The Full Marty: A John Francis Cuddy Story" by Jeremiah Healy. Copyright 1999 by Jeremiah Healy. Reprinted by permission of the author.

"Reliable Witness" by Stuart Kaminsky. Copyright 1995 by Stuart Kaminsky. Reprinted by permission of the author.

"The Case of Johnny Walker Black" by David A. Kaufelt. Copyright 1995 by David A. Kaufelt. Reprinted by permission of the author.

"Document of the Keys" by Peter King. Copyright 1999 by Peter King. Reprinted by permission of the author.

"Machete" by John Lutz. Copyright 1999 by John Lutz. Reprinted by permission of the author.

"The Works" by T. J. MacGregor. Copyright 1990 by T. J. MacGregor. First published in *Sisters in Crime 2*, 1990. Reprinted by permission of the author.

"Framed for Murder" by Harold Q. Masur. Copyright 1977 by Harold Q. Masur. First published in *Ellery Queen's Mystery Magazine*, 1977. Reprinted by permission of the author.

"Instant Replay" by Stuart McIver. Copyright 1995 by Stuart McIver. Reprinted by permission of the author.

"Heartbreak Avenue" by Billie Sue Mosiman. Copyright 1995 by Billie Sue Mosiman. Reprinted by permission of the author.

"Midnight Pass: A Housesitting Detective Story" by Robert Randisi. Copyright 1999 by Robert Randisi. Reprinted by permission of the author.

"Tahiti Junk Shop" by Les Standiford. Copyright 1999 by Les Standiford. Reprinted by permission of the author.

"Heart Throb" by Robert W. Walker. Copyright 1995 by Robert W. Walker. Reprinted by permission of the author.

"Hole in the Boat" by Erik Wiklund. Copyright 1999 by Erik Wiklund. Reprinted by permission of the author.

Introduction

As I sit at my computer writing this, it is the end of January. Through my window I see bright sunlight on the very green leaves of the exotic tree outside. My windows are wide open. A slight wind rustles. If I move fifteen feet to the screened porch, I will look out at my yard and stand a good chance of seeing a hawk perched on the rusting volleyball post or an eagle swooping low over the creek hidden by dense bushes, out of which a family of armadillos occasionally wanders. The odds are even better, however, that I'll see a white heron.

I've lived in Florida a decade. It has snowed here only once in that time, very thinly and very briefly. My family and I make an annual New Year's Day pilgrimage to picnic on the beach ten minutes away to remind us of Januarys in the North.

I grew up in Chicago. My worries were of winter temperatures that froze my car and snows that blocked the streets. I was accustomed to it. I welcomed it. I wrote about it. The North is bleak in the winter, blistering in the summer. Those who were convinced they were tough stayed there, as did those who didn't feel they had much choice. Others stayed because they couldn't believe Paradise was open to them, while some who had tried living in perpetual summer and spring returned because they could not bear the sameness of seasons.

Millions of us have come here from the North and West and discovered that there is a price to pay for living in Paradise, and that price is the stuff dreams, nightmares, and mystery stories are made of. Florida is a lush flatland of surface beauty and hidden marshes of the human mind and spirit.

I live on a very quiet street with quiet, friendly neighbors and reasonably well-behaved kids. Three weeks ago, a fleeing bank robber drove down our street, realized there was a dead end ahead and pulled into my next-door neighbor's driveway. The police caught him as he hid in the bushes. He threw out his gun. We watched from our driveways, discussed it for a few minutes, and went back to work or play.

Florida is a state of contrasts.

Florida is a state of contradictions.

Florida is a state of mind.

For the mystery writer, that state of mind includes sandy coastlines; red tide; hurricanes; inland swamps; the wealthy Keys; Canadian and European tourists; retired elderly; natives in pickups who are often unkindly called rednecks; hustling, stereo-typical politicians; the crowded, automatic, massive theme parks of Orlando; the colossal noise and size of the Daytona speedway; the now-Hispanic city of Miami; gators (both real and those who play football in Gainesville); spring training; land speculation; boat people. . . . The list goes on. Retirees, tourists, writers, and speculators flock to Florida, but so too do drug smugglers, child abusers, and teen gangs who rob and kill each other and tourists. Ted Bundy made his way here. The most famous female serial killer in history, Aileen Wuornos, made her way here.

Florida has become a mecca for mystery writers. Elmore Leonard, Carl Hiaasen, James T. Hall, as well as the authors represented in this book, have helped to move the center of regional mystery writing to our state. Florida is ripe for the mystery: the promise of Paradise, the reality of broken dreams. The contrast between Paradise and consequences is, I repeat, fertile material for the mystery writer. When word went out that this book was being put together, I received dozens of unsolicited stories even after the decision had been made which stories would be included. Some unsolicited stories were terrible. Many were good. A few were very good.

The stories in this collection are generally in contrast to the established tradition of the noir mystery set in the big city. Those stories take place largely at night in the cynical jungle of the city, the shadows in the darkness. In many Florida tales, it is not only the darkness that should be feared but also the bright sunlight. The Florida mystery can be violent. Florida's killers kill on the highways and beaches in broad daylight.

There is no hiding from evil in these Florida tales.

The shark, the jellyfish, the alligator, the drug dealer shooting wildly, the kid with a knife and no conscience, the old man driven mad by broken dreams—they're all out there and they're very real.

There was a time when California was the mecca, the promised land of broken dreams that beckoned to mystery writers. California's mountains, coast, and tarnished Hollywood image have faded, replaced—at least for the present for mystery writers—by the humid, flat, hot promise of a peninsula Paradise, Florida, under whose sun lies as much intrigue and murder as California ever offered. Since the 1920s, there have been tales of crime set in a very vivid and often cynical New York or Chicago. There is hardly a city or town in the United States where a mystery novel or even a series of novels has not been set.

But as a related whole, the contemporary Florida mystery rules. This may change. There are a number of fine mystery novels set in Alaska and a few in Hawaii, but for now—from the oldest city in the United States, St. Augustine, to the new towns that pop up whole and bustling every month or two—Florida is the place to be and to write about.

John D. McDonald knew that, and for a long time he had the genre pretty much to himself. Now the literary offspring of John D. have taken to the computer and word processor to chronicle the ever-changing reality and fantasy that is Florida.

I love it here.

—Stuart M. Kaminsky

MYSTERY
IN THE
SUNSHINE STATE

The Blue Highway

DAVID ASH

I'd promised to take them to Disney World and that's what I was going to do, I thought, no matter what. The windshield wipers slapped back the rain as best they could. But at ninety miles an hour, even the stolen Pontiac's double-wide blades couldn't keep the water from building up on the glass. The road ahead smeared into a shimmering pool of headlights, road signs, and heat lightning, the divider line snaking under the left front fender. It was all I could do to keep her steady.

We came up hard on somebody's taillights, twin red saucers racing toward us through the blue shimmer like Klingon warships coming in for the kill. I jerked the wheel hard left. Rubber squealed on the wet pavement. There was a blinding burst of light. I closed my eyes for less than a second and saw stars dancing in space. The long blare of a horn faded behind us. Then there was nothing. Nothing but us and that blue shimmer and rain hissing through the tires. Pablo struck a match, his hand shaking. The shadows on his face looked eerie, like someone in a gangster move. He lit his cigarette, drew a deep breath and held it in.

"Close," he said and exhaled.

Billy and Gail were in the back seat and Billy just about had Gail's jeans unbuttoned. My driving never scared Billy. I watched them in the rearview mirror as long as I could, until more taillights came up. Billy had his other hand up under her Mickey Mouse T-shirt. The mouse was doing a hula dance. I pushed the old car up to ninety-five.

Billy was trying to work her jeans down while she tried to push him away. She caught my eyes in the mirror. I didn't look away this time. They were as blue as a hot blowtorch. We looked at one another a couple of seconds like two little kids having a staring contest. Billy still working at her jeans.

"Tell him to quit, Danny," she said.

But I didn't say anything. Billy was losing it big time, meteorite coming down, getting ready to burn up in the atmosphere. He didn't need to shoot that old lady. She would've given us the keys. I knew where this was headed. But I didn't know what to do about it.

Gail slapped Billy's face hard.

"Quit!" she screamed.

But he was as big and strong as a wild bull now. Billy and Gail, me and Pablo had been together practically since we were little kids. He grabbed her arms, laughing at her.

"C'mon," he said, like they were play fighting, "give me a quick one."

She struggled up, arms twisting, but he pushed her right back down.

The front left wheel caught the shoulder and the car rocked like a roller coaster, bouncing us up and down on the seats, till I wrestled it back up on the road. Easing her back in her lane. I looked in the mirror. Billy was still on top of Gail. She looked at me over his shoulder. Burning a hole through me with her X-ray vision.

"Let her go, Billy," I said.

Billy turned and looked at me hard but didn't stop. All worked up, his chest heaving. Not wanting to back down in front of Gail.

"I ain't askin' you again, Billy," I said. There was no getting around it. He was bigger than me. But I'd been in more fights than him and ten like him. I'd bust him up good and he knew it.

"We're just playing," he said, mumbling a curse as he started to get off her. Gail shoved him the rest of the way and yanked out from under his arm. She began pulling her jeans back up. Billy looked out his window, cursing to himself, ". . . just playing," he said again, "just playin' with you."

"What are you looking at?" Gail shouted at Pablo. "You want a quick one too?"

Pablo shrugged, "Sure, OK. . . ."

"Stop looking at her," I snapped.

"How 'bout you," she said, struggling with the last buttons on the fly. "Com' on, Danny, how about a quick one? You first."

Maybe Gail was getting nutso too.

"Knock it off, Gail," I said. "Try to enjoy the ride."

"Right," she said.

She tucked her shirt in, sat back and folded her arms. Watching me in the mirror for a second, angry as hell, bumping the post under my seat with her shoe. Then she looked out her window, out at space, the Milky Way, Mars or Pluto or someplace.

A small tick began somewhere deep in the motor. Somewhere in the crankcase, I was thinking. I eased the accelerator back slowly. We were on our way, all right, but I was wondering if we'd ever make it. It wasn't like our kind to make it. I went all the way back down to eighty-five and the big engine was smooth again. Floatin' along on space warp cruise, drifting through the galaxy.

Everyone but me slept on late into the morning. They looked like a bunch of kids all curled up in that big car. The highway began to fill with vacation campers, RVs, and station wagons. We came to a service plaza with a round water tank painted like a big orange. I slowed down to exit, letting the big Pontiac coast off the turnpike. The transmission whined softly beneath the big hump in the floorboard.

I tried to nudge everybody awake. Gail knocked my hand away and Pablo jerked up like the devil was after him. I had to shake Billy a long time to get him to come to, but finally I got them all awake and off to the john to get cleaned up. Meanwhile, I turned from the lobby into the Roy Rogers restaurant to get a bite to eat and wait for them. I picked up a tray and got into the line with some burly truck drivers playing grab ass with one another. The one in front of me, with his sleeves rolled up to his shoulders and thick hair down to his knuckles, was telling dirty jokes to his buddies. They all laughed a lot.

I hadn't eaten since we left Homestead so I was pretty hungry. I piled on the milky scrambled eggs and took a dozen of the little sausagettes, scooped on three clumps of the greasy tater tots, jammed a couple extra biscuits onto the plate, and slid two cartons of orange juice inside my jacket.

"Kind of hungry, ain't ya, Slick," said the big trucker with the hairy arms. Like it was his business or something.

"Oink, oink," he said, snorting like a pig. I didn't say anything but he kept looking back and forth between me and his buddies, grinning, like he was gonna make a joke out of me. I'd seen plenty like him before. Go out of their way to mess with you. Poke fun at you, trying to start something up.

I took a far booth next to the window to get away from the truckers and so I could watch the parking lot. Pablo, Billy, and Gail came in and went through the line with their trays. When they started walking over towards my booth, I noticed that Gail had put on a red bikini top. She looked pretty good. But we were supposed to be trying to lay low, not draw any attention to ourselves if we could help it. She glanced over at me once and turned away. Practically everybody in the place watched her cross the restaurant.

She was moving along trying to swish her way across the floor. She didn't swish too good but I said to myself, *Uh oh, here comes trouble.* Hairy arms was watching too. He and his buddies were jacking their jaws and grinning at her as they forked grits into their big mouths. The one with the yellow Maule Concrete cap wiped his flat nose with the back of his flannel shirt and burst out laughing when Monkey Arms whispered in his ear.

"How come you're wearing that?" I asked, holding a fork full of scrambled eggs in mid-air. Juice dripped onto the plate. I guess I couldn't help but look at her too. Like we were all on remote control. "I ain't speaking to you, fucker," she said, point blank. She jammed her fork deep into the hash browns and swallowed a big glob.

Billy looked at me and his eyes widened. I looked at Pablo but he was shoveling food down his mouth, acting like everything was OK. Billy looked like he was expecting me to do something. Smack her over the head with my tray, maybe.

"Gail," I said, "you run around in a top like that and people'll take notice. We'll stand out." I wiped a spec of grease from my chin with a napkin and looked at it. "It ain't smart."

"Smart?" she asked. She tossed her hair back, glanced at Billy, then back at me.

"That's right," I said.

"You mean like Godzilla brains here?" she asked, pointing a pat of butter at Billy, then squashing it on her toast.

A family of pale Northerners came in wearing matching Mickey Mouse caps. The dad was carrying a little video camera. The mother had a big diaper bag hung over her shoulder and a chubby little brat on her hip, squalling and hollering to high heaven.

Gail crunched off a bite of toast, chewing it noisily, tapping the formica table with the flat of her spoon, *ding-ding-ding*, while the rest of us tried to eat. Billy put his hand over her spoon but then she banged the table leg with her foot. *Clang-clang-clang*, till I couldn't take it anymore. I stomped the top of her flip-flops with the heel of my boot. She went pale and her cobalt-blue eyes flickered and began to water and the corner of her lip quivered. I thought she was going to cry.

But she didn't. She held it in. She hung onto it. Her blond hair shined under the lights. I don't think even I could have held it in that good. It made me feel bad inside. She could have leaned over that table and kissed me or whipped out a pistol and shot me dead and it would have been the same. She sat there holding it in.

I was hoping that we'd make it in and out of the Roy Rogers restaurant with the least bit of problems. Have a breakfast like all the regular people. Drink some coffee. Eat a piece of pie maybe. Then be back on the road and out of there. Seemed simple enough. But when I saw Monkey Arms get up and head our way, I knew nothing in life would be simple for us again. Nothing ever had, I guess. Not that I could remember. Things came looking for me. Maybe it's the way I look. I'm not sure. Maybe it's something more. Something out of my reach. Like the blue shimmer on the road last night. No matter how fast you drive, you ain't never going to get there.

He put his big hand on my shoulder.

"Cleaned your plate to a shine, didn't ya, Slick? How you doing there, young lady?" he said, turning to stare at Gail.

Pablo and Billy didn't look, just kept on eating like they were supposed to. Let me do the talking.

He ran his black eyes over her slowly. Gail didn't say anything. She slid the salt and pepper shakers back and forth across the smooth table top. One of the shakers fell off the edge but Monkey Arms snatched it out of the air before it hit, spilling salt onto the floor.

"Gotcha," he laughed. He leaned closer and his eyes settled on Gail's red bikini top. "Say, little lady, where you headed?"

"She's not headed anyplace. She's with us, mister," I said, straightening.

"Shut up, Slick." He didn't take his eyes off Gail.

Gail looked at him, a glint of cobalt returning, trying to force a smile. She was scared, all right, down deep scared about this whole mess. But maybe she was going to try to play it through to the end. Get this gorilla off our backs. She clenched her hands in front of her.

"That's my rig out there," Monkey Arms said, pointing out the plate glass window. "The big PETER-bilt," he said, laughing, holding his Peterbilt buckle.

"Peter-built, get it."

He slapped the table with the flat of his hand and the plates jumped. Laughing his head off.

I was trying to tell her with my eyes to hang in there a little longer.

"Why don't you join up with me, little lady," he said. "Let me show you the wonders of the road." He roared like it was the funniest thing he'd ever heard.

"We don't want no trouble—"

"Shut up, Slick," he said, putting his hand on her shoulder, leaning close to Gail's ear. "You come out to the truck, give Peter a quick kiss," he whispered. "I won't tell the manager about the orange juice Slick stole and put in his jacket."

Gail glanced up at him, then at me, eyes narrowing. His monkey hand was edging toward her red bikini top, that big shit-eatin' grin.

"Get your fucking hand off her," I said.

I started to push Monkey Arms' hand away, but something hit my throat and began to squeeze. I felt myself being lifted right out of the booth.

"Don't like to tell little punks like you something twice," he said.

His thumbs sank deep in my throat as I tried to breathe. I tried to pull away but he was too strong. Tried to punch at his face, swinging in the air but he held me strong and tight and hard and almost lifted me off the ground. I needed air. The room tilted sharply and turned about me. I couldn't suck a breath of air and felt myself sinking and turning, gasping for air as the ceiling and fluorescent light panels turned and turned. I couldn't breathe. I saw my fingers stretched out in front of me like a man drowning.

Then suddenly fresh air rushed into my throat, filling my lungs. I bent over to cough, spitting, looking at the tiny grains of spilled salt on the white vinyl tile. There was a loud wail behind me. I could just make out Monkey Arms whirling and spinning about, yowling and grabbing at his backside. Pablo's pearl-handled knife was stuck deep in his ass. He spun 'round, back and forth trying to reach for it, knocking chairs and tables every which way, as Gail kicked at his shins. Pablo lept on his back and bit down on his ear. Clawing at his eyes. Chrissakes, it was beautiful. I staggered about like a drunk man trying to get my bearings.

Billy took a lick at Monkey Arms with his right fist but missed and jammed Pablo across the forehead, knocking him into the booth next to where the pale Northerners were sitting. The father began taking pictures with his little video camera, the kid clapped and squealed. My head cleared a bit and I straightened back up. But the fun was up real quick. A chair raised up over Billy's head. The other truckers were on us quicker than stink. The no-neck guy with the flat nose jerked Pablo off Monkey Arms, shaking him like a rag doll. Slapped him across the face.

People ducked as pieces of chair whirled over their heads. The little kid stopped clapping and watched bug-eyed as Billy fell to the floor like a fifty-pound sack of potatoes. Flat Nose still clenched a chair leg in his hand. He drew way back, drawing a bead like he was gonna bash Billy's head in.

"Danny, stop him," Gail screamed.

Some things you got to do, some you don't. We had made a lot of bad decisions up to now but, for the life of me, I couldn't see a way around this one.

I pulled the revolver out from the back of my belt and fired in the air. It was damn loud. Everybody but the little kid and his pop froze like statues. The little kid clapped like the show had begun again. My ears rang from the blast.

I held the gun locked tight with both hands. Pointing at Flat Nose. "Put it down, mister."

He lowered the chair leg slowly.

"Everybody get the goddamn hell down on the floor!" I screamed.

Gail moved behind me. I shuffled over to Billy and gave him a hand up. He and Pablo both staggered a bit as we headed for the door.

"Go on now. You'll be all right," I said. "Help 'em get in the car, Gail. I'll be out in a second."

Billy, Gail, and Pablo pushed their way out the double-glass doors. A man in Gargoyle sunglasses and his pretty wife stopped drinking their fresh orange juice in the gift shop and watched them stagger through the lobby.

"You fellas get down on the floor and put your hands behind your heads and maybe I won't shoot you," I said, sighting down the barrel of the .38 at the three bozos who were responsible for all this. They moved pretty fast for big guys.

"You ought to get some kind of aggression counseling, mister. I know it did me a world of good," I said, shaking the gun in Monkey Arms' face. He just moaned, holding his backside.

I could see the black fry cook through the service window with the phone in his hand, figured I only had seconds to get out of there. Aimed the blue steel revolver towards the cardboard cut-out of Roy Rogers next to the register and squeezed.

Ka-BOOOOM.

The gun lept in my hands. The second shot was louder than the first. Roy had a hole in his chest the size of an Indian River grapefruit. Vapors hissed from a steam cart parked behind Roy. The Yankee zoomed in with his mini-cam as I scooped the cash out of the register. Everybody gave me a clear path as I ran for the door.

Outside I was hit by a hot blast of humid air; the bright sunlight hurt my eyes. I stuck the gun back behind my belt and tried to walk casual-like for the Pontiac. My throat hurt bad and I knew that Billy was banged up too. Gail backed the car out of the slot.

"Get in, Danny," she shouted.

She yanked the shifter into drive as I got in the passenger side, pulling the door shut behind me on the roll. The big Pontiac laid rubber, smoking for thirty feet.

"Easy, Gail, don't blow the rod," I said and put my head back on the seat for a second. I shut my eyes and felt the rumble of the big V-8 growl.

Gail turned off the turnpike three miles down the road. Followed a gravel track along the perimeter fence a couple hundred yards, then ducked in behind a grove of melaleuca trees. We sat there for forty minutes not saying nothing to each other, watching half a dozen troopers speed by us. Then Gail started the engine with a roar, cut the wheel to the right, and busted through a cow gate behind the grove.

The car bucked and rocked through the wet grass across a pasture. The back end slid back and forth as she turned sharply around rocks and holes. Then it lifted high, climbing a small rise, and we almost went airborne, suspended above our seats. Mud sprayed over the hood as the car squatted, jerking us forward, then bottomed out down into a slew of muck and cow pies. But she kept the engine revved, the wheels straight, and we swam right through. Damn, she was good and I was proud of her.

We drove down back-country roads lined with big water oaks hung with Spanish moss. There were many ponds for the cattle, and small lakes and long golden fields stretched between thick groves of palmettos. Snow egrets waded slowly through cane marshes sparkling under the morning sun. A pair of boys in straw hats fishing off a rickety bridge waved at us like they knew us and Billy tried to wave back. The boards clacking rhythmically under our tires.

The sun was going down by the time we stood in front of the gates to the Magic Kingdom. We stood out front staring a long time at the towers of the Cinderella Castle. Pablo looked mesmerized. We'd seen pictures before. But pictures weren't the same. Then we took the Mike Finn keel boat across the lake to Main Street. Billy's eyes were wide and he didn't look like he was feeling any more pain. Pablo said it didn't look real. It was hard to tell what Gail was thinking.

The lights on Main Street were just coming on as I handed each of them their part of the money I'd stolen from the Roy Rogers restaurant. The stores were kind of expensive but we bought some crazy clothes, funny hats, and souvenirs and headed straight for Space Mountain. I'd been on carnival rides but I'd never been on something like that, flying through dark, who knows how fast.

After that we went everywhere. Pirates of the Caribbean, the Swiss Family Tree House, Splash Mountain, you name it—as long as it wasn't some little kid thing, we went there. We saw mechanical parrots talking and chirping, and goofy little dolls from all over the world singing in their own languages. We saw a guy dressed up like Lincoln telling us about our country, went on an African Jungle Cruise, and traipsed around Huck Finn Island. We ate chicken for dinner in some place with huge stuffed bears singing and dancing and a moosehead on the wall talking and winking at us.

At 20,000 Leagues Under the Sea, the water was the same color as around Key Largo, where my old man was a commercial fisherman. The only thing I remember about him was that blue water and him describing Disney World and how he was going to take me there someday. I used to close my eyes real hard and try to remember what he looked like. I wished I had some way to get a message to him, tell him I'd finally made it.

After we came out of the Haunted Mansion, I noticed that Mickey Mouse had been following us, pretending to be just hanging around, keeping the kids entertained. I'd already seen him once, checking us out from the dock of the Jungle Cruise. I was excited then and hadn't thought much of it. But just as a precaution I'd taken the gun out from under the back of my shirt, put it slowly over the side, and let it sink into the dark water.

He disappeared for a while, but somewhere near Tomorrowland, I spotted Mickey again and knew they were closing in on us. I went up to Billy and told him he was going to have to split up from us. Go his own way now. He looked at me and started to cry. I'd never seen Billy cry. He told me he'd never meant to hurt that old lady, it'd just happened somehow. I told him I believed him but it didn't make any difference anymore. It was my fault.

My fault for not keeping a better eye on things. My fault for letting him bring the gun. But it didn't matter anymore. No matter how we felt about it now, it didn't matter, that wouldn't bring her back to life. Billy started bawling real hard and I hugged him like he was my brother. I told him he'd have to get a hold of himself. I told him we were being followed and that he'd have to make a break for it on his own, try to make it to Mexico or Argentina, someplace they wouldn't look for him.

"All right," he said.

He straightened up, looked towards Gail, but she lowered her head. Pablo stuck his hands in his pockets, tried to smile, then turned away.

"All right, then. I'm out of here." He wiped his nose. "Mexico it is."

He stepped back, stumbled a little, and tried to wink, but his eyes were glassy and wet. There was a deep, delayed explosion overhead, then the whoosh and crackle of bursting rockets as they began the fireworks.

"Pretty, ain't it?" I said, pointing at the sky and the banners flying from atop the Cinderella Castle.

He looked up at the colors. Another rocket exploded. He gazed around the Magic Kingdom a moment and tried to smile.

"It's really something," he said.

Then he turned and disappeared into the crowd.

It was about eleven or so, I guess. Fireworks were still going off everywhere. We were getting off the Thunder Mountain Railroad. Mickey, Goofy, Minnie, and Donald were waiting for us at the station. Mickey jerked me into some judo hold while Donald patted me down for weapons. Almost everybody was watching the sky;

only a few little kids noticed and pointed, tugging at their mothers' dresses as Mickey, Goofy, Minnie, and Donald swept us away.

They shoved us through a secret door into a little room where they handcuffed us. The cops took their huge heads off, sweating and cursing the heat. They told us to sit on the bench and keep quiet until the van showed up.

Mickey stepped out of his outfit and stood there in his BVDs and shoulder holster, drinking a Coca-Cola while his partners got dressed.

"Say," he asked, looking at us, "there were four of you. Where's your friend?"

"Dunno," I said.

We all shrugged and shook our heads.

He grinned, touched his hairy belly, and looked at his watch.

"Awright, awright, we'll find him, don't worry."

When the van came to carry us away, we went down a back alley filled with wires snaking all over and huge cables humming away. They had to keep us out of sight, I guess. The fireworks were over and we could hear the people heading back to the parking lot. I wondered what they'd do with the old Pontiac. I tried to put the bad things out of my mind. Tried not to think what they'd do to us this time.

We hadn't slept for quite a while. Pablo put his head on the armrest. Gail leaned against my shoulder and fell asleep. I stroked her long blond hair and felt myself drifting, drifting off into the galaxy someplace with Klingon saucers shooting past castles and snow-capped mountains. From somewhere I heard that goofy music from the little dolls all singing at once in all the languages of the world, saw the little hula girls shaking their hips, dolls everywhere, dancing in space, singing in Spanish now. I wondered if Billy was going to like it in Mexico. 🝰

The Handyman

E. C. AYRES

J ust because my seventh husband drowned, same as my fourth and second, doesn't mean I did it!" complained Vera, as her attorney Sonny Buenaventura escorted her quickly out of the courthouse and across the lawn, through a grove of Spanish moss–draped oaks, and into the waiting brown Lincoln Town Car. I reserved opinion and watched Tom Braithwaite, the crack local reporter from the *Weekly Beach Bugler*, furiously taking notes. Maybe he saw himself getting a Pulitzer for his weekly gossip column in "News from the Neighborhood." He claimed he had a sixth sense: if so, it was the only one that actually worked right, as he'd once confided to his gin-and-rummy partner (at least for the gin part) Freddy the Showboat, who'd immediately told me. If it's secrets you want to keep (or anything else, for that matter), don't tell Freddy about it.

Freddy had gotten his name because he used to mop floors at the Showboat Restaurant on Ulmerton Road up in Largo, before they finally tore it down. "It was a great place, Ernie," he used to tell anyone who'd listen (he called everyone Ernie). "They did

Oklahoma there once, starring Syd Charisse. I watched from backstage. You shoulda seen that gal dance."

You're probably saying, Wait a minute, isn't Sid Charisse a guy? If you are, you're too young to know Bo Diddley, and don't waste my time. You're also probably saying, So who's Ernie? The real Ernie was Freddy's vaudeville partner, back in the old days when he was actually out there tripping over the footlights. Anyways, my name is Jimmy Boyle, I'm a legal investigator (which is the real name for a P.I. in these parts), and this story isn't about Tom Braithwaite or Freddy. It's about Veronica Jones, or Vera for short, and all her dead husbands.

What really got everybody riled up this time around was Judge Gibbs, the same judge who had a nasty misogynistic habit of refusing to grant restraining orders to battered wives "until or unless they wind up dead," and who had fined me more than once for contempt of court, which in his case I certainly had plenty. What he'd done this time was insisted there was no grounds for refusing to give Vera her late husband Alfred Shuttlesworth's insurance benefits to the tune of a half million just because she kept marrying guys who couldn't swim. And so what if his wife of two months just took the insurance out on him two weeks before? "That don't prove nothin'," as the learned and beneficent judge put it. So saying, he also gave her the Town Car and the house on 31st Avenue, right on the bay. When Vera's former, still-bereaved stepdaughter Shelley deigned to object, in rather shrill tones right in the middle of the courtroom, Judge Gibbs slapped her with a $500 fine, her lawyer with another, and court was adjourned for cigars and coffee.

The judge had a lunch appointment, it turned out, with none other than Vera Jones, formerly Shuttlesworth. It was Tom Braithwaite who saw them together at the Shamrock Bar on Shore Drive, so dark inside you could hardly see yourself, which is probably the whole idea. Unfortunately for them, some fool waitress lit a candle on the table while the judge was busy groping Vera, and before his honor could snuff it out, he was spotted. Tom had the good sense, for once, to call me. Having nothing better to do, and owing the judge a return favor or two for his human kindness and public sensibilities, and having once been treated with reasonable kindness and respect by Alfred Shuttlesworth, Vera's most recent husband (who, regrettably, hadn't asked me for my opinion before marrying Vera, much to his demise), I decided to see for myself what was going to happen next.

I entered the bar and pushed my way through the smoke to where Judge Gibbs and Vera were in intimate conversation. You just had to wish you had a wire sometimes—or better yet, a wireless. Anyway, I nodded at Tom Braithwaite, who was beside himself in a corner booth trying to get up nerve to use his camera, walked over to the table, pulled up a chair, and sat down.

"Howdy, Yer Honor," I said. "What's up?"

The judge blinked at me, startled, and his expression changed quickly from hand-in-the-cookie-jar guilt to righteous indignation.

"Boyle, what the hell are you doing here? This is none of your damn business, so you can just get out."

"I don't think so," I told him. "This is a public place over which you don't hold jurisdiction, and I just got here." I turned to Vera, who was trying to disappear through the floor. "So, Miz—er, what? Jones again?—who's next?" I grinned at the judge. "Hizzoner here, with any luck?"

She tried to slap me, but her aim was lousy and she knocked the candle over instead, plunging us into temporary darkness, which caused the judge's own ill-timed roundhouse thrown in my general direction to also miss and take out two Harp lagers and a bowl of chips. At which moment, Tom Braithwaite, bless his soul, filled the light void with a flash photo the likes of which *National Inquirer* wouldn't believe.

"Give me that!" shouted the judge, making a dive for Tom's camera. "You'll be sorry you were ever born, fella!"

I reached out and grabbed his arm, holding him back. "I wouldn't do that, Judge. There's this little thing called the First Amendment."

"To hell with the damn First Amendment!" shouted Gibbs, making another lunge for Braithwaite's camera. "We're talking right to privacy here!"

"Can I quote you on that?" Tom asked, scribbling notes.

I laughed so hard I almost fell out of my chair. It seemed there were a lot of people, lately, determined to uphold one Sacred Right or another and cancel all the rest.

Luckily Freddy the Showboat (You remember Freddy? Hey, it's a small town.) just happened to have started his latest job as janitor at the Shamrock that week, and was Freddy-on-the-Spot with mop, pail, broom, dustpan, and a couple of lame light bulb jokes, like how many husbands does it take to screw in a light bulb, and so on. Vera tried to leave, tripped over my boot in the darkness—still blinded, no doubt, by Tom's flashgun—and wound up sprawled on the floor along with the chips and bottles and all of Freddy's cleaning paraphernalia.

That was enough for Judge Gibbs. "I'm out of here," he muttered, and headed for the door, Vera back on her feet and close behind him.

We had a lot of fun over that, me, Tom, and the bar patrons, elucidating on all the unmitigated gall, judicial corruption, how many blow jobs would it take to get a nice ruling like that, what else she had to offer him, like maybe fifty percent of the insurance money, and so forth. All of which became exceedingly moot when I was rudely awakened the next morning at six A.M. by a phone call from Tom Braithwaite.

"Boyle, you're not gonna believe this," he shouted.

"Then try me later," I suggested and started to hang up. I hate losing sleep over trivia.

It wasn't trivia. "Guess who just turned up dead!"

I woke up the rest of the way. "Don't tell me."

He chose to take me literally, said, "OK, bye," and I had to call him back and chide him for his lack of humor until he told me what he'd woken me up for at six A.M.

"It can't be," I protested. "They weren't even married yet!"

Truth has a way of twisting reality to suit the whims of the gods on Olympus, I suppose. Whoever they are. I told Tom I wanted to go to the crime scene first, then I'd meet him at the Pancake Platter on Beach Boulevard. They had decent coffee if you got there before nine. As I drove west on Gulfport Boulevard in my venerable Studebaker Avanti, that still had most of its parts, I turned on the AM-only car radio to scan the morning news shows. The air waves were full of it, but then they always were: Judge Marvin Gibbs, married, distinguished blah blah blah, was found dead on the beach in Gulfport at five A.M. this morning by some shell collectors.

The early morning sunlight slanted low over the trees along the eastern end of the bay, casting a bright orange glare on the water and the white sandy town beach east of the Casino. The Casino was basically an old-time dance hall. The area was taped off, the usual retinue of law enforcement vehicles parked along Shore Boulevard. I got as close as I could, but the detectives were busy with the forensics team, such as it was. I saw a cop I knew, Ruskin, one of the more off-color characters around town, best known for speed traps.

"You, Boyle, get lost," he suggested, placing his nightstick on my chest and leaning closer than his morning breath warranted.

Tom was waiting for me when I got to the coffee shop around the corner. "Here's the latest, you'll love this," he chortled, waving his cup for a refill. "The old bastard was found buck naked with a giant hard-on, whereas, according to the Gulfport Police, which has jurisdiction at least during working hours, the cause of death was drowning."

"Maybe he got drunk and fell off his yacht," I suggested.

"Yeah, sure," he scoffed. "While porking you-know-who on the flying bridge. Hey, how did you know he had a yacht?" he asked.

"Just a wild guess." I ordered coffee. It was time to join the rest of the world.

"He keeps it—kept it—right down the street at the marina," Tom went on. "Does make you wonder. I never knew Gibbs to go in for midnight swims," he added.

"Then again," I pointed out, "how well did you know Judge Gibbs?"

There was something else he'd gotten wind of as well. Apparently Vera had been seen in the frequent company of a new guy. A handyman type. "It goes back awhile, what I hear," Tom confided, with a glance at the walls, as though in search of ears. "And from what I hear, the kids are seriously pissed."

"What kids?"

"Vera's kids." That was interesting. I hadn't known she had kids. Nor seen or heard about any kids at the trial.

"She has three. All grown up now, more or less."

"Where are they now?"

"Who knows." He made a note. "I'll check that out though."

I walked back to the beach, where the donut brigade had given way to darker, more somber, and better dressed DLE types from up county. Obviously the authorities were pretty bent out of shape about this one. The coroner's wagon was just pulling away. Avoiding the still-vigilant Officer Ruskin, I strolled past Diane Marcoux's seasonal doll tableau in the front window of the Casino and ducked under the pilings on the bay side of the building. If they wouldn't let me near the crime site, I might as well take a walk and think things over. It was a lovely morning. The gulf breeze was warm, the sky pastel. A flock of great white egrets winged their way across Boca Ciega Bay, their dangling feet just skimming above the water. The great wading birds tilted their wings as though in salute and banked past eighty-year-old Tony Pavich on his daily swim through the shallow estuary waters over to the fancy condos at Tierra Verde and back, a good mile round trip.

Someone else was walking on the beach not far from the area where we used to pull shellfish out of the water by the netful. It was a man about five-foot-ten, balding and heavy-set, with tufts of blond hair above his ears. I'd seen him somewhere before. He was using one of those metal detectors, skimming the sand for treasure, but there was something odd about his movements. He didn't seem interested in nickels and dimes. He seemed to be searching for something specific, and all else went straight back into the sand, excepting, from the sporadic glint of sunlight in his hand, the odd silver coin. At one point he glanced around furtively, and I instinctively ducked behind one of the beach park gazebos. I wondered what he was looking for. I decided to find out.

He almost caught me once, looking back suddenly as though sensing someone was on his trail. I turned away just in time. He finally gave up, headed back to Shore Boulevard, and crossed the street to Sebastian's—Gulfport's authentically shaggy, tatter-thatched, open-to-the-elements beach-hut bar. I decided to join him there. The stool next to him was empty, and I slid onto it.

"Name's Jimmy Boyle," I told him, offering a hand which he seemed almost too startled to shake. "You must be new around here," I suggested.

He scowled. "Don Lewis. I work for a lady lives here."

"And who might that be?"

"Vera Jones," Lewis told me, with a look that implied a certain amount of unhappiness with that fact. So this was the infamous handyman Tom had heard about. Small town. Small world.

"I know the name," I said with a smile.

He smiled back, ruefully. "I'll bet," he said. "But I'll tell you what. Things aren't always like they seem."

I nodded and smiled, and we had a beer. I decided to do some digging as soon as I could get on-line. But first I wanted to find what the guy was looking for. We had another beer, exchanged business cards (I always carry a variety and gave him my lawn service version), then he left. As I watched him get into his brand new

Dodge pickup and drive off, I sauntered back out to the beach. The city parks department kept some grooming tools in a little storeroom next to the Casino. It was never locked, and I helped myself to a rake. Sometimes a rake is a better treasure-finder than a metal detector, which can be very unreliable.

I followed the general direction Lewis had taken and doubled back. Sometimes the tide throws you when you're trying to retrace your steps. I noted it was going out, which meant he may have misjudged and been looking too far out from the mean high-water mark. I marked a track five to ten feet further inland and went to work. In short order, I uncovered ten soda cans, six beer cans, two half dollars (which I pocketed), a trowel, and then, just as I was ready to give up, my rake hooked something metallic that flew up out of the sand and arched across the sky, glinting in the afternoon sun, disappearing into a sandcastle a couple of young kids were working on. I barely beat them to it: a watch with a gold Twist-o-flex band. It was a middle-grade, 18-carat gold-plated Benrus, the self-winding type, with an inscription on the back. It said "To Don with love from Vera." Very interesting. I didn't know of too many women who gave watches to their handymen. Slept with them, maybe. But gave watches?

I called a friend on the Gulfport police force and asked her to find out what she could about Don Lewis. Like whether he had a record, for example. My friend, Officer Jane Smithers, didn't owe me any favors. But she called me back an hour later.

"Jimmy?" She always sounded breathless. Granted, Jane had a bit of a weight problem, but I think it had more to do with the heat. Plus she had a few inner fires of her own burning, at times. One of which was a torch she'd carried for me a few years back. I'd requited it the best I could and we'd parted friends—barely. But like I said, she didn't owe me any favors. "It's me," she said. I hate it when people do that. Call you up, don't say who they are, and expect you to know, like they're your most intimate friend. Even if you haven't actually spoken to them in two years. Luckily, I recognized Jane's deep, windy voice.

"Hi, Jane," I said back. "Did you find anything?"

She chuckled. "Sure. What's it worth to you?"

I feigned shock. "Hey! Are you angling for a bribe? If so, that's entrapment."

"What entrapment? I'm angling for dinner. I'm off at six. You can meet me at the Hurricane. Make it seven."

"Fine," I said. "Long as you're out of uniform. I have a reputation to consider."

"The only reputation you have is a bad one, Boyle," she retorted with a throaty chuckle. "Anyway, don't worry about it. I'll hardly be wearing anything at all."

"That's what I was afraid of," I said and rang off.

I had another old girlfriend who did insurance. It just so happened Freddy the Showboat still cleaned her office. It was a useful combination. I made a couple of calls, drove out on 22nd Avenue to a small mini-mall at 49th Street, and parked around back. The timing was good—everyone was out except my aforementioned friend, Katie Donnelley, who was waiting for me.

I flirted with her for a while; she flirted back and flashed me her two-thousand-dollar porcelain smile. "Somebody bought some insurance," she finally informed me, "that you would not believe."

"Yeah," I said. "Vera. It was in the papers."

"Somebody else bought some insurance," she said with a secret smile. I hate secret smiles.

"So," I sighed. "What's it going to cost me?"

She looked angry, hurt, and indignant. "Nothing, nothing at all. Forget it, Boyle." She got to her feet. "I shouldn't even be talking to you about this stuff."

I reached up and touched her arm. "Come on, babe. I'm just doing my job, same as you."

"You don't have a job," she reminded me and showed me the door. I guessed I was going to have to rely on Freddy for this one. But first I had to find him and then wait until closing.

I drove home to my house off 28th Avenue, sank into my little heated spa, and turned on my laptop. I had access to certain data-bases, including the public records of the State of Florida. As I commenced my search, it became clear that the public record on Vera Jones and her past relationships, while extensive and inter-esting, was not necessarily incriminating. There was no mention of any handyman. The way I'd have to find out about him, I decided, was to ask the lady herself.

Vera Jones lived in a lovely waterfront neighborhood with brick streets and an assortment of restored Cracker and Spanish houses on long, thickly wooded lots that sloped to the protected mangroves at the water's edge. I'd gotten her address from the phone book. Some people just can't stand the prospect of not being found. Some people crave company, want to be sought out, and just about hang up a banner. Vera was one of them. Even after all the notoriety. Maybe she liked weird guys calling her up for dates, figuring no way they would be next. Maybe figuring all those dead guys were wimps. Who knows what delusions the male ego can concoct, given the opportunity. I thought about calling her and decided against it. I didn't want to give her the chance to prepare a story. I wanted to catch her off-guard.

The sun was low over the bay as I turned onto the narrow street that led to her house—a small white cottage on a cul-de-sac that ended at the water. I pulled up in front. A white Cadillac was parked in the small circular drive under a moss-hung oak. There was no garage: in typical Florida fashion it had long since been co-opted into a so-called "Florida" room, basically a converted garage that almost always resembled a, well, converted garage, with cheap jalousie windows, concrete floor with low-end carpeting, and maybe a bookcase or two, more likely a cheap entertainment center or wet bar.

Hers was better than most, brightly lit by a nice vinyl multi-paned window that reflected the late afternoon sunlight. The room was reverberating to 40's jazz much too loud to be from one of those radios people leave on to convince burglars with exceptionally low IQs that they're home when it's obvious they aren't. In this case, I was confident the lady was home. Next thing I needed to know was whether she was home alone.

There was no sign of the handyman or his Dodge truck. But it was possible he could arrive any moment, if there was any kind of ongoing assignation in progress. I walked up to the door and knocked.

She answered, her hair all frizzy, her face glowing as though it had been scrubbed. She was wearing a ratty bathrobe, hardly the image of the seductress queen. "Yeah, what?" she demanded, looking me up and down and dismissing me as a likely prospect for husband number eight.

"Hello, Vera," I said. "Remember me?"

Apparently she didn't, which was good. Maybe it had been too dark in the bar yesterday. Maybe she'd been too drunk to remember. Maybe she was lousy on faces. Her eyes narrowed. "I meet a lot of people. What do you want? It better not be about my husband's insurance again. I'm up to here with questions from you damn insurance people."

"I'm not from insurance," I assured her. "So relax. That's all history, as the court in its vast wisdom chose to decide yesterday. You won. Congratulations, by the way, on your ruling."

"You came here to my house to congratulate me?"

"That, and to ask you a question."

She cocked her head and seemed to make up her mind. Maybe that I was harmless. Many people make that mistake. "You may's well come in," she said, leading me straight to the converted garage that still smelled like a garage. "Everybody else does. Get you a drink?"

"You have fresh carrot juice?" I was only kidding, but it's fun to watch people's reactions. God help me the day somebody takes me up on it. I'd probably choke on the stuff and die of terminal health or something.

She merely laughed. "A comedian," she remarked. "I'm having white Zinfandel. Take it or leave it."

I took it, one of those mass production numbers that was only half bad. She perched on a Naugahyde barstool and we regarded each other. "You had a question," she reminded me.

"I assume you know about the judge?" I asked.

"You a cop?"

"Nope. And that wasn't my question. More like an introductory sidebar."

"God," she said. "A journalist."

"Former," I told her. "Now I'm a legal investigator." I handed her one of my cards. She glanced at it, just long enough to register my name, and tossed it aside.

"So, Jimmy Boyle," she said. "What's your game?"

"Tell me," I said, "about your friend."

She looked wary. "What friend?"

"The handyman," I replied and casually took the watch out of my pocket. "The one who owns this."

She stared at it angrily. "Where did you get that?"

"On the beach. He dropped it in the vicinity of where the judge's body was found. I'm sure it was just a coincidence, but the cops might not agree."

She stared, looked nervously back and forth from the watch to me, her jaw working back and forth as though trying to reconnect itself after taking a severe blow. I waited patiently.

"You have it wrong," she said, her voice choking. "Don wouldn't hurt a sand flea."

"Maybe not," I acknowledged, putting the watch back in my pocket. "But like I said, the cops may disagree. It doesn't look good, Vera. You and him, all these dead guys in between."

She looked like she couldn't decide whether to laugh or cry. She opted for the latter. "You don't know shit," she sobbed, groping for the Kleenex I offered her from a nearby box. "You are so wrong it's pathetic."

"So enlighten me. I'm a good listener."

"Donald Lewis," she sobbed, "which you should have known before coming here pestering me about him, so happens to be my sixth husband."

I'd missed that little item. Maybe because he wasn't dead. I stared. "And he lived to tell about it?"

She glared. "I don't find that funny, Boyle. In fact, I find that to be very rude, not to mention slanderous."

"Only if I tell the world," I said. "Don't worry, this conversation is private. Since I'm a licensed investigator, this conversation is protected under the Florida statutes of client privilege. Assuming I have a client."

"So who is your client?" she asked.

"Ah," I said. "Good question. That remains to be seen."

She frowned and regarded me like a side of beef. "All right," she said. "What are your rates?"

"Forty an hour. Plus expenses. You can afford it."

"Very funny. I won't see that insurance money for months, if ever."

"I'm sure you can wait. Me, I'm not so sure."

"Fine, I can pay you. Consider yourself hired and this conversation privileged."

I had to admire her savvy. "OK," I said, beginning to like her a little. "But before I commit to you—a dangerous proposition by all accounts—the next question is, to do what?"

"Do what?" she exclaimed, as though it was obvious. "Find out who killed Marvin, what else?"

"Marvin?"

"Judge Gibbs. Somebody killed him, and it wasn't Don."

"Maybe it was you."

She took that with surprising aplomb. "They haven't charged me yet," she shrugged. "But I guess they will, if they can make a case. But why would I kill him? He's a nice guy."

"He sure was nice to you."

"Last I heard that ain't a crime."

"And did you have to go for drinks right after the trial?"

"It ain't a crime to celebrate."

"Can they make a case against you?"

She shrugged. "I doubt it. What worries me is Don. If they put two and two together like you did, they may make a case against him."

"They may be interested in him in regards to Shuttlesworth as well. You were protected by your friend the judge on that one, but I don't think the cops were wise to this ongoing relationship of yours. It does look kind of suspicious."

She shrugged. "We're friends, is all. Just because we couldn't live together doesn't mean we don't get along. He helps me around the house, odd jobs and such."

"Right," I said. "Odd jobs. A regular handyman."

Her eyes flashed. "You want the job or not?"

I thought it over. If I accepted her as a client, it put me in the awkward position of having to protect her. The way things stood, I'd rather bust her. But a job is a job, as my lawyer friends like to say. I told her I'd think about it. Maybe I'd get a better offer. Such as from one of her kids. Tom had told me she had a few from various former marriages. But when I mentioned this, she didn't take it well at all. She stared at me in sudden recognition. "Hey, wait a minute. You're that sonuvabitch from the bar!"

"That wasn't really very smart, Vera. The bar. I mean, if you wanted to screw the judge, at least bring him back here. Or go with him on his yacht. He does have a yacht, I hear. Or rather, did."

"You slimeball!" she shouted. "How dare you!"

"I don't know," I said. "I amaze myself sometimes."

"Get out!" she screamed and shoved me in the direction of the door, spilling my Zinfandel. I didn't care about the Zinfandel, but it was a shame to have to leave already. I was actually beginning to like her. She had spunk.

I called Don at the number on his card, told him I had the watch and that I had some questions about his former marriage. He agreed to meet me at nine at the rooftop bar of the Hurricane Restaurant in Pass-a-Grille, where I was having dinner. It was a balmy evening, and the sun was just setting out over the gulf when I reached the little colony at the southern end of St. Pete Beach. It was nearly seven, time for my date with Officer Jane Smithers of the Gulfport Police. I went up to get a table, but she was already there. Dressed in a cute but way-too-tight satin blue mini, she waved at me with both hands from over near the bar. It was hard to miss her.

"So," she said when I got over to her table, "what'll you have?" What she was having was a very large margarita.

"What've you got?"

She looked coy and I knew she had me. I smiled and waved the waitperson over. She also wore hardly anything. I ordered a coffee.

Since I was technically unemployed, and also in need of whatever information Jane possessed, I figured there was no harm in giving her my own edited version of the case so far. She saw it as open and shut. "Look what you got," she pointed out, typically breathless. "First you got basically another dead husband for Vera Jones."

"But no proof," I mentioned.

"Yeah, but there's a helluva lot of circumstantial. Now this dead judge, in flagrante. I mean, it doesn't look good."

"No proof I know of there either. Unless you have some." I could tell she was holding something back. I decided not to mention just yet a certain person who was not only Vera's handyman but also her former husband. Apparently they were still pretty cozy. And yet somehow it didn't seem as clear-cut as all that. Like Jane's mini, something didn't quite fit.

"So," I reminded her. "What've you found out?"

She grinned and sipped her margarita. "I were you, I'd watch out for Shelley Shuttlesworth, and pass it on."

"That's news?"

She shrugged, then told me the rest, which was news. "Right now there is an open investigation. Regarding the late lamented judge. I can't talk about it. Except to say some people aren't what they seem."

I thought about the handyman. "That's it?"

"That's it. Sorry."

I looked at my watch. "Oh, well, that's the way it goes sometimes. I'm sorry too. Well, gotta go." I got to my feet.

She looked disappointed, not to mention annoyed. "Why? You hardly just got here. The night is young."

"And so are you," I assured her. "Unlike me. I've had a long day. Tomorrow is gonna be even longer."

"Assuming you live that long," she remarked curtly. I decided she was mostly kidding, but not entirely.

"Rain check?" I cajoled her, as I paid the check and got to my feet.

"Sure," she said, lighting a cigarette. "Rain check." We shook hands, I kissed her cheek and walked away. I made sure she wasn't following me and took the stairs up to the rooftop bar.

Lewis arrived ten minutes early. He spotted me and waved me over to a table near the corner. "OK," he said. "Where's my watch?"

"Not so fast," I responded. "Maybe there's a reward."

He laughed. "You P.I.s. Vera told me about you. Said she hired you to find out what happened to the judge. That right?"

"Nope," I said. "Haven't taken the job yet."

"Why not? Waiting for a better offer?" He was smarter than he looked, which was something to think about.

"You have one?" I asked, ordering an orange juice. Bars always have orange juice.

His look was inscrutable. Maybe he wanted to kill me. Maybe he wanted to hire me. "Me and Vera are old friends," he admitted. "She hires you, I'm with her. Did she or didn't she?"

"Not yet." I produced the watch but pulled it back when he reached for it. "What were you doing on the beach last night, Lewis?"

"Looking for Gibbs," he admitted right off.

My fresh-frozen reconstituted deconcentrated juice arrived. I took a sip, winced, and regarded him closely. "So you knew she was with him?"

"Look, I didn't kill that asshole, and neither did Vera. I was trying to warn him."

I raised my right eyebrow half an inch and put my glass down. "You wanted to warn the judge?"

"That's right."

He was either more brazen than I'd thought, or he was telling the truth. "About what?"

"About a threat Vera'd gotten yesterday. Right after the trial. His name was mentioned along with hers."

I looked at him thoughtfully. "And who do you think made this threat?"

He shook his head and looked convincingly distressed. "I don't know. I have some ideas but no proof," he said.

"Such as?"

"Her kids. From Dudley, Geoffrey, and Frank."

I blinked, fished for my Bic, and started writing on a napkin. "Husbands one, three, and five," he explained.

"You knew their names," I said in admiration.

"Yeah. Beverly is the oldest. Dudley's b-"—he caught himself—"daughter. She got together with Jerry and Gabrielle—"

"Gabrielle," I interjected, scribbling names and arrows and a diagram as fast as I could.

"Gabrielle is this young babe type, but dangerous—" he went on, looking nervously at my napkin. He waved at the waiter. "Can I have a beer? Make it a Bud," he said.

Dangerous babe, I wrote down.

"I know how that sounds, but she is. She's Frank's kid. Her father was a world-class shithead. Cokehead too. A real estate developer. Anyway, her and the other two—"

"—so Jerry is, what, Geoffrey's?"

"Yeah. A real weasel. Anyway, I knew Vera was going to meet him later, after they could ditch those—" He glared at me. "You guys. You and that reporter creep."

I almost laughed. "You realize this casts further suspicion on Vera, don't you? I mean, you weren't with her, you didn't see the judge—or did you?"

"Nope," he said miserably. "But I know she didn't do it. She's not that stupid!"

He had a point there. "And these kids of hers. Are they that stupid?"

He threw up his hands and almost knocked the beer tray out of the grasp of the waiter, who had come up behind him. The waiter caught the bottle in mid-air—accustomed to such foolery, no doubt—and set it down smartly on the table. "You shouldn't come up behind people," I admonished the waiter, "but nice save."

Don sighed. "Look, I'm not about to paste a label on anybody. It isn't my job or my right. But those kids have always been grasping, whining, greedy little shits—"

"Big shits now, I suppose," I interjected. You could almost like the guy.

"And then there's Shelley. She wasn't exactly happy about the outcome of the trial, as you know."

"Good point." I started a whole new diagram, mostly punctuated with question marks. But that would be such an obvious move, and the cops had to be at least smart enough to be questioning Shelley at this very moment. But from what I'd seen of her, murder was certainly possible. And if so, Vera wasn't exactly safe, and there probably wasn't a cop in Gulfport who'd go out of his way to protect her just now. Unless it was Jane.

"Excuse me a minute," I told Don and fished among my numerous jacket pockets for my cell phone. It was the most compact and lightweight model available and easy to lose, but I found it on the third try. "I have to make a phone call."

He was right with me. "Hey," he said, "if Shelley did the judge, she might go after my wife!"

"Your 'ex' wife," I corrected him. "But go ahead and call her first." I handed him the phone. "Tell her to lock the doors and windows, and don't answer the door. We'd better get over there, just in case."

He hesitated, then nodded and made his call. There was no answer. Either he was a great actor or was worried as hell. "We better go," he said. I folded my napkin of notes, put it in a vacant pocket, slapped a ten on the table, and we headed for the parking lot.

We got to my Avanti. When I reached for my keys, I saw Don's eyes looking behind me and widening perceptibly. I ducked and moved to the side in a single movement, spun, and tackled what turned out to be a tiger shark in sequins.

"Leggo, you sonuvabitch!" she shrieked as I pinned her to the Ford Bronco in the next parking space. She was a fiery-eyed brunette with short, straight hair and heavy make-up. She was dressed to kill. Maybe literally.

"Hey!" I heard a quavering male voice emanate from a car I'd noticed idling in the next parking aisle—a black Jaguar sedan. "Bev? You OK?" I could hear a woman's voice as well, in the background, shrill and contentious, drowning out the Jag's car radio. Gabrielle, I assumed.

Bev wasn't OK and let me know it, writhing and scratching and spitting. I revised my assessment of her more towards the panther category. Don had moved away to a safe distance. "Uh, Mr. Boyle, this is Beverly Chalmers. One of Vera's daughters."

I released her, with extreme caution. "You shouldn't come up behind people," I advised her.

"I just wanted to talk to you, you sonuvabitch," she snapped, checking her dress for smudges. Luckily, the Bronco was relatively clean. "That goes for you too, Lewis."

Beverly finished straightening herself out and glanced over at the Jaguar, which was revving its engine in nervous impatience. "Chill out, Jerry, I got it under control."

I believed her. If Gabrielle was the dangerous one, I didn't want to meet her.

"So," I said, "what can I do for you Miz, er, Chalmers?"

She dismissed Don and glared at me. "I understand you're a private detective," she said.

"Legal investigator," I corrected her.

"Whatever. We want to hire you. The three of us."

I glanced at the Jag. "You and your half-siblings?"

She scowled. "Whatever. Yes." She glared at Lewis. "We think this guy has conspired against my—our—mom to steal her insurance. We think he's manipulating her."

"That's a laugh," declared Don from a slightly increased safe distance.

"Shut up," she snapped at him. "You big fat leech."

"I'm not fat," he objected with remarkable alacrity. I looked at him and back at her.

"If I'm for hire, it's to find the truth, not nail a particular person to suit somebody's agenda," I told her.

"Whatever," she said. "He did it."

"Did what?"

"Killed Shelley's dad. For the money. Maybe he killed all our dads."

I played along. "What about the judge? Did he kill him too? Just to keep in practice?"

"They all died, you know," she said stiffly.

I hadn't heard this part. "Yours too?" I asked. She nodded. "How? Drowning?"

She shook her head. "Accidents. Two, four, and seven drowned. One, three, and five had tragic accidents. That's us."

"It does make for an interesting kind of kinship," I noted.

She pointed an accusing finger at Lewis. "And you'll have noticed, he's the only one who isn't dead."

"I didn't even know Vera back then. That's slander," Don protested.

"Fuck you!" Beverly shouted at him.

"Fuck yourself!" he snapped back.

"Shut up, please!" I shouted at all of them, including the two who were arguing in the Jag, for good measure. "I want all of you," I looked at Lewis, "including Vera, at my office tomorrow at noon. We'll sort out who's doing what for and to whom at that time."

"If Vera's still alive," Don said bitterly.

"Shit, we've gotta go," I exclaimed and glared accusingly at Beverly. "We were on our way to your mother's place when you so pleasantly interrupted us," I informed her.

"Jimmy thinks Shelley might be a threat to her," Don added.

"Oh God," gasped Beverly. "That woman's crazy. Jerry! We gotta go, now!" She ran for the Jag without even saying good-bye.

"Let's go," I told Don, and we ran for my car.

It was a race to Vera's house, artfully dodging the Gulfport police, always on the lookout for speeding Jags and such. I knew a better route via the marina and got there first.

The house was dark. "Oh, shit," muttered Don. "What do we do now?"

"You have a key?" He hesitated, then nodded. I could hear wheels screeching as the Jag rounded the corner. We ran to the front entrance, knocked loudly, and I rang the bell. "Vera!" shouted Don, jamming the key into the door lock. We burst in through the door. At that instant we were blinded by the glare of a light thrown directly in front of us.

"Who's there?" demanded Vera, standing in the hallway wrapped only in a large terry bath towel, holding a flashlight in one hand and a large and ugly Colt revolver in the other. Apparently she took a lot of showers. "Don! What the hell?"

"Sorry, honey," stammered Don. "We thought—"

"You what?"

The Jaguar skidded to a halt outside at the curb, and the doors flew open as the occupants piled out like survivors of a plane crash.

"Mom!" Gabrielle shouted. She was the most athletic, I quickly surmised, and first in through the door. Beverly was close behind, shedding sequins, Jerry trailing a distant third. "Are you all right?" gasped Jerry. What a wuss, I thought.

"Why shouldn't I be?" Vera appeared genuinely bewildered. "What's going on?" She was dripping wet. But I noticed that her hair was strangely dry, except the lower ends. She lowered the revolver and turned on some lights.

"It's Shelley," Don tried to explain, looking sheepish. "We were worried she might come here."

Vera looked alarmed. "Shelley? Why? What for?"

They all looked at me. "Mister Boyle thinks Shelley might have killed Judge Gibbs, that she might be after you."

Vera's eyes clouded. "I haven't seen her," she insisted.

Everyone started talking at once. "Hold on, all of you!" I shouted them down. "I didn't say Shelley was after anybody, but it is a possibility. We need to secure the premises, first of all."

"I tried to call you, honey," Don told her.

"Sorry," she said. "I was burned out. I turned the phone off."

I looked around. "Check the doors and windows," I instructed Don. "The rest of you stay here."

"Hey, this is my house!" protested Vera. "I'd know if someone was here!"

We ignored her. Don began to the left side, through the living room and dining area. I headed right, through the salon, a paneled room full of eclectic but interesting Third World artifacts of various sorts—possibly collected by a variety of different men over the years. A large and ugly African Hutu spear hung on one wall; a stuffed barracuda on another. Aside from a bunch of stuffed zebra furniture, the room was empty. I moved on to the now-dark converted garage and the patio behind. I wasn't carrying a weapon. No P. I. in his right mind does, except in rare and dire circumstances. Which maybe this was, but it's hard to plan ahead. I knew how to defend myself if need be, but I could tell the others were nervous about Don and me both leaving them alone like that. I was nervous about that myself. I hesitated at the entrance to the garage room and fumbled for the light switch. Usually there was one just inside the doorway, if not on the outside going in, which in this case there was not.

"There's nobody in there. I think I would know!" Vera called after me, both fear and irritation in her voice.

"Nobody telephoned, nothing like that?" I heard Jerry persist behind my back as I stepped into the garage. I felt my skin crawling as I peered into each dark corner, behind each door and piece of furniture. The room was empty, and so, after a quick check, was the patio outside. I returned to the foyer.

"I told you, I've been here by myself all evening," grumbled Vera, her eyes moving rapidly back and forth, as though seeking affirmation. Or confirmation.

"Ma!" Gabrielle said, a warning tone in her voice. "He's working for us now."

"I didn't say that," I reminded them.

Suddenly a hideous, deathly howl reverberated from the far end of house. The crowd in the foyer stampeded towards the sound, and I was forced to follow behind them. Everyone stood frozen in place when I got to the master bedroom at the end of the hall. They were crowded in the doorway, motionless, trying to keep me out. I elbowed my way through. Don knelt beside the body on the floor. Someone had only half finished trying to roll her up in a fake oriental carpet from Sears when we'd made our untimely arrival. I looked at Vera and saw the reason for the sudden shower, the hastily tied towel, and her mostly dry hair. She'd simply been trying to wash away the blood.

"It's Shelley!" Don sobbed, overcome with the irony of it all. Shelley lay very still, eyes open wide in terminal surprise, a large and ugly kitchen knife protruding from her breast. The pool of blood around her was just starting to congeal.

"I think she's dead," observed Vera.

Don rocked back and forth, weeping. We were all speechless. Finally he looked at Vera, betrayal on his face, dismay in his voice. "Baby!" he sobbed. "How could you?"

"I'm sorry, honey. I really am. But it was self-defense," Vera insisted. We all looked at her. I could tell even her kids didn't believe her. Who would?

I motioned everyone to stand back and stopped Don a moment too late as he reached over, tried to pull the knife out, and thereby incriminated himself. "Don't," I gently rebuked him. "Nobody touch anything else. This is a crime scene." I turned to Jerry. "You're going to have to call the cops."

"Like hell," said Jerry with surprising spunk.

Vera moved to the center of the room and managed to turn our attention away from the dead body on the floor and all the blood. "For God's sake, could we all please get out of here?" she pleaded. We obeyed, and the traffic jam in the doorway was repeated once more, in reverse. We closed the bedroom door and allowed Vera to lead us back down the hall, through the dining room and foyer, to the salon. There she seized the floor. "She was after me, just like he said," she said, looking at me. I looked back as she went on. "But you had it all wrong, just like I told you, about Donny." We all looked at Lewis. I admitted I could sometimes be wrong, and she continued: "She wasn't my kid. You all know that. And all you brats didn't exactly welcome her to the family, either, so don't give me that look." She glared at Beverly, Jerry, and Gabrielle. Don and I glared at them too. They weren't exactly a lovable bunch.

I spoke up. "Turns out Shelley had a couple little policies of her own," I mentioned.

"Insurance? Shelley?" Don gasped. He was still trying to grasp the gravity of what had happened.

"Shelley had two policies out," I explained. "One on her stepmother here, which she may have been trying to cash in on tonight. To go along with cashing in the other one. The one on Alfred Shuttlesworth."

Beverly jumped to her feet. "She had a policy out on Alfred? Her own father?" There was a collective gasp around the room.

"Except he wasn't her father," I said. "He was her stepfather."

"What?" screamed Beverly, Jerry, and Gabrielle all at once. They all looked at each other accusingly, then back at Vera.

"Uh, Mom?" Jerry managed to say. "Exactly whose daughter was she?"

Vera just shook her head. "I don't want to go there," she said. "It doesn't matter, anyway." She looked at the kids. "It wasn't any of your fathers," she added. Don didn't say anything. He just looked sad. Everyone found something inanimate around the room to stare at (which wasn't hard since it was pretty cluttered with marital souvenirs).

"So who was the mother, Mom?" Gabrielle finally blurted out.

"How the hell should I know?" Vera snapped. "What am I, the mother of all mothers? I have enough trouble with you all."

"It doesn't matter," I agreed. "Shelley's mom took off when she was a kid. Left her with Alfred, who did his best." They all stared. "I got sources," I told them. Namely, Officer Jane Smithers of the Gulfport P.D.

"It wasn't good enough," Don murmured, almost to himself. Vera put her arm around him. I liked her again.

"For crying out loud," she exclaimed, "would you all please sit down?" We were her family, you see. Except for me, of course. They all glared at me. We sat down. Except for Jerry, who went and made a phone call.

I went on: "Shelley took out the policy on you around the same time you took out yours on Alfred."

"OK, so we both took out policies," admitted Vera. "I've been unlucky in love."

"No shit," said Gabrielle.

"Except with Donny here," confessed Vera, perching on the edge of the easy chair Don had collapsed into. "He's been real good to me."

"I noticed," I said.

"It worked better for us, divorced," explained Don. It was amazing. They were still together. Through all of it. Maybe Donny didn't mind so much, being used.

"It isn't like you all think!" Vera cried, her eyes flashing. Her robe opened slightly, and Don eyed her exposed knee hungrily. It was still a pretty nice knee.

"Be nice, Mom," said Jerry, coming back into the room. He gave me a brief nod. The kid was growing up, I decided.

The police and meat wagon arrived a few minutes later, lighting up the neighborhood with unwelcome strobes. Don Lewis watched in anguish as Vera got led away, the way a boy looks after an adopted stray pet being taken to the pound. She'd be home again before long. I had a feeling that they'd been partners all along and would remain so. He still loved her, I could tell. But maybe, as her spouse, he couldn't keep her happy. Things got tough, maybe there were some old debts, or new ones. It was Vera who'd come up with the idea. Divorce, remarriage—to somebody with money, power, or both. Like Shuttlesworth. Then a divorce, amicable if possible, and a nice settlement that could tide them over a while longer.

What they hadn't counted on was the mendacity of Shelley. The judge must have dismissed Shelley's complaints with an agenda of his own, like blackmail, and she made him pay instead—with his life. I never did like Judge Gibbs, ever since he got a female friend of mine killed by refusing a restraining order against her old boyfriend, who was waiting for her in the courthouse parking lot and blew her away before shooting himself. Maybe the judge got greedy. Maybe he was just horny. Maybe his yacht needed its bottom painted, or his mansion needed upgrading. The insurance policies Shelley had taken out had been for a million dollars. Maybe he had something else on her, worth part or all of it. Like the drowning of Alfred Shuttlesworth. We might never know.

It was dawn when I left Don at Vera's and shook his hand. "Good luck," I told him.

Tom Braithwaite was waiting by my door, with baited breath. "I got the address from the arresting officer," he said.

"What the hell," I grumbled but finally relented and gave him the story. Maybe now he could write a real story and get a real job. As for me, maybe now I could finally get some sleep. I went to bed.

Good Night, Mrs. Chisholm

WAYNE BARCOMB

J ane Chisholm stood in the upstairs hallway outside her children's room. In the usual commotion of getting the kids off to bed, she hadn't had time to think about Bill's phone call. She leaned wearily against the bedroom door, closed her eyes, and recalled their conversation.

"Honey, I'm afraid I won't be able to get back tonight after all. Duffy wants to run the contract by his lawyer tomorrow before signing it."

"But you said he'd been over it and everything was fine," she had said.

"Yeah, I know, but he says his lawyer wants to double-check everything for him before he signs. The guy's away for the day and won't be back till late tonight. I'm really sorry, sweetheart."

She opened her eyes and moved toward the stairs, stumbling over Jamie's sneaker in the semidarkness. Evening had slipped in upon her. She sat at the head of the stairs, listening to the silence.

She loved the serenity of the house at this time of evening, and she missed Bill. This was their favorite time together. Tonight would be only the second time in nine years of marriage that they would be apart overnight.

She shivered as a breeze drifted through the bathroom window and into the hall. The sound of something hitting the floor startled her. She jumped to her feet and snapped on the hall light.

The sound had come from the bathroom, where she found a shattered mirror on the floor. The sudden gust of wind had apparently blown it off the windowsill, where she'd set it earlier.

After cleaning up the glass, she went downstairs, feeling a little unsettled by the business with the mirror. She switched on the light and checked all the doors, making sure they were locked.

She stood in the ballroomlike front hall, wondering what to do with herself. Even with the lights on, she felt a sense of gloom without Bill. "Mansion of gloom," she said aloud. Funny how that old, long-forgotten phrase of Poe's should come to mind. She had never before thought of her house like that.

It was her dream house, her connection with the New England she had grudgingly left behind when Bill was promoted and transferred to Key West. She'd cried for days over leaving Massachusetts for Florida. But the big old Queen Anne house quickly healed her. Ever since she could remember, she'd wanted such a house. Now, with Bill's promotion, her dream had become reality.

She wandered down the long, narrow corridor, past the dining room and butler's pantry, into the kitchen. The two windows over the sink were cranked open, and the breeze rustled the kids' school papers on the bulletin board. She closed the windows and checked the back door again.

The refrigerator started to hum, reminding her she hadn't eaten. She opened it and spotted the two bottles of champagne still waiting for the festive evening she and Bill had planned to celebrate his contract.

"Damn," she muttered and slammed the door. She snapped off the lights and went into the dining room, poured herself some scotch straight up, and sat on the window seat in front of the massive window overlooking the garden. She crossed her legs up under her and watched the intricate shadows from the sea grapes and schefflera dance across the yard.

The alcohol warmed and relaxed her. She closed her eyes and listened to the wind whispering through the palm fronds.

A tapping against a side window brought her to her feet. She opened her eyes and peered out at the moonlit yard. Nothing. Again the sound, more like a scratching. It was coming from the window in the butler's pantry.

Standing in the darkness of her pantry, about to investigate the sound at her window, her stomach tightened. Half expecting to see a man standing at the window, she peered from behind a shelf and saw nothing but the shrubs and palms. He could have ducked behind them when she opened the pantry door.

An areca palm scratched against the window. The same sound she'd heard from the dining room. She smiled and made a note to trim it in the morning.

Back in the dining room, she sat at the table and sipped her drink. But instead of relaxing, she kept glancing at the wide, curtainless window.

Earlier she'd noticed a battered Toyota pickup drive slowly past her house. Although pickup trucks were common in Key West, she rarely saw one on the upscale street where they lived. It was when it had gone by again, slowing as it passed her house, that she'd felt a little uneasy. The unease had turned to concern when the afternoon paper arrived, with an article about the second burglary in the past week in expensive neighborhoods, the most recent only two streets away.

She thought back to the Toyota, driving past her house, the most elegant and expensive in the neighborhood. She'd considered calling the police, but what would she tell them? "I saw a truck driving slowly by my house." She could hear the cop: "It's a residential street, lady. Vehicles are supposed to go slow."

"Nervous Nellie," she scolded, put out the light, and returned to the grand entry hall.

The French doors at the far end of the hall leading to the back-yard rattled with the wind. She walked toward them. The clacking of her sandals on the polished hardwood floors echoed across the room and up the open stairway.

She opened the doors and stood on the wraparound porch, inhaling the sweet smell of the Confederate jasmine. The earlier breeze was now a full-blown Key West wind. The graceful arc of a coconut palm bending in the moonlight created a picture postcard of evening in the tropics. She had become beguiled by the charm of this far away island retreat of Key West and, much to her surprise, had come to love it.

New England seemed light-years away in contrast to the exotic decadence of Key West. What was it Hemingway had called it? The St. Tropez of the poor. She'd read somewhere that Key West missed being a tropical island by less than a hundred miles, a whim of geography that did little to compromise its Caribbean spirit.

The salt air was heavy with moisture blowing in from the Gulf of Mexico. Although the house sat back several streets from the water, a west wind like tonight's left no question as to what lay beyond.

She noticed the door to the screened-in part of the porch was ajar. She remembered closing it earlier. The wind? She went over to close it. Instead, she stepped in and settled onto the old settee swing that had come with the house. She sat, gently rocking back and forth, the squeak of the settee's springs and the lazy *click-click* of the ceiling fan the only sounds in the night.

She always enjoyed sitting on the porch, but the uneasy feeling was still with her, and her little place of refuge now seemed dark and creepy. Damn, she wished Bill were home.

Back inside the house, she closed the doors, locked them, and drew the curtains. The lock was flimsy, but she'd rejected Bill's suggestion of putting on a deadbolt, not wanting to spoil the natural symmetry of the doors and moulding. The hell with symmetry. She would have the deadbolt put on tomorrow.

She wandered aimlessly into the living room and sank onto the sofa, trying to unwind. The pickup truck came back into her head.

A sudden gust of wind surprised her. Where did it come from? All the windows and doors were closed. She'd checked. A breeze drifted through the house. She felt it on the back of her neck.

A noise in the hallway, something hitting against the wall. Again. She bounded off the sofa and into the hall.

The French door was wide open, swaying in the wind. She went over and closed it, but it bounced open again. She held her body against it, turned the key, and stepped away. The door swung open again. And then she saw why.

The part of the door jamb into which the lock bolt slid was rotted and finally gave way. There was nothing to hold the door closed, let alone locked.

"What a time for this to happen," she muttered and wedged a chair against the door. It stayed closed.

She stood in the hall, nibbling on the cuticle of her thumb, and listened to the silence. It was no longer silence. It was a crushing vacuum of stillness.

All she wanted now was to go to bed, fall asleep, and wake up to the bright Florida sunshine. She turned off the downstairs lights, trudged up the stairs, opened her bedroom windows for some air, and was soon in bed.

Her bed felt as big and empty as the house. She lay back and listened to the gentle snoring coming from the boys' room, reassuring her that she was not alone. She smiled at the thought of seeing Bill tomorrow. They would celebrate tomorrow night, and it would be even sweeter after tonight's disappointment. Her eyes closed and she drifted off to sleep.

When she heard the first noise, she was halfway between sleep and a groggy wakefulness. She knew something had awakened her, but she wasn't sure what. She never woke up in the middle of the night. Never. Bill said she slept the sleep of the innocent.

The second sound, though brief, was slightly louder than the first. She was wide awake now and sat up. Tense. Head cocked.

The wind blew the curtains and whistled through the open windows. Maybe it blew something over again. Yes, that's all it was.

The room was cold, and she was about to get up and close the windows when she heard something downstairs. Was it the wind shaking the doors? Whatever it was, it came from below her.

There. There it was again, like a footstep moving across the floor. There, again. *Oh, God! Someone is downstairs.*

She sat, rigid. Holding her breath, listening.

The house was quiet, except for the wind through the trees.

"This is silly. You're overreacting," she whispered, chiding herself. But she couldn't shake the awful feeling that in another part of the house, someone was standing as alert as she, listening.

She reached for the light and froze. The living room floor creaked heavily—once, twice, three times. The sound moved slowly into the front hall and stopped at the base of the stairs. *Oh, dear God, there is someone in my house.*

The hammering of her heart filled the now-claustrophobic confines of her bedroom. Her eyes landed on the telephone. 911. The police could be here in minutes. She sat up and lifted the receiver, wondering if she could speak softly enough not to be heard downstairs or yell into the phone and let the intruder hear her. Yes, that's what she would do. Let him know the police are on their way.

The phone was silent. No dial tone. Nothing. *Oh, sweet Jesus. He's disabled the phone.*

"Who are you?" she whispered.

One of the bottom stairs groaned, then another. The stairwell acted as an amplifier, hollow and efficient. She curled herself into a fetal position and whimpered. A weapon. Was there something in the bedroom she could use as a weapon? Her mind refused to function, her body unable to move. She was a swimmer struggling toward the ocean's surface against a great weight of water.

Another sound on the stairs. The footsteps moved slowly, one stair at a time. More movement and the creak of a floorboard in the upstairs hall. And then she heard the sound of a man's harsh breathing. He stood not fifteen feet from where she lay.

Too late to scream, too late to move, she closed her eyes and prayed that she could succeed in feigning sleep. *Dear God, let him be just a burglar. Let him take what he wants and leave.*

She half covered her head with the light blanket and closed her eyes, keeping the lids open just enough to see. She faced the open door, where she could see the thin shaft of moonlight slicing through the skylight and across the hall.

The breathing moved closer, and she squeezed her eyes shut. Tears began to form. She opened her eyes to release them, and he was in the doorway. Silhouetted against the moonlight, her nightmare had taken shape.

He stood still, staring at her. She closed her eyes tightly and prayed. *I am afraid. Please help me. Help me. Please, don't let him hurt my children.*

More movement. This time she could feel it. He was in her bedroom. The breathing now directly over her head. She smelled his sour breath and clenched her teeth to bite off a scream, praying to God to protect her and the children. She was losing control, afraid she could no longer contain the terror building inside her.

Then, abruptly, he walked away from her, and she heard him opening the bureau drawers. She opened one eye a slit and watched him sorting through her jewel box, selecting pieces and putting them into a bag.

Oh, God, he is *only a burglar.* She wanted to laugh, and she wanted to cry with relief and thanks. She suddenly realized that her bed was soaked where she lay. The sheet was drenched, and her nightgown clung to her, wet and soggy.

He soon finished, then turned and walked quickly past her and down the stairs. She heard him open the French doors and listened to his footsteps fade away across the backyard.

She sat up in the darkness and put her hands to her face. They were trembling, and her whole body shook uncontrollably. She let all the pent-up emotion of the evening pour out, and when it had run its course, she got up and checked the boys. They were sleeping peacefully.

She went back to her room and picked up the phone. Still dead. Maybe he had only taken the downstairs phone off the hook. She would go down and check.

As she hung up the phone, she noticed a small object lying on the bedroom floor, shining in the beam of moonlight. She picked it up and saw it was a set of keys—two car keys and two others that looked like house keys. The keys were attached to a quarter-sized medallion with the words, "Toyota, I love what you do for me."

"Oh, my God!" she said aloud. "He'll have to come back for these. The boys! I've got to get them out of here, to the police."

She grabbed a robe and hurried into their room. Still afraid to switch on a light, she rummaged through the kids' closet to get their robes. There was no time to dress them.

As she fumbled for Mike's bathrobe, she noticed that she was still clutching the keys. Her heart pounded, and she was shaking badly now.

"Oh, damn! Where is Jamie's bathrobe?"

She started to cry. Drops of perspiration rolled from under her outstretched arms and down across her ribs. It felt cold under her wet nightgown, and she shivered.

Tears and sweat covered her face as she fumbled with the clothing along the rod. Pants, shirts, sweaters flew everywhere. She spotted the robe at the far end and frantically tugged at it. The rod fell to the floor onto the pile of clothes. "The hell with the robe," she yelled, and when she turned, there he was.

They stood facing each other, Jane half in the closet, and he, inches from her, a shadow framed against the muted rays of the boys' night-light. She tried to scream, but nothing came out. Neither of them moved. "My keys," he said, holding out his hand.

And then all of her suppressed horror erupted into one long, shattering, ear-piercing scream.

He backed away instinctively. As he did, she threw the keys in his face and bolted past him out of the room toward the stairs. Behind her, in a cacophony of fright and bewilderment, came the wails of the boys. She had to lead him out of their room, out of the house. She scrambled down the stairs, her shrill shriek of terror echoing through the stairwell.

His heavy panting followed her across the room and down the stairs. She vaguely remembered running through the living room, into the kitchen, and out the door, her howl echoing through the house and into the night. She was outside on the driveway, and the last thing she remembered was seeing the lights go on in three neighboring houses.

When she awoke, she was lying on her living room sofa. A policeman sat in the room, and she recognized four of her neighbors.

"Your neighbors found you lying in the driveway, Mrs. Chisholm. What happened?"

After being assured that her children were all right and were up in their room with two of her friends, she went up to check on them and returned to describe what happened. Talking about it had her sobbing again, and she had to halt several times.

"Well, don't you worry, ma'am. We'll catch him. Give us a description of the man, if you feel up to it, and we'll talk some more tomorrow."

She described the man as best she could and told the officer about the Toyota. "I'm afraid I'm completely drained," she said. "I just need to get some sleep now."

"Janie, dear, we're not going to leave you here alone again after what's happened." Ruth Ryan, her neighbor and friend, hugged her. "You and the boys come home with us."

Jane made a face and looked at the policeman. She didn't really want to haul the kids out of their beds in the middle of the night and go traipsing over to the Ryans. But she wasn't going to take any chances either.

"We're not going to leave her alone," said one of the officers. He turned to Jane. "One of our men outside has volunteered to stay in the house till you're up in the morning, and then I'd suggest you and your kids go to your friend's house until your husband gets back. We'll want to talk some more with you, after you've had some sleep."

Jane looked outside and saw two officers checking out the yard. She smiled. That was much better. She looked at her watch—nearly four. There was no point in calling Bill now and worrying him. Nothing he could do anyway. She would tell him all about it when he returned.

She promised Ruth that she and the boys would be over in the morning, went upstairs, checked on the kids, who were sleeping, and dropped exhausted on the bed. She heard the neighbors leave, chattering, and finally one of the police cars drove away.

She still couldn't believe it had all happened. But somehow she had come through it. There was a police officer downstairs, and Bill would be home tomorrow. She lay back on the bed, sank into the downy pillows, and, slowly unwinding, dozed off.

She didn't know how long she'd been sleeping when she was awakened by a sound in the house. She glanced at her watch. Four-thirty. She hadn't been fully asleep, and now she remembered the sound clearly. It sounded like footsteps on the stairs. Fear gripped her again. Then she remembered the police officer. "What is it?" she yelled downstairs.

"Oh, I'm sorry, ma'am. I'm just a bull in a china closet. Sorry if I disturbed you. I have a headache. You wouldn't happen to have a couple of aspirin up there, would you?"

"Sure. There are some in the medicine cabinet in the bathroom at the head of the stairs."

Hearing his footsteps on the stairs brought back the ugly memories of two hours ago. But this was very different. She smiled, switched on the light, and turned to put on her robe. She couldn't sleep anymore. She would go downstairs, make some coffee, and keep the policeman company.

When she looked up, the policeman stood in the doorway. She blinked and looked again.

He moved quickly into the room. "I'm sorry, lady, but you saw too much of me."

The face leaned over her. It was the last thing she saw before his fingers tightened around her throat.

Sierra Reveals All

NANCY BARTHOLOMEW

I'm an exotic dancer in one of those little clubs off Thomas Drive in Panama City, Florida. Now, before you go getting all self-righteous on me, let me tell you something. We dancers gotta work just as hard as anybody else. We're constantly inventing new routines, working out, coming up with new costumes, and, to top it off, we take a lot of crap. Yeah, we make good money, but we have our bad days too. Let me give you an example.

Monday was about as terrible as it gets. To start with, Bruno (he works the door at the club and he's my boyfriend) gets it into his head to be jealous of Vince. Granted, me and Vince go way back and we're friends, but he's my boss, for heaven's sake, and he's married. So Bruno comes over around noon, without invitation, and starts harassing me until I finally tell him get out and take your stinkin' attitude with you.

Then I spend the afternoon at the dentist getting a crown, and let me tell you that's no picnic. Not to mention that the dentist comes on to me. I'm lyin' there all vulnerable, my mouth wide open, and he wants to get fresh. He says he likes my new implants and I'm thinkin': you could do with a personality implant. I don't wanna say nothin' cause he's working with a drill in my head, you know?

Then I come home and Vince's old lady's there waiting. My mouth is aching. I'm tired 'cause I didn't get no sleep because I was at the dentist, and she wants to yack about do I think Vince is boinking someone else. Give me a break. I mean, I can see why another person would be insecure given what Vince does for a living, but she used to dance, for Pete's sake. She knows Vince ain't shoppin' the talent. It ain't about T and A; it's about dollars and cents.

Oh, but my day's just starting there. This new kid, Marla, just has to jack me up right before I go on for the late show. She comes barging into the dressing room, swinging her little rhinestone pasties, you know, the ones she had done special to look like the United States flag, and calls me out.

"All right," I says, "any time, any place, just wait till I finish my act."

She gets all cocky, 'cause she knows I'm not goin' out to fight, and she says how's about we make it interesting and have a war of the strippers? She wants to get Vince to run some big ad about the two of us battling it out for the title of best dancer. She wants me to agree that the loser leaves the club. Now what kind of crap is that?

She got all belligerent when I said it was a stupid idea.

"Watch your back, Sierra," she says, "'cause I'm coming after you and your friend Vince ain't gonna help you this time."

I was so mad, I almost broke my own rule and kicked her ass, but I remembered and didn't. Every night, before I go on, I spend the last few minutes getting in touch with my inner child, busting free, I call it. I almost let Marla distract me from my meditation, but I'm a professional.

So I go on and I do one hell of an act. I'm Little Bo Peep. Man, they go crazy for that one. Bruno actually had to come down and subdue one of the regulars. The man was making sheep noises and trying to crawl up on stage, and him a professor at the community college. Where's their self-respect?

Bruno thought I should be appropriately grateful to him and invite him back to my place afterward. I told him I wasn't that grateful, just tired. My tooth was giving me fits and I just wanted to go back to the trailer and crash, you know?

I drove all the way home checking my rearview mirror, just in case that wacko professor decided to follow me. It was a quarter past three when I finally climbed the steps of the trailer and fumbled with my key in the darkness. The door just swung open, 'cause I must've forgotten to lock it, again. Fluffy, my Chihuahua, usually starts barking when she hears me, but I figured she'd fallen asleep on my pillow.

I slipped inside the door, reached up for the light switch, and immediately started screaming. Vince was lying in front of the refrigerator. The door was wide open, like he'd been hungry and looking around, but somebody'd gotten to him first. His chest was full of red holes. Fluffy was nowhere to be found.

I don't know how I called 911. I remember standing there with the phone in my hand, shaking too bad to dial. The next thing I remember seeing is maybe five squad cars, more than even the last time they raided the club. They were all outside my trailer, their lights flashing, Panama City's finest. I even recognized a couple of them, but I acted like I didn't. Guys are sometimes embarrassed to admit they frequent a strip joint.

The head man was a short guy, good looking, if you like them clean cut. I've always been partial to bikers, myself. He had me come into the living room and give him the details. I told him I didn't know much, but he said we had to go over the whole thing.

"Were you and Vince close?" he asked finally. He was trying to look like he didn't mean nothing in particular by it, but I knew what he was looking for.

"Detective," I said calmly, "Vince was my friend. He dropped by here sometimes after work, and we talked, nothing else."

"What did you talk about?" His eyes were soft and kind and I stared just a little too long before I answered.

"I guess life in general: his problems with his wife, my love life, the future, the past, the whole nine yards."

He wrote something down in his notepad and was starting to ask me the next question when he was interrupted by one of the uniforms. The detective got up and walked into my bedroom with the officer. In a few minutes he returned and took his seat across from me.

"Got any idea of who'd want to tap your phone?" he asked.

"Get out! You're telling me someone bugged my phone?" I couldn't believe it. Who'd care what I had to say?

"Does anybody dislike you? Do you have a jealous boyfriend? There are lots of reasons why people tap phones. Sometimes they want to keep track of an errant spouse; sometimes they're looking for illegal activity." He paused and looked hard at me. The soft eyes weren't as kind now.

"Oh, yeah, right," I sneered. "I'm a stripper, so I must be involved with drugs or the Mafia. Geeze, you guys don't quit, do you? Am I a suspect or what?"

"It's too early for suspects," he said smoothly. "It's too early to tell who the intended victim was too."

"What do you mean by that?" I asked, trying not to seem scared.

"Who knew Vince was coming to visit you tonight?" he asked.

"No one," I answered, my voice coming out like a squeak. "I didn't even know. Vince is always dropping by. Sometimes he comes over just to relax from the club for a little while. He has a key. He makes himself to home. Sometimes I'm not even here. It don't mean nothing."

"Maybe someone was looking for you."

I told him about Marla and the head case from the club, but I didn't really suspect either one.

The detective folded the notepad over and tucked it in his jacket. The interview was over. Vince was dead in my kitchen and I wasn't sure the bullets hadn't been meant for me.

When Fluffy returned that afternoon, I was sitting at the dinette table waiting for the coffeemaker to finish brewing. She scratched at the back door, yipping impatiently.

"Fluffy, baby, where the hell have you been? You scared Mommy."

Fluffy leapt into my arms, burying her face in my purple terrycloth robe. She was trembling.

"You poor baby," I murmured. "I bet you're starving."

I got up to get her something to eat and was opening the can when she started to growl. I don't know if you know this, but Chihuahuas are very protective of their owners. I turned around to see what she was after and saw her pawing at the bottom of the refrigerator.

"Fluffy, baby, calm down. Mama's fixing you something right now." Probably saving me from a giant palmetto bug, I thought. In Florida we have palmettos the size of Fluffy.

When I walked over to set Fluffy's dish down, I realized she had something.

"Here girl, let me," I insisted, pushing her aside.

Something was hung on the inside of the little black grate that fit across the bottom of my refrigerator. I fiddled with it and finally ended up pulling the whole grate off. A red, white, and blue American flag pastie landed in my hand.

"Hey, Sierra, open up!" Bruno's voice rumbled through my trailer like a train.

I stuffed Marla's pastie into my pocket and went to the door. Bruno was huffing and puffing in the late August sun, and he was angry.

"Bruno, not now. This is not a good time, you know what I mean?"

Bruno is three hundred pounds, mainly in his neck, and he's steroid impaired. We'd only been dating for three weeks, but the relationship was really over before it started. I dated him because everybody kept giving me heat about Vince. I figured I'd show them there was nothing to it by seeing Bruno. I just didn't figure he'd take it so seriously.

"What was you doin' with Vince last night, Sierra?"

"Oh, gee, Bruno, maybe I was fillin' him full of holes. The guy was dead, all right?" The man had shit for brains.

Bruno took a step back, his big dumb eyes filling with hurt.

"That's sick, Sierra. You know what I mean. There was something going on with you two, wasn't there?"

Behind us, Fluffy started to growl. She wasn't going to let some three-hundred-pound gorilla hurt me.

"For Christ's sake, Bruno, go home."

I slammed the door and fastened the chain. In a few moments, I heard Bruno's Camaro start and his tires chirp as he laid rubber out of the mobile home park. Good riddance, I thought.

We did a memorial show for Vince that night. All of us dancers wore black, and for the very last number, we all paraded back onstage and sang "Shall We Gather at the River." It was a touching moment. I know I'll never forget it. All of Vince's associates were there, out in the house, and they were buying for everybody.

The girls were all quieter than usual, each of us remembering Vince in her own particular way. The only one to show her ass was Marla. She made a big show of pulling this table and chair down front by the stage. She wouldn't let anyone near it. She called it the Dancer's Missing Man Formation. Then she did her act in front of the table, crying while she peeled off her bra. I coulda gagged.

Later, when she was catching a smoke outside, I went out to talk to her.

"Marla," I says, with no attempt to be nice, "guess where I found this?"

I pulled out the pastie and swung it just out of her reach. She looked nervous for about one second, then tried to act cool.

"Oh," she says, "my pastie. I was wondering where I dropped it. Thanks."

She made a grab for it, but I snatched it away.

"Not so fast, hot shot," I said. "I found this under my refrigerator. I want to know how it got there."

At first she tries to act like she don't know; but I was on to her. I persuaded her to come across with the truth. Actually, I grabbed a big hank of her hair, wrapped it around my hand and pulled until her face was grazing the rail of the fire escape.

"Now, as I see it, Marla, we can do this the easy way or the hard way. It don't make no difference to me."

She squealed, and I took that as a sign of impending cooperation.

"I . . . I gave it to Vince last night," she gasped. "God, let me up, will you?"

"Why'd you give it to Vince?" I asked, gripping her hair as a reminder.

"I don't know," she groaned. "It was like a souvenir. Will you let me up?"

Slowly I eased my grip on her hair, pulling her gently upright.

"What were you doing at my trailer?" I asked.

There was a very brief hesitation, the kind I used to give Sister Mary Margaret back in Philly when I was in Catholic school. She was figuring the percentages in lying to me.

"I don't know what you're talking about," she said. "I wouldn't step foot in your old trailer. I gave Vince the pastie after last night's show."

Bruno came looking for us then, pushing open the old fire exit and poking his fat neck through the opening.

"Ralph's looking for you two," he growled.

Marla broke away from me and pushed past us into the club. I stared after her, wondering what she was hiding. What had been going on between her and Vince?

Bunny Rabinoski also wanted to know what had gone on between Marla and Vince. As the grieving widow, she figured she had her rights. When I got to the funeral home for the viewing, Bunny buttonholed me. She stood there in her little black dress, with a ridiculous pillbox hat and veil contraption covering her ash blonde dye job. I knew Bunny before I knew Vince. Back in the good old days, before she turned so insecure, we used to hang out. She's the one who turned me on to the profession.

"Sierra," she whispered, as she led me up to the coffin, "you gotta level with me. Was Vince punchin' someone's time clock in private?"

Here we was, standin' over her dead husband, and she wants to know was he fooling around.

"Bunny," I answered, "what does it matter now? He's dead." I crossed myself and whispered, "May he rest in peace."

Bunny looked like hell. Her eyes were red and swollen nearly shut from crying. Mascara tracks lined her cheeks. Was she eating herself up 'cause he was dead or 'cause he was cheating?

"Well, I can't rest," she sobbed softly, glancing around to see if anyone was listening. "I gotta know for sure. Who was it? He'd tell you."

I started worrying about why she didn't suspect me. After all, we spent a lot of time together. In fact, I knew he'd been thinking about leaving her, mainly 'cause she wouldn't let up on him. I didn't say nothing. I just turned and looked down at poor Vince.

"He looks good, Bunny. They done good with him."

Bunny looked up at me like I was nuts.

"How can he look good?" she wailed. "He's dead! Come on, Sierra, you gotta do this one thing for me. Find out who it was. I know it had to be somebody. I think maybe that new girl at the club. What's her name?"

"Marla?" I asked, knowing the answer.

"Yeah, that's it. Marla. You call her up, tell her you gotta talk, get her to come over to your place. Surely, she'll tell you, Vince's friend. Hell, give her a couple a shots of tequila. Do anything, but find out for me. I gotta know. Maybe she done this," she said, gesturing to Vince. "I just gotta know."

I had no intention of calling Marla, but I agreed to do as Bunny asked right away, just to get her shiny red nails out of my arm and me out of that funeral parlor. Those places give me the creeps. Let me tell you something, you don't ever see them guys coming into a strip club. I figure they like their bodies a little colder.

I didn't realize that I was being followed home until I'd already pulled into the trailer park, and by then it was too late. Marla hopped out of her little white Miata and was over by my car door before I could get ready for her. She was dressed in a black dress too, but hers was cut to her navel, with little rhinestones bordering her cleavage like miniature spotlights.

"I gotta talk to you," she said, and her look wasn't taking no for an answer. "Inside."

What the heck, I thought, might as well kill two birds with one stone. At least Bunny would be happy. I let Marla follow me up the rickety wooden steps to the trailer. I no sooner closed the door behind us than Fluffy flew into the room, teeth bared, ready to tear Marla apart. Marla screamed and jumped up on one of my barstools. I would've laughed if I hadn't been so busy trying to subdue Fluffy. The dog was serious about taking a piece of Marla. Maybe she didn't like rhinestones.

"What's wrong with that thing?" Marla asked after I'd penned Fluffy in the bedroom. Fluffy was hurling herself at the door, scratching and barking.

"I don't know," I said, "maybe you got bad karma. Dogs know about that stuff."

Marla rolled her eyes but held her tongue. She seemed to be trying real hard not to get into it with me.

"Listen, I gotta ask you something," she said at last. "About finding my pastie, I'd like you to keep it between us. You know, like don't tell the cops or . . . well, nobody."

I laughed. "Now why should I do something for you?"

"Because you were Vince's friend and because it's just better this way."

She wasn't going to get away with that, I thought. Marla was sitting at the dinette table, staring at her hands, avoiding looking at me.

"That don't cut it, Marla," I said. "How do I know you didn't off Vince?"

That's when she started crying. Marla didn't cry like Bunny. Marla shed one tear at a time. She had a little black lace hankie that she pulled from out of her little black clutch. She dabbed gently at each eye, then put the lace hankie back in her purse.

"I would never off the man I love," she said quietly. "We was planning to be married when his divorce was final."

I was shocked. Marla and Vince? I thought back over all our conversations. He never said for sure that he was seeing someone, but I guess in the back of my head I knew there had to be somebody. He and Bunny hadn't been getting along for months, maybe even years. But Marla?

"It isn't ever going to happen now," she was saying. "So, there's no point in even mentioning it. It would only tear his wife up. What she don't know won't hurt her, I guess." Marla sighed. "I got enough trouble, being the new kid in town, I don't need the owner's widow making my life more miserable." She was watching me, looking for a reaction. "So, we got a deal or not?"

"I'll think about it," I said.

Marla stood and walked over to my chair. She was wearing black-seamed stockings and black spike heels that made her close to six feet tall.

"I would like to think we came to an agreement," she said in a soft, menacing voice.

"Marla, I think I'm the one in the catbird seat, you know what I mean? I'll make my decision when I'm ready."

Marla looked at me long and hard before she turned and walked out.

I went to the cabinet and pulled out the souvenir bottle of tequila I bought in Mexico, the one with the worm. The situation seemed to call for drastic measures. There was a slightly shriveled lemon in my crisper which I sliced into wedges and brought to the table along with a salt shaker. I proceeded to get plotzed.

At some point, Fluffy joined me, having hurled her tiny body against the flimsy bedroom door until it opened. I remember putting her dog food dish on the table and giving her a leftover hamburger. We held a wake for Vince, just the two of us. I cried a little bit and toasted Vince a lot. Fluffy didn't have much to say. Every now and then she'd yip or growl at something outside. For the most part, I just drank and tried to figure out who would want to hurt Vince.

Around two A.M., I woke up. I was lying in my bed, fully clothed, and Fluffy was barking.

"Jesus, Fluffy, quit it! Can't you see I'm trying to sleep here?"

Fluffy ignored me and took off for the living room. I sat up and the room went spinning. I grabbed for the nightstand for balance, missed, and fell onto the floor. I heard Fluffy growl deep in her throat and then sigh suddenly, as if all the wind had been kicked out of her. There was no more noise in the living room. Instead, I heard someone making their way slowly down the hall.

I stayed low, by the side of my bed, waiting. Whoever it was moved slowly, uncertain of their steps in the darkness. They were coming closer, heading straight for me, as if they knew exactly where I hid. I flattened myself and moved under the bed, barely daring to breathe as the person in my room stepped around the bed and headed for the nightstand.

I inched slowly toward the other side of the bed, thinking maybe I could make a run for it. The intruder went straight for the phone. They were looking for the tap. Quietly, they replaced the phone on the nightstand. I inched out from under the bed and was pulling myself to a crouch when I heard the click of the hammer being pulled back on a gun. I froze.

"This is for not tellin' me he was running around," Bunny said in the darkened room. The gun discharged, and I hit the floor, wondering if this was death. I didn't feel nothing. Then I realized she'd shot my pillow, mistaking it for me.

Again I crouched on my hands and knees, ready to run, but I knew I wouldn't get far. I heard the trigger cock again and held my breath.

"And this is for lying 'cause you was screwin' him too. Now the both of you can rot in hell!"

There was a second loud explosion, and I tore into action. They say drunks and people in danger don't know their own strength. Well, I was drunk and scared, so I suppose I was doubly blessed. I grabbed the mattress and flipped it, pinning Bunny against the wall and knocking the gun out of her hand.

Bunny shoved as hard as she could and managed to squeeze out from under the mattress. I tripped her, then jumped on top of her as she tried to run out of the room. It was an all-out cat fight after that. I was beating her with everything I had, and for a while I was winning. Then she grabbed the lamp from the table and conked me over the head. I gotta admit that slowed me down.

She was on top of me, punching my face, when Fluffy woke up. I heard a low snarl and then Bunny screamed as my tiny tiger sank her teeth into Bunny's ass. Fluffy held on for all she was worth, snarling and tossing her little head. When Bunny turned around to try and dislodge Fluffy, I hit her with the lamp. Bunny slid off me like Jell-O melting on a kitchen floor.

"Good girl," I said, petting Fluffy. "You saved Mommy from the mean old Bunny Rabbit." I swear Fluffy was smiling.

The detective was smiling when he arrived too. The uniforms who responded when I called 911 had paged him when they realized what was going on. He'd rushed right over to take my statement. Bunny'd been led away by this time, so it was just me and him in my living room. The crime scene investigators were back, crawling around in my bedroom using that disgusting black powder to find prints and digging bullets out of my favorite pillow.

Detective Harper—John, as he told me to call him—looked at me with those melting chocolate eyes of his while I gave him the details.

"So I think she went off," I said. "Vince was gonna leave her. He was tired of her always following him, accusing him of fooling around on her. I suppose he finally decided to give her something to worry about, and then he realized he liked it. He told her he was leaving that night, and she followed him over here."

The detective was starting to grow on me. He sat on my sofa, his notepad open, forgetting to write down what I said. He had this cute-little-boy look, very different from a biker. When he realized he was staring, he blushed. Now when have you seen a biker do something like that?

"We traced that tap on your phone to a mail-order house. Bunny's name was on the order," he said in a strangled voice. "We figure she must've been trying to get the goods on him or you.

"I guess she thought if she couldn't have him, she could at least keep someone else from getting him and keep the club," I said.

"We'll run the ballistics," the detective said. "Bunny's gun and the one that killed her husband are the same caliber. We're fairly certain it's the same weapon."

We were babbling now. The words were pouring out of our mouths, but we weren't thinking about murder. I was thinking it might be just as exciting to date a cop as a biker. After all, change is good, I thought to myself.

Like I said when I started, it ain't easy being a dancer. There's good days and then there's bad days. Our lives have their ups and downs, just like everybody else's.

Ghosts

DAVID BEATY

It was just before sunset in Biscayne Estates, and the Armstrongs were safe at home. Darryl paced around his study, sipped scotch, and listened on his cordless telephone as a client screamed threats at him in broken English. Finally, he said, "Narciso, old buddy, stay calm. This is a temporary setback." He kept his voice reasonable but firm. "You've been going on about killing me all week. What good would that do you?"

Darryl cleared his throat. He said, "And believe me, I understand your anger. Nobody likes to lose money. But you wanted to play with the big boys, remember? Then the market went limit down three days in a row." He paused, not certain of what he'd just heard. "What? Simultaneous buy and sell orders? Who told you that? That's a lie. I don't care who told you. I've never dumped a bad trade in your account. That one? You gave me a direct order. Well, no, I can't play it back for you because your order came over my untaped line." He winced and said, "Hey, c'mon, you're calling me at *home*."

He took a greedy swallow of scotch and said, "Stop it. That's enough. I need a vacation from hearing about how I'm going to die.

I'll hang up now, OK? But call me if you get any more crazy ideas. Don't sit there obsessing. We're going to work this out. You have my word on that, OK? Bye, bye." He lowered the telephone into its cradle.

While Darryl talked in his study, his wife, Caroline, drifted among the racks of clothes and shoes in her walk-in closet, searching for a simple blouse to wear. She wondered at the forces in herself that had driven her to buy so many bright, costly things. Who was the woman who'd chosen them? Where was the exhilaration and hope they'd represented? She couldn't visualize herself in them now. The sight of them embarrassed her. When she looked around the closet, she imagined an aviary of tropical birds.

Caroline had recently turned thirty-three, and now, with a rueful laugh, she told friends that she was quickly closing the gaps: next year she'd be eighty-eight! Last week she'd resigned from her civic committees, her charities, her mothers' groups: places where she'd been spinning her wheels. She felt herself changing. She was tired of people who thought about money and not much else—and that included herself. She yearned for a more spiritual life. She wanted to break free.

At the moment, however, she felt blocked. A free-floating gloom seemed to hang over her life.

The telephone was driving her crazy. It started ringing as soon as Darryl came home from the office. When she answered it, the caller hung up, but he stayed on if Darryl took the call. Then Darryl would hurry into his study and shut the door. He pretended that everything was fine, but she knew better. Worrying about it—and how could she not?—kept her under the thumb of depression. Caroline turned again in her closet, sorrowing over the constant losses, the daily disconnections from hope, that seemed to define her life now.

Darryl, forced out of his study by the need for more scotch, signaled his availability to Kyle, age nine, and Courtney, age eleven, by cracking open a tray of ice in the bar. They appeared behind him in the doorway, energetic and needy.

He wondered when Narciso would call again. Silence was a danger signal. Silence meant: "Grab your wallet and go out the window!" Darryl poured scotch over the smoking ice in his glass. He had to keep Narciso talking, had to draw off his anger, like draining pus from a wound, or God only knew what that maniac might do. He wondered, But what if my luck has deserted me?

He fled into the patio with the children chattering at his heels like dwarfish furies. He sagged into a white plastic chair and tried to quiet Courtney and Kyle with the promise that if they ate all the food on their plates and didn't give Mrs. Hernandez a hard time, they'd get a big surprise after dinner.

"Oh, what surprise?" Kyle said. Feeling full of the idea of surprise, he danced around the patio. Courtney, who liked to mimic adults, folded her arms on her chest, struck a pose, and said, "Daddy, what on *earth* are you talking about?"

"Something of interest to you, my little madam." He talked to distract them, afraid that they could hear the voice of Narciso raging and threatening in his head. His children circled him—his fragile offspring, driven by such blatant needs. He felt the spinning pressure of their love. What have I done to them? he wondered and abruptly closed his mind against that thought. He offered them a face all-knowing and confident. "If I tell you, it won't be a surprise. Wait until after dark." He drank deeply.

"After dark!" Kyle shouted. "Wow!" Making airplane noises, he skimmed away. He ignored a barrage of furious looks from Courtney and settled into a holding pattern around the patio table. Courtney said, "But, Daddy, you didn't answer me."

Daddy's attention, however, had been captured by the sapphire beauty of his swimming pool, and by his trim green lawn, where sprinklers whispered *chuck, chuck, chuck* and tossed quick rainbows in the evening light, and by the *Lay-Z-Girl,* his sixty-foot Bertram yacht, which seemed to bob in polite greeting from its mooring on the canal. It was a typical view in Biscayne Estates, just south of Miami, and fragrant with the odors of damp earth and thrusting vegetation and the faint coppery tang of the ocean, but this evening its beauty and the achievement it proclaimed seemed like a trap to Darryl. Like one of those insect-eating flowers, but on a huge scale.

At one time, this life was all Darryl had hoped for. Now the prospect of working to sustain it made him think of a photograph he'd seen in *National Geographic*, of Irish pilgrims crawling on their knees over a stony road in the rain.

He felt, on his eardrums, the light percussion of rock music from next door, where Mr. Dominguez, a successful importer of flowers, fruits, and vegetables from Colombia, lived with his young wife, Mercedes, and a son Kyle's age, a sweet boy named Brandon. There was another son, from his first marriage, Jorge, a seventeen-year-old monster with shocking acne, who lived there too. Jorge was forever wounding Darryl's sense of neighborliness with his sleek red Donzi speedboat, his roaring Corvette, his end-of-the-world music, and his endless succession of guests, who used Darryl's lawn to drink and drug and screw and then left their detritus for Courtney and Kyle to puzzle over. Whenever Darryl trotted next door to complain, Mr. Dominguez laid a manicured hand over his heart and said, "I sorry, I sorry," and somehow managed to imply that he was apologizing for Darryl's bad manners, not Jorge's.

Jorge was a painful reminder that there were millions of teenagers out there having a high old time with their parents' money. Meanwhile, Darryl's resources dwindled away. If only he could get a tiny slice of what those parents were wasting on their kids. The idea of offering an Armstrong Education Fund shimmered in his mind, then faded. The word "slice" had turned his thoughts back to Narciso and his death threats.

Darryl didn't want to think about Narciso, so he let himself get angry with Jorge Dominguez. A door creaked open in Darryl's mind, and Darryl scampered down the rough stone steps to the dark arena where he played his special version of "Dungeons and Dragons" with his enemies. There, in his imagination, he passed a few delightful moments clanking around, teaching Jorge Dominguez to howl out his new understanding of the word "neighbor."

And then, from somewhere close by, Darryl heard the sounds he'd been dreading. He raced up from his mental dungeon to see the water empty from his swimming pool, and the swimming pool float into the sky and join the other clouds turning pink in the evening light. After that, the noises of a chain saw and a wood chipper came growling towards him and his gardenia bushes, hibiscus, sea grape, the low hedge of Surinam cherry that separated him from the Dominguezes, and all of his palms fell over, crumbled into mulch, and blew away. His lawn burst into flame and burned with the fierceness of tissue paper, exposing earth the color of an elephant's hide, dusty and crazed with cracks. *Lay-Z-Girl* popped her lines and fled down the canal into Biscayne Bay. Behind him, Darryl heard glass shattering and sounds of collapse and rushing wind, and he knew that if he turned around he'd find empty space where his house had once stood. His world had vanished. Ashes filled his heart.

Then it was over. His vision cleared. He lifted his shaking hand and glanced at his watch and guessed that no more than half a minute had passed. He took a swallow of scotch and saw, with gratitude, Kyle circling the table and Courtney staring at him.

He looked away from them and regarded the *Lay-Z-Girl.* Another broken-down dream. At first, Darryl had retained a full-time captain, but when that became too expensive, he'd found someone less competent who was willing to work part-time. Now he couldn't even afford that. A week ago, without telling Caroline, he'd fired the man. Yesterday he'd called a yacht broker and put the *Lay-Z-Girl* on the market.

Tonight, however, he dreamed of sailing away with his family to a new life. Tortola. The Turks and Caicos. A home on the ocean wave. Yes. He said to Courtney, "Mommy knows I'm here?"

"Mommy knows," a voice behind them said. Caroline, barefoot, dressed in designer jeans and a white linen blouse, closed the sliding glass door on the greenish talking face of the television news announcer and stepped onto the patio, darting shy, uncertain glances at Darryl.

He said, "Baby, you look great." She brightened and gave him a smile and a kiss.

He sniffed the air between them. "Love the perfume too."

The children cut across their current, clamoring for attention. A moment of plea bargaining with their mother ensued, after which Kyle and Courtney trudged away toward the kitchen, where Mrs. Hernandez, a smiling Nicaraguan who was going to apply for her green card any day now, stood ready to dish out their supper before she began her trek out past the guard house and estate gates to the bus stop, and her night off.

"Any better today, Sweetness?" Caroline asked, sitting down and taking a joint from her jeans pocket and lighting up.

The phone rang inside the house. Darryl lurched to his feet, saying, "I did OK in coffee. Made a buck or two. But I got hammered again in currencies. Big time." He stepped into the house, carefully closing the sliding glass door behind him.

"I'm sorry to hear it," Caroline muttered, watching him pick up the phone in the television room. She took a hit off her joint. When she exhaled, it sounded like a sigh.

She smoked and watched Darryl waving a hand and talking. Behind him, the colors on the television screen changed into electric blues, greens, and reds and became a map of Israel, Jordan, and Syria, which was replaced by the image of a handsome young man in a safari jacket talking into a microphone in a desert. Caroline wondered, Would he find me attractive? The correspondent's eyes narrowed, as if he were thinking it over. Then his hair lifted, like the wing of a bird, revealing a bald spot the size of Jordan. Caroline shouted with laughter.

Darryl paced around the television room: tall, red-haired, muscular, dressed in chinos and a blue Izod shirt, moving his right arm as if he were conducting the conversation. Still handsome, Caroline thought. She'd fallen in love with him when she was sixteen years old and he was twenty. He desired her still. She was as certain of that as she was of anything else in this darkening world. Lately, though, he had been making love to her with such a blind, nuzzling intensity that she felt herself recoiling from him. His need frightened her. At the same time, her response left her feeling inadequate and guilty.

Well, she would get him a nice safari jacket for his birthday. She watched the frown on his face and drifted into a fantasy: Darryl was talking to the correspondent in the desert. Together they were solving a knotty international problem. "I told Arafat that he better cut the crap." Something like that.

Darryl slid open the door and returned to slump into the chair next to her.

Caroline glanced at him. "What's happening, Mr. A?"

His face looked drained. "That client keeps calling to say that he's going to kill me."

Dread thumped on Caroline's heart. She blinked and fingered a button on her blouse. "Have you called the police?"

"It's under control."

"Control?" She sat up and flicked away her joint. "Whose control? He's calling you at home?"

"Well, he's upset."

"And you're not? He should be locked up."

"I've got to keep him talking. Calm him down."

"So, are we in danger? And damn you, Darryl, don't you lie to me."

"He'll calm down. And there's a guard on the gate and police on tap. We're safe."

"I don't feel safe. I mean—you're going to do nothing?"

"I've just got to live with it for a while. It'll blow over. Someday I'll kick his ass. He's a jerk. The market turned against him and he started hollering that I'd robbed him."

Caroline asked where the client was from, and Darryl said that, as far as he could make out, he'd begun in Ecuador but had ended up in Panama. Darryl shrugged. "He uses a Panamanian passport. But who knows? He hangs out in Key Biscayne when he's not in Panama."

"He's the only one complaining?"

Darryl looked darkly at her. "In a down market, everybody complains."

"But he says you clipped him? Why would he think that?"

Darryl shrugged. It wasn't what she thought. This guy loved playing the commodities market. Darryl had made a lot of money for him in the past. Last week, however, he'd lost big time—stopped out, three days in a row. Darryl had told him, "Cool off." But he was hot to jump in again. Well, he'd lost again, big time. Now he claimed it was Darryl's fault. He wanted his money back.

"And the threats?"

"You want his actual words?"

She looked away. She didn't want to hear the threats. "Well, anyway, this isn't Ecuador, or wherever he's from."

"Oh, no. Thank God we live in little old Miami, where everybody fears God and pays their taxes." Darryl nodded over his shoulder. "Like that nice Mr. Dominguez."

"This is not a sane way to live."

"Well, my choices are limited at the moment."

Caroline asked if maybe, just maybe, Darryl was getting too old for the commodities game?

Darryl bristled. "You don't like the style of life we have down here? I do it for you and the children. You want to go back to Chunchula, Alabama?"

She gave him a troubled smile. She told him that she surely loved him more alive than dead. And his children did too.

"Lover," he said, calming down. He took her hand and kissed it and admitted that maybe his life was a little too exciting now. That happened in his business. It was part of the adventure. As soon as he was clear of this little problem, they would think about changing things. Right now, he had to sit tight and roll with the punches.

Darryl told her a story about how Napoleon interviewed officers slated for high rank. The last question Napoleon asked was: Are you lucky? If they hesitated, or said no, he didn't promote them. Darryl grinned. "I damn well know what I would've told him."

Caroline had heard the story before. Tonight, it lacked its old magic. An aggressive attitude to luck might help on a battlefield. But in business? She worried that Darryl bragged about luck just to keep himself moving through the scary scenarios he seemed bent on creating for himself these days. Maybe bragging was a fuel. Or a mantra. Or a charm. He'd always been addicted to danger, to the edge, to the thrill of winning big. A little impromptu craziness had made life interesting for him. It used to refresh him. Now it seemed to her as if something else was going on.

She worried about Darryl's attitude towards other people's money. She used to love hearing him romance a client: his voice had carried a weird and beautiful music, rich and deep and sexy—a "brown velvet" voice, somebody had once called it. But over the years she had identified new sounds, less beautiful. Now when the check changed hands, the music suffered a modulation too. She heard dry notes of contempt in Darryl's voice. Darryl acted as if the client had signed away his rights over his own money, and Darryl resisted with bewilderment and outrage any client's attempts to withdraw his account. He acted as if the client were trying to weasel away his, Darryl's, property.

Caroline worried that Darryl was growing addicted to the stronger jolt, the darker thrill, of losing big. She had been trying to identify the signs. Was she seeing another example tonight? She wasn't sure. He'd deny it, of course. Could she tell before it was too late? The fragility of their life worried Caroline, but it seemed to excite something in Darryl.

"Lover?" he said. "Didn't you hear me? I said I'm thinking of making some big changes."

"When?"

"Well, as soon as I get clear of these problems."

They looked at each other, and then away, toward the canal, where the *Lay-Z-Girl* gently chafed at its moorings in the evening breeze.

Courtney and Kyle returned to the patio just as the telephone rang again. Their father went into the television room and returned immediately, shaking his head at their mother.

"So, Daddy," Kyle said. "What's the big surprise?"

His remark startled his parents. They stared at him.

"Surprise?" Caroline said, reaching up to finger the button at her throat.

"Daddy," Courtney said, "you promised us a surprise."

"Oh, that surprise." Their father put his face in his hands and choked with laughter, and his neck flushed bright pink. When he didn't stop laughing, the children grew uneasy. They looked to their mother for guidance and saw her staring at the top of their father's balding head, as if there were something wrong with its color or shape. The phone rang and both parents moved, but their father was faster. His absence left everybody on the patio wordless and uneasy.

He was back in a moment. As he came out onto the patio, Darryl breathed out sharply, clapped his hands, and shouted, "Ghost!" That got everybody's attention. He said, "We're playing Ghost tonight. That's the surprise." He waited for the confusion to subside. They'd played it once before: after their dinner, Mommy and Daddy had turned out all the lights and come searching for Courtney and Kyle.

Caroline said, "Not tonight."

Courtney said, "I hate that game."

Kyle said, "What's the prize?"

"Something really nice," Darryl said. "Now listen up." They'd play for only an hour. Kyle giggled and said, "I'll hide at Brandon's house." No, Darryl told him, nobody could leave the house. Whoever remained free, or was the last to get caught, won the game.

"What's the prize?" Kyle said.

"It's a *su*-prize," Darryl said. The children examined this statement and rejected it as adult nonsense. Kyle gasped, "We're staying up late," and his mother said, "Not too late. School tomorrow. Tonight's special." Why was it special? the children wanted to know, and their mother directed them to their father for their answer. He winked and said that it was a secret. "Why is everything a surprise or a secret?" Courtney said.

"Is this necessary?" Caroline said. She sensed her evening sliding towards a dark corner. But she knew that marijuana stoked her paranoid tendencies, and she was confused about what she really felt, so she went out of her way to enunciate her doubts in reasonable tones. "Do we really need this tonight, honey?" They were eating on the patio. The children had been banished to the television room. Caroline served the food that Mrs. Hernandez had prepared—pork chops and rice, a salad of crispy greens, and a bottle of Chilean cabernet—and then she brought out the portable television so she could keep an eye on a rerun of *Star Trek* while she ate.

Darryl had drunk himself into a mood where he found life piquant. "C'mon," he said. "I need a little lighthearted fun. It's just a game." He laughed. "It reminds me of what my daddy said to me at his own daddy's funeral: 'These are the jokes, so start laughing.'"

"Stop." Caroline put down her fork.

The image of Mr. Spock came on the television screen and said, "Irritation. Ah, yes. One of your earth emotions."

"Darryl, this just doesn't sound right."

He shrugged. "Isn't it like life? You're in your house and it feels safe, but suddenly it's dark as Hades, and out there are people who are coming to get you."

"I forbid you to talk like that." Caroline blinked at the pale light coming down over the canal and felt a heavy downward drop in her emotions. "Let's just take the kids to Dairy Queen, OK?"

They wrangled quietly. "I was joking," Darryl said. "The kids were bugging me. We'll play for an hour."

Caroline, unhappy and distrustful, looked over at the portable television. Mr. Spock, wearing earphones, said, "This must be garbled. The tapes are badly burned. I get the captain giving the order to destroy his own ship."

Caroline told Darryl that she'd think about it. She busied herself with her dinner, even though she wasn't hungry now, and pretended to concentrate on *Star Trek*. Captain Kirk was ordering a twenty-four-hour watch on the sick bay.

And then she thought, Maybe I'm not being fair to him. Maybe I'm not being helpful. He's so edgy tonight. He needs to play more than the kids do. She wavered and then gave in. "OK. OK. But only for an hour." He brightened immediately. She looked away, feeling slightly creepy.

"Let's do it right this time," Darryl said. They discussed ways to turn themselves into ghosts. "We need sheets," Darryl said. "You're not cutting my good sheets," she said. "I'm talking about old sheets," Darryl said. Caroline said that all their sheets were new. She said, "Everything in this house is new."

"But what's a ghost without a sheet?" Darryl said.

From the television, Mr. Spock shouted, "We're entering a force field of some kind! Sensor beam on!"

"Hold it," Caroline shouted. "We're almost ready. But not yet, so you can't come in." Courtney and Kyle wouldn't stop tapping on the locked bedroom door, so their mother, whose hair had suddenly turned white and who was wearing the palest makeup she could find, burst out of the bathroom in her bra and panties, trotted across the bedroom, and shouted through the door for them to knock it off. The telephone rang and she picked up the receiver and said, "Hello?" She waited, and when nobody spoke she muttered, "Oh, fuck you," and dropped the receiver into the cradle and walked to her dressing table and looked at the image of herself with white hair. She shook her head, closed her eyes, and sighed. She felt exhausted.

She reached into a drawer and retrieved a small vial. She dipped her finger, applied it to each nostril and inhaled, rubbed the finger around her gums, and then replaced the vial and went back into the bathroom, where Darryl waited nude in the shower stall singing an old Pink Floyd number about money, and she finished powdering his hair with flour.

She wiped the flour off his shoulder with a towel, kissed him on the lips, tweaked his nipples, and fondled his penis. She stepped back, her eyes hard and sparkling, and considered her handiwork. From the shower stall, Darryl, smiling, red-faced, and drunk, blew kisses at her. "Hmmmnnn," she said. "Hmmmnnn what, baby?" he said. She said, "I just wanted to see how you'd look as an old white-haired cracker with a hard-on."

The children rushed through the doorway and halted just inside the bedroom and almost fell over with fright. In front of them, holding hands side by side on the bed, sat two laughing ghosts with pale, shiny faces, chalky white heads, and bloodshot eyes. They wore flowing white sheets. The ghosts raised their hands in the air, flopped them around and wailed, "Whoooooooo!" and Kyle turned and ran into the door frame.

A ghost jumped up and took Kyle's face in its white-dusted hands and said, "Honey, you all right?" Kyle looked up with one of his eyes shut and said, "Mom?" The ghost nodded. Kyle said, "You scared me." The ghost bent back Kyle's head to examine the bump over his eye and asked, "You sure you're all right?" Kyle nodded. "You want to play the game?" Kyle nodded again. "I guess so." "It's only for an hour," the other ghost said, and Courtney said, "Kyle's so spastic."

"So, if we're all OK. . . ," Darryl said. He reminded them that no lights or flashlights were allowed during the game.

"And Kyle better find his own hiding place," Courtney said.

Darryl told them that the ghosts would wait in this bedroom, then come out and search for the children, *ha, ha, ha.* Courtney pressed her hand to her forehead and said, "Dad, you're weird."

Darryl, noticing a look on Kyle's face, said, "And you can't just give up. If you're caught, you'll have to wait in the TV room—with the TV off. Under no circumstances can you go outside the house. OK?"

Kyle nodded and touched the bump on his forehead and said, "But what's the prize?" "A Peanut Buster Parfait at Dairy Queen," Darryl said. "Tonight?" Kyle said, in a rising voice. Darryl nodded. "Wow!" Kyle said, and even Courtney forgot herself enough to show enthusiasm. "So, we're ready?" Darryl asked.

From where the children waited in the TV room, they caught glimpses of the ghosts floating around the house, turning off lights. They heard, in the gathering darkness, one ghost remind the other about the alarm system. Then the ghosts returned to the doorway of their bedroom, their sheets billowing behind them.

Darryl called out, "Children, can you hear me? Can you hear me?" "Yes," the children shouted. They had ten minutes to hide themselves, he announced. He looked at his digital watch and called out, "From *now.*" He slammed shut the bedroom door, and he and the other ghost groped towards the bed and lay down side by side in the darkness.

He said, "Lordy, think of them creeping around out there like mice." Caroline said that she didn't know if she had the energy to spend an hour chasing the kids around a dark house, and Darryl reached over and touched her nipple and said, "Who says you have to do that? I've got a great idea. Want to hear?"

"Hmmmnnn—probably not," she said. "But tell me anyhow."

As he began to speak she sat up, moved off the bed, and found her way over to her dresser. She quietly opened the drawer, found her little vial, and applied some of its contents to her nostrils and gums, and when her husband paused to ask what on earth she was doing at her dressing table, she sniffed and told him that she was looking for her eye drops, because flour from her hair was irritating her eyes. "I'll take some," Darryl said. "Some what?" she said. "Eye drops," he said, and she said, "Coming right up!" A moment later she started swearing because, she said, she'd just dropped the container on the shag carpet and now she couldn't find it.

Kyle couldn't find a place to hide. Every spot he chose turned out to be too obvious, or it bothered Courtney, who seemed to be playing a game of her own, popping up behind him in every room he went into and hissing at him to *go away*. He finally returned to the living room and squeezed himself under the sofa. Kosmo the cat came over to keep him company and interpreted all of Kyle's efforts to shoo him off as invitations to play, and just when Kyle realized that he'd picked another stupid place to hide, he heard his parents' bedroom door open. His father's voice called out, "Ten minutes is up. This is now officially a *ghost house*. Only *ghosts* live here. Watch out, heeeeeerrrre we come!"

From under the sofa, Kyle looked over and saw the two ghosts standing in the doorway of his parents' bedroom. He whimpered when they laughed like those jungle animals from Africa Kyle had seen on TV. As they began searching through the house, flapping their sheets and making terrible noises, Kosmo finally ran away, and Kyle squeezed himself into the tiniest ball he could imagine and tried not to think about the throbbing bump on this forehead, or about all the places on his body that itched, or the fact that he badly needed to clear his throat, at least once. An hour seemed like forever.

The game glided over Caroline's imagination with the sinister smoothness of a dream bird. She felt more energetic now, and she put her best effort into it. Action kept her paranoia—the panic feeling that she was wavering like an old quarter around the edge of a bottomless pit—far enough away to be bearable.

They swept through the house making ghostly noises, and the first place they looked for Kyle was under the living room sofa, because they both remembered that when Kyle was a little younger he loved to crawl under this sofa and declare himself invisible. Caroline spotted one of his feet and pointed it out to Darryl, who nodded. They circled the sofa, moaning and flapping their sheets, and went on in search of Courtney.

Caroline's senses twitched when they passed the broom closet just off the kitchen, and they stopped and flapped their sheets outside that. While she was dancing around and tapping on the freezer next to it, Caroline felt a stronger twitch of intuition, and she led Darryl to the linen closet by the laundry room. She had remembered that Courtney loved the floral smell of the sachets slipped between the laundered sheets and towels to keep out the smell of mildew. The ghosts wept out her name, and Caroline rattled the linen closet doorknob and felt a sudden pull from the other side. She pulled harder, but the door wouldn't budge. She pictured Courtney obstinately hanging on to the door knob, and a wave of irritation rose up in her, and she felt a wild urge to yank open the door and strike terror into her daughter's heart, and then she felt ashamed. She loved Courtney. Why should she want to terrorize her? Caroline was appalled at herself. This game had gone too far. She turned away and signaled urgently to Darryl. They made one last sweep through the house, then silently departed through the sliding glass door to the patio and fled across the lawn.

Courtney sat on a pile of towels in the linen closet and hung on to the doorknob with both hands. She wept as silently as she knew how. She had felt, through the door, the force of her mother's anger, and it had shocked her. What had she done to deserve it? She knew she was overweight and unlovely, but she couldn't help it. Her father was acting so weird too. She cried harder now, because she wanted to love him but he wouldn't let her, and she felt so alone.

Kyle strained until he thought his ears were going to pop, but he only heard the thumping of his own blood. He waited and waited and *waited* for the ghosts to make a noise, and finally he just had to move his legs, and then he had to scratch all his itches, and after that he couldn't stop himself and he cleared his throat. Time dragged by. He couldn't remember the house being this quiet, ever.

Caroline and Darryl threw cushions down on the dew-dampened afterdeck of the *Lay-Z-Girl* and tore off each other's sheets, T-shirts, shorts, and underwear and made love in the silvery light of an almost full moon, as if they were young again and back in a field outside Chunchula, Alabama. Ah, it was sweet and powerful, the best ever, they told each other afterwards. Sweaty and relaxed, they dozed for a while, until the crisp growl of twin outboard engines, approaching in the canal from the direction of Biscayne Bay, awakened them. The outboard engines shut off close by, and they looked at each other and shook their heads. "Jorge?" "Jorge." Both of them had thought the same thing: young Jorge Dominguez was returning home. Darryl got up into a crouch, looked over the railing, and glimpsed two figures moving across the Dominguezes' lawn. He lay back down again next to Caroline. They decided that Jorge had taken his girlfriend out in his boat, to smoke a joint or fuck in the moonlight.

"Someday," Darryl murmured, lying on his back and tracking the blinking lights of a passing airplane, "I'll get me a sweet little .357 magnum and take Jorge's heart for a spin over the red line. I surely will. I swear it on the grave of my Aunt Alice, who always had a strap handy for uppity children—I'm not joking," he said, turning towards Caroline.

"You're my big strong hero," she said, fondling him. "Sure you are."

Kyle flitted from room to room, growing more and more upset. He was alone, all alone in this dark house. They'd gone away and left him. Even the cat was gone.

Or maybe they were playing a joke on him? Yes, that was it, he thought with a burst of blistering hatred, because Courtney was a bully and she always got what she wanted and she loved to gang up on him, and now they'd taken her side. Now they were all together someplace, laughing at him. They were waiting for him to act like a baby. Well, he wouldn't. He wouldn't call out or turn on any lights.

But what was he supposed to do? Where was everybody? He'd checked everywhere—now he was coming out of his parents' bathroom, leaving a safe zone of damp towels and reassuring smells, the scent of his mother's perfumed powder, his father's cologne. He walked through a house now unfamiliar, pretending not to notice how the walls bulged out at him. It was hard not to shout with fear when he saw the dark hairy animals that had taken the place of the chairs and sofas he had known. He pretended he didn't see them, and the animals stopped breathing and watched with glowing eyes as he passed. He heard their hearts beating; they gave off a rank, rotten smell as they inched nearer in the darkness, on every side. He knew that they longed to touch him.

He slipped into the kitchen, quietly closing the door behind him, sniffing the air and finding faint traces of the pork chop and rice Mrs. Hernandez had served him for supper. He missed her and her kindly, rough hands. He felt so alone. He fetched up in front of the refrigerator, pondering his father's last words: "This is now officially a ghost house." Was that a secret message which Courtney had understood, but which he, Kyle, had missed? Would it be a ghost house forever? Did they have to abandon it? As Kyle repeated his father's words in his mind, they became alien and threatening. He opened the refrigerator door. The light was wonderfully bright and

warm. He reached in, grabbed four slices of bologna, shut the refrigerator door, and stuffed the bologna into his mouth. He stood there
in the dark, chewing.

The more Kyle thought about it, the more he grew convinced
that they were all someplace together, Mom, Dad, and Courtney.
Well, if they weren't inside, they weren't playing fair.

They were together outside. That had to be it. He pictured them
sitting together on the back terrace, near the pool, waiting to see
how long it would take dumb Kyle to figure out their big joke, and
because this picture was the brightest thing in his world at the
moment, Kyle accepted it as the truth. Courtney had gotten hold of
his mom and dad. Now they were on her side.

So now he'd leave the house too. He'd sneak around to the
terrace, where they were sitting around playing their big joke on
him, and he'd leap out of the bushes and give them the fright of their
lives. "Ha, ha, ha," he'd yell. He'd beat up Courtney. He'd wipe
everybody out, *pow, pow, pow*. Then they'd be sorry. Boy, would
everybody be sorry when Kyle the Avenger jumped onto that
terrace. They'd see how Courtney had lied to them and they'd never
ever play a stupid joke on Kyle again.

He grinned as he opened the kitchen door, slipped into the
night, and began trotting toward the back of the house and the
terrace. He was playing that scene over again in his mind, the one
where Kyle the Avenger jumps onto the terrace and frightens the
willies out of everybody, when he heard a noise behind him. He
dropped down on the ground and froze against the side of the
house. He looked back and saw two figures in dark clothes detach
themselves from the Surinam cherry hedge. They had come from
the Dominguezes' yard. They walked directly over to the kitchen
door and opened it, silently entered the house, and just as silently
closed the door behind them. Kyle stared at where they'd been.
They'd moved so smoothly, so quickly, so quietly. Like ghosts. For a
moment, Kyle found it hard to breathe. He felt dizzy and light-

headed; he wanted to clear his throat, but he fought against it, and then he began to gag.

He jumped up and plunged through the Surinam cherry hedge and landed on his hands and knees in the Dominguezes' yard, where he quietly vomited up the bologna. He wiped his mouth with his hand and flopped onto his back in the grass and lay shaking in the darkness. Music poured from the Dominguezes' house, and it felt soothing and familiar to him. Dad hadn't told him there were other people playing the game. Where'd they come from? Why were they wearing dark clothes?

Lying in the Dominguezes' yard, Kyle looked up at the moon and thought of the ghosts in dark clothes. Boy, were they scary. He never wanted to play this game again. He closed his eyes and saw stars and felt dizzy, so he opened his eyes and stared up at the sky and wondered how long he'd have to wait until the game was finally over and he could go home and fall asleep in his own bed.

"Christ Almighty, would you listen to that racket?" Darryl said when the heavy metal rock music started up at the Dominguez house. Darryl and Caroline had dozed off again; the music had awakened them.

"I'm going to the head," Caroline muttered, "and then let's collect the kids. Don't forget we've got to take them to Dairy Queen." She kissed him, then groaned as she got off the deck. "I'm getting old, sweetness," she said, descending the stairs. "Old."

Darryl moved to a chair moist with dew. He looked up at the stars and over at the lurid night sky above downtown Miami. He felt better than he had in a long while. Getting out of the house and away from the telephone and making love to Caroline in the moonlight had brought him to a place of balance between the ever-tightening inner craziness of the last few weeks and a sense of future possibilities. He felt refreshed. Hopeful. He loved his wife and he loved his children. He stretched, feeling sexy and content and not at all drunk. He knew he could solve his problems. He was ready to fight the fight. "Fucking rock music," he muttered, staring at his neighbor's house. How could old Dominguez stand that shit? Was he deaf?

"That client—the one who's been threatening you?" Caroline was coming back up onto the deck.

Darryl sighed.

She peered up at the sky and began to pick up her clothes. "What are you going to do?"

"Make a deal."

"What kind of deal?"

"I'll make them happy. I'm thinking of a way to pay them back."

She stopped dressing and stared at him. "Them?"

"Yes." He looked at her. "I told you that."

"You did?" She began crying.

He touched her, but she moved away. He opened his mouth but didn't know what to say. He pulled on his shorts and T-shirt.

She zipped up her shorts, weeping. "What are we going to do?"

"I borrowed some of their money."

"Borrowed?"

"Something like that."

"Well, for God's sake, give it back." Her head emerged from her T-shirt.

"I don't have it right now."

"What have you done with it?"

"It's gone." He opened his hands. "I'm in a deep hole."

She wept again. "Oh, tell them—anything."

"I've been doing that."

She hugged herself. "This is too much."

"It's business. I can't panic, or they'll be on me like sharks."

"Aren't we talking about your life—our lives? Is it all some kind of a game to you?"

"No." He felt her receding from him and he wanted to set things right between them. He told her that he loved her, and he embraced her, breathing in her smell, waiting to feel her soften. She didn't, so he stepped back and willed a smile onto his face. "Look," he said, "I screwed up, but I *know* a way to get out of it."

"How?"

"My luck's got to hold out a day or so, and then I'm clear. I want a different life. I can't go on like this. And that's a definite promise. We'll sit down and you'll tell me what you want and we'll make a plan."

She stared at him. "You're never going to change, are you?"

He remembered the flour in his hair and felt self-conscious. He must look absurd. "I'm changing," he said. "You'll see."

"I don't believe it."

"My biggest worry at the moment," he went on, rubbing his head, "is how I'm going to get this gunk out of my hair. Go back to the house and round up the kids and we'll go out to Dairy Queen. I'll use the boat dock hose and be right there."

She climbed down onto the concrete edge of the canal and then looked towards their house. It was dark and silent. Compared to the Dominguezes', so bright, throbbing with music and energy, her house seemed like the negative of a house. The children, she thought, were being unusually patient and quiet. She looked up at Darryl. She was angry at him and disappointed. "Oh, hurry up," she said.

"I love you," he said.

She gazed up at him, then turned and started into the darkness. Darryl tried, and failed, to find something reassuring to call after her.

He stepped into the cockpit, groped around, found a key, fitted it into the ignition, and tried to start the twin diesel engines.

The *Lay-Z-Girl* was Darryl's province, one in which Caroline was not interested. She hated fishing, and she complained about sunburn and seasickness.

Lay-Z-Girl badly needed repairs. Now the main engines wouldn't start. He couldn't work the radio. The gauges for the three fuel tanks were hovering near empty. He gave out a deep sigh. How he had loved this boat. And what a mess his life had become. He had told Caroline the truth. He wanted to change. But what was he going to do about Narciso? A solution seemed impossible but at the same time close, very close.

On his way back to the railing, he almost tripped over the sheets that Caroline and he had shed on the deck. He threw them over his shoulder, climbed down onto the concrete dock, turned on the hose, then changed his mind and turned it off.

He'd seen the Dominguezes' lawn explode into low fountains of water. Their automatic sprinklers had come on. In the light from their porch, Darryl saw droplets sparkling on their grass. It was a strange and beautiful sight. His own lawn was dark. So was the house. Caroline hadn't turned on the lights. He halted, uneasy, and stared at his house and around his backyard. He felt that something was wrong with it all, but he didn't know what it was.

His house was perfectly quiet. Darkness seemed to flow out of it toward him in dense waves. He felt a spurt of anxiety and fought to control it. Where was Caroline? Where were the kids?

"Caroline?" he called. There was no answer. He thought that he glimpsed a dark movement behind the sliding glass door to the living room. "Caroline?" he called again. Why didn't she answer?

Darryl studied his house. For some reason, it didn't look like his home. It seemed alien. He didn't like it. He glanced with irritation at all the bright lights illuminating the Dominguezes' house, and he wrestled down his anxiety.

He made up his mind: he'd had enough paranoia for one day. He was tired and he wanted this game to be over. There was, he decided, only one reason for the silence in his house. His family were waiting inside in the darkness to surprise him. Well, he'd play along, even though the notion of moving into that darkness gave him the creeps.

He wanted to be greeted by warmth and light and happy children. He had a vision of them standing just inside the door, holding their breath, waiting to switch on the lights and yell "Boo!" That vision propelled him forward, smiling.

Perhaps, he thought, as he walked up the lawn, rubbing the flour from his hair, perhaps when they got back from Dairy Queen, he'd switch on his porch lights and turn on his sprinklers and show the kids how beautiful water can be, even at night.

The English Tourist

EDNA BUCHANAN

It was August in Miami, the week of the full moon. The shooting never stopped.

Five people had been cut down in six days at the La Roncha Café. A robber shot an owner. A robber and two customers were shot by the cashier, who was shot two days later by the chef, who emptied his .357 magnum, sending bullets buzzing across a busy intersection like angry bees.

Colombian cocaine cowboys and Russian gangsters exchanged high-powered slugs in a riverfront showdown. Jail inmates rioted, demanding satellite TV in their cells, and a fifteen-year-old gunman tried to rob a seventy-seven-year-old ice cream truck driver, who shot him dead in front of a crowded playground.

The temperature soared, the barometric pressure dropped, and the police called in reinforcements.

A man wearing a fake beard, a postal uniform, and a mail pouch claimed to have a special delivery, then shot and killed a Miami man at his front door. I attended the police press conference held to assure the public that "more than likely he's not a real mailman."

Weary and irritable, I dreaded Saturday night. My name is Britt Montero, and I cover the police beat for *The Miami News.* After the press conference, I slipped up the back stairs to the fourth-floor detective bureau to see what else I could learn about the bogus mailman.

A tall, middle-aged man sat forlornly on a hard wooden bench outside the noisy and crowded robbery office. He was pale and bruised, had a short beard, a torn shirt, and a ham-and-cheese sandwich. "Who's that?" I asked the young detective inside.

"You supposed to be up here, Britt?" he asked suspiciously. His muscles bulged against his tight cotton shirt and leather shoulder holster.

"It's lunch time, no brass around. Is he a witness?"

"Nah, a victim. English tourist. Had a twelve-hour stopover and got nailed. I feel sorry for him. Just bought him a sandwich."

"One of those plastic-wrapped ones out of your vending machine? Now I feel sorry for him too. What happened?"

"Carjacked, abducted, and robbed by some guy running amok. He's, lemme see, victim number four, so far. The robber's still out there, must be having a crack attack. Snatched four victims off the street at midday in less than an hour. I'm still talking to victim number two, three's at the hospital, got pistol whipped and thrown out of a moving car."

Another tourist burned in the Sunshine State, I thought ruefully. I visited homicide, returned and found the Englishman listening in open-mouthed wonder to the sorry tale of victim number two, a local businessman. The robber had taken his shoes, along with his tie and jacket. He padded off barefoot to look at mug shots, and I introduced myself to the Englishman. He squinted at me nearsightedly, furrowing his brow. The robber had stolen his glasses.

His name was David Grant, age forty. In Mexico City, where he had flown first on business, he had prudently slipped off his watch and initialed signet ring. Unfortunately, he had slipped them back on in Miami.

He had stashed his plane tickets, passport, and luggage in an airport locker, rented a car, and was soon lost. The man he asked for directions pulled a gun and forced his way into the car.

The robber took his watch, ring, wallet, and camera, his thick-lensed spectacles, and the car. "I was quite certain he planned to kill me," the tourist said quietly. He looked bewildered. "I've only seen things like this in American films."

Welcome to Miami, I thought, taking notes.

Dumped out of the car along the expressway, he was astonished and quite relieved to be alive. He walked for hours before finding Miami police headquarters, then took his place in line to report the crime. He had no money and no transportation back to the airport to catch his flight, still hours away.

"How do you live here?" he asked seriously.

I cover the dark side of the city I love every day, but I hate when others see it. "It's not really that bad," I insisted.

The English tourist remained unconvinced.

While he filed his report, I pitched his story to my editor. He agreed that this was a good opportunity to show the human side of a victimized tourist and assigned a photographer. Lottie Dane is the best news shooter at the paper and my best friend.

"Don't worry," I told the detective as Lottie arrived, her Nikon 8008 slung over her right shoulder, her frizzy red hair long and loose. "We'll see that he gets to the airport." The detective looked relieved, then turned his attention to victim number five, who had just arrived, bleeding from a nasty cut on his chin.

The gentle, soft-spoken English tourist hesitated a moment before folding his tall frame cautiously into my T-Bird. Alone and stone-broke in a foreign country, he had already been abducted by a stranger once that day.

"I can't believe the man actually had a gun," David repeated for the third time. I decided not to mention the revolver in my glove compartment.

We gave him the tour, pointed out the homes of Madonna and Sylvester Stallone, then drove east toward South Beach, past the huge cruise ships at the port and posh Star Island, home to Gloria Estefan, Vanilla Ice, and Leona Helmsley, the Queen of Mean.

"What time is it?" He fretted about making his plane.

"They took his watch," I told Lottie.

Without hesitation, she slipped the Swiss Army watch off her freckled wrist. "Here you go."

"Oh, no, I couldn't possibly accept such a . . ."

"It ain't nothing but a thang," she drawled in her molasses-smooth Texas twang. "I want you to have it."

Graciously, he accepted and buckled the strap around his wrist as we cruised along traffic-clogged Ocean Drive. The sea, sparkling and turquoise, pounded the sandy beach on one side, and stream-lined moderne architecture framed the other, art deco hotels in ice-cream colors with parapets, spires, porthole windows, and eight-dollar valet parking. He probably couldn't see much without his spectacles but seemed to relax. Lottie shot photos as he stood squinting in front of a coconut palm, then we stopped at an outdoor café to drink iced cappuccino, surrounded by gorgeous models, Rollerbladers, retirees, and yuppie motorcyclists.

"You know," David confided, "I've been here before." He had come to Miami twenty years earlier, he said, as an exchange student to study business administration.

"I lived with a family . . . that's why I was here today. I was hoping to find someone. But the city has changed so much, I got lost straightaway. Too late now, and I wouldn't want her to see me like this." He fingered the swollen bruise over his right eye.

"Her?" We both perked up. The demands of our jobs have had disastrous effects on our personal lives. Most of our romantic adventures are lived vicariously.

"My first love," he said shyly. "Althea Rose Peabody, the daughter of the people I stayed with." He glowed as he spoke her name. "She was eighteen. Blonde like you, Britt, suntanned and graceful. She studied ballet and loved poetry. We read Emily Dickinson to each other on the beach."

"What happened?" Lottie demanded.

"My father died suddenly, halfway through my time here, and I had to return to England. I swore I'd be back, but once I got home things became more complicated. I had younger siblings and my mother to think about. I had to leave school and work for a few years." He looked down. "She didn't answer my letters."

"How serious were you?" I asked.

"Very." He shifted uncomfortably in his chair. "In fact, at the time I left, there was a possibility that we would marry much sooner than expected."

"You mean she was . . ."

He nodded. "We weren't sure, but it was a distinct possibility."

"You're not married now?"

He shook his head wistfully.

Moments like this make it a joy to be a reporter. I felt my adrenaline pump, brain cells kick back to life.

"We can find her," I promised excitedly. The poignant tale of long-lost lovers reunited was more than a good story, it would be a happy ending to this week of numbing carnage and unrelenting bad news. Even if the woman were happily married, she would be flattered.

"She wasn't listed in the telephone directory," David said doubtfully.

"We can do it. We'll go back to the paper and run library and computer checks on Althea Rose Peabody."

"Right." Lottie pushed back her chair.

My beeper interrupted. The Miami police had caught the robber and wanted the English tourist to identify him.

Even without his glasses, David immediately pointed out his abductor. His name was Roland, a sandy-haired young punk with a scarred face, a missing front tooth, and a rap sheet as long as he was tall.

"Will I have to return for a trial?" the English tourist asked, dread in his eyes.

"Nah," the detective said. "We've got multiple cases, enough to put him away for twenty years to life. He was already out on bond for cutting off a woman's finger to get her ring during a robbery."

"Good God," the tourist said.

He shook my hand quite properly as we said good-bye at the airport.

"I'm sorry about what happened."

"It's all right," he reassured me. "I'm still alive."

I promised to contact him at once when I found Althea Rose.

It wasn't difficult. The third Peabody I called was a cousin, hadn't seen Althea Rose in years, but said she had married several times, never for very long. The cousin dug out the address.

The full moon was climbing, huge and ripe, as I drove to the small bungalow near Morningside Park. The police scanner in the dashboard crackled with action. My beeper chirped nonstop. A shooting at the port. A bomb scare at the airport. The Vicious Latin Boys and the International Posse were engaging each other and the cops in drive-by firefights. Casualties so far: three innocent bystanders, but I ignored them. I remained resolved, undeterred, my anticipation building. They would have to wait, I thought, until I found the happy ending we all needed.

The door was answered by a heavyset, middle-aged blonde woman with too much makeup on her bulldog face and the smell of liquor on her breath. I searched in vain for a trace of the graceful teenage ballerina.

"Are you Althea Rose Peabody?"

"That's right. That was my maiden name."

I took a deep breath. "I'm writing a story about a series of robberies downtown today. One of the victims was an English tourist. . . ."

"I know, I know." Her bleary eyes swam with tears.

"So you've already heard about him?" I was confused.

"The police called me. Why are they always picking on him? Roland's a good boy at heart, my only child. He's barely twenty." She dabbed at her eyes and looked defensive. "It's not easy raising a child alone."

"No, it isn't," I managed to whisper, "especially not in Miami."

The Great Persuader

STANLEY ELLIN

On the morning of her seventy-fifth birthday, Mrs. Meeker dallied over her usual breakfast of coffee and a cigarette while reading through the pile of congratulatory messages on the table before her. Telegrams, notes, and cards. Messages from the governor of Florida himself, from dignitaries of the city of Miami Beach, from old, old friends who nested as far north as Palm Beach and Hobe Sound.

There was even an editorial in the Miami Beach *Journal* swimming in adjectives and dedicated to her. A half century ago, it pointed out (and the choice of phrase made Mrs. Meeker feel incredibly ancient), Marcus Meeker had brought his fair young bride from the chilly North (tourists take note, thought Mrs. Meeker) to help him shape a glittering wonderland out of the sun-kissed isle of Miami Beach. Honored be his memory. Happy the birthday of the partner who had shared his triumphs, the First Lady of the city.

There was, of course, no mention of Marcus junior, who in his time had provided the *Journal* with even more spectacular copy than his father. The painful memory of her long-dead son rose in Mrs. Meeker. What a charmer he had been. How gay and clever and handsome. But with one fatal weakness. Where the horses were run or the cards dealt or the dice thrown, there he was simply a helpless, useless hulk, sick with the gambling madness. A lamb for the slaughter, easy pickings for the wolves. Because of them he had squandered the Meeker fortune—first his inheritance and then his mother's—had neglected his ailing wife until it was too late to do anything but mourn her death, and had made himself a stranger to his infant daughter. And finally had gone to a bloody and scandalous death, murdered in a dark alley as a lesson to others who might fail in the payment of their gambling debts.

Yes, what an enchanting boy he had been, Mrs. Meeker thought. What a pitiful figure of a man.

She closed her mind to harrowing memories. There was other mail before her to attend to. A solemn warning from the tax commission, a heartfelt plea from the electric company, urgent reminders from various local merchants. Mrs. Meeker dutifully read them all, then contemplated her barren dining room, wondering what was left in the house to sell and what price she could hope to get for it.

Really, she told herself, it was like being captain of a luxurious ship whose fuel reserve was gone and whose precious furnishings had to be fed to the hungry boilers. It became a way of life after a while. Painful at first to see the jewelry go, and then the silver and china and curios and books and pictures and, at last, the furniture, piece by piece; but that was nothing to what her misery would be if she were forced to sell the estate and live out her remaining life elsewhere.

She smiled at the portrait of her husband on the wall. Dear brawling, arrogant Marcus, who had come out of a Boston slum to carry off a Beacon Street princess. He had brought her south with the assurance that he would make his fortune here, and he had kept his word. And once the fortune was made he had built this hacienda, building by building, to her design.

Casuarina, it was named, from the grove of trees around it; and the day she saw it complete, set among casuarinas and royal palms against the pale green waters of the Gulf Stream beyond, she knew that this was where she intended to live out her life. The buildings might be shabby with decay now, but they still stood defiantly against tropical sun and wind; and this was home—this was where the heart was, and life anywhere else would be unendurable.

She was lost in these musings when her granddaughter Polly came down to breakfast, a song on her pretty lips, a birthday gift in her hand. It was a silver brooch, a profligate gift considering Polly's earnings, and Mrs. Meeker swiftly calculated that it might placate the electric company for a month or so without Polly's knowing where it had gone.

Polly was an adorable child, as her grandmother readily acknowledged; she was, along with Casuarina and a passion for cribbage, foremost among the things that still gave life meaning. But she had a head full of confetti, no doubt about it. She had failed out of the university at the end of one semester; she held her receptionist's job at the law offices of Peabody and Son only because young Duff Peabody was hopelessly infatuated with her; and at the age of twenty she had an ingenuousness about life that could be frightening at times.

But, Mrs. Meeker wondered, how does one cope with a breathtakingly beautiful young woman who stubbornly insisted on taking everyone in the world at face value?

Before breakfast was over, a car horn sounded, and Polly leaped to her feet.

"Which one is that?" Mrs. Meeker asked.

To her, the young louts from the university who danced attendance on Polly were indistinguishable from each other. All football players, apparently, and all astonishingly muscular, they had fallen under Polly's spell during her brief tenure at the university and now took turns driving her to her office.

"It's Frank," said Polly, "or Billy. I don't know which." She flung her arms around her grandmother and kissed her loudly. "Happy birthday again, darling, and whoever it is I'll have him pick you up later for your shopping."

After she was gone, Mrs. Meeker had Frazier, the houseman, clear the table and bring her the worn notebook containing the inventory of household belongings. As a young man, Frazier had been majordomo of Casuarina's numerous staff. Now white-haired, he was the sole remaining servant of the house—chef, butler, handyman, and sales manager all in one.

With him Mrs. Meeker combed through the inventory book deciding which of the remaining pieces of furniture must be sacrificed to demanding creditors. There were twenty rooms in the house, most of them picked clean long ago, and her heart sank at the way page after page of the inventory showed how little was left for the market. The only thing of real value remaining was the property itself, and that, it went without saying, was sacrosanct.

With this dismal business at last settled, Mrs. Meeker removed her shoes, donned a broad-brimmed straw hat and sunglasses, and walked down to the shore for solace. She was squatting at the water's edge feeding the gulls their daily ration of breadcrumbs when she saw a man leave the house and make his way through the grove of casuarinas toward her.

She stood up as he approached. He was in his middle thirties, good-looking, deeply tanned, dressed in an expensive suit. Not a bill collector, she decided warily; more the expensive lawyer type.

"Mrs. Meeker?"

"Yes."

"My name is Yaeger. Edward Yaeger. I want to offer good wishes on your birthday and to tell you what a privilege it is to meet you."

"Is it? And what's your business with me?"

Yaeger laughed. "Not my business. I represent a Mr. Leo August of Detroit. And since you evidently like to come right to the point, I'll do that. Mr. August believes you may be considering the sale of this estate, and he wants to make an offer for it. I'm authorized to meet any fair price you set."

"Indeed." Mrs. Meeker pointed her sharp little chin at the row of pastel and glass skyscrapers, the surprising outlines of gleaming new hotels, stretching southward into the distance. "Aren't there enough of these things around here as it is?"

"Mr. August doesn't intend adding to them. He wants this place as his residence. It won't be changed at all. It will only be restored."

"Restored? Does he know what that would cost?"

"To the penny, Mrs. Meeker."

"But why Casuarina? I'm sure he could find a dozen places as suitable."

"Because," said Yaeger, "he's looking for prestige. He's a man who made it to the top the hard way. I'd say that owning the Meeker estate would mean to him what a knighthood means to some successful junk dealer in England."

Mrs. Meeker decided that she did not like Edward Yaeger. Not only was he being impertinent to her, he was being downright disloyal to his client.

"I'm sorry," she said, "but Casuarina is not for sale. I don't know where you got the idea it was."

"Oh, come, come, Mrs. Meeker," said Yaeger playfully. "Your circumstances aren't any secret. Why not take a handsome profit while you have the chance?"

"Because this happens to be my home. So if you don't mind—"

She saw him to the driveway where his car was parked, and after he was gone she stood there surveying her domain. Everywhere were shattered windows sealed with cardboard, roofs denuded of their tiles, stuccoed walls scabrous and cracked, and rank vegetation forcing its way through broken roads and walks. The roof of the building containing the indoor swimming pool had long ago collapsed. The doors of the garage, which had once held half a dozen cars, hung awry on their rollers, revealing bleak emptiness within.

To anyone passing on Collins Avenue, thought Mrs. Meeker resentfully, the place must look abandoned. But it was not. It was her home, and it would remain her home.

However, she soon learned that Edward Yaeger was not one to be readily discouraged. He appeared at the house a week later while she and Polly were at an after-dinner game of cribbage, and he brought with him gaudy temptation.

"I've been in touch with Mr. August," he said, "and when he heard that you won't set a price on the estate, he decided to offer one you can't afford to turn down. A hundred thousand dollars." Yaeger was carrying a leather portfolio under his arm. Now he placed it on the table, opened it with smiling assurance. "In cash."

Polly gasped at the display of packaged banknotes before her. Mrs. Meeker felt somewhat unsettled by the spectacle.

"Your client does have a dramatic way of doing things, doesn't he?" she finally managed to say.

Yaeger shrugged. "He believes that cash is the great persuader. If it is, all you have to do is sign this letter of agreement for the sale of the estate."

"Isn't it risky carrying all that money around?" asked Polly with wide-eyed admiration.

"Hardly. If you look through that window at my car you'll see an unpleasant-looking gentleman whose job is to provide an ounce of prevention. He's one of Mr. August's most loyal employees, and not only is he armed with a gun, but he would have no objection to using it."

"Horrible," said Mrs. Meeker. "Incredible. All this money, an armed bodyguard—really, your Mr. August is too much for me. If I ever did sell Casuarina, it wouldn't be to someone like that. But, as I've already made plain, I don't intend selling."

It was hard to convince Yaeger that she really meant it—in fact, it was hard to convince herself in the face of the offering before her—and that was bad enough. What was worse was Polly's naïve regard of Yaeger, the unabashed interest she was taking in him. He was, Mrs. Meeker realized with concern, something new to the girl—an older man, attractive, urbane, overwhelmingly sure of himself. For his part, it was evident that he had taken close note of Polly with a coolly appraising eye and liked what he saw. Liked it a great deal.

When he finally accepted temporary defeat, he turned his attention to the playing cards and pegboard on the table, obviously looking for an excuse to dally.

"It's cribbage," said Mrs. Meeker shortly. "I gather you don't play."

"No, but I'm a quick learner at cards. Show me the game, and I'll prove it."

"Isn't there someone waiting for you in your car?"

"He'll wait," Yaeger said. "Waiting is his business."

So, short of flagrant bad manners, there was nothing to do but show him the game. In truth, as Mrs. Meeker explained the rules she found herself softening a little toward him. He listened intently, asked shrewd questions, and what more could any devotee of cribbage want than a willing convert? When the time came for a demonstration she shuffled the deck and started to deal.

"Don't we get a chance to cut the cards in this game?" Yaeger asked smilingly.

"Oh, I'm sorry," said Mrs. Meeker. "As a matter of fact, I should be penalized two points just for not offering you the chance to cut. That's the rule that's used for very strict play. But I've been playing so long only with dear friends—"

"That you're inclined to skip the formality," said Yaeger. "Well, I'd much rather have the compliment of being thought a friend than the penalty," and, Mrs. Meeker observed, when it was his turn to deal, he didn't offer her the deck to cut either. After that, it was always a case of dealer cut for himself, as if they were the dearest of dear friends.

As he had remarked, he was a quick learner. At the start, unsure of the best discards, he made several blunders. Then he gave Mrs. Meeker an honest run for her money, losing the first game by a wide margin, but very nearly winning the second. And all this, Mrs. Meeker observed, while he kept up a half-flirtatious dialogue with Polly. It was dismaying to watch the nonchalant skill with which he simultaneously handled both his cards and her moonstruck granddaughter. Somehow it seemed to deprecate cribbage and Polly together, just as the cash thrust under her nose had deprecated the true value of Casuarina to her.

All in all, it was a most disturbing evening.

Others followed. Yaeger came again and again to renew his client's offer, to play cribbage, to court Polly. It led Mrs. Meeker to wonder if she should not bar him from the house. But on what grounds? As for appealing to Polly, that would be useless. All you had to do was look at Polly while in the man's company to see how useless.

So there was only one satisfaction to be gained from Edward Yaeger's intrusion on the scene. He became a superb cribbage player and, as Mrs. Meeker guiltily knew, a good game of cribbage was as heady for her as fine old wine. Other card games had never interested her. Cribbage, she would point out, was the only true test of guile and nerve. The trouble had always been in finding an opponent of proper mettle, but now in Edward Yaeger she had one. Although he lost more often than he won, he made every game a challenge.

She began to relish those nightly duels with him. Nothing had tasted as sweet in a long time as the movement of pegging another victory over this formidable adversary. And to give up this pleasure because she was vaguely repelled by his cocksure manner, his disdainfully smiling self-assurance—well, she couldn't. Simply couldn't.

But she was not unprepared for dire revelation when it came. It was young Duff Peabody who brought it. His father had handled

Marcus senior's legal affairs, and Duff had inherited not only the law office but a vested interest in the Meeker family. Especially Polly. As he had once frankly admitted to Mrs. Meeker, having Polly working for him was a perpetual torment. For one thing, she was gaily and totally incompetent at her work; for another, her presence addled him completely. As far as he could see, the only solution was marriage to her, but, alas, Polly remained deaf to all his pleas.

Now he suddenly arrived at Casuarina in a lowering, gusty afternoon when Mrs. Meeker was at the water's edge attending to the gulls who flocked around her. He was in a really bad state, Mrs. Meeker saw, and she let the gulls fend for themselves while she heard him out. It was a damned mess, he said. Luckily, Polly was innocently pleased to reveal her intention of marrying this thug—

"Thug?" said Mrs. Meeker in alarm. "Marry?"

"Yes," said Duff, "that's the word she used—marry. And now that I've taken the trouble to look him up, I can tell you that your friend Yaeger is no better than a thug. The man he works for, Leo August, is a racketeer who runs a gambling syndicate behind a big-business façade. Yaeger is his front man in these parts. Not that he's faking a good background and education. He has all of that, and that's exactly what he sold to August. From what I was told, August yearns to get into the social swim. People like Yaeger impress him."

Mrs. Meeker found herself both angry and frightened. "But it's all so obvious now. That large amount of cash. That ugly little man who's always waiting in the car—"

"Yes, that's August's pet gunman, Joe Michalik. He's got a few murders to this credit, if not on his record."

"Does Polly know all this? Have you told her?"

"Of course. And when she put it to Yaeger he laughed it off. Made it look as if I was the jealous suitor trying to get rid of him."

"But she knows what men like that did to her father. I've never kept it a secret from her."

"And she refuses to draw any connection. As far as she's concerned, Yaeger is the most glamorous thing that's ever come her way, and that's it. It's impossible to talk to her."

"How awful. Duff, we must do something. What can we do?"

"You mean, what can you do? Well, all this may be Yaeger's way of pressuring you into selling the estate. What if you make a deal with him? You sell him Casuarina, and he says good-bye to Polly."

"Would someone like that keep any such bargain? And suppose he tells Polly I tried to buy him off? Can you imagine how she'd react? No, there must be some other way."

But, Mrs. Meeker knew, easier said than done. She stood there in despair while the gulls wheeled overhead screeching for their dinner, while lacy edges of the tide lapped at her bare feet. On an incoming wavelet rode the pale, blue-fringed bladder of a Portuguese man-of-war, and Mrs. Meeker shudderingly backed away as the garish scarlet and purple of the creature's pulpy body, the slender black threads of its deadly tentacles washed ashore. These men-of-war were old enemies. She had once been stung by one while swimming, and it had felt like a white-hot iron playing over her arm. It had been an agonizing two days before the pain receded, and ever since then she had waged unremitting war on any of the pulps that came into her ken.

Now she looked with disgust at this one helpless on the sand, its bladder inflated and swaying back and forth in the warm breeze.

"Do fetch me that stick of driftwood, Duff," she ordered, and when he had, she thrust it hard into the bladder, which collapsed with a pop.

"The object," she said, "is to deflate and then destroy."

She carried the slimy residue of pulp inshore on the stick and buried it deep in the sand, leaving the stick as a grave marker. "Deflate and destroy," she said thoughtfully, staring at the upright stick while Duff watched her in puzzlement.

She suddenly turned to him. "Duff, I'm going to have a party."

"A party?"

"Yes, this coming Saturday. And you're to be there with a bill of sale for the estate. Can you prepare one on such short notice?"

"I suppose so. But what made you—?"

"Oh, do stop asking questions." Mrs. Meeker knit her brow in concentration. "And I'll have Polly invite her football-playing friends and some pretty girls. And, of course, Mr. Yaeger and that nasty little associate of his—"

"Michalik?"

"Yes. And as for a collation—well, Frazier will have to persuade our shopkeeper friends to extend their credit just a bit further. That means we can have a buffet, then dancing afterwards, and perhaps games."

"With Yaeger and Michalik running them, of course," Duff said grimly. "You sound as if you've gone completely out of your mind."

"Do I?" said Mrs. Meeker. "Well, perhaps I do"—which to Duff's bafflement and concern were her last words on the subject.

She was not minded to offer further enlightenment when Duff arrived at the party Saturday evening. The patio and rooms fronting it were brightly lit and filled with young people alternating between dance floor and buffet. Yaeger and Polly were intent on each other; Michalik, gray-faced, stony-eyed, and dour, leaned against a wall and surveyed the proceedings with contempt; and Mrs. Meeker was being royalty in a light mood, apparently delighted to find Casuarina once again alive with company and music.

She drew Duff aside. "Do you have the bill of sale ready?"

"Yes, but I still don't know why. You said yourself that selling won't really settle matters."

"So I did, but you must have faith in me, dear boy." Mrs. Meeker patted his hand. "Remember that man-of-war on the beach? I handled it quite competently, didn't I?"

"It's hardly the same thing."

"Perhaps you're wrong. Meanwhile, Duff, your job this evening is to stand by me. What I intend to do may seem foolhardy, but you're not to put any obstacles in my way."

"If I only knew what you intended—"

"You'll know soon enough."

Mrs. Meeker left him glowering and went about her business of playing hostess. She bided her time. The cool night breeze rose; couples abandoned the patio and crowded indoors. The hour grew late. And so, Mrs. Meeker told herself, it is now or never. She took a deep breath and moved, serenely smiling, toward Yaeger, who had a possessive arm around Polly's waist.

"Enjoying yourselves?" Mrs. Meeker asked, and Yaeger said, "Very much. But as for our business—"

"I have the papers ready. And I suppose you have the money here?"

"I have. If you don't mind leaving the festivities for a few minutes, we can close the deal right now."

Mrs. Meeker sighed. "I can't say I do mind. I'm afraid I am not up to parties like this anymore. My idea of a good time is a little game of cribbage. Dear me, how angry Polly's grandfather would get when I lured someone into a game during a party. He always felt it was the worst of bad manners, but I could never resist the temptation."

"No reason why you should," said Yaeger with heavy gallantry. "If you want a game right now, I'm your man."

"How kind of you. That table is all arranged. The noise in the room won't bother you, will it?"

Yaeger laughed. "Yes, I noticed that table before. I had a feeling we'd come to this before the night was over."

"You're an old conspirator," Polly told her grandmother fondly. "You really are, darling."

"Oh, sticks and stones," said Mrs. Meeker. As she sat down and opened the deck of cards, she was pleased to see that interested onlookers were gathering around the table—among them Duff Peabody and the dour Michalik. "When it comes to cribbage I don't at all mind being humored. How far would you go in humoring me, Mr. Yaeger?"

"I don't know what you mean."

"I mean, would you mind playing for stakes? I've never done it in all my life, and the idea seems quite exciting."

"All right, I leave the stakes to you. A dime, a dollar—"

"Oh, more than that."

"How much more?"

Mrs. Meeker riffled the cards. She set them neatly on the table before her. "I should like to play you one game," she said smilingly, "for a hundred thousand dollars."

Even at this, she saw, Yaeger did not lose his poise. In the midst of the surprised clamor that rose around the table, he sat observing her with an amused curl to his lips.

"Are you serious?" he said.

"Entirely. Your Mr. August is eager to get possession of this estate, isn't he?"

"He is."

"And I am just as eager to lay my hands on some money. A large amount of money. I think it would be entertaining to settle the matter over the cribbage board. Therefore, I'll wager the signed bill of sale for Casuarina against your hundred thousand dollars. If I lose, Mr. August gets the estate, and you, of course, would have the money for yourself."

"And suppose he loses?" Michalik interposed in a hard voice. He turned to Yaeger. "Forget it, big shot. You don't play games with August's money. Understand?"

The smile vanished from Yaeger's face. "Michalik, remember that you're hired help. When I want your advice, I'll ask for it."

"But he's right," said Duff Peabody. "Mrs. Meeker, this is out of the question." He appealed to Polly. "Don't you agree? Don't you have something to say about this?"

"I don't know," Polly said unhappily. She stood with a hand on Yaeger's shoulder as if drawing strength from him. "After all, Casuarina isn't mine."

"And the money isn't yours," Michalik told Yaeger contemptuously. "So don't take any chances with it."

It was, Mrs. Meeker knew, the worst way to handle any male as arrogant as Edward Yaeger. And, as she could see, Leo August had been right. Cash was the great persuader. In Yaeger's eyes was a visible hunger for the money.

Still he hesitated. But he was wavering. Mrs. Meeker said, "Do you know, in all our games I've had the feeling you were humoring an old woman, that you weren't really playing to beat her at any cost. Now I wonder. Do you admit that I'm the better player? Is that it?"

Yaeger set his jaw. "Do you know what you're letting yourself in for? This isn't like playing for matchsticks."

"Of course."

"And if I win, August gets this bill of sale and I get the money. If you win—"

"Winner take all," said Mrs. Meeker. "Those are the terms."

"One game?"

"One game, and that settles it."

"All right," said Yaeger. "High card deals."

It was only when she picked up her first hand that Mrs. Meeker realized the full enormity of what she was doing.

Up to now she had not allowed herself to think of losing, to think of giving up Casuarina lock, stock, and barrel, and of making herself dependent on someone's charity for survival. Whose, she had no idea, but someone's it would obviously have to be. The thought was so unnerving that she discarded too cautiously, fell squarely into the trap Yaeger had set for her, and at the end of the first deal was already behind in score.

Watching his imperturbable expression, his deft handling of the cards, made it worse. She had meant what she told him. In their previous matches he had never seemed to extend himself. He had always been paying as much attention to Polly as to the game, and even then he had been a tough opponent. Now, relaxed in his chair, his eyes fixed with absolute concentration on his cards, he took on frightening dimensions.

Mrs. Meeker found herself suddenly weak with apprehension. Her fingers, when she dealt, were clumsy. He was a professional— that was what it was. He would never have accepted the challenge unless he knew the odds favored him. So she had baited her trap perfectly—and now had a tiger by the tail.

By this time everyone in the room had gathered around the table, silently watching. Not many understood the game, Mrs. Meeker knew, but all could follow the progress of the pegs moving along the scoreboard—Yaeger's red peg now far ahead, her white peg pursuing it feebly.

They played out the deal swiftly, the tension rising around them. Yaeger turned over his cards. "Fifteen two, four, six, and a pair makes eight." The pegboard clicked merrily as he measured off his eight points.

Mrs. Meeker matched his score and sighed with relief that at least she had held her own for that deal. Now for the crib, the two discards from each player, which was tallied to the dealer's score. It took only a glance for her to see that there wasn't a point in it. It was as if Yaeger had read her mind. Perhaps he had. He knew she would be discarding recklessly to make up lost ground, and he was prepared for that.

She changed her tactics. At the halfway mark she made a little headway; then a lucky deal came her way, a twenty-point hand, and now the white peg was only a short distance behind the red one.

But no sign of concern showed on Yaeger's face.

"Fifteen two," he said, "and a pair makes four."

It was not his face she should have been watching as he pegged his score. It was Polly who said to him with surprise, "Oh, no, you've only made four points. You've given yourself five," and reached for the red peg.

Yaeger's hand caught Polly's wrist in a sudden hard grasp—how hard was easy to tell from her look of alarm. Then the grip was immediately relaxed. Yaeger showed his teeth in a smile. "I'm sorry, dear. I thought it was your mistake, but you were right. Go ahead, put the peg where it belongs."

"Thank you," said Polly in a strange voice. "I will." And after she had done so, Mrs. Meeker saw with gratitude, Polly no longer leaned tenderly close to the man, her hand on his shoulder.

There was not much else to be grateful for. Yaeger, his face growing taut with strain, his eyes narrowed, discarded flawlessly and played his cards brilliantly. Mrs. Meeker, knowing that she must look as drawn with strain, drew even with him, and that was all. One point from victory, the two pegs stood side by side.

One point, thought Mrs. Meeker as she watched him gather the cards together and prepare to shuffle them. One point, and winner take all. Then realization suddenly burst on her. One point was needed, and there were two points waiting for her if he—

She tried to turn her eyes away from those supple, beautifully manicured fingers riffling the cards, riffling them again, but they held her spellbound. Yaeger dealt the first cards across the table, and Mrs. Meeker barely had strength to place a hand protectively over them.

"Two points' penalty for not offering me a chance to cut the deck," she said, feeling as if she were about to faint. "And that means game to me."

It took Yaeger a moment to comprehend what had happened. Then he rose from his chair. "You old biddy," he whispered, "you tricked me into that."

"Did I?"

"You tricked me into it. That means the bet is off. Nobody wins and nobody loses."

"You're wrong, Mr. Yaeger. You lose and must pay. I learned long ago by bitter experience that one must always pay his gambling debts."

"All right, if that's the way you want it, consider yourself paid. And since Polly and I are getting married, consider this money your wedding present to us. Now Mr. Michalik will take care of it. He'll be very unhappy otherwise."

"Who cares about that?" said Polly furiously. "As for marrying you—"

Her voice failed. In his hand Michalik was holding a gun. It was not very large and it was not flourished with menace, but it was clearly and indisputably a gun ready for use. And it was, Mrs. Meeker saw, one of Polly's huge football players who almost indifferently knocked the gun out of Michalik's hand as the bodyguard reached over the table to gather in the money. Others, even bigger and brawnier than the first, surrounded Michalik and took ungentle charge of him.

"Little man," said the biggest and brawniest, Frank or Billy or whoever he was, "the party's over. It's time for you to go."

Michalik struggled wildly and futilely as he was borne to the door; but he managed to point a quivering finger at Yaeger.

"Not without him!" he cried. "You hear me? Not without him. Just give him to me. That's all I want."

The news of Edward Yaeger's murder broke in the Miami Beach *Journal* a few days later. Mrs. Meeker read it with equanimity; Polly seemed badly shaken by it. No matter, thought Mrs. Meeker comfortably, she's young and healthy, and with Duff Peabody on hand for solace, she'll soon recover. For herself, she went down to the shore to enjoy the familiar scene with new zest.

She was there when Duff came scrambling down the sandy slope to the beach, bringing with him a tall, shy young man who seemed uncomfortably conscious of being in the presence of royalty.

"This is Detective Morrissey," Duff said. "After I saw the paper this morning I had a long talk with him. He's working on the Yaeger case and wants to hear your story about what happened the other night. He just booked Michalik for the killing, and he thinks he can land Leo August as the one who gave the orders for it, if Michalik can be made to talk."

"Indeed?" said Mrs. Meeker. "And what about the money?"

"Oh, it's all yours, ma'am," said Detective Morrissey earnestly. "I mean, unofficially speaking, there sure won't be anybody else to claim it. You can take my word it's all yours." Then he said with concern, "Ma'am, hadn't you better come away from there? You don't have shoes on and those things can sting like fury."

Mrs. Meeker raised her eyebrows at the man-of-war drifting toward her on the ripples of the placid sea.

"Not at all," she said graciously. "Really, these creatures are no trouble at all when you know how to handle them."

Flora Africana

DeLoris Stanton Forbes

S he bought the little plant because it reminded her of spring. Since the month was January, and even in Florida, especially in northern Florida, temperatures dropped and thermostats were changed from cool to heat, it was important to Mrs. Craig to be reminded of spring. Spring always had been hope time, good-things-on-the-way time, warm-weather time. Mrs. Craig thrived in sunshine.

"What is it called?" she asked the nice young man in the florist's shop. Mrs. Craig had never been a gardener (Henry had always tended the roses, had hired a man to mow the lawn) so she felt a kind of awe toward those who could plant a seed and make it grow.

"It's an African violet, ma'am. We have a fine selection." He directed her attention to a mass of greens and purples standing leaf to leaf, flower to flower on a long, low table. "Almost any color you might fancy."

Mrs. Craig put out a gloved finger, tentatively touched the dark leaves of the plant nearest her hand. "This one is pink," she said. "I've always been fond of pink." The leaves, such a deep shade of green, stood out around the pot on rubbery arms. Each reaching leaf had a furry look as though it wore a fine cashmere sleeve, yet was somehow translucent. A thick outer coating, surmised Mrs. Craig, protecting a tender inside. The lovely pink flowerettes stood upright, swayed in the breeze as if someone somewhere opened and shut a door. "Are they hard to care for?"

The young man smiled. Mrs. Craig thought he really was a most polite young man, unlike so many these days. "Not at all," he said. "There are a few little tricks. They need light but not too much light. And you'll notice that the pot is set in a liner. You water from the bottom, from inside the liner, and use warm water. You water every three or four days, whenever the liner is dry. Then, about every six weeks give it a taste of . . ." he produced a bottle of dark blue liquid from behind the cash register, "this." The label read African Violet Plant Food.

Mrs. Craig bought the violet and the violet food and took them home.

Not home, she amended as she unlocked the apartment door. Home had been the house that had been sold while she was in the hospital. "That big old house was just too much for you, Mother," her daughter Evelyn had said. "We're going to get you a nice little apartment where you won't have all those responsibilities. A nice safe apartment where we won't have to worry about you."

She carefully set the African violet down on an end table and took off her gloves. She had to admit it was a nice apartment. Nice. Its inoffensive neutrality was designed to appeal to the general taste. Pale beige walls, pale gray slip covers, pale drapes, pale ceilings, pale floors. Lately Mrs. Craig had the feeling that the little rooms (little, oh, yes indeed!) were fading into complete neutrality, taking her with them. Now the old house, that had been a mass of color, a decorator's nightmare, no doubt, but so—interesting. Enough about the old house. It was gone.

And now the plant—the sturdy yet fragile-looking little plant— struck a positive note in this monotonous symphony.

"You're very nice," said Mrs. Craig to the African violet. "I hope you like it here." She went out into the kitchen—everything in the kitchen was yellow like an egg yolk turned bad, Mrs. Craig thought. She preferred white kitchens, big white kitchens with touches of bright red and green and a braided rug on the shining hardwood floor. She turned on the faucet with a brisk motion, ran water into the tea kettle. She told herself, and firmly, too, what's done is done and there's no sense in complaining.

She made her cup of tea and drank it in the living room sitting near the African violet.

The next day was Sunday, and John and Evelyn brought the children to visit. There was something about being with her family that tired her, Mrs. Craig decided. They were so big, even the little ones, big for their ages. Even Evelyn, slim as she was, was a tall girl and so vital. They all laughed so much and talked so loudly. If the children cried, which they seemed to do at regular intervals, they cried more loudly than Mrs. Craig ever remembered children crying.

"Have you had a good week, Mother?" Mrs. Craig's daughter, as Mrs. Craig and Evelyn herself had often been told, was a real beauty. Mrs. Craig looked at her now, hardly hearing the question, so intent was she on seeing how her daughter looked, really looked, really seeing it—this thing that made her beautiful. After three children (John Thomas Trent III, Fredericka, and Ashley), Evelyn's figure was as svelte as ever. Her chestnut hair was as wavy, as lustrous at thirty-six as it had been at twenty. Her face was as unlined, her dark eyes as brilliant. It was still, always would be, Mrs. Craig supposed, a pleasure to look at Evelyn. So that was beauty.

"I said—what kind of week did you have?" Evelyn raised her voice a few more decibels. As though I were deaf, thought Mrs. Craig with annoyance.

Mrs. Craig searched her mind for small details that Evelyn might like to hear. "I had lunch on Tuesday," she said, "with Millie Crockett." Mrs. Craig stopped in the middle of her narration, cast an anxious eye at the children who were now involved in a wrestling match, even the girls. They were, Mrs. Craig thought, perilously near the table that held the African violet. I shall have to find a better place for it, she told herself.

"That's nice," said Evelyn. "Where did you eat?"

"Hey! You Indians!" John Thomas Trent (the Second) had been a star halfback at Florida State. He loomed large when he rose to separate the young grapplers. "You're making your grandmother nervous. Cut it out."

Evelyn stood up. "They're getting restless," she said. "I suppose we'd better take them home before they attack the settlement." She reached out, took her mother's hand. "You're sure you're feeling all right?"

Mrs. Craig smiled up at her. "Of course I am."

The beautiful face frowned. "I don't know, John Thomas. What do you think? She still looks so—so sort of peaked."

Mrs. Craig's son-in-law bent over her from his tall height, peered into her face. "You are all right, aren't you, Mom?" he asked without waiting for, perhaps not expecting, an answer. "It's just the operation, Evie." Mrs. Craig still winced inwardly whenever she heard her lovely daughter called 'Evie.' Just as she did when the children were referred to as 'John-Tom, Freddie, and Ash.' Mrs. Craig loved nice names. "It was a major operation, honey," John Thomas was going on. "It takes time to get over it."

Evelyn smiled, evidently reassured. "Of course. A few months of this lovely peace and quiet will make a new woman of you, Mother." And then they were busy donning coats and caps and collecting assorted toys and games, all of which took an inordinate amount of time, and it wasn't until long after they'd gone and the echoes of their being there had died away that Mrs. Craig realized they hadn't even noticed her African violet.

That night she gave it a name. She called it Tamara.

Bright and early Monday morning Mrs. Craig bought two more African violets, one white and one dark lavender. She brought them back to the apartment, arranged the trio in a window that got the morning sun. The white one she named Blanche, the dark one she called Liliom. It took her quite a while to select the appropriate names. She spent the rest of the morning arranging then rearranging them, then sitting back to enjoy their strange beauty.

Imagine! Violets in Africa!

She had wanted a pet when she'd learned about the apartment. Her house sold, her furniture in storage ("Honestly, Mother, it isn't worth moving. The pieces are so big and heavy—they'd crowd you right out of the apartment."), she'd felt quite acutely the need for companionship. If only Ebeneezer were still with her. Ebeneezer had come to live with her and Henry when he was just a kitten. But they'd had to put Ebeneezer to rest when she'd become so ill—unable to care for him. It hurt—it still hurt—to think of it. So she wouldn't. She wouldn't even hint that the hurt was still with her. She'd be matter-of-fact. She'd simply point out that she needed someone—something alive.

"A puppy? Or a cat?" Despite her resolution, she'd broached the subject timidly to Evelyn. Evelyn had never been what she'd call an animal lover.

"But, Mother, you can't!" Evelyn's fine brows climbed up her noble forehead. "You know how you get attached to animals—and, besides, the apartment house won't take pets."

"Now, Mom," John Thomas had stepped in close to the hospital bed, put out a comforting hand, "you know any kind of animal or bird requires a good deal of care. Why, this apartment we've found for you even has weekly maid service. We don't want you to have to do a thing."

"And remember, Mother," Evelyn had added, "a pet ties you down. We want you to be free." She made a gesture with her expressive hands. "Free as the breeze."

And now Mrs. Craig was glad. She didn't have an animal or a bird. She'd found something much better. Her African violets.

On Tuesday it seemed to her that Tamara had grown a bit. But Blanche—she wasn't absolutely sure of this, but she thought

Blanche looked a wee bit less hearty, her leaves a little tired, a little pale. She studied the water depth in the liners, decided they might need a little plant food. After all, she concluded, they'd suffered a sort of shock. They'd been moved from their home (not a big house with white curtains, true, but the florist's shop) to this apartment. She read the directions carefully, prepared the mixture, and filled the little cups.

At noon when the sun was at its brightest, when the rays cut in through the window and caused a glare, she carefully lowered the shades, raised them again after trial and error at three when the sun had moved away. The windows were in a sort of bay that looked down on a small enclosed area, the apartment house's excuse for a yard. Now, in this Florida winter, the annuals had died their predetermined death and the pines looked tired and rusty. Clearly horticulture was low on the complex's priority list; everything here was so ugly. So ugly. Except for the violets.

On Wednesday she bought Dianna and Andrea. Dianna was just a shade lighter than Liliom, and Andrea was a smidgen darker than Tamara. That was the day she had a luncheon engagement with Vera Hogarth. Mrs. Craig called and cancelled it, said she had a headache. The truth of the matter was, she didn't dare go out. She would have to leave the apartment shortly after eleven and—remembering Vera's long-windedness and her penchant for shopping trips—she probably wouldn't be back before five. Mrs. Craig knew she couldn't pull the curtains and take the sun from her charges from eleven to five—they would starve for sunlight—and, conversely, she couldn't leave the shades up. The nice young man at the florist's shop had told her they needed filtered sunlight at noon. So—she'd called and cancelled.

Mrs. Craig cooked herself an omelet and brought it into the living room. "Africa," she said. "Do you really come from Africa? You must—because of your family name. Tell me—I've never been anywhere—what is it like in Africa?"

And she sat in the semi-gloom and let her omelet grow cold while she heard wonderful stories of jungles of primeval green and striped black-and-white zebras and tawny lions and smoke-gray elephants and small jeweled snakes and . . .

The phone rang.

"Mother, are you all right?"

"Yes, Evelyn, of course I'm all right."

"Mrs. Hogarth called. She was quite upset." Evelyn's voice took on an edge. "In fact, I guess you could say she lit into me."

"Lit into you?" repeated Mrs. Craig. "Whatever for?"

"Oh, you know Mrs. Hogarth. She believes in speaking her mind. According to her, I am the worst sort of ungrateful child. She said I had no business installing you in that apartment all by yourself. . . ." Her daughter's voice broke. "You are all right, aren't you? You are happy there?"

Mrs. Craig's answer was sure. "Of course I am."

She could hear Evelyn's sigh of relief. "Honestly, Mother, you don't know how I've worried about it. We wanted to have you with us, of course, but the house isn't big enough even for all of us. There's absolutely no place to get away from one another. Sometimes I think . . ." she stopped, began again, "well, John Thomas and I thought the children would just drive you mad and the doctor warned us . . ." she hesitated, seemed to be choosing her words, "the doctor said your operation might cause some psychological repercussions. After all a hysterectomy is a dangerous thing. . . . And at your age. . . ."

"Evelyn." Mrs. Craig cut her short.

"Yes, Mother." Funny, just then she sounded like the little-girl Evelyn with the long, curling hair and the sunny disposition.

"I'm fine. You did the right thing. Don't worry."

As soon as she could, she left the telephone, but the violets were napping in the diffused light and Mrs. Craig couldn't go back to Africa. Not right then.

So instead she went back to when Evelyn was little and Mr. Craig—dear Henry—was still alive and they were together in the big house with the high ceilings and the wide-ruffle–curtained windows. How happy they had been—how the years had flown and then, before she knew it, Evelyn was married and then Henry was gone and there was nothing to give her any pleasure but going back.

Going back. There—she was doing it again, and that nice young doctor had told her she must look ahead. "Make a new life," he had said. "There's a big interesting world out there and you're still young enough to enjoy it."

Well, she was. She was making a new life, following orders. The doctor's orders, her daughter's orders. "Mother, don't look back, look to the future!" But they didn't plan on this, Mrs. Craig told her friends on the sill. They didn't plan on Mrs. Craig's traveling to Africa.

On Thursday Ursula was due. Ursula was the weekly maid, much too hit-and-miss for Mrs. Craig's taste. She usually redusted and remopped after the maid had gone. In addition, she broke things. Mrs. Craig thought it best if Ursula didn't come in before she'd provided safe quarters for her friends, so she called downstairs and told the manager she'd be out for the day: "Please tell Ursula I won't need her this week. I don't like anyone in the apartment when I'm away." Then, so she wouldn't be a liar, she went shopping.

She bought a special stand to hold her plants, a stand with glass shelves so it wouldn't matter if the water leaked a little, and she also bought Virginia, Helene, Eloise, Gloriana, and Melisande. She would have bought more but the nice young man at the florist's shop opened her eyes to yet another world.

"I don't want to seem impertinent," he said, "but you seem to be awfully keen on Africans and I wondered if you knew how easily they reproduce?"

"Reproduce?"

"African violets reproduce asexually. That is, a leaf from an African violet planted in the right sort of soil will produce another African."

Mrs. Craig stared in wonder at Gloriana—she had just now named her—in her hand.

"You mean, I can grow my own?" She was bemused.

"Yes, ma'am. A whole forest of them if you want to." The young man produced a plastic bag of potting soil and a series of little pots with small holes in the bottom, even a bag of pebbles. He showed her exactly how to pinch the leaf, how to put a few pebbles in the pot for drainage, how to mulch the potting soil.

He packed the whole business up and helped her to her cab. The cabbie gave her a hand in bringing everything to the doorman, who carried the collection up to her floor. She tipped him and told him she could manage. She could, and she did.

By Saturday evening Mrs. Craig had started a leaf from each of her friends—her children? She was tired, so tired that she was confused. Possibly she'd tried to do too much all in too short a time.

But she was done now and proud of her work. The neat little rows of babies (really too many for the plant stand she'd purchased) . . . how wonderful it would be when they, too, were grown and full of flower, to then have their own babies, to go on and on forever and ever while Mrs. Craig sat by and watched. No, not only watched. This was an important thing. They needed her—needed her to feed them and water them, to keep them alive.

It had been so long since she'd been needed. Not since dear Henry was alive. And then the operation, the horrible operation that had left her a shell of a woman—an empty, useless creature. How foolish she was being! She must stop this feeling sorry for herself, Henry used to say . . . she must stop this feeling of worthlessness. And besides, it wasn't true anymore.

Virginia? Yes, Virginia and Dianna were beckoning to her, whispering, but she was so tired, so very tired. She would just take a little nap right there in the chair, and when she woke up she'd be rested and ready to go.

Pyramids and the Sphinx and the long-necked ones—the giraffes and the ostriches and the people with rings stretching their necks upwards (she'd seen them once in the circus when she was small). . . and diamond mines, yes, diamond mines that sparkled like— diamonds (of course) in the morning sun.

The buzz from the foyer brought her back. She'd ignored it at first . . . where was she? What day? (The sun was shining). What time, what did it matter? But the buzzer was so insistent that she excused herself and attended to it.

"Mother! You frightened me, you were so long in answering. We're here for our Sunday visit."

Mrs. Craig looked into the tunnel of the speaking tube.

"Whom did you wish to see?" she asked.

"Mother! John Thomas, she sounds so funny. . . . Mother, it is you, isn't it? You sound so far away. Mother, this is Evelyn. John Thomas and the children are with me. Mother, are you all right?"

"You must have the wrong apartment," said Mrs. Craig kindly. "I'm leaving today. I'm taking a trip to Africa with a large group— my children, my friends. I hope you find your mother."

As she came back to them, those who eagerly waited, she took time to bolt and double-lock the door.

"Now," said Mrs. Craig over the far-off noise of the buzzer. She sat on the sill beside them and she looked down below onto a lush tangle of green, green, green: forest green and emerald green and apple green and spring green, jungle green, every green there was was down there . . . dark-skinned Basuto maidens and tall, strong Zulu warriors, child-sized Pygmies and king-sized Balubas, the Nile and the desert and the jungle, the land, the sky, the water . . . she moved smoothly toward it, through it all, going with them (naturally they led the way), deeper and deeper and deeper into the thick, dark, rich green.

"I tell you—something is wrong with my mother." Mrs. Craig's daughter let her apprehension make her voice shrill. "You must let us into the apartment."

The manager frowned, reached for his keys. He had managed apartments for many years, and he was sure of his ability to size up a prospective tenant. Mrs. Craig, unlike some he could mention (that couple in Three B, for instance), he had labeled 'no trouble, no trouble at all.' And now, if she were ill or had met with an accident. . . . He sighed inwardly and led the way to the elevator. The daughter and her husband and their three noisy children followed close on his heels.

The manager rapped on Mrs. Craig's door. First he rapped easily, politely, then more loudly, urgently.

The daughter asked sharply, "Do you hear anything?"

"Open the door, man," said the son-in-law. His tone was carefully unemotional. "Now don't worry, Evie. She's probably taking a nap."

"But I just spoke to her. . . . Do you hear anything?" the daughter asked again. Her voice had risen. The manager put his keys in the locks, turned one, twisted the other.

The door gave a little; the chain lock held it, gave them a six-inch view of neutral carpet, walls.

"Where's Grandma?" asked the littlest girl. "Momma, where's Grandma?"

The boy tugged roughly at her curls. "Shut up, Ash."

The bigger girl jostled him. "Leave my sister alone!"

"John Thomas. . . . " The daughter's face was ashen. "Something's terribly wrong." She whispered the words.

Her husband moved back, preparing to rush at the door. "Just a minute," protested the manager, "if you break the chain lock you'll splinter the door jamb. Who's going to. . . ?"

"Hurry, John Thomas, we've got to get in!"

"Grandma! Grandma!"

"We'll pay for any damages," said the son-in-law and hurled himself against the panel. They heard the tearing of wood; the rattling chain fell aside and the door swung open then, wide open.

"Mother!"

The room was empty. The daughter and her husband looked at each other. "Wait here," the husband said and walked briskly across to the kitchen. The daughter clutched the shoulders of the boy, called the girls to her with a low word.

The son-in-law came out of the kitchen, the door swinging wildly behind him. He didn't look their way, turned into the bathroom. The manager looked uneasily around. He was pleased to see the apartment looked neat, clean, well-cared for . . . hadn't Mrs. Craig cancelled Ursula this week? No matter. Apparently.

The son-in-law reappeared, his big square face expressionless. Mrs. Craig's daughter took a step toward him. "The bedroom? She's in the bedroom?" He shook his head, made a hopeless gesture with his hands.

"Oh, no," said the daughter. She began to cry. Like a child, she began to cry in shuddering sobs.

"No," her husband spoke quickly, harshly. "She isn't—that is, she isn't here. Anywhere. She's out."

The manager swung around to face him. The daughter stopped her weeping, stared at him with open mouth as though caught in the formation of a new wail.

"Isn't here . . . ?" asked the manager. "But—the chain lock . . ."

"Isn't here?" echoed the daughter.

"Where is Grandma?" The little girl was crying now, absorbing her parents' emotions. The other two joined her in an ear-splitting chorus.

"It's impossible," said Mrs. Craig's daughter through the din. She started for the kitchen. "She's fallen somewhere—or she's shut in somewhere—try the closets, the fire escape. . . ."

The two adults moved in opposite directions, calling, searching, opening and closing doors. The children joined in, making it some kind of macabre game: *bang, bang, bang* went the doors.

The manager stood, keys dangling from his hand. The room was hot, he thought, very hot, even though the shades in the bay were drawn and the thermostat (he checked) was at its normal setting. It was, oddly enough, an almost tropical heat.

And all those plants—massed at the windows in the bay. What were they? Oh, yes, African violets. He'd never seen so many and had never seen them so large. Huge, green clumps of them, their pink and white and purple blooms waving at the ends of slender stems as though they trembled. Air current, he supposed, yet it was still, yes, almost like a jungle.

He moved toward them, realized suddenly the center window behind them was open. Wide open behind the shade, wide open to the winter air, yet in here it was so still, so hot. He moved closer, mentally denying the sudden surge of apprehension.

He heard the sound as he came closer to the window, and it surprised and puzzled him. He thought one of the children might be making the sound until he understood—those tenants in Three B, three stories underneath, had their television turned too loud again. And after he'd warned them repeatedly. . . .

No matter that it made no sense, no sense at all, he always remembered that he clearly, most clearly, heard the harsh beat of native drums—just before he looked down.

Death by Pliers

CAROLINA GARCIA-AGUILERA

My beeper had just gone off for the third time. This last call was different—it had the 911 emergency code. I recognized the number. It was Michael Maloney, a criminal defense attorney I had done a significant amount of work for in the past. He was a good client. Definitely, this was not a call I could afford to ignore.

My dilemma was that he had started beeping me as I was standing in line at the Toys 'R' Us in South Miami for forty-five minutes, waiting to pay for my three daughters' Christmas presents. The cashier was tantalizingly close. Only two more ahead of me and I was there. The beeper went off again. Shamelessly, I reached into my purse and switched the function button from beep to vibrate. I could still feel it shaking angrily in my purse for the ten minutes it took to pay. I returned the call as soon as I was comfortably seated in my car in the parking lot.

"Where the hell have you been? Why isn't your cell phone turned on? I've been beeping you for over an hour now." Typical. Michael wasted no time with small talk.

"Don't exaggerate. It's only been twenty minutes," I replied sweetly. "So, what's up?" I had turned off my phone on purpose—my monthly bill was astronomical, and I still had to get through December and its budget-breaking Christmas shopping.

"Listen. I just got this case. Murder Two, court-appointed but largely circumstantial. Not too much money in it for either of us. It caps out at twenty-five hundred dollars for legal and five hundred dollars for investigative fees. It would have been First Degree Murder if our client had planned it beforehand, but because it happened during a drunken argument—victim had both cocaine and alcohol in her blood—he's charged with a Murder Two instead." With typical arrogance, Maloney had assumed I was already onboard. "Our guy's a migrant worker in Homestead charged with killing a hooker. I got him a real sweetheart plea, seven years if he pleads guilty to manslaughter, but he won't take it. Says he didn't do it."

"They all say they didn't do it. Why are you so surprised?"

"No. You don't get it. He says he really didn't do it. I got him seven years with gain time and good behavior and all that shit; he might serve a third of that. The State has since passed a law that States' inmates must serve eighty-five percent of their sentences before being released, so he's lucky he squeaked by under the old timetable. The penalty for second-degree is capped at twenty-five years—under the guideline sentencing range—so he could be facing that in the worst-case scenario. The guy won't take it. I explained to him that if we go to trial, he's looking at twenty-five big ones." Maloney repeated in wonderment. "Guy wants to go to trial. Can you imagine?"

It was rare that Maloney's clients did not take a plea. Hell, it was rare in all of Dade County. The overburdened judicial system in south Florida loved pleas: the judges loved them because they could move their cases out fast; the prosecutors loved them because they could reduce their caseloads; the defense lawyers loved them because they would not have to prepare for a trial they were likely to lose;

and the defendants loved them most of all because they would get off easier than they would if found guilty in a jury trial. Without question, in Dade County a plea was definitely the least-painful, most-efficient resolution to a case. The victims of crimes were seldom happy with pleas, but that's a different story—they are often overlooked in the judicial system.

"Look. I want you to go to the jail and talk to him. Get the story. You're going to have to do it in Spanish, 'cause the guy doesn't speak any English. You know how to shmooze him. I want to know what you think."

This was not an unusual request. I was known for having a nose for bullshit. I had developed it the hard way—I'd had four husbands. When I started in the business over ten years ago, I was a rarity: a Cuban-American female investigator with an MBA—and no drug habit. From the beginning, I had never lacked for clients. I knew my reputation. I was known for being smart, honest, and relentless. The fact that I spoke Spanish was a definite asset in a city that was approximately 64 percent Hispanic. Most important, Maloney trusted my judgment.

"I had Lola draw up an authorization for you to go see him. He's at the Guilford Turner Knight Jail behind Jackson. It shouldn't take you too long."

Maloney must have sensed my hesitation. I was burned out. I really wanted some time off. My daughters were on Christmas vacation from school, and I wanted to spend time with them. It had been a long, tough year. I was too exhausted to even be annoyed with Maloney to be so confident I would take the case that he had already had his secretary type up an investigator of record letter.

"Just talk to the guy. That's all. He's been in there since July. I only got appointed last week. Come on, it's Christmas. Be generous. I need you to do this."

I sighed. "OK. I'll do this, but that's all. I'll go talk to the guy and report to you. That's all," I repeated.

Maloney's office was located in the northwest part of Miami, in a dingy building on an even dingier street. I really did not like going there as it was just starting to get dark, but I wanted to get the assignment over with. Maloney refused to move out of the building he had been in for years. He liked to say his clients came in for his services, not for the amenities. If they wanted a view of Biscayne Bay, they could just go over and hire a lawyer in one of the high-rises downtown and pay for it.

It did not take long for me to pick up the legal authorization form needed for access to prisoners in any Dade County jail. Maloney had left the letter taped to the door outside his office. He had also left a note saying he had gone to the Alibi Lounge at the nearby Holiday Inn to have a few cocktails. I was to report to him there after speaking with our client. Nothing new there.

Maloney had told me our client was being held at the jail directly behind Jackson Memorial Hospital, just a short drive away. That relieved me, as it was one of the easier jails to visit. The Dade County Stockade, for example, was a nightmare. Not only was it far away, on the other side of the airport, but visiting inmates there was an all-day affair—even longer if they were having a lockdown.

I read the file when I stopped for red lights as I drove to the jail. It was as Maloney had said. Our client was accused of murdering a young hooker, Lindsay Farrow, his sometime girlfriend, during a drunken fight outside the apartment building where they lived. Cause of death had been a blow from a blunt instrument to the back of her head. Channel lock pliers. No identifiable prints on weapon. It was too rusty. Could work both for and against our client.

I read the last of the file as I waited in the visitors' room of the jail. I wanted to know as much as possible before meeting the client. I passed through the metal detector and just before handing over my personal effects to the corrections officer at the desk, even though I had not felt a vibration, I took a last quick check of my beeper. It would be the last chance I would have for a while.

Different jails have different rules for visiting inmates. Some will let you take in files and pen and paper to take notes. Others require that you surrender everything, including your files. None of them will let you take in a purse. Some jails have lockers inside the waiting room in which you have to put all your belongings; in others, you have to leave them with one of the corrections officers. Savvy visitors will lock their possessions in the trunks of their cars prior to entering, only taking in their professional identification and driver's license.

The toughest screening, by far, is at the Metropolitan Correctional Institute, the federal jail in the southwestern part of Dade County. There, visitors are not allowed to take anything in at all. The metal detectors are so sensitive that they will pick up the nails used to join the heels to shoes. It is not uncommon to see a visitor take off his or her belt, shoes—any object that will set off the machine. I personally have had to almost undress in front of everyone there until the offending article of clothing was identified. Usually I try to plan ahead and dress in such a way as to avoid that, even to the point of choosing a bra without underwire, but sometimes I get caught unprepared.

The corrections officer, after reading the authorization letter from Maloney and inspecting my credentials as a duly licensed private investigator of the State of Florida, escorted me down the hall to the interview room where I was to meet my client.

By now, I was experienced enough to know at which times to visit inmates. Regular visitors had to adhere to a posted visiting schedule. As a private investigator, I had the luxury of going at odd hours, but experience had taught me to avoid mealtimes, prisoner count time, or change of shifts of the corrections officers; otherwise, I would be waiting for hours. Breakfast was never a problem, as the prisoners were given their first meal of the day at 4:30 a.m.

No matter what jail I'm in—and, believe me, in the ten years I've been in the business, I've been in all of them—the smell that they have in common is the same musty odor of disinfectant. It's a smell that, once experienced, is never forgotten, evoking visions of Proust and his Madelines. I have never encountered that odor anyplace but in the Dade County jails.

I waited fifteen or so minutes in the cramped, ugly interview room before my client, Tirso Fernandez, was brought in. He was a small, squat, muscular young man with black hair tied back from his face with a rubber band. He had the traditional broad face common to Central American Indians. He was respectful, almost courteous, in waiting for me to ask him to sit in the only other metal chair in the room. If he was surprised that the investigator his attorney had chosen to send him was a woman, he did not show it, or maybe he was just past being shocked by anything. He waited in total silence for me to address him.

Maloney had warned me that he did not speak much English, so I conducted the interview in Spanish. I started by asking him a few basic questions—not really necessary since Maloney had done so already and I had the information I needed—primarily to put him at his ease. Besides, I had a copy of the police report, commonly known as the "A" Form. The "A" stood for "arrest."

According to the background I had on him, Tirso was a twenty-one-year-old Mexican migrant worker who lived several months in the winter in Homestead, picking fruits and vegetables. This had been his third year of doing so. His was not an unusual story. He lived with several other male migrant workers in town, under spartan, primitive conditions so they could save as much money as possible to send to their families back in Mexico.

During his narration, Tirso was calm and composed. It was only when we got to the part about the murder that he became agitated. He stood up, gesticulating wildly. With apprehension, I looked at the black button in the wall bell, located by the door, that was used to summon guards. I figured it would take me three steps to reach it. Even then, there was no guarantee that there would be an immediate response. I regretted not having returned to my self-defense class for the complimentary yearly refreshment course. The interview rooms, I knew for a fact, were soundproof.

"I swear to you, Señora! I did not kill her. I did not!" Tirso implored me to believe him. Suddenly, to my shock, he started unbuttoning his shirt, and I started inching towards the bell. To my relief, he stopped and showed me two pink, plastic rosary beads he was wearing around his neck, hidden under the shirt.

"My mother." He crossed himself. "My mother, bless her sainted soul, said to always tell the truth! On my sainted mother!"

"Tirso, if you did not kill Lindsay, then who did?" I asked him.

"I don't know. I had too much to drink. There were a lot of people around. I don't remember who was there." He sat down and put his head down on the table. "I know I did not do it, Señora."

"Tirso, start at the beginning. Tell me what happened that Saturday in July. Take your time. I know you have told the story many times before to the police, the detectives, Mr. Maloney. But, please, tell me."

"Si. Okay. We get paid on Saturday, after work. The boss, Mendoza, gives out the checks. I cashed my check at the Easy Quick. Like I always do. Then a couple of friends and me went to the market to buy food and beer. We wanted to make a barbecue. You know, have a few friends over. We like to do that. We got the stuff and went back to the house. I share that house with five or six muchachos. It's a dump, but it's cheap, you know?" Tirso fingered the rosary beads. It was not difficult to visualize the Saturday afternoon's activities. So far, so good. "I take a shower and start to drink beer. Watch TV. A little while later, Lindsay comes in with her friend, the other hooker, Caryn." Tirso pronounced the name "Linsee." "They were high. They always got high on 'piedras,' you know, crack. I hated that. I hated when she smoked. She acted stupid. We had a fight. I hit her a few times, not hard. She ran behind the building. That's the last time I saw her until the police found me. That's all. I hit her, yeah. I did not kill her. When she ran away, she was alive. I swear it!" Tirso kissed the rosary beads. He was very agitated. I attempted to calm him down.

"OK. OK. Now I am going to ask you a few questions, OK?"

"OK."

"Tell me about Lindsay."

"What do you want to know?" Tirso shifted around in the chair. "I don't know too much about her."

"How did you meet her?" I asked him.

"She just hung around. She was a hooker. She was on crack. Everyone knew that. She turned tricks for crack. I didn't know her too long, maybe one month. I liked her, but I didn't like it that she took drugs. Drugs are very bad. Very bad." Tirso shook his head.

I shook my head too. Here was a guy facing minimum twenty-five for killing a hooker, and he was pontificating about the dangers of drugs. It was hard to see him as one of Nancy Reagan's foot soldiers in the war against drugs.

"Did you live together?" I asked.

"No, no." Tirso almost looked insulted at the question. "She came over sometimes."

"I thought she was your girlfriend." I had to know the nature of the relationship. "Was she your girlfriend?"

Tirso shrugged his shoulders. "I slept with her sometimes. I didn't like that she was a hooker and that she smoked. We had fights when she smoked. I didn't like that."

"Did you fight a lot?" I held my breath. There were bound to be witnesses to any fights.

"No. I mean, I don't speak English and she don't speak Spanish. We didn't talk much."

So much for bilingualism. "OK. Explain to me about the fights. If you couldn't communicate, how did she know how you felt about her taking drugs?" I asked even though I already suspected I knew the answer.

"Sometimes I yelled at her. Lindsay, she had been in trouble with the law because she took drugs. It was the drugs that got her in trouble. Always—she smoked too much. I didn't want any trouble. I get into trouble, I get sent back to Mexico. I just wanted to mind my own business, but Señora, you have to understand, Lindsay smoked more and more. I hit her sometimes when she did drugs. Not hard, but I had to let her know I wasn't kidding about that. Sometimes I knocked the pipe out of her hand. Stuff like that." For the first time in the interview, Tirso was avoiding looking at me.

"You have to tell me the truth. How hard did you hit her? Did you ever hit her really hard? Did she ever pass out on you?"

"Maybe once. Maybe more. Not that hard, just a slap. It didn't hurt her." Tirso shrugged his shoulders in a weary manner. "She is used to men hitting her."

I wondered how he knew that. Probably wasn't going to get much more out of him on that subject, so I let the subject drop. "Anybody see you fighting with her those times you had, before the day she died?"

"I don't know for sure. Probably yes. It was in the afternoon. There's always people around. Look, I swear on my mother and the Virgin I didn't kill her," he repeated, crossing himself, his eyes pointing upwards. Looking for a sign? I wondered.

Tirso had stopped pacing around the room and had, mercifully, sat down. Throughout the question-and-answer period, he had never taken his hands off the rosary beads. Suddenly, in one smooth, practiced motion, he took them off, reverently laid them on the table, and carefully covered them with his callused hands.

"Señora. I swear to you, I did not kill that girl. The last time I saw her, she was alive. She was running away behind the building. She was alive. I swear on the memory of my sainted mother." He crossed himself with the rosary beads, reverently, kissing the crucifix at the end. "Señora. The lawyer, Mr. Maloney, he said to me he can get me a deal. He said if I say I killed the girl by accident in a fight— that I was drunk—then, he said, I only have to go to jail for seven years. Probably less, maybe two years and some months. He says if we go to trial and we lose, then I go to jail for twenty-five years, for sure."

"That's right," I answered him. "Mr. Maloney said that he had explained all that to you, but you refused the plea." I knew from Maloney's notes that he had even brought the prosecutor in to explain the situation to Tirso.

"Señora. My mother." He crossed himself. "My mother, she always said to me, 'Tirso. You always tell the truth and the Virgin will look after you.' Well, Señora, I am telling the truth. The Virgin will look after me. I know that. My mother." He crossed himself yet again. "My mother, she loved me. She would not tell me something wrong. She is looking out for me from heaven."

I sighed. So help me, I believed this guy. Maybe there was something to what his mother had told him. I'm a mother; I believe in mothers. His mother might be looking out for him, but his mother for sure did not know that the total budget for the miracle was three thousand dollars. Plus, as far as I knew, there were no Virgins in Dade County. Weren't then and still aren't now.

In my line of work, I seldom have a client who I believe is innocent. The majority of my clients lie to me. I don't take it personally, as I know they lie to everyone. Some people will lie just on principle, primarily because they are so used to doing it. I knew Maloney's theory on lying clients. He believed that clients are never forthcoming in candor with their attorneys or investigators and that the tendency of human nature is to relate a story most favorable to oneself. Sometimes my clients are innocent of the crime they are charged with, but they are guilty of something—they just were caught for the wrong crime. Rarely do I believe a client the way I believed Tirso. Maybe, statistically, it was time that that happened. I was becoming too jaded.

"OK, Tirso. Tell me again—this time in detail. What happened the day Lindsay was killed." I sighed. This time, I would listen to him as I would listen to someone who was innocent—a totally different stand for me. I hoped I could cope with this new attitude.

As he spoke, I could see that the detectives in Homestead had used what Maloney called the Casablanca method of investigation. They had rounded up the usual suspects—migrant workers, pimps, hookers, dealers—and by process of elimination, had narrowed the field down to where only Tirso was left. Although no one had seen him hit the girl with the channel lock pliers, he had been arrested because he was her boyfriend at the time and had just had a fight with her. They had a history of violent fights—not in Tirso's favor. The thinking was that Tirso satisfied the three elements required for murder: motive, means, and opportunity.

I could just see them, pleased as could be by their crack investigative skills. I bet not one of them had canvassed the neighborhood looking for witnesses. They had just rounded up a few of the local characters and leaned on them for a while, until Tirso's name came out of enough of them.

I was almost done when I heard the sirens go off in the hallways. This ear-shattering noise was followed by shouts of "Lockdown!" I groaned, as I knew what that meant.

Before I was led out of the interview room, I had one last question for Tirso. "Do you own a pair of channel lock pliers?"

Tirso just shook his head sadly. "No, I did not even know what those were until the police showed me." I could hear the guard's footsteps quickly approaching.

"Do you know who owned the pliers that killed Lindsay?"

He shook his head again.

The corrections officers quickly ushered all visitors to the lobby of the prison, where we waited for the next two hours, watched over by guards. It seemed one of the prisoners had set fire to the mattress in his cell and the administration wanted to make sure no one had escaped in the confusion. After a lockdown, all prisoners have to be accounted for. Only then are the doors of the jail opened up again.

I was in a foul mood when I arrived at the Alibi Lounge to meet Maloney. I knew him well enough to know that he had wasted no time in getting into the holiday spirit. A few of the regulars were sitting on the stools around him, exchanging war stories. They all reeked of alcohol.

Maloney put his arm around me and pulled me to him. He faced the lounge lizards on either side of him. "Here she is—the best P.I. in Miami. The best! Not bad, huh?" I knew it was a matter of minutes before he patted me on my ass. I hated it when he did that, so I moved away. Maloney was completely oblivious to the sexual harassment furor in this country.

"Maloney, I'm in no mood for this shit from you. Can we talk about the case? I've just come from the jail."

"What took you so long? I've been sitting here, waiting for you." He took a large gulp of his gin and tonic. It was difficult for me to sympathize with him. I was tired and hungry and had a trunkload of Christmas presents still to wrap.

The barmaid was shooting daggers at me. I knew she and the lawyer had a sometime thing going on, but Maloney's love life was no concern of mine. I was not in the mood to play games. I just wanted to get this over with. I had told the kids I'd take them to the movies, but here I was, at almost ten o'clock at night, four days before Christmas, at the Alibi Lounge, talking to a ginned-up lawyer with overactive hormones about a case I was going to lose money on. I did not need any extra aggravation.

"Maloney, I believe the guy. Don't ask me why, but I do." I shrugged my shoulders. I knew what was coming.

"What was it that got you—the part about the mother and the Virgin looking out for him, or was it the rosary beads?" Maloney was no fool. He knew that you can never take the Catholic out of the girl. "Come on, you can tell me."

"I just don't think he did it. Stop with the cheap analysis." I ignored his references to motherhood and Catholicism. He was Irish Catholic. I was Cuban Catholic. There was nothing to explain.

"I'd like to stop by your office tomorrow morning and get a copy of the complete file. Then I think I'll drive on down to Homestead and do some checking around."

"Fine. I'll have it ready for you."

I was confident that it would be as he promised. Whatever Maloney's shortcomings as a person, he was reliable in his work. I knew from long experience that, even if he was tanked the night before, regardless of whatever sins he had committed, if he said he would do something, it was written in stone. I also knew him to be an outstanding trial attorney. He had spent some years in the pit as an assistant state attorney. With some lawyers, I had so little confidence in them that I would hope and pray the case would not go to court. I hated public humiliation. More than once, a mediocre lawyer had left me on the stand to fend for myself. It was not a pleasant experience, believe me. Maloney would never do that.

One quick pat on the ass, one more glare from the barmaid, and I left the Alibi. I knew I would have some fast talking to do at home to explain away to my daughters yet another outing that did not take place. Being a working single mother will fine-tune anyone's guilt, anytime, guaranteed.

Early the next morning, I was on my way to Maloney's office to pick up the complete file on Tirso Fernandez. As promised, Maloney had it waiting for me. I locked myself in the conference room and began to read. I read the file three or four times until I was familiar with it. I read the official documents first: the "A" form, medical examiner's report, crime scene reports, and the like. Then I took out a yellow legal pad and started writing. I made two lists: the first had to do with problems in the case—that is, the fight Tirso had had with Lindsay prior to her death, their history of violence, his alcohol consumption at the time, the cocaine and alcohol in her system. Facts which hurt our case. On the other, I wrote in detail a to-do list. I decided to start with the witnesses, as that seemed the weakest link in the case against Tirso. I also wanted to check out the apartment building and grounds around it. I wrote a memo to Maloney, telling him what I planned to do.

It took less than one hour to get to Homestead by the back roads. As I drove through the fields, I could see the migrant workers in the distance, bent over, picking legumes. Every so often, there would be a truck nearby with giant containers in the back filled with drinking water. At certain times, I could see the workers clearly. They were mostly muscular young men with the same broad facial features Tirso had. I pulled over to the side of the road and watched for a while. The two-lane road I was on, Krome Avenue, was traveled mostly by agricultural-type vehicles—pickup trucks, tractors, and the like. I felt like a city slicker there in my German car.

A few minutes later, I started up the engine and drove into Homestead. The city was laid out north to south, with Krome Avenue being the main artery. It was not difficult to locate the side street where the apartment building was. Although there was brilliant sunshine that December morning, I felt uneasy being there alone. I was reassured by the gun I had brought along, but I had to admit to myself I would have been happier with another investigator along.

The apartment building where Tirso had lived was located in a devastatingly poor part of town. The street was unpaved, with deep potholes filled with water from the last rainstorm. On the south side of the street, one block away from the apartment building, was the grocery store where Tirso said he had cashed his paycheck. Wooden shacks lined both sides of the street. The poverty and resulting despair were palpable.

I drove slowly, made a U-turn, and headed for the police station. It was a modern building located just a few blocks away. I went upstairs to the Records Department, introduced myself to the officer on duty, and filled out a request for official documents on the case. Although helpful, the officer was curious as to what I hoped to find out. As far as he was concerned, the guilty man was in jail. I was just wasting taxpayers' money investigating the case. It was open-and-shut.

As it would take a while to compile the information I had requested, I left, telling the officer I would be back later. He called out to me to be careful if I were going out to the location of the crime, as it was a rough neighborhood. It was not reassuring to me to be warned about that by a cop, especially in broad daylight.

I went back to the street where Tirso lived and parked across from his building. Before getting out of my car, I checked in my purse for my gun, a Colt .45. Although I knew I was paid up on the insurance on my car, still I prayed as I locked it that it would still be there when I returned. I walked around for a while, trying to get the feel of the place. There wasn't much to feel. It was a dump. Scantily dressed children congregated around me as soon as I took out my camera. I knew it was highly unlikely Maloney would ever step foot in the place, so I wanted him to see the scene clearly.

I wasted no time in starting to knock on doors, trying to locate witnesses. This was the most time consuming, my least favorite part of any investigation, but a necessary one. I asked the same questions of everyone.

"Did you know Tirso Fernandez? Were you there on that Saturday night in July? Did you see anything? Did you hear anything? Do you know of anyone who might have seen or heard anything? Did you know Lindsay Farrow? How about her friend, Caryn Smith?"

Just as I had expected, no one had seen or heard anything. I was not particularly discouraged, as this was only the first go-around. I would have to come back several times to establish a personal relationship, to assure the residents that I did not represent the authorities. I was just trying to help one of them. I knew it worked in my favor that I was a woman who looked Hispanic and spoke Spanish—I was a less threatening presence than some huge Anglo cop.

I took notes on who was home and who was not, and I planned to contact the people who were not at home on that first visit. Next time I would talk again to the ones I had already met. I knew from past experience the number of times that witnesses would come forward upon being recontacted. It was as if they needed time to make up their minds to speak to me. Sometimes it was only on the third or fourth visit that useful information was forthcoming.

I left my business card with the people I interviewed, even though I was fully aware that the chances of anyone taking the initiative and contacting me were slim at best. Although I stressed that I was not a law enforcement officer, I knew that it would take much persuasion on my part to convince the residents of that fact. For the most part, their contact with authority had not been pleasant. Anything to do with the courts was to be avoided at all costs. Nothing good would come of it.

When I returned to the police station, I discovered that word had gotten around that there was an investigator from Miami asking about the case. I spoke briefly with two of the officers there, both clearly skeptical about my efforts to clear Tirso. They were polite and helpful, probably because they felt they could afford to be generous because of their anticipated victory over me. I paid for my copies at the cashier and left, heading back to Maloney's office.

"Well, what do you have?" he bellowed at me as soon as the receptionist told him I was in the conference room.

"I went down there and looked around. I dropped off the pictures at the one-hour developing at Eckerd's. They should be ready in about fifteen minutes. I picked up the records of all the witnesses at the Homestead Police Station. Not a Mother Teresa in the bunch. They all have priors, starting with the dead girl and ending with her best friend, Caryn Smith. I also requested incident reports for the building and the houses immediately adjoining. I have pages of incident reports. Here. Look."

I handed Maloney the printouts detailing all the occasions police officers had been called out to a certain address and the reasons for the calls. Mostly they were for drunk and disorderly behavior, but sprinkled in there were some assault and battery along with breaking and entering. The majority of the incidents took place on Saturdays after cashing checks, no doubt, and when the partying began. Tirso did not live in a desirable neighborhood. No wonder the cops had warned me about going there.

The incident reports confirmed my impression about the roughness of the neighborhood. More interesting, however, was that Lindsay Farrow's boyfriend before Tirso had been shot and killed in a bar three weeks before her own death. Coincidence, or maybe relevant? It was early yet in the investigation.

Lindsay herself had a couple of priors—possession of cocaine, solicitation, theft—the last one involving a man, a john, she seriously injured in a hotel room after he found her stealing from him. According to the police report, she had hit the guy on the head with a radio when he tried to stop her from taking money out of his wallet. I did not like to play "blame the victim," but this girl did run with a rough crowd. It was almost inevitable that she would get hurt sooner or later.

Her pal, Caryn Smith, also had a record for similar offenses, mostly involving drugs. Neither of them, however, had done time. For some reason, no action had ever been taken on any of the charges against them.

In the middle of reading reports, Maloney reached into his briefcase and took out a brown paper bag. "Here." He threw it at me. I barely caught it, the contents were so heavy. "Open it."

I carefully looked inside the bag and took out a large, heavy object. I held it for a second before placing it on the conference table. I kept staring, fascinated.

"Channel lock pliers. Just like the ones that killed the girl," Maloney informed me. "I got them at the hardware store. Pretty ugly, huh?"

He picked them up and held them in his hand. "Heavy. The medical examiner's report says she was struck just behind the right ear. You read that, right? Come here. You're about the same height as the girl. Five-five, right?"

Before going along with Maloney in his experiment, I reached over and started reading the coroner's report. "What was the angle of the wound? Was it a blow from above or below or what? If it was from above, it can't be our client, because he is only five-seven. I don't see anything about that in here."

"No. You're right. There's nothing about the angle of the blow in there. That's a question I'm going to have to ask the medical examiner at her deposition. That's a real important point." Maloney made a note of it.

For the next two hours, we went over the information we had. Lola, Maloney's secretary, went out for the photographs. I explained the layout of the neighborhood to Maloney. We drew a diagram of the area and numbered the sequence of events as noted. I told him I had checked with the weather service for information on the weather that day. It was important to know beforehand if there was enough visibility for the witnesses to be able to see clearly what happened. The report had come back that on that Saturday in July there had been clear weather, a full moon, affording good visibility to any witnesses. We discussed the problems of the case and how to approach them.

Maloney and I decided that I should first interview the individuals on the prosecution's list of witnesses. I had already conducted background checks on them, so I was prepared. Using the telephone in the conference room, I set up appointments with the ones I was able to reach. Quite a few numbers were disconnected, not a good sign. As for the others, I would just have to show up on their doorsteps and hope they were home. After that, I would be finished for the day. I still had to finish my Christmas shopping.

First on my list, simply because his office was in Miami, was a trucker who had been making a delivery to the grocery store across the street from the apartment house in Homestead at the time of the crime. According to the statement he had given the police, he had witnessed the fight between Tirso and Lindsay. He said he had seen Tirso hit Lindsay but had not seen any object in Tirso's hand when he had done so. I pressed him for more details but he said he was not talking about it anymore. There was no point in antagonizing him, so I left. Maloney would be able to get more out of him at a deposition, I figured. At that point, it was unclear whether his testimony would help or hurt us, so I took notes on what he had said.

I have found that people differ in their reactions to note taking. Some will speak to me on the condition that I don't take notes. On those occasions, I concentrate hard on what they are telling me, then run out to my car and write it all down. In all the years I have been doing this, I have trained myself to have almost total recall. If I let time pass—even just a few hours—it will make a difference in my recollections. I then write my official report from those notes. No one will ever talk if I have my recorder on. It's too threatening and distracting.

After writing up the trucker's report, I headed down south to Homestead to see three other people who were present that fateful Saturday. On the way, I telephoned Maloney and told him what I was doing. He told me to be careful. I made sure the Colt .45 was easily reachable in my purse.

The three other witnesses tried to be helpful, but they all basically said the same thing as the trucker. There was a fight, Tirso hit Lindsay, she ran away, he was fast on her heels. The next thing anyone saw was that she was on the ground, the pliers next to her. And Tirso was nowhere to be found. No one had seen the actual crime. I now had the same story from the State's four main witnesses. I had to come up with something else, or Tirso, if forced to serve out his whole sentence, was going to go away for a very long time, Virgin or no Virgin.

In Homestead, I canvassed the neighborhood again. This time, as it was late in the afternoon, I had better luck; more people were at home. I revisited the same homes I had been at before, plus I hit three new ones, widening my canvass area. In one of them, a Mexican woman said her nephew might be able to help me, but he was not there at the time. She said she thought she had heard him talking about the murder of the Anglo hooker, but she could not say for sure. I asked her if either she or her nephew had spoken to the cops about that. She replied that no one had come by, that the cops had not asked them any questions. No surprise there. I asked her to please have her nephew call me but did not hold out too much hope for that. Next trip to Homestead, I would try again.

When I returned to my car, I found a woman standing by it. I recognized her immediately from the photograph clipped onto her criminal record file. It was Caryn Smith, the dead girl's friend. She looked terrible, unwashed and scruffily dressed. She was also scratching herself constantly, as well as sniffing. I recognized the symptoms. Two suspicious-looking Hispanic guys were lurking behind a pickup truck parked close by. I was starting to get very nervous. I reached in my purse to free the Colt .45 in case I needed it. I did not like the scene at all.

"Are you the detective from Miami?" she asked me. Her pupils were huge. Her nose was red and dripping.

"Yes. You're Caryn, right?"

"Yup. That's me. You're working for Tirso, right?"

I started to answer, but she cut me off.

"Why are you trying to help him? He killed Lindsay! She was only twenty years old! She was my best friend! I hope they give him the chair for what he did to her!" She started screaming at me, all the time fumbling for something in the pocket of her jeans. I went on top alert, all my senses heightened.

"You were there, right? Did you see him actually kill her?" I asked.

"He did it! He did it!" she yelled at me, a crumpled-up cigarette in her hand. I relaxed a bit. All she had been searching for was a smoke.

According to the reports I had, Caryn had given the police three different versions of what had happened. She was not a reliable witness. No jury, especially not a Dade County one, was going to buy her story.

I was not going to worry about her at that point. Maloney could take care of her.

I went back to the apartment building, this time carrying in my hand the diagram that Maloney and I had worked on. I walked around the complex trying to duplicate the scene according to the information I had been given by different sources: Tirso, witnesses, police reports.

As I saw it, the weak point in the State's case was a blind spot behind the northeast corner of the building, where, according to all reports, Lindsay ran past with Tirso chasing her. That area was not visible to any of the witnesses standing in the places where they said they were standing at the time the deadly blow was struck.

Tirso claimed he had returned to the apartment after the fight, when Lindsay had run away from him. That was the last time he had seen her. According to all the other witnesses, the last time any of them saw Lindsay alive was when Tirso chased her. They assumed she had just kept on going until she reached the street behind the building, and she had been stopped by the pliers thrown at her. Her friend Caryn was the one to find Lindsay on the ground, lying there without moving. The trucker stated he had come over as soon as he heard Caryn's screams when she found Lindsay. In his statement he said that he had seen the pliers, dirty and rusty, lying close to her body.

I sat down on an old tire lying on the ground and just kept looking the scene over. It simply did not make sense. If Tirso did not kill her, who did? There were no fingerprints on the pliers. The lab said it was because they were in such bad condition. They thought those pliers had been lying there a long time for them to be like that. Someone else had to have been there behind that building. If Tirso was telling the truth, then that was the only possibility. Lindsay obviously did not slip and fall and bang herself on the head behind her ear on channel lock pliers lying on the ground. Maloney and I had actually discussed that improbable scenario. I wondered if that someone could have been involved in the murder of Lindsay's boyfriend in the bar a few weeks previously.

The only fact I was certain of at that point was that it had to have been an opportunistic murder. It had not been premeditated, thought out in advance. No one knew for sure that Lindsay was going to run behind that building when she did. According to the lab, those pliers had been lying there for quite some time, so they were obviously just grabbed at the last second and used.

Before going home, I went back to the jail to see Tirso. I showed him the photos and diagram and had him show me exactly what had happened that day. It was just as Maloney and I had marked off. I asked him to tell me the whole story again, in detail. It was just as before. I asked him who he thought had done it. He still had no theory. I asked him every question I could think of, so much so that I think he was starting to question my state of mind. I left before he started to lose confidence in me. I suspected he was thinking he was better off relying on the Virgin and the pink plastic rosary beads.

By then, I had put in so many hours that I was way over the five hundred dollars the state had allotted for the investigation of the case. I knew Maloney was over his twenty-five hundred dollars as well. Although we had not discussed it, we knew we would continue. We were convinced that our client was innocent. I was on a mission. I wanted to prove Tirso innocent, but in addition to that, I wanted to find the killer. Plus, of course, I wanted to prove that my judgment had not been impaired in believing in a client.

It was now two days before Christmas. My daughters' presents were still in the Toys 'R' Us bags in the trunk of my car. I had woefully neglected my children in my quest for the truth. I resolved to spend that night with them, case or no case. I had to get my priorities in order. My children came first.

My resolution crumbled fast as my beeper rang while I was turning into the driveway of our house. Glancing at the screen, I recognized the exchange as a Homestead one. My heart started beating for two. Sitting in the car, I called the number on the cellular phone.

"You the lady detective? The one who has been coming here to Homestead?" a deep, heavily accented male voice was asking.

"Yes, that's right. Who are you?" I felt a familiar tremor of excitement.

"I know who killed the girl."

"Who was it?" My heart was beating so hard and fast, I was sure the man could hear it.

"I don't want to talk on the telephone. I want to meet with you." I could hear my informant inhaling from the cigarette he was no doubt smoking.

"OK. Tomorrow. Tell me when and where and I'll be there."

"No, it has to be tonight. Tomorrow I'm going back to Mexico and I won't be back for six months. Tonight, or I don't tell you. You have to come to Homestead tonight."

I groaned. No, not tonight. However, I knew I had no choice. I had to go. My good intentions would have to wait. Without going into the house, I pulled out and headed south. I prayed my children had not spotted the car in the driveway. I tried to reach Maloney at his office before leaving, but with no success.

I called Maloney's service and left a message with them.

I called the Alibi and cursed as I recognized the barmaid's voice. She said Maloney was not there. I did not believe her, but I had no choice. I told her to have him check his service for a message from me, that it was urgent. I hoped she would pass it on to him. I was uneasy about driving back to Homestead without anyone knowing where I was. I briefly considered stopping for another investigator, so I wouldn't have to go by myself, but I didn't. I'm stubborn about situations like that. I know I'm in an overwhelmingly male profession, so I hate to demonstrate any weakness at all. I could handle it; besides, the adrenaline was pumping. I knew, of course, I could be on a wild goose chase, that this guy could very probably stand me up, or worst—he could be the killer himself. But this had been the only break in the case.

As I sped all the way, the trip down to Homestead took less than thirty minutes. My informant, Alberto, had chosen to meet behind the dumpster at the grocery store, the same place I had seen Caryn. I was starting to wonder about Homestead. Everything seemed to happen at that grocery store.

The parking lot was deserted when I drove in. I took the Colt .45 out of my purse and slipped it into the waistband of my skirt. Then I untucked my shirt and let it drop loose, hiding the gun. I took the safety off and prayed I would not shoot myself. The Colt .45 weighed so much I was listing to the right. I hoped Alberto would not notice the imbalance, but it was so dark in the parking lot, that would be unlikely. I was not about to get out of my car and walk around the building under those conditions, so I waited.

A few minutes later, a tall Hispanic guy stepped out from behind the dumpster, scaring the shit out of me. I jumped a few feet up in the air, frightening myself that the gun would go off. Apparently he figured out it was me—a woman alone, sitting there in a foreign car with the lights on. No one else would be that stupid. I got out and walked over to him, carefully patting my gun.

"You're the lady detective, right? I'm Alberto."

As he approached, I had a chance to study him closely. This guy did not look like a migrant worker to me. He was sharply dressed, with designer jeans, tight black cotton shirt with the top three buttons undone, and cowboy boots. I was engulfed in Dakkar cologne.

"You talked with my aunt today. She told me."

"Oh. Now I know who you are. You're the nephew, the one who has information." I suddenly remembered the lady who had mentioned her nephew. "So tell me. Who killed the girl?"

"You're probably not going to believe this, but it's the truth."

Given that I had already driven down there and had no other leads, I was willing to listen. What did I have to lose?

"It was an eight-year-old boy."

Alberto was right. I didn't believe him. I didn't say anything. I simply started to walk toward the car, cursing under my breath that I had wasted my time on a wild goose chase. Alberto started following me, choking me with Dakkar. I quickened my gait.

"Wait. Wait. It's the truth. Let me tell you how it happened. I'm leaving tomorrow, and I won't be coming back for a long time, if I ever do return. I have to tell somebody what happened. You're the only person I'm going to tell, and I'm only telling it once. My aunt told me to talk to you. She liked the way you looked. She thought you were nice. She thinks it's the moral thing to do. You told her that Tirso could go away for twenty-five years for something I know he did not do." Alberto took a deep breath. The Dakkar was suffocating me as he got closer to me, making me gag. "I saw it happen."

"You saw it? You were there?" I stopped in my tracks.

"I saw it. I was there. Tirso and the girl had a fight. He hit her a few times. She started running away and he followed. They ran behind the building, but she was too fast for him. He was drunk and could not keep up with her, so he went back to the apartment. She kept running. The boy saw her run away from Tirso and wanted to stop her so he threw the pliers at her. He saw the pliers lying there on the ground, picked them up, and threw them. He didn't mean to hit her—he just wanted to scare her into slowing down so Tirso could catch her."

"You expect me to believe that? Who is this boy? Where is he now?"

"He went back to Mexico with his parents. They got scared and left. Someone told them that if the police found out he had killed the girl, they would take him away from his family and they would never see him again."

"No, no. That's not what would happen. He's only eight years old. They wouldn't put him in jail. It was an accident. Look. It's hard to believe the story you've just told me. Do you have any proof of all this."

"There is no proof. You just have to believe me." Alberto shrugged his shoulders.

"Why didn't you tell this to the police?" I knew I was asking a stupid question even as I was mouthing the words.

"They never asked, and I wasn't about to volunteer. Listen, lady, now you know what happened. My conscience is clear." He turned and walked away, back into the shadows.

"Wait, wait, please!" I ran after Alberto. I tugged at his sleeve.

Alberto looked at me quizzically. "I just told you who did it. What else do you want?" He sounded annoyed, like a man in a hurry who wanted to be on his way.

"Please, I need a statement from you. I am a notary. I'll write down what you dictate to me. You sign it and I'll notarize it. To make it official and legal." I was not past begging. I knew instinctively Tirso's future hinged on this.

"I do this and I can go?" Alberto asked. I nodded as I searched through my purse for a steno pad, a pen, and my State of Florida notary seal.

Alberto started talking, and I started writing, including as many facts and details as I thought necessary. It was quite a thorough statement.

It was a miracle I didn't crash driving back to Miami. I didn't know what to think. I was completely confused. I had to digest what I had been told.

The next morning, I went to Maloney's office to report on the previous evening's activities and show him the notarized statement given to me by Alberto. He telephoned the prosecutor handling the case and informed him of the most recent developments.

Tirso Fernandez was released from jail soon afterwards. His case was *nolle prosequi*. He never called either of us to thank us. We never heard from or spoke to him again. As far as we know, no action was ever taken against anyone else. As I sent the State of Florida a bill for my services, I calculated I had worked for twenty-seven cents per hour. I hoped the Virgin had noticed.

The Full Marty

JEREMIAH HEALY

D el Wonsley reached for my suitcase. "John Cuddy, good to see you again."

"And you."

After we shook hands, I let him take the bag as he guided me from the terminal at Key West International Airport out into the surprisingly cool late-February air. Wonsley, about five-eight and thirty years old, had added a little weight since I'd known him in Boston, but more as muscle than fat if the wide-neck T-shirt was any indicator. He'd lost the pencil mustache and mushroom haircut, though, in favor of the razor-close look he sported now. Wonsley's skin was a shade darker than even the near-ebony he'd been as the partner of Alec Bacall, who'd hired me as a private investigator to look into death threats against a friend of his.

I said, "How long have you been in Key West, Del?"

Wonsley swung his head absentmindedly left-right-left, as though he'd lost track of where he'd parked his car. "I came down here a month or so after . . . losing Alec to the epidemic." Wonsley now looked up at me as we waited for a truck to go by. "You know, John, he never forgot your coming to visit him at our house."

I pictured the gay activist, lying in his bed near the end of his fight against AIDS, trying to be cheerful. "Neither have I."

Crossing the street to a candy apple–red Austin-Healey Sprite, Wonsley said, "I'm glad you don't have a bigger suitcase."

"Your car?"

"Marty's, until . . ."

I waited.

Wonsley fumbled a little with the trunk key. "Until I lost Marty too."

"This is lunch."

We'd driven from the airport on the southeast corner of Key West for roughly a mile and a half to an elegant, lushly landscaped neighborhood. Leaving the classic Sprite tucked up on the grassy shoulder, Del Wonsley brought me through a beautifully restored building to a beachfront deck. Blue umbrellas and seat cushions complemented white wrought-iron tables and chairs. As our waiter settled us under a spreading tree, he said, "Del, good to see you. And we're so sorry about Marty."

The man had a slight but unusual accent.

Wonsley simply said, "Thank you, Luc."

"Can I get you gentlemen anything to drink?"

Wonsley looked at me. "Wine?"

"Either white or red is fine."

Without looking at any list, Wonsley said to the waiter, "A King Estate Pinot Gris, the ninety-five if you still have it."

"Right away, Del."

As Luc went away with our order, Wonsley smiled at me without showing any teeth. "Say it."

"Say what?"

"What you're thinking right now."

I looked after our waiter. "I was wondering what accent that was."

Wonsley seemed a little surprised but said, "Dutch. He and his wife spend five months here, four on Nantucket up by you, and three back in Holland or vacationing."

"Sounds like a nice life."

Wonsley regarded me for a moment without the smile. "I thought you were going to say, 'How did a poor black child from the South Side of Chicago come to know the wine list at a fancy restaurant by heart?'"

"I remembered the Chicago part."

A real smile now, with teeth. "One of the reasons Alec both liked and trusted you, John. You're different and straight—in both senses of that word." A cloud over his eyes. "Which, unfortunately, is a combination I need just now."

"Because of this 'Marty'?"

"Marty Kriss. I was down here about two months when I met him, and a month after that, we were living together at his place."

I was about to follow that up when Luc brought our wine. After pouring a dollop for Wonsley's approval, Luc described the specials of the day. Wonsley ordered a swordfish dish with herbed butter, arugula, and endive. I went with a simple grouper sandwich. Then Luc filled our glasses halfway—the right way—and left.

Wonsley raised his glass. "To absent friends."

I nodded and clinked mine off his. The wine itself was both flinty and smooth.

"What do you think?"

I said, "Superb," with no exaggeration.

Wonsley smiled wider. "Marty loved wines. Oh, Alec did too, but Marty really studied them toward introducing friends to good new ones."

"He in the business?"

"The . . . you mean liquors?"

"Yes."

Wonsley shook his head. "Marty was a dentist, John. One of the gay pioneers down here in the early sixties, according to everybody else."

"Everybody else?"

"I didn't know jack shit about Key West until I was mourning Alec, when people in Boston told me I had to see the place. Marty never bragged about anything, but his *friends* here quickly let me know what a *catch* he was, both in terms of status and wealth."

A little bitterness there. I took another sip of wine.

Wonsley set down his glass. "Meow."

"Meaning?"

Barely a smile. "I sounded stereotypically catty, didn't I?"

"Probably depends on what you have to be catty about."

He looked at me. "You know much about Key West, John?"

I thought back to a different case. "I was here once, briefly."

"How briefly?"

"Overnight."

Wonsley nodded. "Historically, Key West was a pretty rough town. Wreckers would salvage what they could from ships that foundered offshore. Hemingway wrote something like two-thirds of his books here while he fished and drank. The naval station was vital during World War Two and later against Castro in Cuba."

Now Wonsley looked around the deck. "This place used to be owned by a wrecker. Eventually it became Louie's Backyard, a pretty unpretentious name for a fine restaurant, especially one ecologically sound enough to keep this great mahoe tree we're sitting under."

I guessed Del Wonsley had a point, so I let him get to it.

Now he looked out to the ocean, a motorboat going by towing a parasailer a hundred feet off the surface, the multicolored panels of the chute giving an abstract-painting effect against the almost artificially blue sky. "I know all these things because Marty talked about them. He felt it was important for us to know about the history and culture of the island."

"For *us* to know?"

Wonsley came back to me. "Younger gays. Marty had to fight a lot of battles when he came down here, John. Discrimination in housing, in jobs, especially governmental ones the Conchs thought were theirs forever."

I'd heard the expression on my other visit. "The people born here."

"Right. Well, maybe I saw in Marty a lot of what I saw in Alec, only with Alec, the battle was against AIDS, ongoing and . . . frustrating."

"While with Dr. Kriss . . . ?"

"The battles had been mostly won. And Marty could now enjoy all the things that being a successful dentist let him afford."

Luc brought our entrees. Wonsley insisted I try a triangle of his swordfish, which was wonderful, though for me more a dinner than a lunch. My grouper sandwich tasted as though the fish providing the filet had been swimming an hour before.

When Luc was out of earshot, I said, "Like the Austin-Healey?"

"Like? Oh, the things Marty could afford?"

I nodded.

Wonsley set down his fork. "I've been kind of dribbing and drabbing information to you instead of giving you 'the full Marty,' so to speak, and that's not the way for a client to talk with a private investigator."

"Frankly, Del, I'm kind of used to it."

The real smile. "And you're licensed in Florida?"

"Since last month."

"OK. Where to begin?"

"How about you enjoying your lunch first?"

Del Wonsley gave me an even better smile. "Yes, Mom."

"Actually, we could have walked here from Louie's, but there's generally plenty of parking." Wonsley left his car at the curb, and I followed him onto the beautifully maintained grounds. There were the usual monuments, but most of the area was filled with white-washed honeycombs, almost condolike. Four levels high, twenty units long.

Wonsley said, "You visit cemeteries much, John?"

I thought of my wife, Beth, asleep in her hillside overlooking Boston Harbor. "Now and then."

"Before Alec died, I never did. But after I came down to Key West, Marty told me about this one. The crypts had to be moved here from another part of the island after a hurricane in the eighteen forties basically washed them up."

Some maintenance workers were weed-whacking near a monument for the men killed on the USS *Maine* in Havana Harbor in 1898, the event that sparked the Spanish-American War. The monument itself was a solitary bronze sailor holding an oar, looming over little white headstones, rural mailboxes turned vertically. All around us were small graves for children, carved lambs or angels atop them, and some elaborate crosses for whole families.

Pointing at one of the crosses, Wonsley said, "Yellow fever epidemic."

I nodded as we passed one of the condolike structures, the names and dates carved into the tablets that would have acted as the end door when the bodies were interred. Many Hispanic names, and several of these had head-and-shoulder photos glazed and shaped into the oval of a cameo.

Then we stopped near the end of the next structure, in a part of the cemetery that I thought was particularly quiet. Not all the tablets were inscribed yet, but the one in front of Wonsley read "MARTIN G. KRISS, FEBRUARY 13, 1937–FEBRUARY 11, 1998" and, under that, the epitaph, "KNOW A MAN BY HIS DEEDS."

I said, "Just before his birthday."

"Yes."

I quickly did the arithmetic. "Dr. Kriss was only sixty-one?"

The thirtyish Wonsley turned to me. "A kind way to put it."

"What was the cause of death, Del?"

Wonsley looked back to the tablet. "For his sixtieth birthday last February, we went to New York City, which royally pissed off a lot of Marty's friends down here. But he hadn't been feeling great, and I thought a controlled trip with me would be better than the craziness of a mini-Fest."

"Mini-fest?"

"Every Halloween down here, they have what's called 'Fantasy Fest,' kind of a Mardi Gras. For birthdays, a lot of people have smaller versions as parties."

"Got it."

"Well, when we were in Manhattan, I took Marty to Chelsea—the hip center today of things gay. He was going to bring me to Marie's Crisis, an old haunt for his generation, but then Marty heard of this newish restaurant in the West Village called Lips. It's basically a raucous place where the hostess and waitresses are all transvestites—men dressed as women?"

"I think I can picture that."

Wonsley smiled weakly. "Well, to kind of ease the rift over our going up to New York, whenever people called the hotel from here to wish him a happy birthday, Marty would tell them we were going to Lips. And it was fun, John. The waitresses served food and drinks, but every ten minutes or so, music would come on, and one or more of them danced and lip-synched a Streisand or Garland number. Marty enjoyed it immensely, but . . ."

"But?"

"On the way back to the hotel, he suffered a heart attack in the cab. Fortunately, the driver knew the closest hospital, and Marty pulled through. But the doctor up there said no strenuous stuff for a while. So, we came back down here and basically dodged that kind of thing."

"Dodged it?"

"Yes. If people called us for tennis or dancing, we'd just decline."

"You didn't explain about his condition?"

"No. Marty insisted. He wanted no one—except for his dental assistant—to know he'd come so close."

"Why?"

"Marty felt it would be too much of a downer, when the epidemic already provides all the pessimism our crowd needs."

I could see the man's point. "Then what?"

"Well, Marty started following doctor's orders. Lost some weight, began low-level aerobic exercise in our house. He was pretty good about it, too, until he got the flu over Christmas and kind of relapsed."

"Another attack?"

"No. Just shelved the cross-trainers and went back to his old ways of food and drink." Wonsley shook his head. "Then, two weeks ago, Marty was found dead in his dentist's chair."

"The heart?"

A long, slow swing of Wonsley's face toward mine. "Supposedly."

I looked toward the crypt, then back at him. "Maybe we'd better sit down."

There was a bench nearby, and he joined me on it. When we were seated, Del Wonsley began speaking in a low but steady voice.

"I met Marty at a party thrown by his then-boyfriend, Bo Smith."

"Bo is the first name?"

"Actually, it's short for *Boz*-few-lett."

"Spelling?"

"B-O-I-S-F-U-E-L-L-E-T."

"I can see where the guy would prefer 'Bo.'"

"Yes, well, unfortunately for Bo, Marty preferred me. I think his thing with Bo was breaking up anyway, but I was the catalyst, no question."

"And that didn't make this Smith very happy."

"No, but he still came to Marty for dentistry work."

"Dr. Kriss was that good?"

"More like Bo was that cheap. Marty felt badly about the way their relationship ended, so he'd do Bo's teeth as a freebie."

"Generous."

"The kind of man Marty was. Another of his friends from down here—just a friend, by the way, *not* another former lover—is an accountant, Fred Ippoletti. When Fred's partner was dying, Marty lent Fred the money to allow him to care for the man over his last six months."

I pictured the way Alec Bacall had been, that time I'd visited their house in Boston, Del Wonsley doing the same for him.

"John?"

"Sorry."

Wonsley nodded, a little uncertainly. "Marty wasn't just generous that way, either. As I mentioned at the restaurant, he also took the lead in civil rights. Marty supported the gay guest houses that opened in Key West during the seventies, and later he pushed the city to hire an openly gay police officer named Jerry Finneran. In fact, Marty once told me he'd never felt prouder than when he watched Jerry at a formal ceremony, wearing that dress uniform and parade hat."

I tried to pull together what Wonsley had told me. "You think all these good deeds had something to do with Dr. Kriss dying?"

Wonsley looked at me squarely. "You mean, do I think some gay-baiting asshole killed him in a way that would seem like a heart attack?"

"Yes."

"No, John, I don't. As I said, most of those battles have been won. Key West measures only two miles by four miles, but about twenty percent of the population is now gay."

Nearly the same voting clout as my Irish in Boston. "Then what do you think?"

Del Wonsley looked away from me, back toward the tablet we'd read. "I think Bo Smith, Fred Ippoletti, or Jerry Finneran killed him."

Over the noise of the Sprite's engine idling at a stop sign, he said, "They were scheduled for three appointments in a row. Fred, then Bo, then Jerry."

"Was that unusual?"

"Ask Lorna."

"Lorna?"

"Marty's dental assistant slash receptionist slash bouncer. You'll love her."

"I'll need Lorna's last name to use the phone book."

Wonsley slapped a palm to his forehead. "Oh, where is my brain? Here." He slipped a piece of paper from the briefcase behind his seat. "Addresses and telephone numbers for all the people I've mentioned."

I glanced at the list as Wonsley shifted into first and we turned the corner. Five entries, including Lorna Hernandez and his own, but no further details.

Pocketing the paper, I looked over at Wonsley. "Back in the cemetery, you said Ippoletti is an accountant and Finneran a police officer."

"Jerry got promoted to detective a few years ago, if that makes a difference."

"What does Smith do for a living?"

"Bo? As little as possible. He's sort of a gay gigolo, John, despite the toupee."

"Toupee."

"Yes. When it's misbehaving, he wears an Atlanta Braves baseball cap to hide his baldness. But he has the body of a Greek god, and that attribute really appealed to Marty. Bo maintained his own apartment, but he sort of lived off Marty. Not that I didn't, too." A sidelong glance toward me. "And pretty much still do."

"I'm not sure I get that last part, Del."

"When Marty died, I was his sole beneficiary. Or 'soul' beneficiary, as Bo wrote to me, probably intending the misspelling."

"Romantically or racially?"

Wonsley gave me the good smile. "Not afraid to ask difficult questions, are you, John?"

"What people hire me for. Including you."

"Point taken." Wonsley slalomed around a guy with long hair on a bicycle, a bulldog wearing a pink bow riding in the front basket. "On Bo, I'd say more the racial than the romantic."

"He resented you because you're black?"

"It helped."

I was having a little trouble following Wonsley's train of thought. "Del, just what do you want me to do?"

He made another turn onto another narrow street. "Everybody we've talked about is a long-timer down here. I'm not. I want somebody like you—somebody I trust who's an outsider with no private agenda—to try and find out if Marty really died of natural causes."

"Wouldn't this Detective Finneran be a better choice for that?"

"Because he might 'owe' Marty for getting him on the force?"

"And because he'd have access to the autopsy report, lab—"

"John, the reason I suspect Jerry Finneran is because he says Marty was dead when he went in for his appointment."

"Point taken."

Wonsley switched to a grim smile now. "And, as executor of Marty's estate, I finally found out just how much Fred owed him."

"And now owes you."

Wonsley tick-tocked his head. "Not. In his will, Marty forgave all his debtors."

Motive. "Just how much 'forgiveness' are we talking about here?"

"A hundred large, as my friends up in the Second City might say."

Motive squared. "A hundred thousand dollars."

"Ninety-nine thousand, seven hundred and eighty-four, to be exact." Wonsley sniffed. "Fred may be a parrothead—that most uncool of all fan addictions—but he's still an accountant."

"Parrothead?"

"You'll see tonight."

"What's tonight?"

We came to a stop in front of a small building beside a large gate. "This is where I've booked you. I thought it would be easier for you to stay at a hotel."

"Looks more like a guest cottage."

"Wait'll you see your room. I scouted it myself."

I came back to Wonsley. "You said something about 'tonight'?"

"Enjoy the city. On Marty's and my dime, John. Then start in tomorrow. Oh, and you won't need a rental car."

I tapped the pocket holding the list Wonsley had given me. "All the people within walking distance?"

"Except that you might want to cab it to Fred's office on North Roosevelt. Otherwise, Old Town Key West is like Harvard Square with better weather."

As I got out of the Sprite, Del Wonsley said, "Call me if you need anything."

Including, I guessed, the answer to my "parrothead" question.

-2-

"Hi, I'm Jennifer. This your first time at Simonton Court, Mr. Cuddy?"

"It is," I said, walking behind the bouncy young woman in placket shirt and shorts who'd insisted on carrying my suitcase.

"Well, this path takes you past all our cottages. The swimming pool and hot tub are at the end, where we'll turn left for the Mansion."

"The Mansion?"

"Yes. Mr. Wonsley has reserved the Bird of Paradise room there."

Bird of. . . . I shook my head.

We turned left. "This bar area between the pool and the Mansion is where we serve breakfast, which is included in your room charge."

Jennifer led me up a staircase past discreetly partitioned decks to the third floor. "Number six, at the end of the hall."

When she opened the door, I could see a large room with vaulted ceilings and suspended fans, the bedspread and upholstery in bright, Caribbean pastels. Entering, I nearly bumped into a spiral staircase on the left.

Setting down my suitcase, Jennifer said, "That leads to your widow's walk."

Or widower's.

"If you need anything, don't hesitate to contact the office."

"Thanks."

After Jennifer left, I climbed the staircase. At the top was a skylight trapdoor on a nut-and-bolt hinge mechanism that reminded me of the shim used by car thieves on spring-locked door buttons. The widow's walk itself was a small roof deck, with picket railing surrounding two white resin chairs and matching cocktail table. The view was more a vista, facing west toward the ocean and the coming sunset.

I decided to forgo unpacking long enough to get a soda from a vending machine by the swimming pool. Back on the roof, I sat in one of the resin chairs and put my feet up on the railing. For the next twenty minutes, some ancient biplanes performed an air show over the ocean before flying off in formation. After that, I watched the horizon evolve from orange to pink and from pink to charcoal gray, the fiery ball that gives us all life—and at least some hope—eventually disappearing for the night.

Quietly I said, "Beth, you'd have loved this."

Then I downed the rest of my soda and decided to get some dinner.

I had a great duck dish on the outdoor patio of Thai Cuisine, an unassuming restaurant that shared its signpost with an auto body shop. After paying the tab, I made my way down to Duval Street, which I remembered as being the main drag of Key West nightlife. I figured to work off dinner by walking first to the south, then back again north.

About halfway down the first leg, I found out what a parrothead was.

The Margaritaville Café was in the five-hundred block of Duval. Nearly everything bore the imprint or image of singer Jimmy Buffett. In the café itself, a band performed, rabidly supported by a dozen or so men and women wearing parrot paraphernalia, including hats with life-size bird replicas on them, all such available for purchase in the adjoining shop.

I stayed for a beer, deciding that I probably wouldn't want accountant Fred Ippoletti standing between the I.R.S. and me.

Continuing my walk, I saw taxis painted pink, bike racks mounted on their trunk lids. Blue pedicabs went by, the men and women at the handlebars in terrific physical shape. Paint jobs on cars mimicked autumn leaves, rhinestones, and tropical fish. Bumper stickers on more "normal" vehicles read "EAT RIGHT, STAY FIT, DIE ANYWAY" and "REHAB IS FOR QUITTERS."

At the end of Duval, I turned north again. There were other bars to drink in and discos to dance in, bordered by enough swimsuit, T-shirt, and other souvenir shops to service twenty cruise ships, no waiting. Instead of spending any more time "on the town," though, I took Eaton Street to the right and went back to Simonton Court, letting the Bird of Paradise room lull me into a deep and restful sleep.

-3-

The next morning, I knocked on the door of a little peach cottage with wind chimes hanging from every crossbeam on its porch. They gave off so many ping and pong noises that I found myself reading the MARTIN G. KRISS, DDS sign aloud. I was pretty sure somebody had to be inside, because an Italian racing bike leaned against one of the posts holding up the porch roof.

When the door opened, a woman stood staring out at me over half-glasses worn halfway down her nose. She was bird thin, dressed in a halter top and spandex biking shorts and sneakers without socks. The bangs of her jet-black, Prince Valiant pageboy nearly reached her eyebrows. However, if the hair said she was thirty, the crow's feet around the eyes pushed her to forty, and the leathery skin over heavily veined hands might have skipped fifty altogether and gone right to—

"You weren't one of Marty's patients."

"No, I wasn't. Ms. Lorna Hernandez?"

"Who the hell else would be sitting in a dead dentist's office?"

Good point. I showed her my Florida identification.

She looked up from reading it. "You the one Del imported from the Great White North?"

"Boston."

"That's far enough."

"I wonder if I could ask you some questions about Dr. Kriss and his death?"

"Why not? It's not like I don't still have a hundred letters to send out."

Hernandez turned and walked away, over her shoulder with, "Well, don't just stand there, Boston. Come on in."

The cottage living room was a reception area, a door at the back open with several farther doors off it.

"Opertories," said Hernandez from behind the counter separating her from the chairs, me in the closest to her.

"I'm sorry?"

"About what?"

"The word you just—"

"Opertories? Just a fancy name for the two little cubicles Marty alternated between, torturing the poor slobs couldn't remember to brush and floss twice a day." Hernandez stuffed an envelope. "I thought I'd try a limerick."

"Limerick?"

"Don't tell me you don't know that word, either?"

"I know it, I just—"

"To let his patients know he was gone, though I suspect most of them must have read the story or obit in the Mullet Wrapper."

"The mullet . . . ?"

"Key West *Citizen*, our local rag. Still, I thought all the patients should be *notified* of Marty's *demise*. And it seemed a limerick might take the edge off the bad news, only I couldn't come up with one that rhymed right."

"Bold idea, anyway."

Hernandez studied me over the tops of her half-glasses. "All right, we've established that I'm smarter than you are, but that after taking a punch, you can throw one. Now, why don't we get down to whatever the hell it is Del wants you to ask me."

"He wants me to look into Dr. Kriss' death."

"Look 'into' it? Well, Boston, you can 'look' into anything you want, but it won't change much. Marty ended up the way I told him he would, he didn't stay off the fatty food and on the exercise routine."

"Heart attack."

"The old blood clot break dance, right in number two."

I didn't say anything this time.

Hernandez smiled, but not kindly. "Bravo, Boston. You're learning. Opertory number two, the one directly behind me."

"Can I see it?"

"He was slumped right there, getting a taste of his own medicine."

I looked from Hernandez to the dentist chair itself. "You saw Dr. Kriss before the emergency people took him away?"

"When I got back from the concert that day. Place was a madhouse, what with Marty's one-forty-five getting here a little early to face the music only to see police and ambulance and I don't remember what else."

"I thought Dr. Kriss died around noontime?"

"Lunchtime, anyway."

"But you were at a concert?"

"Yeah. Open-air thing, this new punk group I'm following. They grunge up their act a little more, I might even be interested in touring with them."

I tried not to shake my head. "You were the doctor's receptionist, so—"

"Receptionist, bookkeeper, assistant to hold down the ones couldn't take the pain." A softening of her features. "Myself, I'd've strapped them into the chair, but Marty was a kinder, gentler sort."

"What I mean is, you would have booked his patients' appointments."

"Of course I would." Exit the softening. "The hell you think a receptionist does, Boston?"

"I'm interested in the three men coming in around lunchtime that day."

"Easy enough. Fred Ippoletti was the nooner, account of his business makes him nervous enough he doesn't like to be out of his office except around then. Bo Smith, the arrogant son-of-a-bitch, was twelve-thirty, and Jerry Finneran, the one o'clock."

"And?"

"And I went for lunch just as Fred came in with a shopping bag. We exchanged meaningless small talk for as long as I could stomach it—an accountant isn't your most scintillating of conversationalists. Fred went into Marty, and I took off for my concert."

"Then what happened?"

"Well, obviously I don't know since I wasn't here. But apparently Marty did the prophylactic—a general cleaning, Boston, not a condom check. And Marty complained to Fred that he wasn't feeling great."

"Had Dr. Kriss said anything to you about that before you left?"

"Nada. But he always tried to show the world a brave front, the roly-poly pea brain. Anyway, Marty was still upright when Fred left. Then Bo says he got here late for his appointment."

"How late?"

"Bo don't wear no watch—he's from Georgia originally, and he really talks like that. By the time he thought to get up from a chair in reception and look at the clock by my counter, it was going on one. Bo claims he knocked on the door to the opertories but didn't get any answer. He was already out on the sidewalk when Jerry arrived for his appointment. Because he's a cop, I guess Jerry had the sense to be worried, so the two of them came back in. When Jerry opened the door there, he could see Marty crumpled on this chair. Jerry says he did CPR while Bo called nine-one-one, but the fickle chicken of life had already flown the coop."

"Did it seem odd to you that these three men would all have consecutive appointments?"

Hernandez regarded me differently. "You know, I thought about that."

"What do you mean?"

"Well, Fred's a wimp about pain, so he usually likes me around to hold his hand, even for just a cleaning. That's why, when he called three weeks ago for the prophylactic, I told him I'd be at this concert. Fred said no problem."

"How about Smith?"

"Well, Bo, he don't usually like for his lunchtimes to be—I told you, he really talks like this. But Bo called the same day Fred did and wanted that twelve-thirty spot for his cleaning, so I gave it to him."

"And Finneran?"

Hernandez closed her eyes a moment. "A bit odder still, what with him being on a six-month notice for as long as I can remember."

"How do you mean?"

"Jerry had been in just before Christmas."

"Finneran give you a reason for coming back so soon?"

"Yeah. Said he had a hot new sailor he wanted to be sweet for, and tartar can play hell with your breath."

"When did Jerry Finneran call to make his appointment?"

"Late afternoon of the day Fred and Bo did."

"You're sure?"

"Of course I'm sure. Generally, things don't fill up that smoothly. Schedule of appointments looks like a checkerboard until a few days before, when everybody needs to see the doctor yesterday for this awful toothache, or a—"

"But all three of these men were looking for just cleanings, right?"

"Right."

"And if they didn't get them done?"

"What, the prophylactics you mean?"

"Yes."

"Well," said Lorna Hernandez, "nobody ever died from tartar."

Suddenly, the softening flowed back over her features. Both eyes welled up with tears above the half-glasses, and she began to cry like a baby. "Damn, but I'm gonna miss that fat tooth fairy."

-4-

"Mr. Ippoletti?"

"Yes?"

"My name's John Cuddy."

The man held a key in his hand, I assumed the one that would open the office door we flanked on the third floor of a building on North Roosevelt Boulevard, maybe a mile from the Old Town area. Ippoletti was about Del Wonsley's height but blockier, as though he spent a lot of time lifting weights in the gym. He wore a parrot-patterned Hawaiian shirt over hiking shorts with lots of flaps and buttons. His hair was curly but thinning on top and combed across the head in a way that highlighted his balding more than it hid his scalp. The open face seemed genuinely surprised that someone would be waiting for him at eight o'clock on any morning.

"Do we, uh, know each other, Mr. Cuddy?"

"No. I'm here about Dr. Martin Kriss."

"Marty?" Ippoletti shuddered visibly. "Just the thought of that dear, dear man, so in love with life, and now all closed into a tiny crypt in . . ." Another shudder, then a focusing. "I don't recall Marty ever mentioning you, though."

"We never met. I'm investigating his death, and I'd like to speak with you."

"Investigating . . . ? You're not with the police?"

"Private." I held out my Florida identification, but Ippoletti barely glanced at it.

He said, "But who . . . ?" then shook it off. "Perhaps you should come in."

Unlocking the door, Ippoletti flipped some switches that brought up the lights and brought on an air-conditioning hum. His office had just one desk, the walls festooned with posters of Jimmy Buffett, some of which I recognized from the café the night before. Mercifully, the parrothead hat that Del Wonsley had mentioned was nowhere in evidence.

Ippoletti waved me to a chair across from his desk, file folders stacked neatly on one corner. A computer monitor and keyboard were off to the right, an elaborate phone system to the left.

When we both were seated, he said, "I don't quite understand why you're here, Mr. Cuddy."

"I already told you. I'm investigating—"

"Yes, but Marty's death, however, uh, tragic, is closed."

Closed. A term the police often use and regular citizens usually don't. "Someone thinks otherwise."

"Oh. Oh, my."

"I wonder if you could go over with me the details of that day."

"Details?"

Ippoletti suddenly seemed to be on a different plane of existence. "For starters, when did you make your appointment with Dr. Kriss?"

"When? Uh, well, I don't know."

Not exactly a stump-the-band question, but Ippoletti still seemed thrown by it. "Ms. Hernandez said it was three weeks ago, a week before he died."

"I guess Lorna would, uh, know better than I."

"After you called her, Mr. Smith and Mr. Finneran did too."

"They did?"

Ippoletti was asking more questions than I was. "Ms. Hernandez said you were the doctor's noon appointment because you didn't like to be out of your office except at lunchtime."

"Yes. In fact, I went there directly from here."

"Directly."

"Yes."

"When you arrived that day, how did Dr. Kriss seem to you?"

"Seem?"

"Your impression of him."

Ippoletti looked around his own office. "He—Marty—seemed, uh, a little . . . peaked."

"Peaked. Like he wasn't feeling his best?"

"Yes. Yes, exactly."

"Did you and he talk about that?"

A nod.

"And?"

"He said he wasn't feeling . . . his best."

"Quite a coincidence."

"What?"

"That he'd use the same term then as I did just now."

"Yes, well, it's, uh, pretty common."

"Down here."

"What?"

"In Key West."

Ippoletti looked as though he was trying to decide whether I meant the term was common or that a lot of people on the island weren't feeling their best. Time to cut to the car chase.

"Mr. Ippoletti?"

"Yes?"

"You want to tell me what really happened?"

"What . . . ?"

"You told me a few minutes ago that you went directly from your office to Dr. Kriss' office."

"I, uh. . . . Well, that's right."

"But Ms. Hernandez said you were carrying a shopping bag."

"Uh. . . . Well, I don't recall."

"Do you recall that you owed the man money? Nearly a hundred thousand dollars?"

"Actually it was ninety-nine—"

"Go with my ballpark. That makes me wonder if maybe you didn't have a motive to see Dr. Kriss removed from the ranks of your creditors."

"Removed?"

"Via the debt-forgiveness clause in his will. Surely you know about that."

Ippoletti stiffened. "Here's what I 'know,' Mr. Cuddy. Marty never once asked me to pay that money back. As a friend, he knew I couldn't, and Marty was prepared to wait forever."

I stood up. "I guess now he will."

There was no answer to my knock at the ground floor apartment in the first really seedy building I'd visited on the island. I knocked again, then basically hammered at the door with no better results. There was a broken gate at the side of the structure that gave onto a weedy path leading around back, so I took a little stroll that way.

The rear yard was small, with a lot more weeds in the flower beds. A man lay on a tri-sectioned lounge chair, one of those whose head and leg parts could be raised and lowered independently by ratchets at the hinges. In the kind of shape you'd see on the cover of a bodybuilding magazine, he wore a baby blue thong bikini, a pair of matching, egg-cup eye goggles, and the earphones to a Walkman. I pegged him at a little under six feet, his toes twitching in time to music loud enough for me to catch some of it as I moved toward him.

Three feet away, I got a whiff of coconut oil and said, "Mr. Smith?"

No apparent response.

I moved up to the side of the lounge and tried again.

Nothing again.

I leaned down and flicked away the right earphone. "Mr. Smith?"

He sat up abruptly without taking off the eye protectors, the few wisps of blonde hair on his head giving him the appearance of a space alien and making me wonder where either his toupee or baseball cap was. When the goggles fell off from gravity, Smith said, "And just who the Sam-fuck would you be, boy?"

Southern drawl, like Lorna Hernandez had caricatured. "John Cuddy." I opened my ID holder for him, but he never bothered to look at it.

Smith shucked the other earphone without turning off the music. "What are you doing here?"

"Investigating the death of Martin Kriss."

His eyes closed for a moment. "Jerry said. . . ." Then he opened the eyes but wider. "Wait now. Let Bo see that thing again."

I reopened my ID case.

"Boy, this here says you're private?"

"Correct."

He put the earphones back on and reached toward his lap for the goggles. "Then Bo don't have to say Sam-fuck to you."

I waited until Smith was lying back again comfortably before leaning down and flicking away the right earphone as I had once already.

He sat bolt upright again, not waiting for gravity to take off his eyewear this time. "Boy, is Bo gonna have to throw you out of here?"

"We already are."

A troubled look in his eyes. "Are what?"

"Out. As in outside."

Smith stared up at me now, flexing.

I said, "So, where would you throw me, Mr. Smith?"

He came off the lounge, but with that drag on quickness you see from people who use weights without cross-training in other sports. I caught his right wrist and turned it, locking his elbow.

"Hey?"

"Mr. Smith, I'd like to just talk."

"Hey, man." Louder now. "No shit, that hurts."

"Then why don't I let go so you can sit and talk to me?"

A male voice above and behind me rang out with, "What's going on down there?"

I didn't turn around. "Nothing I can't handle."

The voice seemed to come from a second-story window. "Bo, you want me to—?"

"No!" said Smith sharply, and not from anything I was doing to him. "No, Paul, Bo's OK."

"You sure?"

"Every little thing's fine. Just butt out."

Paul's voice grew snippish. "You're welcome."

I said to Smith, "Same deal on you sitting and talking."

"OK, OK. Just let go of—"

I did.

Smith rubbed his right elbow with the other hand. "You don't have to get rough, boy."

From man to boy again. "Tell me, how did you come to pick that day for your appointment with Dr. Kriss?"

"Bo didn't 'pick' nothing. I called up, and his espanola gave me a time."

I don't speak Spanish, but I'd never heard "espanola" as a word before. "Not the way Ms. Hernandez tells it."

"Well, you can believe 'Ms. Hernandez' if you want, no skin off my ass."

"Could be you're mistaken there. Describe what happened when you found Dr. Kriss."

"What happened? Nothing happened. Old Marty, he was history, boy."

"When you first went in his opertory?"

"His what?"

"The room where he worked on his patients."

A wave of the hand. "Whatever. When I opened the door, old Marty was in that big chair of his, dead as the cow that gave the leather for it."

"I thought it was Detective Finneran who opened the door."

Smith seemed to lose a little of his tan. "I don't remember who pulled on the Sam-fuck door. I just remember seeing my . . . friend lying there."

"Trouble you at all that Dr. Kriss broke off with you in favor of Del Wonsley?"

"Yeah." A little fire now. "Yeah, it 'troubled' Bo. But old Marty decided to cut himself a piece of dark meat, he got to live with the con-se-quences."

"And what consequences are those, Mr. Smith?"

"I guess old Marty's been spending the last few weeks finding that out from his Maker."

I wasn't quite to the sidewalk in front of Bo Smith's building when a dark sedan pulled up to the curb. The driver was the only one in it, and even he wasn't there very long.

Over the roof with, "You John Cuddy?"

"That's right."

"Get in."

"How about some ID first?"

The man came around his car without bothering to close its door. About my height but thinner, no more than one-eighty stretched over his six-two plus. He didn't wear a jacket, but the short-sleeved dress shirt was accompanied by the first tie outside my own that I'd seen on the island. His pants were straight cut, a badge and a semiautomatic resting near each other on the right side of his belt.

Up close, the hair was sandy brown and crew-cut, no sideburns. The nose ran straight and narrow, the green eyes burning.

He tapped his badge. "You seen enough?"

"Let me guess. Detective Jerry Finneran."

The cleft chin jutted out a little. "Show me your license."

It seemed kind of unnecessary, since he already knew my name, but I pulled out the Massachusetts one first.

Finneran looked at it, then grinned. "That carries zero weight down here."

I opened the Florida version. "Like this one any better?"

The grin evaporated. "What the hell are you doing?"

"My job. How about you?"

You could see the jaw working under his skin. "Get in the car, mister."

I glanced across the street. "There's a nice bench over there. Why don't we both take a little fresh air with the roust?"

Now I could hear teeth grinding, but Finneran spun on his heel and went to the car door, slamming it as he crossed the street in five strides.

I followed him at my own speed and lowered myself gently onto the opposite side of the bench.

Finneran said, "What's your game, Cuddy?"

"No game. Just a job."

"Being?"

"Trying to figure out what happened to Dr. Martin Kriss."

"Del Wonsley hired you."

"Would that make a difference to you?"

Finneran started to escalate, then took himself down a notch in a way that made me admire him a little. "Look, Cuddy. Marty Kriss was overweight and didn't exercise. The man had a heart attack. End of story."

"Somehow I don't think so."

"Why?"

"You made an appointment to see him out of your usual rotation."

Finneran scowled. "And that's it?"

"Depends."

"On what?"

"On whether you can give me the name of the sailor who supposedly—"

"That's none of your business, mister."

"But your appointment just 'happened' to follow Ippoletti's and Smith's? Come on, Detective. Without knowing anything about the landscape and players down here, I rattled one of them enough to call you and the other enough to nearly swing on me."

Finneran kept the scowl. "Cuddy, Marty Kriss just plain died."

"I can see where you couldn't know I was on the case until I visited Ippoletti this morning. I can even understand why neither of you could reach Smith, since Mr. Universe was in his backyard with enough music blaring through his ears that any telephone might as well be ringing in Miami. What I don't get, though, is why the police officer who found the good dentist's body didn't just work his own caseload until an out-of-town investigator came by to see him."

Finneran, deadpan now, watched me.

I watched him back. "I'm told you got on the force thanks to Dr. Kriss' being a civic activist. Now that you're a detective and in a position to investigate his death, don't you owe him the truth?"

Detective Jerry Finneran said, "I know who I owe, Cuddy, and for what." He stood up and began striding back toward his car. "And everybody'd be better off, you just went back to wherever you came from."

"Massachusetts," I called after him. "Says so on my other ID."

-5-

I spent the rest of the day checking the circumstantial stuff. Back issues of the Key West *Citizen*, a better paper than Lorna Hernandez had led me to believe. There were three stories on the death, none telling me anything I didn't already know. Asking around at maybe a dozen bars for any scuttlebutt on island dentists in general, I didn't hear a word about Martin Kriss in particular. At five, I called Del Wonsley from a pay phone near Mallory Square with a summary of my activities. He seemed appreciative and told me to keep on it.

After hanging up, though, I couldn't think of more "it" to keep on. Wonsley's loss of Martin Kriss was real and, being so recent, painful as well. But I wasn't sure the puzzle was solvable.

I left the pay phone and walked down into the square. Mallory is the waterfront area where some good folk of Key West and about a thousand tourists gather to watch the sun go down over the ocean, and I'd done it myself on my last visit. The guy who could make house cats perform like Clyde Beatty's lions and tigers wasn't there this time, but the Southernmost Bagpiper in the U.S.A. still strutted his kilted stuff to "Scotland the Brave" and other skirling tunes. A ponytailed guy on a high wire did some pretty impressive things as well. The largest portion of the crowd gathered around him before the setting sun itself reminded them of why they'd come to Mallory Square in the first place. I lingered a little longer than most, the cool air of near-night not bothering my Boston thermostat, the beautiful colors—even as they darkened—chipping away at my own memories of loss.

It was maybe six-thirty and black as pitch as I made my way along a side street that would intersect with Simonton and lead me back to the hotel. I figured on taking a shower, then going out for dinner and maybe some jazz or blues.

What I didn't figure on was being yanked into an alley by some-body strong enough to hurl two hundred pounds of me a good ten feet.

Both of them wore ski masks and sweatclothes. The shorter one—no more than five-six—had a broom handle, sawed off to four feet of riot baton. The taller one bent down to pick up a miniature baseball bat, the kind kids get in ballpark promotions everywhere.

Only this one had the distinctive logo of the Atlanta Braves on it.

Shorter rushed at me ninja-style, brandishing the broom handle like a sword. He finally dropped the melodrama and just jabbed the end of it at my stomach. I parried his thrust with my right palm, then grabbed the wood with my left and yanked. When the guy came forward without letting go, I clocked him with the heel of my right squarely on his left ear.

It's a pretty painful blow to unprotected cartilage, and he dropped the stick, clamping his hands to both ears under the mask like someone suffering a loud noise.

The taller guy looked from his partner to me but didn't move. I reached down and picked up the broom handle, holding it like a quarterstaff. As Shorter retreated toward the mouth of the alley, I tilted my head toward the bat in Taller's hand.

I said, "Mine's bigger than yours, Bo."

When Taller still didn't move, Shorter took his right hand off the good ear and tugged his partner by the sleeve of the sweatshirt, finally getting him to break into a lumbering run as they cleared the mouth of the alley and were gone.

In the thrall of my adrenaline rush, I thought about giving chase. Then I realized finding them wouldn't be that hard.

Back at Simonton Court, I lay face-up in the Bird of Paradise bed, staring at the ceiling fans. I'd pretty much made up my mind what to do when the phone rang.

"John Cuddy."

"John, it's Del Wonsley. I've . . . I've decided not to go forward with the investigation after all."

I gave it a beat. "First you might want to hear what happened to me a while ago."

"It doesn't matter, really. I . . . I just want to thank you for all you've done so far. Please feel free to stay through tomorrow if you'd like."

"Del, are you all right?"

A forced laugh. "Of course I'm all right."

"You want me to come over there and—"

"No, John!" Then more normally, "Really, I'm fine. Nobody's got a gun to my head." A better laugh. "If they did, I wouldn't be saying you could stay another day, now would I?"

Hard thing to judge over the telephone, but Wonsley sounded more nervous than stressed.

"John?"

"Still here."

"Simonton Court will charge me directly for the room. I'll let you arrange any flights back to Boston you want, and you can send me your bill for fees and expenses whenever."

"Del, are you sure about this?"

"Positive, John. And truly, many thanks for all your efforts."

Wonsley hung up.

After replacing my own receiver in its cradle, I laid my head back on the pillow. Thought about what I'd learned and how my client had just sounded on the phone.

Then thought about it some more before deciding to do what I was planning on anyway.

-6-

By 7:30 the next morning, I was camped anonymously at a bus stop catercorner from the building on North Roosevelt Boulevard containing Fred Ippoletti's office. He arrived for work twenty minutes later in a compact Nissan four-door, some shade of dark green.

After Ippoletti went inside, I gave him enough time to be sure he hadn't forgotten anything in his car. Then I walked over to it and copied down the plate number.

Anyone watching my actions for the rest of the day would have graded me a diligent tourist. I visited the Little White House at the Truman Annex, a museum to Plain Harry becoming a bit crowded by residential development. I moved reverently through the Hemingway House on Whitehead Street, stepping carefully around the uncountable cats roaming freely. I ate lunch at Sloppy Joe's, a bar Hemingway favored, with more photos of Papa than his own house held. I toured the Key West Aquarium, joining a crowd mesmerized by the sharks eating their meal. I took a solitary walk through Nancy Forrester's Secret Garden of meshing trees and spectacular plants. Spreading Del Wonsley's money a little wider, I had dinner at Captain Tony's, thousands of business cards tacked to the walls and hundreds of bras and bikini tops hanging from the rafters.

In fact, about the only non-touristy stop was a late afternoon buying spree at a hardware store, the clerk who helped me smiling pleasantly as she bagged an adjustable wrench, a pry bar, and some duct tape.

That night, I got lucky. From a corner stool in a place diagonally across from the Margaritaville Café, I saw Fred Ippoletti walk into his favorite performer's shrine and sit down, though still without a parrothead hat. I waited till the barkeep put a beer in front of him before walking in the direction Ippoletti had come from.

I crisscrossed the streets until I found a dark green Nissan, checking its plates to make sure I had the right one. When nobody was in sight, I took out the hinge mechanism from my skylight at Simonton Court. The adjustable wrench had been just right for undoing the nuts and bolts holding the contraption at the top of that spiral staircase. And the mechanism itself smoothly shimmed the lock button on one of Ippoletti's rear doors.

Once inside, I pushed the button back down and hunkered on the floor behind the driver's seat to wait, hoping the wrench would be just right for another task that night.

It was.

At ten-twenty by my watch, Fred Ippoletti keyed the driver's door to the Nissan. After he was in the seat and reaching for his safety belt, I rose partway up and used the business end of the wrench to sap him lightly behind the right ear.

Ippoletti slumped to the left without a sound. I got out of the car and shoved him over to the shotgun seat in front, not needing to say "Friends don't let friends drive drunk" to any passersby.

Ippoletti didn't wake up until he was already over my shoulder. Bound by the duct tape at hands, ankles, and mouth, all he could manage was a little wriggling and some muffled groaning.

I wasn't sure I could find the right spot in the dark, but the moon came out helpfully just long enough for me to get my bearings. Two minutes later, we were in front of the crypt holding Dr. Martin Kriss among his many neighbors.

I laid Ippoletti down carefully in a sitting position against a headstone five feet away. As the moon went back behind a cloud, I wished I'd remembered to buy a flashlight too, but then noticed that, even in the darkness, I could see the name etched across from us.

So, apparently, could Ippoletti.

Over his huffing behind the tape, I said, "After we talked yesterday morning, I remembered you didn't seem to like the thought of graveyards."

Ippoletti stopped making noises but began blinking at me rapidly.

I took out the pry bar. "I'm pretty sure I can get that facing tablet off with this. If there isn't enough room in there for both of you, I'll try one with no name on it yet."

Now the blinking stopped as his eyes flitted from one tablet to the next in the honeycomb across from us.

"I don't enjoy doing this, but last night a couple of guys jumped me. I'm pretty sure one of them was Bo Smith, and I still need answers to some questions about what happened to Dr. Kriss."

Ippoletti's eyes came back to me.

"If you promise to be quiet, I'll take the tape off your mouth. Any noise, though, and I'll hit you again. We clear on that?"

A series of very abrupt nods.

I laid the pry bar down and reached over to the duct tape, pulling it as gently as I could across his face.

The second that Ippoletti's lips were free, the words began tumbling out. "It was all Bo's idea, but we went along with it."

-7-

Later that night, I stood in front of the address Del Wonsley had listed on the sheet as his own. Or his and Martin Kriss'.

It was one of the bigger houses I'd registered in Key West, yellow clapboard with white trim and elaborate fretwork. There were several gables breaking up the roofline, the facade displaying both first- and second-floor porches with white wicker furniture. The windows beneath the upper overhang reminded me of eyes peering out from under a craggy brow.

I went up the front steps and knocked on the door. When I heard Wonsley's voice say "Coming," I made myself comfortable in one of two peacock chairs near the porch railing.

The door opened and Wonsley peered out, having to take a step onto the porch to see me. "John?"

"That's right."

"What are you—"

"Visiting my client. The one who wanted a private investigator who'd be 'straight' with him."

"Uh-oh." Wonsley's face dropped. "You know, don't you?"

"Only because I nearly terrified Fred Ippoletti into telling me the truth."

Wonsley looked around, then said, "Maybe we should talk inside."

"It's a nice night, Del. I promise to keep my voice down."

He came out farther onto the porch, then took the other chair. "I swear, when I asked you to come down to Key West, I had no idea what really happened."

"I know. I also know this isn't easy for you. But, Jesus, Del, you could have saved everybody a lot of trouble—"

"—if only I'd been honest with you. I know. But when Jerry Finneran showed up last night, he said he'd tell me only if I swore to keep it a secret."

"And to call me off."

"Yes," admitted Wonsley.

"OK. So now that I know, there's no reason we can't talk about it, is there?"

"No reason, but no purpose, either."

"Indulge me." Looking around, I didn't see anybody, but I lowered my voice anyway. "For a while before February eleventh, the three of them—Ippoletti, Smith, and Finneran—were all a little pissed off at you."

"Because I vetoed their 'big party' for Marty's birthday."

"But only because you knew what they didn't, about his heart condition."

Wonsley nodded.

I said, "So Bo Smith gets probably his first bright idea of the nineties. Why not treat our long-time friend Marty to a 'little party,' one he might enjoy almost as much as last year's blast without us."

"At Lips in New York."

"Where you 'spirited' Dr. Kriss to after you 'took over' his life."

"Fred said that?"

"Exact quote, though I got the feeling all three felt it."

"The bitches."

"Anyway, Smith wants to show his old lover that he's still a friend, and Ippoletti is genuinely appreciative of the no-strings loan he received. They persuade a hesitant Finneran—who owes Dr. Kriss his original job as a patrol officer—to join them."

"I know it must sound silly to you, John, but—"

"—kind of thoughtful, actually. They all call Lorna Hernandez and schedule consecutive appointments on a given day around lunchtime, a period that Ippoletti found out she wouldn't be in the office. He arrives first, with a shopping bag, making sure Hernandez is on her way before Smith and Finneran join him, all three 'with their hats on.'"

Wonsley nodded, smiling a little despite what eventually happened.

I said, "Ippoletti dips into his bag for the parrothead number and probably Smith's Atlanta baseball cap and even Finneran's parade hat from his dress uniform."

Wonsley smiled a little more.

I didn't return it. "And then they hustle Martin Kriss into that opertory, push him into the patient's chair, and do a striptease to the tune from that British movie about the laid-off steelworkers."

"*The Full Monty.*"

"Only while the birthday boy is pleased, it's all a little too much for his heart."

Wonsley dropped any pretense of smile, shaking his head. "They meant well, and I'm sure Marty did enjoy it."

"Ippoletti panics and leaves the room, but Finneran has the presence of mind to have Smith call nine-one-one while he attempts CPR. As Finneran realizes that's not going to work, he comes up with a story that he sells to the other two. A story that sounds fine until you hire me to start tugging on the strings here and there because of Ippoletti's and Smith's apparent motives."

"John, put yourself in Jerry's shoes. He's a fine police officer, but a gay one too. If the truth got out, Bo maybe loses his new lover—Paul—and Fred maybe some of his clients, straight and gay. Jerry, though, would be laughed off the force for sure, even if he wasn't fired from it for contributing to the cause of a death."

"So after I rattle some cages, Ippoletti calls Finneran, and Finneran rousts me. Then Smith—with friend Paul—tries to beat me bloody in an alley."

"But Fred and Jerry had nothing to do with that, John, and neither did I."

"Because Smith and his sidekick decided to jump me before Finneran leveled with you here."

"Exactly. Even Jerry didn't know about your being attacked until Bo called him, all worried because Paul was developing a cauliflower ear."

"Which made Finneran finally realize he had to trust you before things blew up in everybody's face."

"Yes." Shaking his head, Del Wonsley closed his eyes. "And all because Marty's older friends couldn't 'level' with his new lover over what happened—unexpectedly, tragically—from what should have been just a fun show."

I thought, *The Full Marty*, but kept it to myself.

Reliable Witness

STUART KAMINSKY

"Taradish, his name was Taradish, or Taradash, I'm sure,"
said the little man, hugging his overcoat tightly around his
chest.

"Taradish?" the cop asked.

"Or 'dash.'"

"Or Taradash?"

"Or Franklin. Might have been Franklin."

"Franklin doesn't sound anything like Taradash."

"It's not the sound. It's the feel," said the little man.

The cop's name was Conners. He was fifty-six and vaguely
worried about his left knee, which had recently begun to inform
him that it might want to retire and stop supporting him. Conners
had a mane of pepper-white hair and a belief that he had seen just
about everything a Sarasota cop could see: cult murders, drive-by
murders by twelve-year-olds, ninety-two-year-olds in a suicide love
pact. Name it. Conners had seen it.

"Koffer, this is definitely a mistake on my part and I know I'm
gonna regret it, but why are you wearing a coat?"

The information that he was wearing a coat seemed to startle the little man, who stood suddenly and looked down at himself.

"The temperature is ninety-five degrees outside," said Conners. "Humidity almost one hundred percent. It's not much better than that in here."

Koffer looked around Conners' small office in the hope, perhaps, of discovering some truth about the temperature.

"It was Flynn," said Koffer, sitting again.

Conners looked at the little man. He was wearing a ratty coat, a pensive look, and a pate with a few hundred strands of yellow hair, each of which took its own direction. Conners figured the little man for forty at most. He could have been anything from an eccentric department store heir to one of the growing number of the city's homeless, drawn by weather that couldn't kill them in the winter.

Hell, what troubled Conners was that Errol Koffer was the only witness to a murder.

Conner considered sitting to appease his knee, but if he had any chance of getting sense from Koffer, he knew he had to make him uncomfortable, block the light.

"Flynn," said Koffer, looking at Conners now with confidence, wanting to please. "I'm sure. Write it down."

Conners did not write it down.

"What were you doing in the restaurant?" asked Conners.

"It is," said Koffer. "It really was Flynn, Lieutenant."

"Sergeant. And . . ."

"They played 'Happy Birthday' on the loudspeaker. A tape, and gave me a cookie with a candle."

"And then?" Conners prompted.

"I blew out the candle."

"No, the two men. In the other booth. The only other customers in the place at ten in the morning."

Conners wished the Chief were watching and listening. Raymond Conners had a reputation for impatience. Actually it was much worse, but Conners preferred to think of his explosions as "brief moments of understandable zeal," as his wife expressed it. At the moment, Conners, with his knee and a coming headache, was straining to be reasonable with this man.

"A gift," said Koffer.

"A gift?" repeated Conners.

"The coat," explained Koffer, rubbing the top of his head to put the wisps of hair in some uniform direction. They refused, looking worse when the little man's hand came down. "The coat was a gift from a guy. I treasure gifts."

"You have a job, Mr. Koffer?"

"Deep pockets," Koffer said. "Look." He stood up, dug his hands into his pockets, and came up with a fist full of bills. "It's good for carrying moolah."

Ray Conners rested his ample rear on the edge of his desk. Since his head was now definitely beginning to hurt, he gave in to his knee.

"No one says 'moolah' anymore, Koffer," Conners said, looking out his second-floor window down onto Main Street. The sun was shining. A lone palm tree stood next to the parking structure. A chubby kid was trying to get the chain off a bike locked to the tree. From the trouble he was having, Conners figured the kid had lost his key or was trying to steal the bike from in front of police head-quarters. Conners figured the latter. He turned back to Koffer.

"I like the way it sounds," said Koffer. "Moo-lah. Moo-lah."

"Where did you get that money, Mr. Koffer?"

"Earned it," said Koffer. "Almost twenty years in the accordion repair business in Holland, Michigan. Couldn't stand listening to another bar of 'Lady of Spain' or the 'Beer Barrel Polka.' Sold my half of the place to my brother, pocketed the money, went south before the winter came. My brother said I was crazy. I ask you, who's back listening to 'Maleguena' in four feet of snow?"

Koffer looked up triumphantly, and Conners tried to imagine lunch at the Melody on the North Trail. The prospect of the lunch special usually helped to calm him. Not this time.

"The two men," said Conners.

"Franklin and the other guy," Koffer said, looking up with a knowing nod.

"I thought you said his name was Flynn?"

"I was testing you," said Koffer, playing with the buttons on his coat.

"Testing me?"

"You weren't writing," said Koffer. "I wondered if you were taking me seriously."

"I'm taking you seriously, Mr. Koffer. A man is dead, murdered. You say you heard the conversation between the dead man and the man he was with. You are the only witness. I'm taking you seriously." Conners was up now, his fists clenched. "How about you taking me seriously?"

Koffer thought for a moment, then, putting his hands firmly on the arms of the chair, he rose. Conners had moved so close to his witness, when Koffer stood they were almost nose to nose. Koffer smiled and sidled to his right.

"I remember better when I walk," Koffer said. "I go through lots of shoes. But I buy good shoes. That's important. Good support for your feet and knees."

"I'll remember that," said Conners. "Murder."

"Murder," agreed Koffer with a nod, pacing, moving his arms, his heavy coat swishing as he moved. "The man who was killed . . ."

"Sbarzki," Conners supplied, taking the chair Koffer had vacated.

"I never heard his name," said Koffer. "Guy who shot him. I heard his name."

"Taradish, Taradash, Franklin, or Flynn," said Conners wearily.

"Sounds like a law firm," said Koffer.

"That it does," said Conners with a deep sigh, putting his hand to his forehead.

Koffer plunged a hand into his right coat pocket, fished around, and reeled in a small bottle. A few bills fluttered to the floor. Koffer picked them up and handed the bottle to Conners.

"What's this?" said Conners.

"Chinese, for headaches, pain. Comes from the mainland. It's got ground stag antlers, ginseng, good stuff."

Conners started to hand the bottle back.

"Try," said Koffer.

Conners looked at the ceiling of his office, beyond which, he hoped, God was not watching.

"What the hell?" he said, opened the bottle, took out two light blue oval pills, and drank them down with the dusty glass of water he had poured himself more than an hour earlier.

"The man, the one who shot Mr. . . ."

"Sbarzki," Conners supplied.

"I'm not good with names," Koffer admitted, grinning at the policeman apologetically.

"I've noticed."

"You did?"

"I'm an experienced cop. Look, can we continue this later, or maybe Officer Breen can . . ." Conners said, starting to rise.

"But," Koffer interrupted, "I'm great with numbers, small things. Accordions have more parts than you think."

"I have never," said Conners, "thought about accordion parts."

He knew he should get up and see if the kid was still trying to steal the bike, but he didn't move. It had been a long night and a bad morning.

"Man who shot him was five-feet-six, weighed one hundred sixty-five or sixty-six," said Koffer, resuming his pacing. "He had brown hair with a fringe of gray, but it was a wig. I'd say he was sixty, sixty-one tops. His suit was blue with a single navy stripe down the trousers. I'd say a Kuppenheimer a couple of years old. Shoes were good, Florsheims, black. Briefcase was real leather, cowhide. He was a lawyer, office on the sixth floor of the . . . I don't remember the name, but the address is thirty-four fifty-four Ringling Boulevard."

Koffer stopped and looked at Conners, whose mouth opened slightly. "That help?" asked Koffer.

"That helps," said Conners, reaching for a phone.

"They were arguing over a bill Mr. . . ."

"Sbarzki."

"Sbarzki," Koffer repeated. "He said the other guy owed him thirty-four thousand one hundred thirty-four dollars for some account."

"Breen," Conners said into the phone. "Get in here."

Koffer had wandered over to the window and was looking out.

"Kid over there's stealing a bike," he said.

"And Breen," Conners said into the phone, "there's a kid across the street stealing a bike. Send someone over to get him."

Conners got up. His knee wasn't half as bad as it had been minutes ago.

"How's your head?" Koffer asked, turning from the window. "Chinese stuff is great. Food. Medicine. Natural stuff."

"How about after Officer Breen talks to you, I take you over to the Melody Restaurant for a birthday lunch?" asked Conners.

"Sounds great. Thanks, Lieutenant. . . ."

"Conners," said Conners gently. "Sergeant Raymond Conners."

The Case of Johnny Walker Black

David A. Kaufelt

I swore on a stack of Bibles that I'd never return to Fenton Beach in this lifetime, but money, particularly inherited money, has a way of changing such youthful vows.

Located on the western and lesser coast of the Florida peninsula, a spit away from that capital of glamour—St. Pete—Fenton Beach likes to think of itself as a publicity-free Palm Beach. Fat chance. The twenty blocks or so of Victorian houses built by my Midwestern grandpa and his minor mogul buddies could easily be mistaken for a Cleveland suburb, circa 1910. Only in this instance, the potted palms are on the outside. There's no real money anymore.

The only people who live here year-round do so because they have to. What used to pass for culture was a rickety theater located in the old Carlson barn, long since burned down. It looked like a stage set for a Mickey and Judy movie, and the productions (your *Oklahoma*s, your *South Pacific*s) were popular among the winter tourists from Indianapolis because of "the old tunes."

The Red Barn was created, owned, and managed by a dragon of a woman who must then have been in her seventies, Arden (née

Janet Yates), who attempted with no little success to pass herself off as a madcap forty. It was only when Arden had her famous stroke in the shopping center Walgreens—blood all over the candy display, I'm told—that the Red Barn went dark. In time, her nephew, Raymond Yates, an aspiring play*wrong*, returned from college with the express goal of making the Red Barn into something more than a vehicle for his auntie's overdisplayed talents.

This is also where I entered, stage right. I had left Fenton Beach some years earlier to become a theater actress (and not in the great Arden tradition, I assure you) and had met with some success. That year I had the second lead in an Edward Albee play waiting for me in the fall but not enough resources to get me between May and October. Luckily, my brother—often billed as the fanciest man in America—died without issue and I suddenly found myself the owner and occupier of the old family manse on Bay Street.

Phineas had been nuts about Fenton House. There was a provision in his will to the effect that I had to spend six months a year in residence if I were to benefit from the Byzantine trusts he had set up. My attorney said there was no way I was going to worm out of that. Dear Phineas. Not unexpectedly, I was bored out of my gourd, having forgotten how hateful and pretentious, not to mention sweltering, Fenton Beach in the summer could be. So when Raymond Yates asked if he might call to discuss a play he had written, I said certainly.

Raymond was handsome in the wide-shouldered, dimple-chinned, earnest, gray-eyed, dirty blond–haired manner that the young William Holden had made popular. I found myself, well, receptive. We sat facing one another in the mustard yellow living room on mother's heat-generating navy blue horsehair sofas Phineas had refurbished at enormous cost. Raymond was pouring Johnny Walker Black down his throat as if it were designer water, and I was sipping at a pony of Hennessy. It was a gray sweltering day—Phineas hadn't believed in A/C—and one could smell the white jasmine hedges blooming outside the oversized French windows. Heady stuff, jasmine and booze.

I found myself entertaining thoughts of leading Raymond up to my private sitting room (pale, pale salmon and linen white—not a success) and then into my embrace. Spending a sweaty hour with Raymond in the gilded sleigh bed Phineas had insisted upon seemed a not unappetizing way of killing the afternoon.

Raymond was single-minded, however, and sex with me was not on the agenda. His father had been the golf pro at our sad excuse for a country club, and Phineas used to say, "Well, of course, dearie, he's not one of us." He could have fooled me, his arrogance right up there with Phineas'.

"I have a play I want you to read for," the dopey bastard actually said. Even then, Lettie Fenton didn't "read" for plays. But I liked his drugstore cologne and the way he slugged down his scotch.

"What's it about?" I asked. I was wearing tennis shorts (not that I played but I looked good in them) and crossed my legs a couple of times, but it was clear that Raymond wasn't paying attention.

While he told me about the play, yet another Southern family drama, the thought crossed my mind that I should introduce him to an actor chum of mine. Perhaps he liked the man thing.

"You're not listening," he said, looking up, his gray eyes attractively stormy.

"'Anne walks across the room, lights a cigarette with trembling hands, and starts to cry.' I heard every word."

"Want to hear more?"

"Certainly not. I loathe being read to. Reminds me of mother." I topped off his glass.

He knocked it down in that manly way and said, "I guess you're not interested." He had a thick, pouty lower lip. Snake eyes. He moved nicely. He was terrifically attractive.

I chug-a-lugged my brandy to prove I could be as butch as he and said, "I'll tell you after I've read it—to myself—and after we've made love."

He put the manuscript down on the distressed pine table and looked at me for perhaps the first time that afternoon.

"You despised me in high school."

"You never seemed quite clean." I stood up and headed for the stairway. "Your fingernails always looked as if they were in mourning." He filled his glass and wanted to know where I was going. I didn't answer; he knew very well. He followed, clutching his damned play in one hand, the Baccarat whiskey glass in the other. I think it was his reluctance that made the experience so piquant.

Needless to say, I agreed to play Anne in *Reflected Glory*, a character as intellectually challenging as Snow White. With one proviso: that Raymond would continue to sleep with me. I don't know what got into me, you'll excuse the expression. I had slept with a number of men and boys and one memorable woman, and I never had felt like this before: as if my entire life depended on those moments when we were together; like Bette Davis in one of her weepies. I didn't even fight it. I couldn't.

He cast the other actors—of course he was producing and directing—with what passed for talent in Fenton Beach. He had new lighting installed and the barn walls painted somber gray and the bills sent to me. Rehearsals were the nightmare anyone might have predicted, taking into consideration Raymond's limited, collegial experience; his drinking; his temperament; his monumental misunderstanding of theater and human nature.

A partially recovered Auntie Arden kept having herself wheeled in to give advice. Finally he barred her from her theater. He looked and sounded like a nervous breakdown to come. Nor was his performance in bed anything to alert the Academy about. I suggested he hire an assistant to look after "the little stuff. Raymond, you can't do it all."

There was a time when that line would have made me giggle. But I was beyond shame, his disinterest fanning the flames. He said he would think about it, and two days later he announced he had taken on Jean Norton as production assistant.

Jean's Chicago grandmother owned a great big Victorian pile not far from our house. Thinking that the rest of Florida was hopelessly vulgar, she wintered each year for half a century in Fenton Beach. No hopeless vulgarity here, more's the pity. Jean was then a perky, well-bred, blunt-cut blond, a Lake Forest deb of a girl, murder on the tennis courts. Everyone liked her. Coincidentally, her granny had died a few days after Phineas. She had left Jean the house and what was then not a bad income.

"I've never met anyone like Raymond," Jean told me, making me feel a thousand years older than she.

We were sipping lemonade on the front porch of her house a few nights before Raymond's play was to open. It was a rare, not unpleasant summer Florida night, a Cecil B. deMille moon in the sky. The terrifying sounds of the VFW band slaughtering "When the Saints Come Marching In" down on the town pier swept in on the tepid bay breeze. Even the fireflies, usually overrated, provided amusement. It was a night for confidences. Jean wanted to talk about Raymond; there wasn't much to say about his play. She wasn't stupid and she knew how dismal it was.

"Have you ever met anyone like Raymondo?" she asked, giving the name a Spanish inflection.

Big romantic stuff this, darling. I wanted to say Raymondos were a dime a dozen on every Eastern college campus that gave scholarships, but Jean had that look in her puppy-dog eyes.

"He's exotic," I contented myself with saying. "Maybe it's his Polish Jewish background. All those beatings by the Cossacks and those endless salt mines and deserted steppes."

"Raymond's Jewish?"

"I don't think he practices," I said, to see if that would help. I had forgotten about the infamous Midwestern Brahmin propensity for anti-Semitism. But it was *au contraire* in both our cases. The truth of the matter was that I was in love with Raymond. You would think that I, now a big-city girl, would have laughed uproariously at Raymond's smoldering and patently unconvincing sensuality. But there's something about pathetically innocent men who believe in their own integrity that makes me want to hold them and whisper sweet reassuring nothings in their ears. I fought it and I hated it, but I had come to the conclusion that after the play failed and Raymond was in a particularly vulnerable mood, I would pop the question.

I was wondering what our issue would look like when Jean broke into these thoughts by saying, "I always wanted to be kissed by a Jewish boy." She had a martyred expression on her Miss Porter–pretty face as if she were confessing to wanting to be embraced by a mutant.

I reached for my lemonade—how I despise the stuff—and muttered what I had just then realized, "I bet he's more than kissed you."

Her heart-shaped face turned bright pink. "Lettie," she said, turning to me. "You're my best friend here and I've got to tell someone. We were married last week in Georgia." She dug around in the décolleté of her little white dress and pulled out the modest wedding band she wore on a chain around her charming neck. "We're not going to announce it until after the play opens."

"How nice for you, dear," I said, getting up out of the rusting porch glider, nauseous, spilling the damned lemonade, going to my house and Phineas' telephone and telling my agent, that blond, Bronx-bagel beauty, that I'd changed my mind and certainly I'd do *Tiger at the Gates* at the Cherry Lane in August. Be marvelous prep, I said nonsensically, for the Albee play in the fall.

Early in the morning I gave the tough old bird of a housekeeper instructions and was on my way. "What about Raymond Yates' play?" she called after me.

Reflected Glory opened with a local beauty in the lead and got exactly the reviews and audience it deserved. Jean and Raymondo stayed on in her house, he writing plays no one in his right mind would produce, she playing tennis and involving herself in Fenton Beach cultural pursuits, an oxymoron if I ever heard one. I went on to a fair amount of success, lots of lovers, and a wardrobe filled with Galanos gowns.

Cut to twenty odd years later. I am, if not the darling of the American theater, at least its favorite witch. I do evil so well. Raymond is still officially writing plays and has become the town ex-alcoholic, the sort that can't look at a drink without needing one. He is overweight and overbearing and spends most of his time sailing a boat Jean bought him when her trust fund meant something. Jean herself is a washed-out drab, an emaciated tennis aficionado, too tan and too sinewy. Childless, she has spent the last couple of decades trying to make her income stretch while jumping ("How high, darling?") when Raymond, that unproduced, unwritten genius, snaps his fingers.

So it was winter, it had rained hard, and the temperature had gone down to fifty, which is considered Arctic weather in Fenton Beach. The bay had overflowed and the streets were impassable by car. And yet Jean had braved the elements and come to sit with me by the hearth of the overly adorable Victorian fireplace with which Phineas had seen to outfit the drawing room.

I was, as we say in the theater, resting that winter and uncomplainingly so. If it was fifty in Fenton Beach, it was in the teens in New York, and I didn't for a moment miss the snow or the drafty dressing rooms or the steam heat which dries out my skin and nasal passages. I would long for it all in a month or so and then I would go back and presumably pick up some TV. Maybe Clytemnestra in a new public TV production, Lord help me.

Jean, normally the sort of woman who makes a great thing of keeping a stiff upper lip, looked especially blue and down at the heel. Speaking of which, her feet were bare. "He didn't give me time to grab my flip-flops before he threw me out," she said, sipping at her brandy, talking to the fire and herself.

After twenty odd years of Raymondo, Jean was no longer perky. There was a new and bitter lilt to her chat which made her, for me, more companionable. "I thought he was off the sauce since the doctor told him he'd be dead in a year if he didn't stop." I told Mary—the new but no less sour housekeeper—to get Jean a pair of house slippers. "Didn't Raymond go to AA last spring. . . ?"

"No, he did not go to AA." That once heart-shaped face now looked as if it had been drawn by a five-year-old, the lines going this way and that. "He thought the AA people were a bunch of sissies. 'What do those fruitcakes know about real drinking?' he asked.

"He quit all by himself. He had me load up his damned boat with life-giving produce—*Prevention Magazine* is his bible—and then he sailed out to the middle of the bay. He returned two weeks later. Dry. Hasn't had a sip since, though he can't look at a grape soda bottle without salivating. That's why he rarely leaves the house. He's developed a new addiction. TV game shows. It will be easier when the rains stop and he can go out on the boat. There's no temptation on the low seas."

She put her head with its boy's hairdo on the sofa and looked up at the Venetian glass chandelier Phineas had caused to be hung in the center of the room. "Trouble is, Lettie, I liked him better as a drunk. At least he'd eventually pass out. Now his rages go on for days. He's so damned paranoid. Tonight he accused me of stealing his non-alcoholic beer."

"You don't actually drink non-alcoholic beer?"

"Tell me. But in his dementia he forgot that. Claimed I was out to drive him crazy. I said it was a short ride and he hit me."

"Stop," I begged. She lifted up the sleeve of her sweatshirt. There was an amoeba-like bruise taking shape where a sailor would have a tattoo. "Dear Lord," I said, wondering if I should go to her. But neither of us is that sort and so I stayed put in the understuffed ladies' chair, genuinely shocked.

"Then he threw me out of the house. Dragged me down the front steps."

She closed her eyes for a moment, and I was afraid she was going to go the limit and cry. Thankfully, she didn't.

"His anger had nothing to do with the non-alcoholic beer," Jean said, pouring herself more brandy, something the old Jean would never do without asking. "Did you know his Auntie Arden finally died this week? Knocking me about was his way of celebrating. He's rich now. Or comfortable. He doesn't need me and my pittance of an income anymore. Soon as the estate is probated, come spring, he's jumping ship, he said. Taking the boat and never coming back. He'll be rid of me."

I hate to admit I was losing patience. I was never one of the girly girls who loved confidential chats—truth is, I don't like women much—and I said, with some asperity, "I thought this was what you wanted. After all, you'll be rid of him."

She looked at me then and smiled. "You've never been in love, have you, Lettie?"

"I've been in love once and in lust often." My one love, of course, was Raymond, but I wasn't going to admit that. This kind of conversation makes me uncomfortable. The only part of me I like to thoroughly examine are my cheekbones. She downed the Napoleon, asked to use the phone, and left me for a few minutes, during which I contemplated my unloving life. Raymond and I would have lasted twenty minutes, I knew. But it would have been a memorable twenty minutes.

"He's OK now," she said, returning from the phone. So was she. The only real victim of the night was yours truly. "Why?" I asked, as she opened the thick glass doors, letting in the unlikely chill, and prepared to step out into the rain. "He's still a great kisser," Jean said, remembering the house slippers, kicking them off, going barefoot into the night.

I didn't see much of her during the rest of the winter. An occasional luncheon meeting of the Annual Literary Arts Seminar (ALAS), usually held at one of the overpriced, old-fashioned eating houses those elderly, sentimental girls prefer. A couple of times at the movies over in St. Pete, Raymond on her arm, ignoring me. I suppose the movies were one public place he could go where liquor wasn't a temptation.

And then in late April—I had decided not to go back to New York for any number of work-related reasons—I met her coming out of the ratty supermarket (we call it the Moscow I.G.A.) out on the highway. One of the stock boys was putting a big carton in the back of her Honda station wagon.

"I didn't know you shopped here," I said. "Though you get far better value for your money than in town. Especially if you cut the coupons out of the Sunday papers."

Jean was distracted. She said yes, that was a great idea, she had to start saving coupons. She gave the boy a dollar, which was fifty cents too much, and took off. It was later that same day when I was down at the Fenton Beach excuse for a yacht club, paying my annual dues (these small Florida towns nickel and dime one to death), when I ran into Jean again. She was sitting on a park bench, bleached-blue eyes focused on the green bay waters.

"You look as if your puppy just died," I said, sitting next to her. It was pleasant sitting there, watching the boat owners fool around with their rigs and masts and whatever they do; they don't seem to spend much time on the water.

"He's left me. As promised. I had just enough time to get supplies aboard."

So like Jean in her martyr mode. Seeing her man off with food. She stood up and put her hands in the pockets of a sad windbreaker and moved off to her grim little station wagon. I called after her but she either didn't hear or didn't want to. It occurred to me as I sat there that there was a goodly amount of irony in the fact that Jean's I.G.A. purchases for Raymond's voyage of good-bye had been packed in a liquor box.

Though it was late in the season, there were several hurricane warnings that week, the seas getting nasty. If I thought about it, I would have guessed that Raymond had taken shelter over on St. Pete Beach. But after it cleared, early on Saturday morning, his body washed up on the yacht club beach, scaring the hell out of the life-guard (well, that boy needed a good jolt) and a couple of senior citizen joggers. They found the boat, or what was left of it, over in nearby Indian Harbor. Raymond, they said, had lost control in the storm and had scuttled it on the rocks. But any sailor as experienced as he should have known how dangerous Indian Harbor shoals were.

Jean said that perhaps he had been drinking.

Document of the Keys

PETER KING

A light breeze sent puffs of white sand scuttling along Siesta Beach. Pelicans squawked in protest as their flight paths were interrupted, then flapped awkwardly out into the Gulf of Mexico in search of calmer air. Buoys bobbed gently in the rippling water, and further out, a lone sail cruised serenely.

Mack Dennison smoothed down his ruffled white hair. "Good of you to agree to stay over a few days, Will. This is just your kind of thing—and you'll get a kick out of it, I know." His weather-beaten, reddish-brown face, his hair, and his erect six-foot frame made him a noticeable figure even to those beach strollers who didn't recognize the councilman, prominent in local political and social circles.

Will Greenaway stepped over a section of a sodden palm tree, half-buried in the sand. Three inches taller than his companion, his long legs and lanky body made it easy. "As long as I get back to the university by Monday, that's fine. You've certainly got me intrigued, Mack. We're out of microphone range here, I take it?"

Mack Dennison grinned. "Nothing quite that cloak-and-dagger." The grin faded. "At least, I hope it doesn't turn out that way."

A biplane rattled overhead, its banner advertising an arts and crafts fair. When its noisy engine had died away, Dennison resumed. "As a historian, you'll be particularly interested in this, and as a regular visitor to Sarasota for years, you'll feel even closer to it."

Will Greenaway nodded. "For twenty-three years, Lucy and I came down here every year. When she died two years ago, I thought I would never come again. Then the snowstorm that came through Jersey last week made me recall what it must be like here." He waved a hand at the clear blue sky and the late morning sun, already warm. "I had a few weeks' leave coming, and I decided any memories of Lucy that this place brought back could only be happy ones. So here I am. Now, come on, Mack—what's all the mystery?"

"Cast your mind back," said Dennison, "to the seventeen nineties. As relating to Florida."

The other frowned. After a moment, he said slowly, "Under Spanish rule and remained that way until the United States purchased it in eighteen nineteen."

"Spanish rule, yes. But more specifically? Who really ruled it?"

"The governor at that time was Don José Alvarez. He ruled it from Havana. I wrote a monograph on him while I was down here one year. He had a lot of territory under his control—almost all the Caribbean islands as well as Florida. Did a better job than many governors."

Dennison nodded as they walked on, waves lapping a few feet away. "Go on. What was Alvarez' big worry?"

"He had a lot of worries. . . ."

"Foreign invasion one of them?"

"Napoleon was flexing his military muscles, casting covetous eyes at Louisiana and Florida, so there was a threat of a French invasion, yes. Then, Florida had previously been under English control so there was a strong possibility of their wanting to get it back and check Napoleon's conquering imperative at the same time."

"Well done, Professor," said Mack Dennison with a grin.

Greenaway's lean, New England features took on a mock-stern impassivity. "Not another word until you tell me what this is all about!"

The winter sun was getting warmer and Dennison loosened his jacket. "One of our famous stately homes is being torn down. The Barrington mansion. You probably remember it?"

"Yes, I do. Not to make room for another twenty-screen multi-plex, I hope?"

"It just died of old age. Shame, but it wasn't preservable any longer. Anyway, a team was going through the library to decide what to do with the books when they found a document."

Dennison's ominous pause caused Greenaway to turn to him. The councilman went on. "It's an agreement between Spain and the United States that the two countries would join forces to resist an 'invasion by a foreign power,' as the document puts it. They meant, of course, France or England. As a result of the alliance, the United States would be given the mainland of Florida and Spain would get the Florida Keys—to be administered by the government of Cuba."

"The Florida Keys. . . ." mused Greenaway. "Are they named?"

"They are identified. Some of the names have changed but there's no doubt about their identity. Key West and the others—well, they have their problems but we have our own. Included also are some of the west coast barrier islands, namely Siesta Key, Longboat Key, Casey Key—thousands of people, scores of multi-million dollar homes, real estate beyond estimate."

"Whoa, wait a minute!" Will Greenaway held up a restraining hand. "Even if this document had any validity—which would have to be established—no way is Spain going to press an ancient claim on some little Florida islands." He smiled at the changing expression on Dennison's face. "I know they're important to you, Mack, but after all, they are only—"

"That's not what we're worried about. Spain—OK, they're not likely to raise any hackles over this. But, you see, the document says 'the government of Cuba.' It meant the Spanish governor at the time—but it has a different meaning today."

"Ah." Will Greenaway breathed the monosyllable. "Right now, Washington is having severe disagreements with Cuba on a number of matters. Whether this document has any validity or not, the Cubans might well make an issue of this . . ."

"Exactly. So now you see why I asked you to stay over. You are a professor of history and you know this period well. You've authenticated old documents, and you even did some sleuthing over that Monticello business. You're the perfect choice to look into this. I've talked to my colleagues at city and county levels and they agree. Needless to say, even the thought of Cuba's collecting the taxes on our Keys has everybody here in an uproar."

Will Greenaway stopped to throw back a football to some youths on whose field of play they were infringing. "You were right. It is fascinating. You've got me, Mack. How can I resist? The first thing I want to do is see the document."

"I'm afraid you can't do that." Dennison's words were spaced. "The document left by courier yesterday for Tallahassee. The vehicle was in an accident at the Skyway Bridge tollbooth, and afterwards the document case was found to be missing. You see, now, why I added that bit about sleuthing?"

The Historical Resources and Documentation building is a small structure on State Highway 41 as it goes through the city of Sarasota from north to south. It is overshadowed by its two larger, neighboring buildings—the Municipal Auditorium with a large sign outside advertising a Stamp and Coin exhibition, and the Visitor Center, its parking lot full of cars with Northern state license plates.

Inside, Will Greenaway was chatting with one of the staff while Mack Dennison, taking the opportunity to check on a zoning change, was poring over a large map.

Jenny Rodriguez was a lively fifty-year-old, quick in speech and movement. She slapped a large sheet of paper on the table where Greenaway sat. "Copy," she said briskly. "We made several, naturally."

Will's pulse increased slightly as it always did under such circumstances. The language was flowery, but the words were written large and were very legible. Jenny's sharp eye noticed a slight frown. "Need any help with the translation?"

"Thanks, I'm OK at the moment." He went through the document twice. There was no doubt that it stated exactly what Mack Dennison had said and gave Cuba the ownership of the Keys and the right to govern—and tax—them. Mack came over.

"Signed by Don José Alvarez on behalf of the King of Spain and by the Secretary of State on behalf of the president of the United States," Will murmured. "Seems authentic but obviously we need the original to determine that. Washington has been informed as well as Tallahassee, I presume?"

"Yes. They declined to comment."

"Very wise," murmured Will.

"We shall fight them on the beaches and in the supermarkets," said Jenny in a passable impersonation despite her light voice. "We shall fight them in the parking lots and in the Opera House. Longboat Key will never surrender."

Will chuckled. Mack managed a weak grin.

"Who knows about the discovery of this document?" Will asked.

"Everybody," said Jenny promptly. Mack's agreement was a grimace.

"There are quite a few Cubans in the vicinity, aren't there?"

"I'm half-Mexican," Jenny said quickly, "but yes, there are."

"I suppose people know about the theft of the original too?"

"Too many," shrugged Mack. "Margaret West, our indefatigable girl reporter, will have it in the *Herald Tribune* tomorrow."

Will heaved his long body out of the chair. "Let's talk to that courier."

Frank Janowicz had been a courier and driver for the county for fifteen years. He was chunky and looked tough enough to hold his own against any two men. Whoever stole the document case might have known that, Will thought. So they had contrived a minor collision and taken the case in the ensuing confusion.

"A dark blue Ford pickup," Janowicz told them. "Ninety-three or ninety-four. I'd just come through the tollbooth—the lanes narrow, there was a lot of traffic. It hit me in the side, I pulled over. I wasn't expecting anything; I mean, all I had were some papers, right?" Will nodded encouragement for him to go on. "This guy got out, was examining the side of his pickup, waving his arms, getting excited. It didn't look that bad to me—that must have been when another guy got out and took the document case."

In answer to Mack's question, Janowicz described the first man. "Mid-thirties, medium build, dark beard and mustache, dark glasses, a red bandana 'round his head. Bit of an accent—"

"Hispanic?" asked Mack.

"Might have been. Then he was calming down, said something about his deductible. We said we'd exchange names, addresses, insurance, the usual. We both went back to our vehicles, and next thing I knew he'd driven off."

"That's when you noticed the case was gone," commented Will.

Janowicz looked a little shame-faced. "Not exactly. I phoned in to report the accident. I was driving away—then I noticed."

La Perla Ristorante was almost full. The buzz of Spanish filled the air, already redolent of garlic and onion. The tiled floor and the plastic-covered tables were not haute cuisine, "but the food's good," said Mack Dennison.

"And your other reason for bringing me here?" asked Will Greenaway.

"Can't fool you, can I?" smiled Mack. He lowered his voice. "A detective on the local force said it was the meeting place for the 'Free Cuba' movement."

Will glanced around. "Which ones are the revolutionaries?"

"About half, Ernesto says."

Will raised an eyebrow. "Ernesto?"

"Who better?" asked Mack.

The waitress was a good-looking woman with black hair, black eyes, and a swinging stride. "Specials today are grilled grouper with black beans and rice, spare ribs with Cuban sauce, and shrimp Santa Clara." She took their orders, snapped her pad closed, and asked, "Any luck finding the parchment?"

Mack groaned. "Does everybody know?"

"A parchment?" said Will innocently. "Is that what it is? I hadn't heard that."

"And what would you like to drink?" asked the woman, looking him boldly in the eye.

"Chardonnay," said Will. "Any of these fellows here know anything about this missing, er, parchment, do you think?"

"I'll ask around," she said, still looking him in the eye.

They strolled along Main Street in Sarasota, "walking off those Caribbean calories," as Mack put it. Will stopped to look in the window of a pawn shop. "We don't have any of these anymore," he commented. Next to it was a Japanese restaurant with a sign on the ornate door saying that it was closed and would reopen soon as a Northern Italian restaurant. "They come and they go," shrugged Mack.

The next shop was a hardware store. "The tools look like antiques, I know," Mack said, "but they're not." Then came a stock-broker's office and next to it a bar with a flashing Michelob sign and some loud music. A man stepped out of the doorway.

He was clearly Hispanic. He had olive skin and a ponytail of black hair. "Still looking for the document?" he asked insolently.

"You were in La Perla," Mack said.

"Right. Heard you talking to Carlotta."

"Do you know anything that would help us?" Mack wanted to know.

The man's dark eyes ranged from Mack to Will and back.

"I'm with the 'Free Cuba' movement. That document wouldn't be any use to us."

"Who would it be of use to?"

"Gotta few Castro-ites around these parts. They might want to get ahold of it."

"What are they doing here?" Will asked casually.

The man grinned, showing brilliantly white teeth. "Keeping an eye on us mostly."

"I'm Mack Dennison—"

"Yeah, I know."

"Let me know if you hear anything."

The man's gaze rested on Will but Mack made no effort to introduce him. Instead, the two walked on. The man watched them for a moment, then went back into the bar.

"Think he's telling the truth?" Mack asked as they walked on past a jeweler's, a delicatessen, and a gun shop.

"Could be," Will said laconically. "Best you can hope for is that the 'Free Cuba' people might want to score a few points. They might pass on something."

"Guess you're right. Now where, Professor?"

"I was thinking we might go back to the origin."

"Origin? Oh, you mean where all of this started?"

"Yes."

"Concannon's Bookshop is just a couple of blocks ahead. Colin Concannon is usually there—"

He was there. Big, bearded, and boisterous, Colin Concannon obviously loved books almost as much as life itself, and within minutes, all three of them were up on the top floor of the building, among Colin's "private stock."

The bookshop itself was a bibliophile's delight. Old carpets covered the creaky wooden floors and armchairs were scattered here and there, mostly occupied with customers from fifteen to ninety, all deeply engrossed in the written word. A Mozart string quartet played soft and appropriate music as the men climbed the wooden stairs and entered the book-lined study, where piles of books, pamphlets, catalogs, and brochures crowded the fax machine, the computer, and a simmering coffee machine.

Will Greenaway confessed his fascination with books, and he and Concannon compared tastes and preferences, fingered a dozen volumes, and were on their second cup of coffee before Mack managed to steer them back on track.

"I told Will you'd explain exactly how you came to find the document."

It was a first edition of Francis Parkman's *France and England in North America* that had contained the document. Three massive tomes, Morocco-bound with gold lettering, they had apparently not been opened in many decades. When the Barrington family had moved to Florida from Connecticut, they had brought an already sizable library with them, adding to it frequently. After John Barrington died, his wife, Edna, lived in the mansion for fifteen more years. When she died recently, her children, squabbling over the estate and the terms of the will, agreed on very few things, but one of them was the prompt sale of the contents of the library.

"How did you come to open the book?" asked Will curiously. "Sounds as if there were thousands of volumes there."

"In the usual way with a library like that," Concannon explained. "We pick out all the sets, all the quality bindings, all the oversized books, all the gold-engraved covers. These we can sell off individually after checking their value. All booksellers have lists of customers and their special wants. Americana is always a popular category."

"So you pulled out this set?"

"Yes. I took two of our staff with me, both youngish but developing a good eye. Kelly was the one who brought over this set, and she also had a couple of interesting sets on the Revolution. I was looking through them to make sure that no pages were missing, that no one had scribbled notes in the margins, no damage to the spines—that kind of thing—and this document fell out."

Mack suddenly took an interest. "A parchment, somebody told us it was."

"It was on heavy paper, official looking, very old . . . you could call it a parchment, yes."

"Did you realize what it was right away?" Will asked.

"No, I didn't. My Spanish is rudimentary, to say the least. Brian was able to make sense of it, though, and that's why I took it to Historical Resources."

"Any theories on how the document came to be in the book?" Will wondered.

"An earlier Barrington was in the diplomatic service. This could have been one of several copies," Concannon told him. He looked at Mack. "Is the situation past desperate and now getting serious? Should we be thinking about calling out the Casey Key Cavalry? They could make do with their polo ponies."

"Thanks, Colin," said Mack, heading downstairs.

"Give me a few minutes to browse down there," Will said. "Can't resist books."

Back on Main Street, the afternoon sun was warm. "Any of this making sense?" Mack Dennison asked.

"Oh, yes, we're moving in the right direction."

Mack looked at the lanky professor, whose face indicated deep thought. "Where does the trail take us now?" he asked.

Will Greenaway pondered a few moments longer. "Let's try the Municipal Auditorium."

The "show" inside the Municipal Auditorium was attracting a lot of collectors. Under plastic sheeting, stamps from every nation were a dazzle of color, and the more subdued soft silvers, coppers, and bronzes of the coins made a pleasing contrast, livened by the occasional glitter of gold. Collectors and dealers stood around in small groups, earnestly discussing ages, values, and prices, arguing and haggling.

"Haven't been in here since the antiques show last year when Eulalia was hunting for an old Welsh dresser," Mack said. He followed Will as they went from stand to stand. "Are we looking for something?"

Will did not answer immediately. "We'll know when we find it," he said, and moments later he breathed, "Ah, here we are!"

Mack stared, then listened curiously as Will chatted with the man and woman at the stand. Then they went on to the next stand.

That evening, they sat at a window table in the Chart House. Lights twinkled on outside as the sun settled into the Gulf of Mexico with a splendid display of riotous reds. Will had insisted they fill their plates from the lavish salad buffet before he would answer any questions. Even then, he ate most of his salad before he began to satisfy the eager Mack's curiosity.

"Is it really reasonable to suspect Castro supporters of stealing the document? That was the thought that came to me when I decided I ought to be a little more open-minded and survey some of the alternatives.

"The 'Free Cuba' movement? Would they steal it? Why would they? Just to keep it out of the hands of Castro? Well, maybe. Another reason might be to sell it to the Cuban government and then use the money to fuel the movement against them."

Mack smiled. "That would be ironic."

"But perhaps a little preposterous. What other possibilities? I began to think on more pragmatic lines then. Forget politics—what about plain greed, a much more common motive for theft?"

"You mean sell the document simply as a rare commodity—like a valuable coin or stamp."

They finished their salads and sipped wine as they awaited their main course.

"That's right," Will confirmed. "Such crimes can be planned or simply spur of the moment."

"Steal something if the opportunity occurs, then figure out later what to do with it." Mack was getting into the spirit of the discussion now.

"Exactly. However, there was some planning here. The document didn't just disappear, snatched suddenly at an unguarded moment. The theft was planned—the pickup truck, the clever choice of a tollbooth, where there are scores of cars and an easy chance for a getaway."

"But it doesn't seem as if the document is valuable enough to make it worthwhile," said Mack. "That couple at the auditorium certainly sounded knowledgable and they didn't think so."

"True. So what would be the next logical thought?"

"Ah, that's why we moved on to the next stand!"

"Right."

"I knew kids collect autographs of baseball and football players, pop stars," said Mack, "but I didn't realize that it went any further than that."

"The document was signed by two men. The signature of Don José Alvarez is not likely to be of value, but the American Secretary of State at that time was Thomas Jefferson."

"I couldn't read his signature," complained Mack.

"He varied it considerably. Sometimes his handwriting was fine and precise, other times it was large and sprawling. When he became president years later, it made his signature more sought after, of course."

"Are all presidents' signatures valuable?"

"Not at all," said Will firmly. "Perhaps the most valuable collection of signatures in this country is one which contains the names of those who signed the Declaration of Independence. Ever heard of George Read, Arthur Middleton, William Williams? They signed it, but one of the most valuable signatures is that of Button Gwinnett—another name you have probably never heard. That's largely because he got himself killed in a duel shortly afterwards. He was only forty-three, so very few examples of his signature remain."

"So who stole the document case?"

"A friend or relative of Brian, the young fellow in the bookshop."

"How do you know that?" Mack asked.

"Remember Hilda Lawrence at the autograph stand saying how surprised she'd been when a man in his twenties offered her a Thomas Jefferson?"

Mack smiled. "I remember she said she asked how much the fellow wanted and he asked for five thousand dollars."

"For a signature worth perhaps fifty thousand," Will added. The waiter arrived with venison for both, and they eyed it with relish. Will went on before they commenced eating. "Hilda knew she was dealing with an amateur. She told him she wasn't in the market."

"And as she comes up from Naples, she hadn't heard the local gossip yet about the document," Mack said. "Even so, she said he showed her only the signature. There was no trace of the document."

"Oh, he was an amateur but he knew the autograph had some value."

"How do you know that?" asked Mack curiously.

"When I said I was browsing downstairs in Concannon's bookshop, I was asking first Kelly then Brian if they had a copy of Meltznick."

"What's that?"

"The bible of historical autographs. Kelly said yes and promptly took me to it. When she was out of sight, I asked Brian. He's not an experienced liar. He looked flustered, then said they didn't have the book. When they were both out of sight, I looked for the listing on Thomas Jefferson's autograph. It said a good one could fetch five thousand dollars. Brian had obviously gotten his information from it. The book was well thumbed, and it's the nineteen fifty-eight edition. Later editions will show big increases in value since then."

At Sarasota International Airport, Mack Dennison was walking with Will Greenaway to the check-in. "I just talked to the police," Mack said. "They found the pickup, blue and with scratches. It belongs to Brian's roommate. Brian may have been in it at the time of the robbery, or he may have merely been indiscreet in telling his roommate about the document. Hilda Lawrence has identified a photograph of the man who offered her the autograph. It matches Dave Janowicz' description of the pickup driver."

"No trace of the rest of the document?"

"No," Mack said. "Probably destroyed."

"Sighs of relief echoing through council chambers from Tallahassee to Key West," Will said dryly.

"I can't deny it," said Mack. "Even if it is a priceless historical document, it had the potential for being a huge headache."

"So you won't have to pay taxes to Castro on that condo of yours," murmured Will, hoisting his bags onto the scale.

"Didn't really think I would," said Mack slowly. "Still, I was ready to volunteer for the Sarasota Rifle Brigade if it came to that. We fought over taxation by a foreign power once before, you know."

"So I've heard," murmured Will, handing over his flight ticket. "So I've heard." 🦫

Machete

John Lutz

Miranda Herrera shrugged. "I'm paid through the month and I'm going there anyway, so I might as well clean up the blood."

Gull South Condominium manager Wallace King looked at her, this short, frail woman still in her twenties. At the left corner of her mouth was a curved scar—said to be from when her ex-husband attacked her with a broken drinking glass—that made her seem always to be smiling slightly with a beguiling sadness. She was a woman who made men yearn to take care of her, but Wallace knew she lived with her mother in a rough section of town and was raising two children from her bad marriage. Maybe she was tougher than she looked.

"You gotta understand," he said, "this snowbird was hacked to death with a machete." He wheezed twice like an indecisive tea kettle in the sunny, quiet office. He was a short but wide man with bushy, receding red hair and a great deal of fat around the heart, and he wheezed often during the simple act of breathing. "There's blood all over the bedroom. You're just a flusher. You don't have to do this."

"Part of the arrangement was that I'd do light cleaning."

"*Light* cleaning? I said a *machete*, sweetheart!"

"Don't call me your sweetheart, Wallace. And I know what a machete is—a long, heavy knife used to cut sugarcane. I've used them in the fields. What about the rug?"

"Huh? Oh, I see what you mean. Biggest mess of all, other than Mrs. Mulhaney. It's been taken up. It's out back in one of the dumpsters, waiting to be hauled away."

"Then whatever soaked through should be no problem. Those floors are tile."

Wallace wheezed and studied her in a way she didn't like. "Wouldn't be surprised if the place was haunted."

"I'm not superstitious, Wallace. And I still have the key the Mulhaneys gave me when they hired me."

Wallace picked up a sheet of paper with typing on it from his desk and pretended to be busy reading, but he was unable to keep himself from glancing at her tanned, bare legs. "You get scared over there, sweetheart, you come right back here and let me know."

Miranda smiled as she opened the office door to leave. "And if you get scared here, Wallace, you come see me. I know how to use a machete."

Miranda was what in Florida is known as a flusher. Northerners who buy condos and spend only occasional time in them need someone to look after them once a month, walk through them and make sure there are no problems like vandalism, mildew, and, most of all, plumbing problems. Thus an occupation to fill a need: flusher. So-called because some of the duties are to flush the toilets and run tap water to make sure the plumbing is in working order. Flushers also check thermostats and make sure sofa and chair cushions are angled up to allow airflow and prevent mildew. Drawers containing clothes need to be left slightly open for the same reasons. Florida in the off-season is hell on everything built by man.

So the snowbirds—folks who flock south for the winter—need the flushers and pay them enough so there can be a decent living in the job if a flusher has enough clients. Miranda knew of a flusher in Punta Gorda who'd made herself wealthy, but she wasn't supporting a mother and two children and having no luck in locating an ex-husband who wouldn't accept responsibility for the bills she was slowly paying down. Sometimes Miranda cursed her missing Richard, but what was the use? She should have known from the beginning he wasn't husband material. He was a violent man without character.

She drove her rusty Dodge station wagon along palm-bordered Gull Way and parked before the tan stucco building that contained the Mulhaneys' ground-floor, corner unit. As she carried her cleaning equipment along the sidewalk, she could feel heat from the concrete radiating up through the thin soles of her sandals. A bead of perspiration trickled like a wayward insect down her ribs beneath her faded Devil Rays T-shirt. It would be cooler inside the condo, but not much cooler. The owners economized by keeping thermo-stats set just low enough to prevent heat and humidity from damaging furniture and belongings.

Miranda had gotten to know the Mulhaneys slightly when they'd hired her as a flusher. Doris Mulhaney was an attractive woman in her early fifties, still with a trim figure and still something of a flirt. Her husband, Rollo, was a tall, bull-shouldered man who seemed friendly and rather absentminded. One day last month he had come home from a round of golf and discovered his wife dismembered on the bedroom floor. He'd managed to dial 911 before succumbing completely to shock. Local TV news had played the 911 tape of his call over and over for almost a week. It always made Miranda cry, so she began switching off the TV whenever it came on. The police still had no suspects. Rollo Mulhaney had returned to the family home in St. Louis, broken and despondent.

Miranda felt a cool draft on the nape of her neck as she entered the warm condo. It was true that she wasn't superstitious. Not in the way Wallace meant. Yet she knew there were ghosts of a sort Wallace never imagined. The dead left the world gradually and reluctantly, especially those who had died with violent unexpectedness.

Leaving the master bedroom for last, she immediately got to work, examining the other rooms and hall bathroom, testing the spigots and flushing the toilet. Everything was in order, as it usually was in Gull South condos; this was a newer development, expensive if not luxurious.

Perspiring from her previous effort, and with a caution she knew was unnecessary, she entered the master bedroom.

It wasn't as horrible as she'd imagined. The blood-soaked mattress and box springs had been removed, as well as the plush blue rug. But there were blood smears on the walls, and an L-shaped pattern of blackened dried blood on the gray tile floor where the rug had been pulled away or rolled back near the bed.

Miranda was curious about something. She had one day pulled the nightstand drawer open slightly to encourage air circulation and noticed the checked butt of a small revolver. She went now to the nightstand and opened the drawer. The gun was gone. Rollo Mulhaney, or possibly the police, must have had taken it.

The bathroom was a surprise. Its beige and white tiles were splattered with blood, and there was a ring of blood around the drain in one of the washbasins in the twin vanity. Miranda remembered the newspapers had said the killer washed the blood from himself after the murder.

Using the back of her wrist to wipe her damp forehead so perspiration wouldn't sting her eyes, she got busy again. Old blood, once it came into contact with water, cleaned up easier than she'd expected.

When she flushed the toilet she saw the water become discolored as it swirled and disappeared. The killer must have used the commode to dispose of bloody Kleenex or bathroom tissue. She bent down, craned her neck to the side, and saw that there was still dried blood caked beneath the rim of the porcelain bowl.

Miranda sighed, switched off her imagination as she did the TV when the 911 tapes came on, and set to work.

It was late afternoon before she was finished. If Rollo Mulhaney ever returned to the condo, which Miranda doubted, there would be nothing other than his saddened memory to suggest a murder had occurred there.

She glanced at her watch and decided she barely had time to check the three more units on her day's schedule. One of them was in this building, the other two in the building next door.

It was in the first of the next-door building's ground-floor units that Miranda noticed something interesting. When she flushed the toilet off the master bedroom, the water became momentarily discolored, pink with dark flakes. She got down on her hands and knees, looked carefully, and discovered the same pattern of dried blood she'd cleaned from beneath the rim of the Mulhaneys' toilet bowl.

There were different reasons for blood in toilet bowls, Miranda knew, but she was struck by the similarity in the patterns. It was as if someone had used tissues or toilet paper rather than towels to clean up a great amount of blood, so they could be easily disposed of. But when flushed away, they momentarily clogged the drains so the bowls backed up to leave a dark excess beneath the rims, where it wasn't visible. And both toilet bowls had been gleamingly clean—except for the hard-to-see blood.

The condo unit was owned by a retired telephone executive from Chicago, Jack Leary, who used it during the winter months and intermittently throughout the year. Miranda remembered seeing Rollo Mulhaney and Leary in a heated argument outside Leary's garage the week before Doris Mulhaney was killed.

Of course that probably meant nothing. It was Doris and not Rollo Mulhaney who was murdered. And the sixtyish, gentle Mr. Leary was the last person Miranda could picture hacking anyone to death with a machete. When she was ten she'd seen two men fighting with machetes behind the shack where she and her mother had lived in the barrio, and she still recalled the terror, the *chunk*ing sounds whenever blows landed, the whisper of flung blood staining the pavement. The horror of that event would occasionally cause her to deny it had happened, to black out and not remember anything of the matter for weeks. It was difficult to place Mr. Leary in such a terrible scene.

Still, she knew from reading detective stories and watching TV that murderers could look and act like everyone else. If they didn't start out that way, they learned to be that way to avoid suspicion.

Miranda walked from the bathroom and sat on the edge of the bed, her knees still aching from kneeling on the hard tile floor.

She rested. Her imagination didn't.

She didn't finish cleaning the bathroom. Before leaving the Leary condo, she used a knife from the kitchen to scrape some of the blood from beneath the toilet bowl rim. She carefully placed the scrapings in a small plastic bag, also from the kitchen.

With an extra bag she'd taken, she went to the dumpster behind the condo office and found the rolled-up rug that had been removed from the Mulhaneys' bedroom. She collected dried blood scrapings from the rug and placed them in the second plastic bag. She didn't use the same knife and was careful not to mix the scrapings. There would be no polluting of evidence here, as in that endless trial she'd wasted so much time watching a few years ago on television.

She placed the bags in her car, then went into the office and told Wallace the heat was bothering her and she was leaving for the day. She felt depressed, yet at the same time she was excited. She sensed she'd grabbed on to something important and revealing, and it was pulling her forward, like Mrs. Mulhaney's hand in hers.

"You sure it's only the heat?" Wallace asked. He was still seated behind his desk, as if he hadn't budged since this morning.

"I'm sure, Wallace."

"Then Doris Mulhaney's ghost didn't jump up and scare you?"

"Yes, it did," Miranda said solemnly. "I wouldn't go there if I were you, Wallace."

He laughed, taking her in with his eyes in a lightning up-and-down glance. "You solve the murder while you were down there, sweetheart?"

"Maybe."

"Oh?" He raised his bushy eyebrows almost to his receding hairline. "You gonna tell the police?"

"Not till I'm sure."

She didn't elaborate, and he was wheezing and staring dumbfounded at her as she went back out into the late afternoon heat.

Miranda had taken the samples to a friend named Iris Lopez, a nurse who worked at one of the local clinics where they did a great deal of blood testing. Iris was a very heavy woman with short black hair and a trace of dark mustache. She had beautiful brown eyes that seemed never to stop moving, as if they were searching for something long lost.

"The samples matched," Iris said to Miranda when they met the next night in a back booth at the Sarasota Brewing Company, a tavern where the various beers Iris liked so much were served. She took a sip of dark lager, leaving a cream-colored foam mustache on top of her own shadowy one. "Both are type A-positive."

"Is that a rare type?" Miranda asked. She was drinking iced tea from a glass with a large lemon wedge still stuck on its rim.

"Second most common," Iris said.

"Then you can't say both samples are from the same person?"

"Not with any certainty. But somebody owes me a favor. I can have the samples sent away to a lab for DNA testing and to see if they contain the same antibodies. It'll take a couple of weeks to get the results, though."

"A couple of weeks. . . ."

Iris took another sip of beer and licked foam from her upper lip. "Sorry, Miranda, that's how it is. They can't be rushed."

"And could this lab make a definite match?"

"It'd hold up in court," Iris said.

Miranda stared beyond Iris at the tape of a basketball game running without sound on a TV mounted on the wall. "All right," she said.

Iris studied her over her beer mug. "You seem sure the samples will match."

"I am sure."

"What's going on, Miranda?"

"I'm trying to find out," Miranda said. She watched a player leap straight up and arc the basketball through the rim from at least twenty feet away. Amazing. So much in the world that seemed unbelievable was actually possible.

Miranda was in fact haunted by Doris Mulhaney. She couldn't stop thinking about the murder. Even when she was marketing, dressing Hortensia for school, feeding Alex, or helping her mother with the cooking and housework, Miranda found herself imagining how Mrs. Mulhaney must have felt as she was being hacked to pieces with a machete. Miranda dreamed about that, and she would awaken suddenly and sit straight up in bed, wondering and perspiring in the hot night, impatient for the results of the blood tests. Justice was a yearning; the guilty had to pay. If the blood samples from the two different condos definitely matched, she would go to the police. They'd have to listen to her.

But suppose it was already too late? Jack Leary might have murdered Doris Mulhaney, washed off the most visible blood from himself and his clothes in her bathroom, then returned to his condo to finish scrubbing away the evidence. Then he had gone into hiding. Maybe even left the country.

Though it was almost midnight, Miranda got Leary's Chicago phone number from her condo schedule and called it. She only wanted to hear him answer, so she could be sure he hadn't run away and didn't suspect anyone had made a connection between him and Doris Mulhaney's death.

Instead a recorded voice told her in a polite, bored tone that the number was no longer in service.

That was the end of her sleep for the night.

The next morning, though it was a day early on her schedule, Miranda checked her units at Gull South. She watched carefully from windows as she went from job to job, until finally she saw Wallace leave the office unattended. He was walking away with a man she knew was an electrician, and Miranda waited until they were out of sight before crossing the sun-baked street to the office and ducking quickly inside.

It didn't take her long to search the files and find Jack Leary's new address and phone number. He'd moved, but he was still in Chicago.

Miranda had to be sure. Since it was a long-distance call, she left Gull South and drove her station wagon to an outside public phone at a Texaco station down the street.

After feeding the phone most of the change she'd gotten inside the station, she stood with one finger plugged into her left ear to block traffic sounds. A grouping of three palm trees provided some shade, so it wasn't unbearably hot there, but the brilliance of the day made Miranda's eyes ache. Without diverting her gaze from the swift rush of traffic, she reached into a pocket for her sunglasses and put them on. She listened to the phone ring on the other end of the line in Chicago. It continued to ring as a mosquito did aerobatics around her and tried several times to flit up her nostril.

She was about to hang up when the phone was answered.

A woman's voice said hello.

Miranda didn't know what to say. She didn't want to waste the call, knew she should answer. And she didn't have to identify herself or say where she was calling from.

"Is Mr. Jack Leary there?" she asked.

There was a pause. Then: "I'm afraid not. He—Well, this is— was—his fiancée. He's passed away."

Miranda hadn't expected this. "Mi Dios, that's terrible. He was ill?"

"No, he was killed in a hit-and-run accident. He didn't suffer." The last statement sounded more hopeful than knowledgeable. "Who is this?"

Miranda quickly let the receiver clatter back into its cradle.

Her hands were slippery with sweat. She'd suddenly realized the woman might have one of those devices that indicated where a call had originated. She tried to convince herself it didn't matter, since she'd used a public phone. Only the city she'd called from would be identified, and maybe not even that. Miranda wasn't sure, though, since she'd never owned one of the devices.

She got back into the ovenlike interior of the station wagon and tried to think what this all might mean. It was possible, she knew, that the woman was lying, that Jack Leary wasn't dead. What better way to hide than to fake his death?

The thing to do, she finally decided, was to go to the police.

They listened politely to her in a cool office cubicle, both of them nodding from time to time, jotting pertinent notes in black, leather-bound pads. But within minutes Miranda sensed that they weren't really paying attention.

Lieutenant Foster, the tall, gray one behind the desk, exchanged a glance with his partner, a man named Gardner, and nodded a final time to Miranda when she was finished with her story.

"What does that mean," she asked, "that nod?"

Foster smiled. He had eyes like tiny blue diamonds, with much light but without feeling. Miranda didn't like him. Gardner was better, a fat little man with a squashed nose who was chewing on the inside of his cheek and seemed to be considering what she'd said.

But it was Foster who was in charge. "We'll look into what you told us," he said. "And we appreciate you coming here with the information." He stood up behind his cluttered desk, raising his shoulders and hitching up his wrinkled gray pants with both hands.

"You'll let me know?" Miranda asked, still seated.

Foster cocked his head to the side. "Let you know what?"

"Whatever it is you find out about Jack Leary. Whether he's really alive."

Another exchange of looks between the two policemen. "Still alive? But you said he—Well, sure, that'll be easy enough to determine."

Gardner stared curiously at her, and she thought he might show more interest and question her further. But he merely extended his hand. Miranda shook it and stood up. There was nothing more to say here.

She didn't look back at them as she left the station.

Obviously the police weren't yet interested. They preferred to leave things as they were, trusting Mrs. Mulhaney's killer would drop into their laps like a ripe coconut.

Miranda was an honest woman, but she decided that circumstances made it reasonable and honorable for her to search the Leary condo.

It would ruin her professional reputation if anyone found out that during her duties as a flusher she'd rummaged through owners' belongings. People might not understand her reasons, so she had to be careful. Wallace would understand, perhaps, but he would still have to notify the tenants and she would be fired, probably told never to be found again on the lush green grounds of Gull South.

But the chance had to be taken.

She waited until the next afternoon.

Her key fit both front and back doors to the Leary condo, so Miranda parked the station wagon a block away on the street, slipped between tall hibiscus bushes, and made her way to the unit's screened-in verandah. The outdoor furniture had been placed in the garage for the off-season and the screen door was unlocked. She entered quickly, then unlocked the main back door and stepped inside, out of sight of any neighbors' eyes.

The condo seemed even warmer and quieter than usual, but maybe that was because of why she'd come here. There was a low click, then a steady hum. The air conditioner coming on, to keep the temperature below eighty. The monotonous hum seemed only to add to the sultry silence as Miranda began opening drawers and standing on her toes to peer to the backs of closet shelves.

Like most snowbirds, Leary didn't leave many possessions in his unit between visits. He'd driven north, taking most of his clothes with him, so the closets were empty except for a ventilated plastic hanging bag containing half a dozen shirts, a few pairs of pants, and a pastel blue sport jacket. The medicine cabinet held only a half-used tube of toothpaste and an empty aerosol can of deodorant.

Back in the front bedroom, Miranda looked out the window and saw Wallace strolling along the pale concrete sidewalk toward the office. He glanced over at the window, startling her, but she stepped back and was sure she hadn't been seen. The bright Florida sun turned windows viewed from outside into mirrors.

When she knuckled sweat from the corners of her eyes and peeked out again, Wallace was nowhere in sight. She breathed easier and decided to leave the condo.

But as she took a step toward the back door, she stopped. Maybe the police had gotten the information by now, if they'd actually bothered to contact authorities in Chicago. She might be able to call from here and find out. Condo owners often left phone service uninterrupted when they were going to be gone for only a few months.

She heard a dial tone when she lifted the receiver.

Miranda called her home number. Her mother answered on the third ring.

"Has anyone called for me?" Miranda asked.

"Yes. A nice Sergeant Gardner. With the police."

"He left a message?"

"He said to tell you they checked and Mr. Jack Leary really is dead and buried in Chicago. He said not to worry anymore about this matter but to call him if you learned anything else. What are you doing, Miranda? What kind of risks are you taking, dealing with the police?"

"He was only being polite, Mama. He really doesn't want me to call." *And Jack Leary might really be alive.*

"That isn't the point, *niña.* You've been acting so strange lately, thinking deep inside yourself where only you can go. What's—"

"I have to hang up, Mama. See you this evening."

Miranda lowered the receiver. Explanations could be made later.

She was outside and halfway back to her car when she realized she'd left something undone. She should search the Mulhaney condo too. Jack Leary might also have left a clue there.

Her bulky key ring clutched in her right hand, she cut across a green expanse, stepped around rich, dark mulch still damp from the morning watering despite the heat, and hurried toward the back of the Mulhaneys' ground-floor unit. As she reached the flagstones, a tiny brown lizard alertly scurried out of her way but not far, as if caught up in her apprehension as well as its own.

This unit was more cluttered than the Leary one, mostly because two people had stayed here. But what was left behind was much the same: some clothes suitable for Florida's tropical climate, a few tools, some old underwear and socks in a dresser drawer. Various items, trivial and inexpensive for people as wealthy as the Mulhaneys. Miranda found nothing unusual.

Until she entered the storage closet that held the condo's air conditioning unit and water heater and searched a cardboard box that was on the top wire shelf.

She placed the box on the floor and was still stooped over it when she heard a slight noise behind her.

Holding her breath, she slowly turned.

First she saw the shadow. It was unmistakably that of a man standing and holding a long object in one hand. A baseball bat? No, it was slightly curved, angled at the end. Suitable for cutting sugar cane. And other things.

A machete!

Miranda heard her own shrieking inhalation when Rollo Mulhaney stepped into view in the center of the room. He looked calm in the way Richard had sometimes before beating her. That scared her much more than anger.

"I've been watching you," he said. "No one knows I'm back in Florida, but I've been following you for days, weeks. I overheard your conversation at the Sarasota Brewing Company and thought I'd save you the suspense: the DNA tests will show that both blood samples are from my wife."

"Then you—"

"I murdered her because she was having an affair with Leary, who seemed proud of it and gloated when I confronted him. And I made sure I killed her when they thought I'd be away for a while and he'd be coming to see her. To lie down with her on our bed, my bed. I wanted him to find Doris waiting for him as they'd planned, only she'd be dead."

"Then that was how the blood got in the Leary condo," Miranda said. "He discovered the body. But he never told the police."

"He couldn't. He would have been the main suspect. Besides that, he had a fiancée in Chicago. There was even blood all over his clothes, in his condo. He had to clean everything, make it all seem normal in case the police questioned him."

"But he must have known you killed your wife!"

"He suspected and eventually might have gone to the police. Which is why I drove from St. Louis to Chicago, waited for the opportunity, and ran him down with my car. I thought I was safe after that, but I had to continue the flusher service or attract suspicion. Then it occurred to me that when you were cleaning here you might find something I'd missed. I was right. You were always so diligent about your job. I know what it is you found. I figured out what you saw in both condos."

"You didn't tell me the whole story," Miranda said. She was still crouched awkwardly over the cardboard box, the way she'd been when she was interrupted. "About how you came in through the bedroom's sliding glass door from the verandah, how you could be sure your wife wouldn't hear you and shoot you for a prowler."

"You're an intelligent young woman," Mulhaney said. "I've always liked you and I wish I didn't have to silence you." He moved toward her, the machete raised.

"I found more than just the blood in both condos," Miranda said.

"Really? I think you want to talk as long as possible, hoping against impossible odds. I commend you for not screaming." He raised the machete higher, gripping it with both hands, and took a long step toward her.

"I also found the gun you removed from the nightstand drawer before the murder, so your wife couldn't defend herself."

Mulhaney paused, the machete held high.

The look of realization and terror moved into his eyes first, then his face became stiffened and contorted.

"Found it today where you put it in this box," Miranda said and raised Doris Mulhaney's revolver and shot Rollo Mulhaney through the heart.

"I've been paid through the month and I'm going there anyway," Miranda said a week later. "I might as well clean up the blood."

Wallace leaned back in his desk chair and laced his fingers behind his thick neck, grinning up at her. "You're really something, sweetheart, you really are. Hard to figure out and get next to. Way you talk in those cute little riddles."

"I don't talk in riddles, Wallace. It's just that you don't want to understand me."

"There. See what I mean? Anyway, if you get scared over in that haunted condo, you know I'll come keep you company."

"I won't be scared, Wallace. I'm not superstitious. And the condo isn't haunted any longer."

"Two ghosts now," Wallace said, not hearing her.

Miranda shrugged and stepped outside into the brilliant morning, closing the door behind her.

The Works

T. J. MacGregor

I know how it is down here on the beach for the old ones now, what with rising prices and traffic and crime. They're afraid to go out at night. Their Social Security checks barely cover a month of meals at Wolfie's. They feel like Miami Beach's postscript.

The Art Deco craze did it, you know. Ever since folks decided Deco was in again, those little hotels over on Ocean Drive are booming with business, charging prices like I can't believe, and, yeah, people pay them. I mean, seventy bucks for a room no larger than a closet, five dollars for a hard-boiled egg and a slice of bread that's hardly toasted, two bucks for coffee. The old ones can remember when coffee in these places cost a dime.

There's a haughty look to the hotels that really gets me too. They stand so prim and proper at the edge of the sea, all spiffed up in pastels, windows so clean they gleam like jewels. The old ones feel like they can't afford to even walk there, and when they do, shuffling in their tired bones, under the weight of eighty or ninety years of memories, they're nearly trampled by the youthful crowds rushing to this hotel or that bar.

So I keep my prices low and do what I can. When an old one is troubled or sad, sick or too drunk to stand, I take him or her in. Word has gotten around that Millie's Place is where you go when it's gotten bad.

Like tonight, for instance.

Toby wandered in off Washington Avenue a few minutes ago, out of the thick night heat, looking about as bad as a man can look and still be alive. He's ninety-four years old, with a spine so bent he can hardly lift his head, glasses thicker than his arm, a heart that just won't quit.

He's counting one-dollar bills from a tattered envelope with SOCIAL SECURITY ADMINISTRATION in bold black letters across the top. If I remember correctly, he worked nearly half a century for an auto parts plant that merged with another plant, and most of his pension got lost in the transition. His Social Security check amounts to about three hundred dollars a month, and we all know what that buys you in Miami Beach.

"The room's only six bucks, Toby," I tell him when he keeps counting out the bills.

"Want a meal too," he mumbles, moving his dentures around in his mouth because they hurt his gums.

"Eight bucks, then."

"And the Works. I think I want the Works, Millie."

"You'd better be sure. It's a bit more expensive."

His head bobs slowly. It reminds me of a beach ball, rising, falling, riding a wave, and I want to stroke it, embrace it, kiss this old, beautiful head. It's as hairless as a Chihuahua, with a mass of wrinkles that seems to quiver and dance to the back of the skull. Not so long ago, on a rainy afternoon down at the Ace Club, some of the old ones and I gathered around Toby's head to see if we could read our fortunes in the wrinkles, like they were creases in a palm.

"I'm sure," he says softly, depositing an old canvas bag on the counter, straining to look up. "How much?"

His eyes behind those thick glasses are alarmingly small, almost transparent. I feel like they might disappear at any second. "Twenty-five. I guess you know what all the fee includes."

His smile creases his mouth and, like a widening ripple in a pond, touches all the other wrinkles in his face. For a moment or two, his features shift and slide, rearranging themselves. "Sure. I came with Mink, remember?"

Mink: right. She was close to a hundred, small as a toy doll with white hair that had fallen out in spots, exposing soft pink patches of scalp. She had cancer and the radiation or chemo or whatever it was they'd used on her had rotted her from the inside out, but her heart ticked on. She took baby steps, I remember, like a toddler learning to walk, and drooled a little when she talked.

It's true that decades stretch between infancy and old age, but children and old ones aren't all that different. Both are afraid. Both have special needs. Both require love. I understand that and they know it.

"There. Twenty-five." He taps the stack of bills against the counter, straightening them, then slides the pile toward me.

"Sure?"

"Positive."

"Okay, let's go take a look at the menu."

I ring for Sammy to man the desk and he shuffles in, big as a truck and all muscle. He's not an old one, but he was living on the streets until I took him in and now I don't know how I'd run this place without him. I've never heard him speak. I don't know if it's because he can't or just that he chooses not to.

I come out from behind the counter and Toby hooks his old, tired arm in mine. The kitchen is in the back and while it's not as grand as the ones in the fancy hotels on Ocean Drive, it feels like home to me. The fridge is always filled with everyone's favorites—home-baked pies, drumsticks, potato salad, coleslaw, cookies by the dozens.

When I was doing private-duty nursing a long time ago, I made a point of cooking for my patients. They appreciated it. A lot of them were old ones too, and I learned to prepare the food to accommodate dentures, taste buds that had gone smooth and dull as river stones, noses that no longer worked right. It taught me the importance of spices, sauces, garnishes that dressed the food well enough to make your mouth water.

Toby's mouth is watering now as we peer into the fridge together, I can tell. He points at what he wants. One of those, one of these, this, that. His finger is curved into a permanent claw from arthritis; just looking at it hurts me. That's how it is with me and them. That's how it always is when someone I care for is in pain. It becomes my pain.

"And cookies," he finishes. "Chocolate chip cookies."

"They've got nuts in them."

"Soft nuts?"

"Not really."

"Aw, so what. Nuts are fine."

Together we remove the items from the fridge and set them out on the counter. Before I begin preparing the meal, though, I show him to the best room in the house. It's on the top floor, in back. There's a skylight over the huge bed, a color TV and VCR, forty or fifty videocassettes for him to choose from, and an adjoining bath with a sunken tub that swirls like a Jacuzzi, where fluffy towels, a silk robe, and matching pajamas are laid out. He sighs as his feet sink into the thick carpeting on the floor and sighs again as he eases his tired bones onto the bed and peers up, up into a sky strewn with stars.

"You'll tell me when dinner's ready?" he asks, frowning as though he doesn't quite trust me now.

"I'll bring it up here. Feathers is going to smell that chicken. You mind if she comes up too?"

"No, no, of course not," he says, hooking his hands under his head, lost in the stars. He doesn't hear me leave, but Feathers hears me enter the kitchen.

She's a white Persian who has a definite fondness for chicken and old ones. She likes to curl up on their chests and knead their soft bones with her gentle paws. I toss her tidbits as I prepare the meal and explain the situation to her. She blinks those sweet amber eyes as if to say she understands perfectly and follows me upstairs when I take Toby his meal. He's perched on the wicker couch in the black silk pajamas and robe, squinting at the TV, watching *Cocoon*. It's a favorite with all the old ones. I set his tray down on the table and pull up the other chair.

Feathers flops over Toby's feet, covering them like a rug, and he looks down at her and laughs. I can't remember the last time I heard him laugh and I've known Toby for ten or twelve years, since he moved down here after his wife died. I don't know if he has kids. He's never spoken of them if he does. But that's how it is with a lot of the old ones. When they get too old for their kids to deal with them, when there's talk of nursing homes, of confinement, they get scared and run away. Who can blame them?

"Watch this, Millie," he says excitedly, stabbing a gnarled finger at the screen. "This is where they swim in the rejuvenation pool."

I divide my attention between the screen and the chicken, which I cut up into small, manageable bites for him. I pass him a napkin, which he tucks under his throat like a bib, and pass him his plate. He sets it on his lap, impales a chunk of meat, and dips it into a scoop of dressing. His hand trembles as it rises toward his mouth. A dab of dressing rests on his chin, but he doesn't seem to notice it. He chews slowly, thoughtfully, eyes glued to the screen.

"Will it hurt?" he asks, not looking at me.

"Of course not."

"Are you sure?"

"You were here with Mink," I remind him. "Did she look like she hurt?"

Mouth puckering around a cranberry: "She always hurt. From the cancer. Or the radiation. From something."

Physical pain or psychic pain—the difference isn't that great. Shift your focus and one becomes the other. Mink knew that. "She's OK now, though."

"You talked to her?"

"Sure. I talk to her pretty often."

"And she's OK?"

"A lot better."

This is a game we play, Toby and I. We both pretend we don't know the truth.

"She's finished with the beach, Toby."

He mulls this over, nods, dips his fork into the steaming squash. "Can you do me a favor, Millie?"

"Sure. Anything."

He reaches into the pocket of the robe and pulls out a sheet of notebook paper. The words on it are printed, almost illegible. I can see Toby hunched over the bar at the Ace Club, where some of the old ones hang out, moving a pen up and down against the paper, putting his thoughts in order. I get the point. "OK," I tell him and slip the sheet inside the old canvas bag, which slumps on the floor beside the bed like an aged and faithful pet.

"Can I watch another movie after this one?"

"Whatever you want. When you get tired, just pick up the phone and ring the desk. I'll be up to tuck you in."

"Don't go," he says quickly. "Stay here with me, Millie."

I pat his hand. "Let me get some iced tea and your slice of pie and I'll be right back. Was it pumpkin or apple that you wanted, Toby?"

"Both." He grins mischievously, dark spaces in his mouth where there should be teeth. He's removed part of his denture.

"Both it is."

Feathers doesn't move as I get up; she knows the routine.

From the kitchen, I fetch iced tea for myself, two slices of pie for Toby, and some Friskies for Feathers. In my bedroom, I bring out the Works, running my hands over the smooth, cool leather, remembering. I change into more comfortable clothes, cotton that breathes, that's the color of pearls. Makeup next. A touch of eye shadow, mascara, blush, lipstick. The way I look is part of the Works. Sometimes the old ones ask me to hold them, stroke them, caress them, make love to them. Other times they want to listen to Frank Sinatra and dance or they ask me to walk on the beach with them in the moonlight. Their requests are as different as they are, and I always comply. But with all of them, there's a need for a special memory, an event that perhaps reminds them of something else. It's as if this memory will accompany them, comfort them somehow, like a friend.

Toby is still watching the movie when I return. His supper plate is clean. His eyes widen when he sees the pieces of pie, and he attacks the apple first, devouring it with childlike exuberance, then polishes off the pumpkin as well. We watch the rest of the movie together, Feathers purring between us on the couch. Now and then, Toby's chin drops to his chest as he nods off, but he comes quickly awake, blinking fast as if to make sure he hasn't missed anything.

While the movie rewinds, I fold back the sheets on the bed. They're sea blue, decorated with shells and sea horses, the same ones Mink slept in. "Can we listen to music?" he asks, crouching in front of the stereo on the other side of the room.

"Sure. Whatever you want. Choose an album."

Harry Belafonte.

Toby holds out his arms and I move into them. I'm taller than he is, but it doesn't matter. We sway, his silk robe rustling. I rest my chin on his head and feel all those wrinkles quivering, shifting, warm as sand against my skin. He presses his cheek to my chest, eyes shut. The lemon scent of his skin haunts me a little, reminds me of all the old ones who have come here for the Works. I've loved each of them, and love them still.

When the record ends, Toby and I stretch out on the king-size bed, holding each other, talking softly, the moon smack in the heart of the skylight now. He falls asleep with his head on my shoulder, and for a long time I lay there just listening to him breathe, watching stars against the black dome of sky above us.

The window is partially open, admitting a taste of wind, the scent of stars, the whispering sea. I imagine that death is like this window, opening onto a pastel world where everything is what you will it to be. Yellow skies, if that's what you want. Silver seas. A youthful body. A sound mind. A family who cares. A state of grace.

And that's my gift to the old ones.

I untangle my arms and rise, drawing the covers over Toby. His wrinkled head sinks into the pillow. I bring out the leather case. New York. My old life. The business with the nursing board. Such unpleasantness, really. Like the old ones, I have my secrets. I take the syringe from my leather case and fill it. I have trouble finding a vein in his arm. They're lost in the folds of skin, collapsed beneath tissue, and I have to inject the morphine into his neck, just below the ear.

And then I wait.

Always, in the final moment, there's something that seems to escape from the old shell of bones and flesh, an almost visible thing, a puff of air, a kind of fragrance, the soul released. It leaves Toby when he sighs, fluttering from his mouth like a bird, and sweeps through the crack in the window, free at last.

Funny, but the wrinkles on top of his skull don't seem quite as deep now. His spine doesn't look as hunched. If I tried, I know I could straighten out his fingers. But the most I do is kiss him good-bye.

I get rid of the syringe. Sammy will take care of getting Toby's body to the pauper cemetery. There won't be a headstone, of course. I do have to make some concessions. But the burial will be proper, with an old pine box and all.

I unzip his canvas bag for the sheet of paper I slipped in there earlier and read it over. The list of who gets what is simple; all the names are old ones who hang out at the Ace Club. His belongings are in the bag. I sling it over my shoulder and walk downstairs, where Sammy is still at the desk. He looks up and I nod. He reaches under the desk and switches on the VACANCY sign outside. I take his place at the desk, and he leaves to attend to Toby.

Most of the old ones will know about Toby before they hear it from me. They'll know because the only time the VACANCY sign goes on is when the Works are finished.

Tomorrow, when I go down to the Ace, I'll also pass out my card to newcomers. After all, I've got to drum up business just like anyone else. MILLIE'S PLACE. CHEAPEST RENT ON THE BEACH. GOOD FOOD. SPACIOUS ROOMS. THE WORKS.

Framed for Murder

HAROLD Q. MASUR

A forty-nine-cent ballpoint pen saved my life. Literally. It still writes, but I do not use it. I keep it as a talisman, a reminder to count my blessings in times of adversity.

The pen was in my attaché case when a taxi deposited me in front of the Southern Trust Company on Broward Boulevard in Fort Lauderdale late Monday morning. Carl Steiner arrived on foot at the same time. "Counselor," he greeted me. "Prompt as usual."

"Hello, Carl."

Steiner represented the sovereign State of Florida through its Department of Taxation and Finance. We shook hands, entered the bank, and marched past the tellers' windows toward the desk of branch manager Walter Knox. With his usual air of Olympian detachment, Knox was explaining something to a woman. She turned suddenly, her face shocked; she blinked in recognition and came stumbling toward me.

"My God!" she whispered. "He's dead, Mr. Jordan. The man says Victor is dead."

"Yes, Angela. He died Friday evening. Hadn't you heard?"

She shook her head. "I was out of town, drove back last night. How did it happen?"

"Coronary occlusion. During dinner, at his hotel in Chicago. There was nothing they could do. He was gone when the ambulance arrived."

She looked stunned, marooned in a private world of grief or despair. Angela Lowe was Victor Rosemont's assistant at the Rosemont Gallery. And according to Rosemont's estranged wife, she was something more than an assistant.

"What brought you to the bank?" I asked.

"I'm here at Victor's request. He needed some papers in Chicago. I have a power of attorney for the safe-deposit box, and I was supposed to fly them out to him this afternoon. But now the man says Victor's box is sealed."

"What kind of papers?"

"He found a customer for the Picasso and wanted to show him the authenticating documents."

"When did he call you?"

"He didn't. He couldn't reach me. So he called his wife and told her it was urgent and asked her to give me the message. When she finally got through to me on Friday, it was after three o'clock and too late for the bank. So I phoned Victor and told him I would do it today. Now Mr. Knox won't let anyone open the box without a court order."

"Customary procedure, Angela. Look, go back to the gallery and hold the fort. I'll stop by later."

Her steps were slow and tentative—she was a forlorn figure. I opened my attaché case and handed a paper to Walter Knox. It was an order from the surrogate directing the Southern Trust Company to open the box of Victor Rosemont, deceased, for the purpose of removing his last will and testament and filing it for probate.

As Rosemont's lawyer, I had drawn his will and knew that he had named me as executor. The drill was a familiar one. Strict compliance with all rules was mandatory. That's why Carl Steiner was present. When a man dies, Florida wants its full share of estate taxes. To make sure nobody secretly disposes of any property, the state sends a representative to itemize all the box's contents when it is first opened. A bank official also attends and is charged with delivering the will safely to court.

Knox cast his jaundiced eye over the order, found it satisfactory, and led the way down a flight of marble stairs to the vault area. He spoke briefly to the man behind the steel bars. Keys changed hands. The attendant produced a large metal box, convoyed us to a small conference room, and discreetly withdrew.

We sat. Steiner got out paper and pencil and smiled in anticipation. My attaché case yielded a legal pad and the ballpoint pen, so I could make my own list as Steiner announced the contents.

Knox slid the box to me, and as I passed it across to Steiner, my ballpoint rolled to the floor. I had to duck under the table to retrieve it, hearing Steiner say jovially, "All right, gentlemen, let's see what we have here."

They were the last words he ever spoke.

The world blew apart. There was a blinding flash, an ear-shattering concussion. I felt as if an elephant had stepped on my back. Wood splintered, plaster fell, acrid smoke choked the air. And then a deep, dead silence.

I stumbled to my feet, dazed, coughing. The room was a shambles. A jagged hole gaped open on the corridor. The door hung askew on a single hinge. I saw Carl Steiner and turned away. Sitting over the booby-trapped box, he had caught the full brunt. Walter Knox lay hunched in the debris, comatose and bleeding.

Faces materialized in the corridor. The vault attendant, a retired cop, picked his way through the wreckage and got me out of there. "Knox may still be alive," I mumbled. "Somebody call an ambulance."

A diligent young resident at Manhattan General did a quick workup and found me sound. He put four stitches in my cheek and said I was lucky. He suggested twenty-four hours of bed rest. Detective Lieutenant John Nola, waiting outside the emergency room, offered me a lift.

In the police car he told me that Carl Steiner was dead and that Walter Knox was in surgery, his condition critical. Of the three men in the bank's conference room, I was the only one presently capable of speech, and Nola wanted my version.

Nola was an old friend, precise and incorruptible, so I dealt off the top. I told him about Victor Rosemont's fatal heart attack in Chicago, about Rosemont's will and my appointment at the bank with Carl Steiner of the Estate Tax Section. How somebody must have planted a bomb in Rosemont's safe-deposit box. And about Angela Lowe's narrow escape when she failed to gain access earlier that morning. I painted a brief profile of Rosemont, a prominent art dealer operating out of a highly prestigious gallery on Las Olas Boulevard.

"The Lowe woman," Nola said, "what was she looking for?"

"Certain papers Rosemont needed. He was in Chicago on business, and as usual, he carried transparencies of various paintings. One of them was a Picasso, and apparently he'd interested a prospective customer. But, of course, he could not complete the sale of any important canvas without the provenance."

"Without the what?"

"Provenance—documents detailing the origin and background of a painting to establish its authenticity. Collectors seldom pay large sums of money without proof that the work is genuine. He wanted Miss Lowe to get those documents from his safe-deposit box and fly them out to Chicago. When he failed to reach her, he called his wife and asked her to relay the message."

"Hold it, Counselor. You just told me that Rosemont and his wife were separated."

"Temporarily. Margot Rosemont is a very possessive and jealous woman. She suspected her husband of some extracurricular activity with Miss Lowe. She wanted the woman booted out of the gallery. He refused and she left him. This is the third time. But she always came back."

"Any basis for her suspicions?"

"Probably. Angela Lowe is a very attractive dish, and Rosemont was an incurable chaser. Margot knew that angle of his personality—she used to be his assistant at the gallery herself before they were married. Anyway, they stayed in touch, even though she'd walked out. And since it was inconvenient to keep making long-distance calls, Rosemont got through to Margot, and she reached Miss Lowe last Friday, too late for the bank. So Angela went there this morning to follow instruction. She'd been out of town and did not know that Rosemont was dead."

"And she had a power of attorney for his safe-deposit box?"

"Yes. Because Rosemont traveled extensively, searching for art treasures, Angela remained here, in charge of the gallery. In case of a sale, the provenance had to be available. And those papers were too valuable to be lying around loose."

"The wife also had a power of attorney?"

"Probably."

Nola reflected thoughtfully for a moment. "So we have a very jealous wife, with access, who calls her husband's mistress, with access, and directs her to open a box that's been wired with lethal explosives."

"You're suggesting that Margot planted the bomb?"

"It's a possibility."

"I can't buy it, Lieutenant. Suppose Margot was unable to reach Miss Lowe. Suppose Rosemont flew back and went to the box himself."

"You drew his will. Who's his chief legatee?"

"His wife."

"So he opens the box and good-bye husband. They're only separated. She inherits his money, his gallery, his paintings, the works. Either way, she can't lose."

Cynicism. An occupational hazard. Even so, I pondered the notion. If Rosemont had not suffered a fatal heart attack, if the box had not been sealed, Angela Lowe instead of Carl Steiner would now be lying in the morgue, with nobody available to testify that Margot had phoned and prompted Angela's visit to the bank.

I shook my head. "The bomb was in Rosemont's box. I think he was the primary target."

"Who else had access?"

"Me."

"How come?"

"Rosemont gave me a power of attorney six months ago when both he and Miss Lowe flew off to Japan. The art market there is wide open."

"You having any problems with Rosemont?"

"That's a dry hole, Lieutenant. Don't waste time drilling it."

"Well now, Counselor, let's give it a thought. Three men are in a small conference room at the bank. A bomb explodes. One man is killed, one is critically wounded, and the third walks away alive and kicking. He just happens to be under a heavy table at precisely the right moment."

"I thought you were my friend."

"A policeman investigating homicide has no friends."

"But I haven't been near Rosemont's safe-deposit box in over five months. You can check the vault records."

"I already have. It's a bum system. You sign a slip, the attendant matches signatures, then discards the form. No records. They say they don't want to bury themselves in paper." He looked at me. "I'm going to visit the widow now. I want you to come along."

Margot Rosemont admitted us to her temporary quarters at the Sutton Towers. She had style and presence and a deceptive look of vulnerability. Her husband's body had been flown back from Chicago on Saturday and buried on Sunday. We had agreed that I should proceed at once to probate his will so that business affairs could be carried on without delay.

"Scott!" she exclaimed. "What happened to your face?"

She gaped in dismay when I told her about the explosion, adding, "This is Lieutenant John Nola, in charge of the investigation."

Nola said, "Jordan believes the bomb must have been intended for your husband. Did he have any enemies?"

Her fingers were a bowknot of distress at her throat. "All successful businessmen have enemies. But I don't see how any of them could have gotten into his safe-deposit box to plant the bomb."

"Well, a number of people had access, Mrs. Rosemont. You, Miss Lowe, the counselor here."

"Please, Lieutenant. I was not one of Victor's enemies."

"You left his room and board. There must have been some friction."

She smiled minimally. "Show me a married couple who do not have friction. Oh, yes, we fought, we separated, but always there was a reconciliation. As a matter of fact, he phoned me Friday afternoon before he died."

"We know. He wanted you to contact Miss Lowe and direct her to remove some papers from his vault."

"Yes. He couldn't reach her. She was not at the gallery."

"I take it you are not charmed by Miss Lowe."

"I detest her."

"Is it your impression that she was trying to steal your husband?"

"If she could, yes."

"And you would have done anything to prevent that?"

"Within reason."

"If she had followed your instructions and opened the safe-deposit box, any relationship between them would have been effectively terminated."

"She was lucky, wasn't she?"

"Two other people were not so lucky. Do you have any proof that your husband actually phoned you on Friday?"

Her eyes opened wide. "Do you doubt my word?"

"Skepticism is a tool of my trade."

"And a very unbecoming one. Of course I have no proof. I did not record his call on tape, if that's what you need."

"Then we have only your word."

She studied him in a wintry silence. "Lieutenant, I have just been through several very difficult days. I'm really not prepared to cope with such innuendoes at this time."

"A suggestion," I said. "The switchboard operator at Rosemont's hotel in Chicago should have a record of any long-distance calls he made. It's easy enough to check."

Nola walked over to her telephone and made a note of the number. He would check it from his office later.

Margot turned to me. "You told me that under the circumstances the court will probably accept your copy of Victor's will. And if they don't, I'll inherit the estate anyway, as his widow. Isn't that true?"

"It is."

"Then the gallery is mine. I want that woman off the premises. I want Miss Lowe fired. Today. This afternoon."

I shook my head. "Not so fast. As Victor's executor, I need her on the job. She's familiar with all current and pending deals. When the estate is settled, do as you wish."

She thought about it and shrugged. "All right. But it seems wasteful to pay rent for two apartments. Is there any reason I can't move back into my own place?"

Nola had no objection and neither did I.

"Then I'll do it tomorrow," she said.

Outside, Nola and I parted. He was anxious to question the bomb squad. Sifting through the rubble, they might have found a clue he could work on. I headed east toward Las Olas Boulevard.

The Rosemont Gallery was an elegantly appointed showplace with an air of high-priced exclusivity. Victor's specialty had been the impressionists and post-impressionists: Monet, Cezanne, Gauguin, Degas, and all the rest of that brilliantly innovative crew. He had been a surpassing salesman, a man with an imperious presence who spoke in sonorous Shakespearean cadences that both charmed and intimidated important collectors. Dealers fortunate enough to acquire one of the modern masters willingly split their commission with Rosemont, knowing that his ability and his connection would invariably command astronomical prices.

Angela Lowe was supervising a rumpled, gnomish figure in the arrangement of new pictures. She came over to me. When I explained the bandage on my face, she blanched, her eyes huge.

"Mr. Knox is critically injured," I said, "and Steiner, the tax man, is dead."

"It—it could have been me," she whispered.

"Yes. We were both lucky."

She closed her eyes. "Who could have done such a thing?"

"I don't know. But we have to carry on."

"Yes. There's so much to do. We're opening a new Klaus Helman exhibit this week. Klaus," she called, "come here for a moment and meet Mr. Rosemont's lawyer. This is Scott Jordan."

He had a sallow face and paint-stained fingers. "My second show in twenty years," he told me. "Sold one small canvas that time. Forty dollars. Mr. Rosemont was a genius, a man who could recognize talent. The only dealer in this whole crazy business willing to gamble on me. Only names they want. Famous names." He leveled a scornful look. "Because it's a good investment, not because it's beautiful. Imbeciles. Excuse me, please. I have much to do."

Angela watched him for a moment. "Victor had been planning this exhibit for a long time. He pulled strings. He wanted the major critics to see Helman's work. We sent out notices weeks ago. I know he'd want us to open on schedule."

I surveyed the man's work. A landscape, a still life, a figure study, watercolors, oils, gouaches—all extravagantly colored and skillfully rendered, but to my eye, somehow derivative, reminiscent of the Fauves, those so-called wild beasts of the famous Paris exhibition in the Salon d'Autonme around the turn of the century.

Angela and I went back to Rosemont's private office. She seemed preoccupied, unable to concentrate, burdened by the responsibility of managing the gallery on her own and shaken by her narrow escape from the bomb in Rosemont's safe-deposit box.

"Such a strange way to commit a murder," she said.

I nodded. "Someone wanted to eliminate Victor. So even without that heart attack, his days were numbered."

Understandably, she was concerned about her job, anticipating her dismissal when Margot took over. I did not disabuse her. There was a knock on the door; it was Klaus Helman asking for her advice on the placement of a canvas.

Alone, I sat back, wondering if the gallery could survive without Rosemont's expertise. It had been so essentially a one-man operation. The phone rang and I answered it. A high-pitched, excited voice assaulted my eardrum.

"Mr. Losement, you are a clunk. I speak to my royer. He say you must give back the money or go to plisson."

"Who is this?" I asked.

"You know me too damn well. Sama Kosuri. Kosuri Electronics, Osaka, Japan. I come now for a check, yes? I give you back your no-good Vlaminck, yes?"

"Mr. Kosuri, what seems to be the problem?"

"Plobrem is fake Vlaminck. Give back money and my royer don't sue. But soon. Day after tomollow, I fry back to Osaka."

"There seems to be some misunderstanding. You are not talking to Mr. Rosemont. My name is—"

"No more tlicks." His voice scaled a full octave. "Hundled and twenty thousand dollah too much money for fake."

Angela opened the door, saying "Did I hear the phone?"

"A Mr. Sama Kosuri," I said, offering the handset.

She took it, pronounced her name, and listened, lips compressed. "Now Mr. Kosuri," she said in a conciliatory tone. "I don't think that would be wise. In twenty years, no one has ever impugned the integrity or the reputation of this gallery. We allowed you to take that Vlaminck and to have it examined by experts at both the Museum of Modern Art and the Center for the Fine Arts in Miami, establishments of such international eminence that nobody would presume to question their judgment or their probity. They inspected the provenance and the painting and vouched for its authenticity. Are you now charging them with fraud? Or collusion with us? That would be foolhardy, Mr. Kosuri. Your so-called expert is mistaken. And for your information, I might add that Mr. Rosemont is no longer with us. He died several days ago."

He hung up on her. She gestured helplessly. "These Japanese! They're so bright. They make such marvelous products, and we've bought so many television sets and cameras and motorcycles from them they seem to have more dollars than they can handle. So they've been investing in art, mostly the impressionists.

"About a month ago, Mr. Kosuri walked into the gallery. We had a perfectly splendid Vlaminck, a major work, priced at one hundred and twenty thousand dollars. Mr. Kosuri fell in love with it, but Victor insisted that he have it authenticated. When Kosuri was satisfied, he brought us a certified check for the full amount. He thought the frame was all wrong, so after Victor had another one made, he personally delivered the painting to Mr. Kosuri's suite at the Hilton."

She made a face. "Now the man wants his money back. He's found some buffoon who claims the Vlaminck is a forgery. Which is absurd. The Museum of Modern Art itself would have bought the painting if they hadn't been short of cash."

I sighed. I had more than enough to handle without the added headache of a potential lawsuit for fraud, whatever its merits. A lawsuit could tie up the estate for months.

"Are you positive the Vlaminck is genuine?"

"Absolutely."

"Do you have copies of the original provenance?"

"Of course. Every important document is copied in triplicate."

"Let me have a set."

I borrowed an envelope because my attaché case had been shredded in the explosion. The only part of me that did not seem to ache at the moment was my sideburns. Nevertheless, I went back to my office. I found a stack of messages and a reporter from the *Sun-Sentinel*, eager for information. I referred him to Lieutenant Nola. One of the messages surprised me: phone Mr. Stanley Kemper on a matter of considerable urgency.

Kemper is a fussy and humorless lawyer, a nitpicker, a corrosive misanthrope. I filed the message in my wastebasket, and twenty minutes later, his strident voice was on the line.

"Jordan? I understand you're the attorney for Victor Rosemont's estate."

"Correct."

"Rosemont was a crook."

"You're slandering a dead man, Kemper."

"With justification. He defrauded one of my clients. A Mr. Sama Kosuri. Sold him a fake painting, a forged Vlaminck."

"We deny the allegation."

"I have a sworn affidavit from a recognized expert."

"Tell him to see a good optometrist. And take another look at the provenance. What more does Kosuri want?"

"He wants his money. One hundred and twenty thousand dollars."

"I hope he knows how to whistle."

"We'll sue the estate."

"Your privilege, Kemper. That's what the courts are for."

He struggled for control. "Let's take the painting to any expert you name and see what he says."

Well, I thought, why not? Anything reasonable to avoid litigation. "Agreed," I told him. "Set up an appointment at the Museum of Modern Art and let me know."

He called back in half an hour, saying that arrangements had been made for the following afternoon. I promised to be there. I knew that I would accomplish nothing constructive that afternoon. What I needed was rest, so I decided to take the doctor's advice and go home to bed.

A new day had dawned when the telephone awakened me. In my ear, the Widow Rosemont's voice sounded thin and tense. "Please come quickly," she said. "I'm in Victor's apartment."

Twenty minutes later, I was at the entrance of a renovated apartment in Harbor Beach with my finger on the bell. Margot Rosemont drew me in and pointed, her face white. Utter chaos. The place had been ransacked by vandals. And in the midst of all the carnage lay a rumpled figure. Alongside the ruined skull was a Giacometti bronze.

"Klaus Helman," I said. "You found him like this?"

"Yes."

"When?"

"Two minutes before I called you."

"Tell me about him, Margot."

"He's an artist, not very successful. I remember we tried to sell some of his work at the gallery, but no one seemed interested. He was always begging Victor to give him a one-man show."

"He'll have to give it posthumously," I told her. "It was being arranged yesterday."

She stared. "At the gallery? That's insane. There won't be a single customer."

"It was Victor's decision, not Angela Lowe's."

She seemed at a loss. "I don't understand. It was not Victor's style to indulge people. And anyway, who killed him? What was he doing here? Can't you have the body removed?"

"Not me. It's a job for the police. I want you to call them after I leave. Don't tell them I was here. And then make a full inventory. Did Victor keep any valuable artwork in the place?"

"Very little. The insurance was too high. Almost everything was at the gallery, protected by all sorts of alarms and devices."

"All right, Margot. I'll be in touch later. Can you take care of it?"

She nodded indecisively and watched me leave.

It was time to meet Stanley Kemper, and I headed for the Museum of Modern Art. He was waiting in the lobby, Kosuri's Vlaminck wrapped in heavy kraft under his arm. We nodded but did not shake hands. The resident expert was J. Zachary Barnett, bearded and smugly assured; he told us to be seated and took the painting to another room. Time spent alone with Kemper is about as rewarding as watching deodorant commercials. I listened to a dozen semantic fandangos on the laws of consumer fraud.

At last the museum's art expert returned. He shook his head sadly. "Gentlemen, you've been taken. This is not a Vlaminck. Vlaminck's style, yes. A genuine Vlaminck, no. It is definitely a fake, but a remarkably good one. What the forger did here is most interesting. He found some vintage canvas, probably in Paris. I would say that he mixed his own pigments and copied from the original. And then, apparently, he sprayed the finished work with a special restorer's varnish that helps to dry the oils more quickly and produces a craqueleur, as you can see here, these tiny veined cracks generally found in old paintings." Barnett shook his head in admiration. "I would truly like to meet this man. Behind bars, of course. He's a menace. God alone knows how many gullible dealers and collectors he must have duped. At a rough guess, I would say this painting is worth, at most, maybe a hundred dollars."

"You see? You see?" Kemper was jumping triumphantly. "What did I tell you? Rosemont was a crook."

I ignored him and said to Barnett, "Less than a month ago, your people authenticated this very same Vlaminck."

"No, sir. We authenticated one that looked like it. Not this one."

"What are you going to do about it?" Kemper demanded.

I gave him a pitying look. "Your Mr. Kosuri is a lulu, Kemper. He digs up a fake, hides the genuine Vlaminck, and then demands a refund."

It brought him so close to apoplexy that I almost relented. Instead, I walked out of the room. He dogged my heels, yapping outside a telephone booth while I called my office and learned that Lieutenant Nola wanted to see me without delay. I lost sight of Kemper's rancorous face when a taxi carried me off.

At the precinct, Lieutenant Nola sat behind his desk and regarded me for a long moment, his dark eyes speculative, his mouth tight. "Well, Counselor," he said finally, "we've got another one. A new corpse. Laid out in Rosemont's apartment. The widow found him. Little fella. Some kind of an artist. Klaus Helman. Know the name?"

"I met him once, briefly. What happened? Heart attack?"

"You could say that. Brought on by a cracked skull."

"When?"

"Sometime last night. Mrs. Rosemont went there this morning, and there he was. Somebody had torn the place apart. She was in no condition to talk. And, incidentally, there is no record of any call from Rosemont's hotel room in Chicago to his wife. Was this Helman a good painter?"

"I'm no art critic, Lieutenant."

"We checked his studio. Very unusual. Three locks on the outside, a police lock on the inside. And a strange cache of artwork."

"Strange how?"

"One of my lab men—this new breed, college fella—he's an art buff. Said it looked as if someone had looted the Louvre." Nola consulted his notes. "Pictures that looked like Matisse, Gauguin, Degas, Cezanne. And hidden away in a closet, we found a steel box

with papers, some of them made out to the Rosemont Gallery—
records of sale, certificates, affidavits. What was that word you
used?"

"Provenance."

"Yeah. A lot of them. So we have to run a check on this Helman."

My mind was racing. "By all means," I said.

A small card in the window cordially invited the public to view
the work of Klaus Helman starting on Saturday the nineteenth. But
Angela Lowe was not especially sanguine about sales. She looked
harried when Nola and I walked in. "Klaus didn't come in today.
Nothing has been hung in the back room yet, and I can't seem to
reach him at his studio. Usually he's very dependable."

"Helman won't be in at all," I told her. "He's dead."

Sudden distress flashed across her face. "Oh, no," she moaned. "I
can't take much more of this. First Victor and now Klaus. What
happened?"

She listened and then fled to the office. Nola shrugged. We gave
her a couple of minutes to compose herself. She was sitting behind
Rosemont's desk, staring into space.

"Angela," I said quietly, "we need your help."

She swallowed and nodded.

"How long have you known?" I asked.

"How long have I known what?"

"That Klaus Helman was an expert art forger. That he'd been
counterfeiting the impressionists for some time. That he knew every
trick in the book. That he connived with Victor to supply the gallery
with spurious works of art. That somehow Victor had lost his moral
compass and exploited his reputation to deceive and defraud his
customers. Did you know from the beginning?"

After a long moment, she found her voice. "I never really knew
for certain, Mr. Jordan. But recently I had begun to suspect that
something seemed out of focus. And then after Mr. Kosuri

complained about his Vlaminck, it began to explain a number of strange incidents."

"Such as?"

"Giving Helman a one-man show when he knew it was doomed from the start, just to keep Klaus happy."

"Do you have any idea how many forgeries may have been sold?"

She gestured helplessly. "It's a mess, Mr. Jordan. Victor had customers all over the world. Two months ago he sold a Degas pastel to a West German banker. And before that, a Renoir watercolor to one of the oil sheiks from Kuwait. He sometimes accepted cash, and the transactions never appeared on our books."

"So Victor must have salted away quite a bit of money."

"I suppose."

"And you, Angela? How about you? Have you put away a lot of money?"

She blinked at me. "I beg your pardon."

"Money, Angela. True, at first you only suspected a conspiracy between Victor and Helman. And then, somehow, you stumbled onto hard evidence. And you began to shake him down. Because you realized that he would never divorce Margot to marry you, so you demanded a piece of the action. Security for your future."

Her face was stiff with restraint. "You're insane. That's absolute nonsense."

"Ah, Angela, such righteous indignation! And such brash conduct. You should have known that Victor would never hold still for blackmail. He'd know that it never ends, that no matter how much he shelled out, you might still blow the whistle on him someday. He really had only one solution. Nullify the danger by eliminating you. And since he was a devious man, he cooked up an elaborate scheme.

"It was Victor himself who put the bomb in his safe-deposit box. The implication, of course, would be that someone had tried to kill him. But it was really meant for you, Angela. He called his wife from Chicago and asked her to instruct you to open his box. But he used a pay phone booth so there would be no record of the call. And if his wife talked, he would deny phoning her. Margot had access to the box. It was common knowledge that she blamed you for her separation. Which would make her a prime suspect. She might even be tried and convicted. To Rosemont, everyone was expendable."

"What tipped you?" Nola demanded.

"Your discovery that Rosemont's authentication papers were hidden in Helman's studio. Victor was a greedy man. Those documents were too valuable. He would not allow them to be destroyed in the explosion. So he removed them from the safe-deposit box. He had no reason to do that if he hadn't arranged the booby trap himself."

"He trusted Helman?"

"Sure. They were partners in the conspiracy. They needed each other."

"Why was Helman killed?"

"Because he had forged a Vlaminck, copying an original that had already been authenticated and sold. Rosemont substituted the forgery for the genuine painting while he was arranging for a new frame. Then Rosemont suffered a heart attack. Helman knew that the real Vlaminck was probably hidden in Rosemont's apartment and decided to retrieve it for himself. It was, after all, worth a lot of money.

"But someone else had the same idea. Our friend Angela. She guessed what had happened when the buyer of the Vlaminck complained. And as a special friend of the boss, she had a key to Rosemont's apartment. She probably got there before Helman and took cover when she heard him at the door. Then she sneaked up from behind and brained him."

She appealed to Nola. "Make him stop. He doesn't know what he's talking about."

I said, "What about those fingerprints you found on the Giacometti, Lieutenant?"

"Listen," she said frantically, "I rearranged that statue on Victor's mantel many times."

"Yes, but will you be able to convince a jury?" I asked. "Or explain how you managed to get possession of the Vlaminck? The police know how to search, Angela. They'll take your place apart. And they'll find the painting. They'll find witnesses who must have seen you in the neighborhood. They'll find unexplained sums of money you extorted from Victor."

She seemed to shrink before our eyes, suddenly ill. Nola took a slip of paper from his pocket and began to read the lady her rights. Then he turned to me. "I'm curious, Counselor. You had no idea what kind of rank specimen you were representing in this Rosemont?"

I looked at him aggrieved. "If I had known, would I have accepted the fee he paid me last year? For twelve months of legal services. Claimed he was short of cash and offered me a small Modigliani nude. Which I grabbed before he could change his mind." I shook my head in disgust. "Probably something Helman knocked out one morning before breakfast. Worth maybe fourteen dollars. Why, the damn frame cost me more than that."

Instant Replay

STUART McIVER

I n the dim moonlight, Lamar Carruthers looked out at his soldiers huddled around their campfires. They'd be talking about tomorrow's battle and about the charge through the jagged sawgrass stretching across the wet prairie just to the west of their camp and on down to the shores of Lake Tustenuggee.

"Captain, they tell me that sawgrass cuts you up real bad," said Freddie Ames, barely old enough to shave.

"Mebbe so, but we got no choice," said Carruthers. "Nine A.M. we move out. Old Chief Sam Jones Be Damned is out there waiting for us, him and his warriors. More damned Seminoles than we got any use for."

A nervous quiet settled over the camp, broken only by the croaking of frogs and now and then the bellow of a bull gator.

Beep, beep, beep.

"What the hell," shouted Carruthers. "Who brought a beeper in here?"

Sheepishly, a soldier, stylishly trim in his dark blue uniform, stepped forward and handed the captain his beeper. Carruthers threw it in the dirt, then planted his size-12 boot on it and kept grinding it into the ground until it stopped chirping.

"What's the matter, soldier? Don't you know this is eighteen thirty-seven?"

Yuppies, they'll never get it right, he thought. *As coordinator of the Third Annual Most Holy Reenactment of the Battle of Tustenuggee, I've got the responsibility for transporting these boys out of this miserable, high-tech, back-biting, screwed-up world we live in and back into nineteenth-century Florida. Back to the days when a man could be a hero. I got to make 'em dress like Seminole War soldiers and Indians, bear arms like soldiers and Indians, and at least try to talk like people did then. They can't even chew Clinton out. They gotta go after Van Buren. They gotta stay in character.*

Carruthers shook his head. *Beepers, cellular phones, portable radios, wrist watches: how do you stamp 'em out?* Then through the quiet night came the roar of an eighteen-wheeler rumbling along Route 27. *Sometimes you just can't win. At least the weather looks good for tomorrow.*

And on Saturday the weather was as perfect as he had hoped, only a few wispy clouds and just a touch of chill in the December air. Nearby the army men were finishing breakfast. Far off, on the other side of the marsh, Carruthers could see the Indians back under the trees preparing for the battle. He walked over to the tent of Colonel Tom Haney, commander of the U.S. troops. A stocky man in his early forties, the colonel fought off the morning chill with a cup of black coffee.

"We charge at nine, Captain," said the colonel. "These men damned well better be ready."

"They'll be ready, Colonel. Once they stop grousing about that sawgrass charge."

"Let 'em grouse. I'm here to give orders, they're here to take them."

Carruthers saluted snappily. "Yes, sir," he said and headed on down among the tents. From behind Major Charles Brent's tent, he overheard two enlisted men.

"Way I hear it, Major Brent wanted a flanking movement. We'd be on high ground, north of that swamp. Going straight in makes us sitting ducks. The word I get is Colonel Haney didn't want any advice from any Tennessee Volunteers, 'specially if it's right. He won't listen to anything but regular army."

Carruthers moved on past. He didn't blame them for being sore. *Sawgrass could cut you up. But that was the way it was in 1837 and that was the way it was going to be today. The colonel is the boss. Then and now. And today's colonel is as big a bastard as the 1837 model. Maybe bigger. He's got a lot of people sore at him.*

On high ground east of the swamp, the men had assembled for safety inspection. It seemed to be going well. Then came a roaring sound. Carruthers shook his fist at a jet airliner overhead.

"Too early in the day to get your bowels in an uproar, boy." Carruthers turned suddenly to face Wilbur Austin, sheriff of Tustenuggee County. Tall and thin as a skeleton, the sheriff gazed down at the coordinator, a half smile flickering behind his eyes.

"I missed the last two battles, Lamar. Thought I'd better catch this one. When you get that many men out there with guns, I worry about somebody getting hurt."

"So do I, Sheriff. That's why two master sergeants are out there right now, inspecting every rifle, every cartridge case. We use nothing but blanks."

"All well and good, Lamar. But what's to keep a killer from slipping a couple of bullets in if he really had a grudge?"

Carruthers paused.

"Nothing. If they really wanted to, they'd find some way to do it. Just like spectators could smuggle in a bomb. What could you do? We do what we can. We inspect. Boy, do we inspect!"

"Sometimes just looking isn't enough."

Major Brent had assembled his Tennessee Volunteers on the high ground at the east end of the battlefield. Fifty yards to the west, the sawgrass marsh blocked the approach to the hardwood hammock where a small band of Seminoles waited, invisible in live oaks, cabbage palms, and Spanish moss.

"Men," said the major, "I'm raising on high the sword Captain Thomas Claiborne Brent used at the Battle of Kings Mountain. When I drop my arm, we march into that swamp and we don't stop till we've demolished old Sam Jones and his hostiles."

The men cheered. Brent raised his sword, its shining steel glistening in the bright Florida sunlight. Then he brought the sword down decisively, and his men charged into the sawgrass.

Fifteen minutes later the Tennessee Volunteers were only sixty yards from the hammock bristling with Seminoles. A shot rang out. A young Tennesseean collapsed in the marshy grass. Suddenly the air echoed with the sound of gunfire and the cries of falling men.

One who fell was Major Brent. The Volunteers moved ahead but soon their broken ranks retreated. The Missouri Infantry surged forward past the fallen Volunteers. Now the Indians were beginning to fall back. Time for Colonel Haney to pluck the fruits of victory. From the high ground to the north of the marsh, he rode triumphantly on his chestnut steed.

"On with it, men."

His men moved swiftly forward. The Indians vanished back into the dense thickets. Colonel Haney swung his sword in the air and shouted:

"Go get—"

He never finished the sentence. The colonel fell off his horse and lay still on the ground.

"That's funny," said Carruthers. "He wasn't supposed to go down. Wasn't even a good fall. Oh, well, the son of a bitch always does what he wants to do."

Haney's Regulars stormed on into the hammock. The whoops of the Indians grew louder. Then silence. Carruthers signaled to an artilleryman. The soldier nodded and fired off his cannon. Abruptly the shooting stopped. Lamar walked over to Vinnie Dominici, Channel 8's cameraman.

"Hope you got it all, Vinnie. That's it for today."

Vinnie grinned at him, then signaled an "O" for OK.

Time to relax, thought Lamar, *time to calm down my churning stomach. So many details to coordinate, so many loose ends.* He had rounded up over three hundred reenactors to recreate a battle more famous for Colonel Ambrose Haney's personal vendetta against Major Brent than for its meaningless outcome. What a coup! Whoever thought he would locate a direct descendant of Brent in Memphis and pair him against a descendant of Haney? Getting Tom Haney was easy enough. He lived right here in Tustenuggee City. To nail him, all Lamar had to do was to tie the battle in with that monster development of his, Tropic Highlands, out on that flat prairie. Haney even agreed to underwrite the event. Which meant money to put on a good show. And if Lamar could just make Seminole War reenactments catch on around the state, sales at his West Palm Beach store would just take off. Weaponry, uniforms, shoes, books about the Seminole War—a whole new market. Not as big as the Civil War but nothing to be sneezed at. He could even get a satellite dish. "How would you rate this reenactment, Lamar?" asked the sheriff, who suddenly reappeared out of the crowd.

"Sheriff, I guess, maybe on a scale of one to ten, I'd give it about a six. Good crowd, looks like maybe five thousand. The food, arts and crafts booths, and the beer trucks are all busy. Press and TV coverage is good."

The reenactment had clearly pumped welcome excitement into the sleepy, Old Florida town of Tustenuggee City, joining the rodeo and the Speckled Perch Jamboree. The battle was a festive occasion all right, men in jeans and cowboy hats, a few overdressed city boys who never quite get it right. And plenty of nifties in mini-skirts and cowboy boots. Carruthers' eyes flicked appreciatively over to Monica Abernathy. *Boy, does she know how to strut in those tight-*

fitting jeans, low-cut blouse, and sassy cowboy hat. A moment earlier he had seen her husband, Dexter, limping by in his Seminole outfit. *How does a scrawny little guy like Dexter land a woman like Monica?* he thought. *Money, I guess. After all, he is Haney's lawyer. And he's a first-rate reenactor. Always dresses right for the battle and the period, knows more Florida history than anybody I know, and he sure knows how to handle firearms. But in this gun-loving town everybody's got a shooting iron.*

Carruthers saw Royce Langley from Channel 8 walking toward him. "Just the man I'm looking for," said Royce, carefully combing his thick brown hair. "We're ready now to tape our segment."

The correspondent stepped in front of Dominici's camera and motioned Carruthers to join him. Then the gooey, rich tones of the TV personality poured forth.

"It was a major battle in the Second Seminole War, the Battle of Tustenuggee. It came to life today at the site where brave men fought over a century and a half ago. Lamar Carruthers' expert corps of reenactors from all over south Florida camped out here last night, then bright and early this morning skillfully brought the battle home to all of us. It used to be nearly all the reenactments were Civil War battles. Now we're seeing more and more from the Seminole War."

"It's the fastest growing war in Florida," said Lamar.

"And a lot of the credit for that belongs to Billie Jumper for recruiting men from his tribe to participate. They bring in real authenticity. And I believe he is a descendant of the great Sam Jones, who led the Indians a century and a half ago."

"That's right, Royce, and Billie's not the only one tracing his roots back to that bloody battle. Colonel Ambrose Haney, the deadliest of all the Indian fighters, was impersonated today by one of his descendants, Tom Haney. He's building Tropic Highlands right here on the lake. As you know, Tom helped underwrite this reenactment.

"And all the way from Tennessee, we have Charles Brent, a descendant of Major Brent, sent to his death by Colonel Haney's flawed battle plan. There was even a Congressional investigation of Haney for this blunder. But that was long ago, and there's no bad feeling today between the colonel and the major or, for that matter, Billie Jumper, whose tribe was decimated by the war. They've put it all behind them. Great Americans all."

After the interview, Langley asked Lamar to round up the three great Americans.

"We want to film them together in a warm-hearted post-battle reconciliation."

Carruthers easily located Brent, relaxing at the beer truck with a long-necked Bud. Billie Jumper, a heavy-set Seminole already marked for leadership in his tribe's expanding business ventures, was talking rapidly to a local attorney.

"Hey, Lamar," said Jumper. "We did pretty good out there. After all, you had us outnumbered. The next time I'm in a reenactment, I want it to be one we win. How about the Dade Massacre? Maybe the Battle of Withlacoochee."

"Get your boys ready, Billie, and we'll find a battle for them."

But where was Colonel Haney, a major advertiser with Channel 8? He was not at his tent. His horse was waiting for him at the makeshift corral. But no one had seen him.

Lord, there's still one place I haven't looked, thought Carruthers.

Near the northeastern edge of the hammock, Lamar finally found Colonel Haney. He was lying in the soft grass, right where he had taken his phony, unscripted fall. A pool of blood lay beneath him, and the blue jacket of his uniform was stained red. It was a little too realistic, thought Lamar.

"Come on, Tom. You gotta be kidding."

Lamar turned Haney over, then recoiled suddenly. He ran to look for a doctor. In a few minutes, Dr. Fred Upthegrove, official physician for the event, gave him the bad news.

"Dead, probably instantly. Gunshot wound."

There was no way to keep the curious crowd back. Dominici moved relentlessly in with his camera, and Langley trapped Sheriff Austin, happy to talk in an election year.

"Not much we can tell you right now," said the sheriff. "It looks like a terrible accident. Them reenactors are supposed to shoot blanks, but it looks like a real bullet got into one of them guns by mistake. Only way I can figure it. Tom Haney was an important man. He's putting in a big development right smack up against this battle site. Tropic Highlands means jobs for a lot of people, and it puts valuable property on the tax rolls."

"Any chance of foul play?" asked Langley.

"Looks like an accident but you never can tell."

The sheriff's easygoing, good-ol'-boy manner changed as soon as he collared Carruthers.

"Boy, you need to fill me in real quick. You're running this show so you've got some ideas 'bout what happened out there today."

Lamar squirmed uncomfortably.

"I never saw anything like this before, Sheriff. Now and then some powder burns, or a man getting hurt falling off a horse or out of a tree. Fact is, we had one of the men fall out of a tree today. He's still hobbling."

"How did a real bullet wind up in one of those guns?"

"I don't know how. I told you we inspect every single gun just before the battle starts. Every flintlock, every breechloader, every cartridge box. We don't tolerate any careless mistakes."

"How about they shoot one round, then reach into their pocket, not their cartridge box, and reload with the real thing?"

"No reenactor would do that. It's against the code. Besides, we pat 'em down. I'll stand behind them. My boys are true blue."

"And Tom Haney's true dead."

Overhead a December cold front was moving in. The wind from the north was picking up, and skies were turning an ominous dark gray.

"Doc tells me the bullet came in sorta up high and exited lower down. Since he was on a horse, the only way anybody could shoot down on him would be from a tree. Way it looked to me, the only people in the trees were Seminoles. That about right?"

"Well, yes. But we inspected them, too. They were—"

"They were just like everybody else. They could have switched ammo."

Carruthers said nothing.

The two men walked over toward the crafts area. The Seminoles were selling fry bread, beads, children's dolls, and brightly colored jackets and skirts.

"Want to tell me about that old feud between the Haneys and the Brents?"

"That's a hundred and fifty years ago, Sheriff. These guys barely know each other. And if you're so concerned about feuds, Billie Jumper has as much reason to hate Haney as Brent. Colonel Haney was a bloody, vicious, treacherous, Indian-murdering son of a bitch. But that was a hundred and fifty years ago, and these people, far as I know, just met at this reenactment. You're looking at some kind of weird accident."

"Don't know, Lamar. Seems to me anybody but a halfwit would know if he loaded a bullet or a ball into his shooting iron instead of just powder or blanks."

"Well, as a matter of fact, they couldn't even load a ball very well into a flintlock without a ramrod. And without attracting attention. Be easier to load a breechloader. And whichever one fired, there'd be a recoil."

"Enough to notice."

"Sure. With a blank there's no kick, although some of our reenactors fake it to make it look realistic. They act like there's a recoil even if there isn't one. But you put a real bullet in there, and you'll know it when you fire it. If you were expecting a blank, a real recoil could knock you over."

"All right, Lamar. I want every reenactor rounded up, and I want him to bring his gun. My deputies are on their way here now, and they're going to check every gun before this bunch leaves. Don't tell me this was an accident. Everybody knows Haney's got enemies. Ever since he came up here from Miami, he's jerked a lot of people around. And he's chased a lot of people's wives. Caught a few of them, too, the way I hear it. Have all your reenactors over by your tent in fifteen minutes. With guns. Nobody leaves."

The clouds were growing darker, and a cold wind was whipping across the field. The sheriff zipped up his windbreaker, headed for his car, then flipped on his car radio.

"Jim, you finding out much about Haney?"

"Word I'm getting is he had a slew of enemies," said Deputy Jim Hamilton. "With all his money, he just figured he could push people around anytime he wanted to. Pete Ledbetter says he swindled him out of his land. That environmentalist fellow from the Audubon Society, Joe Newton, is after him for draining the marsh and breaking up that ibis rookery with all that heavy equipment. And he sure goes for the ladies. He's been messing around with Monica Abernathy, and ol' Dexter has found out about it. He's got business enemies and he's got unhappy husbands out there. It's a big list."

"Keep after it, Jim. We gotta come up with some answers in a hurry. I can't keep everybody here forever. This whole town's got their TVs primed for this afternoon's Dolphins-Chargers game."

Royce Langley was just getting ready to leave when the sheriff and Carruthers caught up with him.

"What's your hurry, Royce?" asked Austin.

"Gotta get back to West Palm to put this story together. We've got a big one here, Sheriff. Haney was a powerhouse."

"Your cameraman cover the whole reenactment?"

"Most of it. One man can't cover it all."

"I want to see that film or tape or whatever the hell it is you use."

"Too late. Vinnie's already on his way back to the station. Besides, Sheriff, you know how sticky the station gets about having its tape turned over to the police. Using reporters to do your job for you. You're into freedom of the press, First Amendment stuff."

"So just let me look at it as a friendly, cooperative gesture, all in the cause of good government."

"I'll let you know, Sheriff. It's not my call."

The crowd was thinning out as Sheriff Austin walked across the field to the headquarters tent. Already some two hundred reenactors were gathered in front, looking anxiously up at a stormy Florida sky.

"Lamar, that bullet probably came from a breechloader, didn't it?"

"Yep, probably from a Hall's rifle. Turns out we've got about nine of them."

"I want to look first at the Hall's rifles that were in the trees. All of them were Seminoles, right?"

"Yes and no. They were all playing Seminoles. But only about five actual Indians were in the reenactment. The rest of them are regular reenactors, mostly Civil War specialists, just wearing pancake makeup and Seminole clothes."

"I'm hoping I can have a look tomorrow at all the film Channel Eight shot. Maybe I'll see something."

"You don't have to wait for Channel Eight. Battles Relived has got three cameramen here today. They'll have more coverage than a TV station anyway. It's their business. They put these tapes together and sell them to reenactors, not just the ones here today, but you've got people all over the South and East who buy these things. Wish I'd thought of the idea."

"Lamar, you got a list of all the reenactors?"

"Just happen to have one right with me," said Lamar.

The sheriff searched for familiar names. Most of the reenactors were from out of town, from the bigger Florida cities where enthusiasm for the war games ran high. Three familiar names caught his eye—Brent, Jumper, and Dexter Abernathy.

"I want to see those videotapes."

It took producer Larry McClelland about an hour to pull all his tapes together. The sheriff found a VCR in the office of Sonny's Bait and Tackle Shop, about a half mile from the battlefield.

"Just set 'em up here, Sheriff," said the rotund Sonny. "Can I get you boys a beer?"

Austin took him up on the offer. He sipped a Bud as the reenactment began to unfold, slowly at first as Battles Relived covered the preparation for the event.

"You realize, Sheriff," said McClelland, "that in a reenactment you take a lot of pains to set the stage. Our people stay in character, and for a little while at least, they actually live a little pocket of history."

"Can we fast-forward to the place where Haney falls off his horse?" asked Lamar.

"Sure. It'll be near the end. In every sense of the word."

A good ten minutes went by before the director found the right spot in the tape. From a vantage point to the east, the camera showed Colonel Haney's regulars moving in from the right flank. It was a wide shot, but the colonel was easy to follow. He started to call out to his men, then stopped suddenly and fell from his horse.

"Play it again," said Austin. They ran it through three more times, each time freezing the fall. The results were always the same. The scene showed nothing. The shot that killed Haney came from offscreen.

"Larry, let's have a look at the tape from the cameraman shooting toward the trees," said Lamar.

Once again the producer fast-forwarded his way through the tape, then near the end found the place to begin viewing. This was a better angle, a camera position behind the colonel.

Again Haney approached the hammock. From the trees, the Indians fired down at the regulars. Once more the colonel led his troops forward. He raised his sword on high and called to his men.

Then he fell from his horse.

At almost the same instant an Indian fell out of a tree.

"Let's see that again," said the sheriff. "Lamar, what kind of gun was that Indian using."

"From here it looks like a Hall's breechloader, Sheriff. It's the kick of his gun that knocked him out of the tree. A gun that fired live ammo."

"Damned shame. Looks like I've got to arrest me an Indian. If it's Jumper, it'll be hell to pay."

Lamar shook his head slowly.

"You won't have to arrest a Seminole. The man who fell out of the tree wasn't an Indian."

"I like to think you're going to give me his name, Lamar."

"One of our best reenactors. A sharpshooter. A man you know well. A prominent attorney. A man with a mighty good-looking wife."

The rain was just beginning as they walked over to the reenactors' tent. They found Dexter Abernathy sitting on a wooden chair, nursing a swollen ankle.

"Feels like it's broken, Lamar," he said in a shaky voice. "Guess we made Florida history just too realistic."

"It's not that you made it too realistic, Dexter," said Lamar. "It's just that Old Florida collided with New Florida. And instant replay won."

Heartbreak Avenue

BILLIE SUE MOSIMAN

Old Sam moved around through the streets in the neighborhood, sometimes mumbling to himself, sometimes smoking his cigar and jabbing it at the air just above his head. The moon was full, creamy as homemade butter tonight, and he expected mayhem. He had witnessed more than his share, living on the street as he did, hoping to be of assistance, keeping his eyes and ears open.

He saw the young man around eleven o'clock. Odd how he walked along, looking at street signs, talking out loud as if to ghosts. He was not a denizen of the night, judging by his garb. He was a stranger, lost perhaps, possibly in need of a friend.

Sam moved stealthily into position behind him, keeping his distance, amused and curious.

It was something to do.

It was the television movie that started the whole thing. I couldn't find anything else to watch and I was bored, you know how it is. I sat watching this thing, this dumb, two-handkerchief movie about a guy cheating on his wife, and the wife finds out. The reverse situation had me by the throat in my own life, and I couldn't stand it, couldn't bear to look at the screen.

Hollywood, boy. They'd putzed around pulling heartstrings in their hokey way—mainly for the bon-bon, couch-potato crowd with your two-digit IQ—and caught me squarely where I live. Grabbed me by the shirt front and waltzed me around in a two-step.

It shouldn't have gotten to me that way. Not silly, sentimental crap getting to me—me, the least sentimental fool I know. Wouldn't have, but I was vulnerable to stories about lost love, all that schmaltzy stuff.

That was last night, the movie. I lost Sandra last month. Last week I lost my job, so what's new? When things go sour, that's how it happens, all in a bundle—ask anyone. You can't wreck your car and then win the lottery or something. You can't one day lose your wife and the next meet a gorgeous babe who's going to bring you breakfast in bed. Oh, no, bad things happen all at once like a ton of garbage dropping out the back of a payloader on your head—boom, you're stinking all over with coffee grounds and limp lettuce leaves and moldy bread. Lousy luck with all capital Ls.

Tonight, no TV. I'll walk the streets until I'm tired and can get some sleep. I might stroll on by where Sandra's staying with her college man. Just for a look-see. I don't do it often. Not more than twice a week if I can help it.

Besides, there's a street I've been looking for.

Sandra told me once there really was a street in this city called Heartbreak Avenue. I laughed when she told me. I said, "That's the Elvis Presley song, 'Heartbreak Hotel.' You got it confused." She said no, there really was. I asked if Heartbreak Avenue might be the place where the King got the lyrics for his gold record. And if so then it couldn't be in Fort Lauderdale, Florida. It must be in Memphis. Sandra said I wasn't funny, she was serious, I didn't believe her I could look it up on the city map. I thought she was fooling with me.

She wasn't. I found Heartbreak Avenue on the city map. One of those odd little side streets, sandwiched in between the numbered streets, just on the south side of the New River. Not too far from Sweeney's or the new country-and-western place that opened. It's supposed to only be a few blocks from here, and close to where Sandra moved. Imagine the guy's troubles who named that street.

It's a little cooler out tonight, autumn coming on. I should be coming up on Heartbreak any minute if I've followed the map right. It's where I should live. It's the geography I belong to. Heartbreak Avenue or Desolation Row. Not that I'm into self-pity—don't get me wrong, I hate self-pity. This walk around town is just a way to keep me busy so I won't think too much about the movie I saw and the wife I miss and the job I don't have. Sometimes I think I must have fallen into a country-and-western song.

This tape recorder? Well, I thought if I could just open up a little, Sandra might see she made a mistake. I thought I'd send a tape of my thoughts to her in, well, like a diary or journal form. Let's call it a project, OK? I know it sounds like I'm some high school twit, but I can't help that. I needed something and this was all I could come up with. Sandra said I never talked to her; she hardly knew me after four years. She said I was boring, she couldn't take it anymore. Maybe if she gets to know me, the real me, she'll love me again. I may not be able to dazzle her with history lessons and elegant language, but if she could just find out I'm a real person with feelings—and that I love her, I really do—she might give that guy up and come back. Anything's worth a shot.

I'm supposed to turn left here, follow Andrews over the river, turn right on Sixth, go down two streets, and the next one is Heartbreak. I used to work on the other side of town at the cement plant. I've never been over this way.

"Hey, mister, you got a match?"

"What? Oh, I didn't see anyone around. You startled me."

"A light for my cigar? You got one?"

"Sure, just a sec. Here's my Bic."

"Thanks."

"You live here?"

"Not . . . exactly. But I hang out around Heartbreak. You lost?"

"That's where I was headed. Where's Heartbreak Avenue anyway?"

"A couple of streets over." He pointed. "Thanks for the light. You wouldn't have a dollar or some extra change, would you?"

"Sorry, no."

Jesus, what a bum. Old damn drunk. You oughta see how he's stumbling off the curb and weaving across the street. Smelled like a distillery. They ought to lock guys like that up for their own good. That cigar wasn't nothing but a stogie out of some gutter. Now let me see, I gotta look around here, find out where I'm at. I think straight ahead should be Ramada.

Wonder if I should drop by where Sandra lives first. She's on a side street, LeGuin, LeGoon, something like that. Ah, here it is: LeGuane.

That house. Right there. The one with the lights in the upstairs shining. I can see silhouettes. I see you in there, Sandra! But would you care if I took a stroll over to Heartbreak Avenue and recorded all this stupid stuff? Dumb idea. Stinking armpit idea. This goes to show just how far down I've sunk. I can't even think how to get you back. All I do is wander over here and stare like a lovesick schoolboy at your shadow behind the shades.

Uh, oh, here he comes. It's the old dude again, the old drunk. What's he doing ducking into the dark around the corner of the last house on the block? Maybe he's a burglar. Nah, couldn't be. He's just an old rummy lost here in a once-genteel neighborhood that's rapidly going to the dogs.

Sandra, you must be wearing that flowing gown I gave you last Christmas. It moves like a breeze when you walk past the window up there. I wish. . . .

"You sure you don't have a spare buck, son?"

"I wish to Christ you'd stop coming up behind me like that!"

"I thought you saw me."

"I saw you down at the corner. Whatta you doin' anyway, casing these homes?"

"Nope. Just wandering, same as you. I see you have a tape recorder. And you seem to be doing some 'casing' yourself, come to that."

"It's . . . it's just a project. I was taping my thoughts. Not that it's any of your business, but that's my wife in there."

"Wife. Upstairs with some other man?" The old guy glanced at their silhouettes in the lighted window. "That's too bad. Maybe you oughta stay away from here. You come often to watch your wife like this?"

"I don't have to answer any questions from you."

"Her new man seems to be going out somewheres."

"I'll see you around, pal. I have to scram."

"He finds you peeping, he's not going to be happy, eh? Bet she ain't either."

"C'mon, let's move on down the sidewalk, will you? You're going to get me in trouble."

"You got some change for a drink?"

"Sheesh, let's talk about it down the street, OK, all right?"

"If you got some money, I'm wit' you."

"Stop turning around looking back there. You're going to make the professor suspicious. He's gonna know I've been watching the house."

"Betty's Bar, it's just two blocks over. Can we go there?"

"Anywhere, just not around here."

"She took up with a professor, eh? Rich guy?"

"I don't know if he's rich or not. It ain't none of my business."

"She's your wife, right? That makes it your business. So, is he rich and good-looking?"

"I told you I don't know about the man's finances! Will you drop it? Look, there's Betty's. I'll buy you a drink. One drink. Then you leave me alone, deal?"

"Sure, why not. It's a deal."

"Barkeep, get us two beers. Draft."

"That's mighty cheap. I bet the professor, he'd buy me a real drink. Whiskey. The good stuff."

"Well, I'm not rich. I lost my job last week, and you're drinking draft if you're drinking on me."

"That's double tough. Lose your wife, lose your job. Gonna wind up like me, on the street."

"Not on your sweet ass, no insult intended, of course. I'll have another job. Tomorrow, maybe."

"Wonder where the professor was going, this time of night."

"Look, drink your draft and forget about it. I've gotta go."

"Can I have just one more? For the road?"

"You sure know how to push it, don't you? Here, take my last five bucks. Have a party."

I don't know how I could have given away my last cash to that bum. See, Sandra, what you make me do? Is this recorder still going? Yeah . . . good. I ought to leave this tape on your porch tonight. Let you know how now I'll have to get into the savings because I'm so broke. Remember how we saved for the down payment on the new Mustang you wanted? You remember?

Who cares. You already have a nice car. Your new guy drives a BMW. Does he have bucks? the bum wanted to know. More than I've got, that's for sure.

Where was he going this time of night? What if he's cheating on you already, Sandra? He sure can't be teaching any classes on Aztec history at midnight.

I guess I could walk back past your place just once more, then I'll head over to Heartbreak, just to check it out, before heading home. Some home. It's gotten pretty bad since you left. I don't have much get-up-and-go after you got up and left. I still feel like I'm stuck in some kind of country song—my dog died, my wife left, I'm broke and broken-hearted. . . .

Imagine that old bum saying I'd end up like him on the street and all! No possible way.

Ah, there you are, downstairs now. I can see you moving around the living room. You keep some late hours, just like me.

Whoops, here comes the BMW. Lover's back. Had to go get you cigarettes, did he? I know how you run out in the middle of the night sometimes and. . . .

Let me get back here behind the hedge where he can't see me. Gotta keep quiet till he goes inside.

There. He's inside. Carried in a small package wrapped tightly in brown paper. Wonder what . . . ?

Wait, I'm going up on the porch, listen in through the window.

"Yo! Mr. Tom Peep! Whachu doin' up there?"

Jesus.

"They almost heard you. Whassa matter with you, calling out like that? You want to get us arrested?"

"I already run outta money. I bought two good whiskey shots. Betty don't give me no credit."

"Why do you keep dogging me? I told you that was my last fiver. I don't have any more money."

"'S all right. Whachu was doin' up there at the window?"

"I was checking on something."

"You need to go to a doctor about that. Woman leaves you, don't mean you should peep on her."

"I saw her boyfriend bring something home. And it wasn't a quart of milk."

"Wha wuz it then?"

"Do you have to hiccup so loud? Let's move down the street before the neighbors see us hanging out here."

"Wha wuz it he brought home?"

"Might have been drugs."

"No."

"I think it was. I saw him dribbling some kind of white powder out on the coffee table and start cutting it with a razor blade. He had a lot of little plastic bags all over the place."

"Blow, man. Them educated types and their recreational fun."

"It was too much just for fun."

"You think he deals that bad stuff?"

"Maybe."

"We oughta call the cops. Where's a phone?"

"No, wait. I have a better idea."

"Waz that?"

"What if I go back there and blackmail the bastard? I tell him I'm gonna turn him in if he don't give me back my wife."

"She might not wanna come back, no how. You have to think of things like that, just in case. . . ."

"She sure won't want to go to prison, do no telling how many years just to stick with that lowlife."

"You gotta point. Tell you what. I'll hide out in the bushes and you go up to the door and tell him you want your woman back. Maybe she'll have some change she can spare 'fore you two go on home together."

"Okay. And I'll tell him I've got it all on tape. Here, take this recorder. He doesn't have to know it's audio tape. He'll think I got him on a videocam."

"Oughta shake 'im down, get some cash too, while you're at it."

"That's not the plan, friend. I just want Sandra back. She can't stay with a guy messing around with illegal substances."

"You want I should turn this thing off?"

"Yeah, why not. I don't need it now."

Old Sam flicked the off button and hunkered down at the edge of a flowerbed. He was getting his shoes dirty, but this promised to be worth it. In front of him was a hedge shielding him from view. Prickly thing, that hedge, kept sticking him when he tried to peer above it.

He watched the young man walk bravely to the door and knock. The door was opened by a man who looked good, like a man who knew what to do with people knocking on his door in the early morning hours.

"I'm Robert Kline. Sandra's my wife. Can I see her, please?"

"I don't think so, Mr. Kline. Do you know what time it is?"

"Sandra? Come to the door. You should hear this too."

"What's this about? I know you must be upset, but your wife doesn't want to see you."

"Listen, clown, I know about the cocaine. I saw you come back with it tonight. I saw you cutting it and putting it into little bags. What, is it your side job, selling it to your students? Sandra!"

"I think you've made a mistake." His voice was ominous, and he began closing the door.

Old Sam thought he was going to pee. He hadn't been involved in a squabble like this in months. He silently rooted for his erstwhile drinking buddy. He almost cheered when he saw him stick his foot in the door to keep it from closing.

"There's no mistake. Oh, there you are. Sandra, you come with me, or I'm turning this jerk in. You can go to jail with him."

"What are you talking about, Robbie?"

Sure, Sam thought, watch her weasel outta this one.

"I'm talking about the drugs. I'm talking about the riffraff you've taken up with. How long has this been going on? Did you know he was into this before you left with him?"

"I think you better go, Robbie. You shouldn't be here. You're getting yourself into something dangerous."

"No, wait, why don't you come inside and let me explain," the professor said, stepping back, taking Robert by the arm to lead him inside.

The door closed. Old Sam swore softly. He crawled up the steps on his hands and knees, not willing to be robbed of the drama that might unfold inside the house.

Just as he neared the front window and peeked through the tiny slice of opening afforded by the drawn drapes, he heard a shot and then a scream that was quickly muffled. He scrambled backward like a crab, half fell down the steps, and hurried along the sidewalk. He was out of breath when he entered Betty's Bar.

"Lemme use the phone!" It must have been his face, drained of color, that kept the barkeep from telling him to go piss up a rope. He swung the desk phone onto the bar counter. Sam called the police and reported, breathlessly, what he knew. Less than five minutes passed and sirens wailed, splitting the quiet night.

The ambulance attendants took out Robert. The police took out the professor and Robert's wife in handcuffs.

Sam knew what hospital these cases were sent to. He trundled off at a steady lope. Wouldn't take him long to get there. Maybe a half hour. After all, he still had the young man's tape recorder. He had to give that back. And he had nothing better to do with his time.

Sam waited all night in the emergency waiting room. A lovely old soul, an old widow who might have seen in him her lost beloved, gave him three one-dollar bills. He had a package of chocolate cookies that tasted like cocoa dirt, a Payday bar, and two cups of scalded coffee that made his eyes roll over in a wince. When morning came, he found out what room Robert had been given. When no one was looking, he shuffled into the elevator and rode to the fourth floor. Hospital workers rattled breakfast carts down the long hallway. The smell of eggs and bacon wafted through the air, causing his mouth to fill with water. Nothing ever bothered him as much as hunger—not the chill winter winds, not sheeting rain, not summer sun that baked him sweaty.

Robert was sedated when Sam came into the room. But at least he was alive. There was a big, thick bandage around his chest, but his color was good. Sam looked in the mirror over the bathroom sink and thought the wounded man's color was better than his own. But what the hell, that shouldn't have surprised him. He hadn't looked well in twenty years. He took a chair and drew it to the bed. And then he fell asleep.

"Who are you?"

Sam woke, blinking and licking his lips. Needed a drink. Needed it bad. "Wha?"

"I'm Sergeant January. Who are you, sir?"

"Uh, just a friend of this here young man. I was with him last night when that fancy professor fellow shot him."

"Do say."

"I do."

Robert's eyelids fluttered. He tried to sit and couldn't. He moaned.

"Robert Kline? I'm Sergeant January. Do you feel like talking to me this morning?"

Sam got to his feet and made himself as unnoticeable as possible during the interview. He fiddled with the maroon blinds at the window. When Robert mentioned anything that involved Sam, he turned, nodded his head, and said, "That's right. He's exactly right."

"Well, I have to tell you, Mr. Kline, that you're a very lucky man. We've been watching Professor Saller for months. He flies all over to deliver lectures on his specialty in history, but we've suspected for some time he was transporting drugs into and out of different cities. We didn't have enough to go for a search warrant, or we'd have caught him sooner."

"What about my wife? She's only known him a month. If you've been watching him, you know that. She didn't have anything to do with all this."

"We don't think she did. As a matter of fact, she's agreed to testify against him, and in return no charges will be brought against her."

Sam heard Robert sigh in relief. After the officer left, Sam moved over to the bed. He handed over the small black box of the tape recorder, pushing it gently next to the young man's arm on the sheet. "This here's yours, son. I was just keeping it safe, making sure you got it back."

Robert grinned, then grimaced and touched his chest gingerly with his fingertips. "Hurts. Listen, that was pretty nice of you to come to the hospital and bring this back to me. It wasn't really that important."

"I thought you might want to give that tape to the missus. Make it into a keepsake."

"Thanks. It was you who called the cops, wasn't it? I guess you saved my life. When they got me in here last night, they said I was losing a lot of blood."

Sam nodded shyly. "Just doin' my civic duty. Now I got to be going. Getting real thirsty."

"Hey. . ."

"Yeah?"

"I'll catch up with you at Betty's Bar sometime. Give you a proper reward."

"Cheap draft?"

"Whiskey. The best."

Old Sam smiled a toothless grin and reached into his soiled coat pocket for his stogie. "You got yerself a deal, son. You sure do."

Once he had stepped outside the room and closed the door, Old Sam waited a beat and listened. Presently he heard what sounded like Robert talking to himself, but he knew it was the tape, rewound and playing. He heard something about old sad movies, lost jobs, and Elvis Presley, and then he moved toward the elevator, but not before snagging a biscuit and a slab of ham to stick in it from a food cart that happened to be right in his way.

A body had to eat to keep up his strength. It was a long walk back to Heartbreak Avenue.

Midnight Pass

A "House-Sitting Detective" Story

ROBERT J. RANDISI

-1-

The only thing Truxton Lewis and his son-in-law ever agreed on was that he should go to Florida. . . .
As Tru Lewis unpacked his suitcase, his daughter's words echoed in his ears as she had spoken them in the living room of his house in Queens, New York, just days before.

"You're sixty-two years old, Dad!"

"Sixty-one."

"Sixty-one," she said, "sixty-two—what's the difference?"

He'd smiled at his thirty-five-year-old daughter and said, "When you're sixty-one you'll know the difference, sweetie."

"My point," Margaret Lewis Statman went on, gritting her teeth, "is that you're too old to go traipsing off into unknown territory—"

"You make it sound like I'm going gold panning in the Yukon, dear," Tru had said, cutting her off. "I'm going house sitting in Florida."

"You don't *know* anybody in Florida—"

"Sarasota, to be exact."

"My *point* is—"

"Or to be truly exact," he'd gone on, "Siesta Key."

At that she had turned to his son-in-law, the Jewish dentist, and asked, "Murray, help me out here."

To his everlasting credit, Murray Statman said, "I think it's a good idea, Maggie."

"What?"

"Since your mother died," Murray went on, "I've thought your father should get out of this house, and now—a year later—he is."

"Thank you, boychick," Tru Lewis—who was not Jewish—had said.

For the first time since they'd met, they'd agreed on something. . . .

Now Truxton Lewis, ten years removed from his job as a detective with the New York City Police Department and a widower for just over a year, was unpacking his suitcase in a two-bedroom condo on Siesta Key on Midnight Pass Road, the Key's main drag. He had put some ads in newspapers all over the country—well, papers from places he wanted to go—that said MATURE MALE IN 60s AVAILABLE FOR HOUSE-SITTING. NON-SMOKER, NO PETS, WIDOWER. Actually, he'd gone back and added the word "early" in front of the "60s" part. He'd been delighted to get a call from a realtor in Florida about a condo in Sarasota—on Siesta Key—that needed looking after for a couple of months, and he'd jumped at it.

He stopped in the middle of unpacking and walked to the sliding doors of the balcony off the living room. He unlocked them, slid one door open, and stepped outside. While there was a parking lot just below him, Midnight Pass went right by the condo, and he could see the water beyond it. The Gulf, he thought, although he wasn't all that sure. The sand was white and there was a lot of beach, only dotted with people rather than packed the way the New York beaches were. It was January, just after New Year's—off-season down here. He thought he could see a couple of women in bathing suits, but for the most part the people seemed to be wearing long pants and windbreakers.

He decided to put off his unpacking and take a walk down to the beach.

Tru Lewis did not own a pair of Bermuda shorts, white shoes, or a white belt. He was determined *not* to dress like an old man or a tourist. Oh, he knew he was old—sixty-one was old in any society—but he didn't *feel* old, so he refused to dress like some out-to-pasture golf duffer. He put on a pair of lightweight khaki pants, a light blue T-shirt, and a light brown windbreaker. The only concession he made to the fact that he was in Florida was a pair of black sandals—but not the kind where he had to have something between his toes. He hated that. He put a Yankees cap on his head to cover his full complement of white hair because it was breezy out, left the condo, and headed for the beach. He made sure he had the key to the front door before he locked it behind him. That reminded him that he still had his Brooklyn house key around his neck. He used to lock himself out of the house all the time when Virginia was alive, but he'd had to learn not to do that over the past year, because she was no longer there to let him in.

He started down the hall toward the elevator when the door of another condo opened and a woman stepped out.

"Oh!" she said, putting her hand to her chest. "You startled me."

"I'm sorry," he said, "I didn't mean to. I'm Truxton Lewis, your neighbor."

"My . . . neighbor?"

"Yes, I'm in . . . fourteen?"

She appeared puzzled for a moment, then brightened and said, "Oh, you're the house sitter?"

"That's right."

"I'm Evelyn Smith," she said, extending her hand. "Mr. . . . Lewis, did you say?"

He shook her hand and said, "Yes, Truxton Lewis."

"Truxton," she repeated, "that's an unusual name."

"Yes," he said, "it is. My friends call me Tru."

"Did you just arrive today . . . Tru?" she asked.

"Yes," he said, "I haven't even finished unpacking. I thought I'd go for a walk on the beach."

"Well," Evelyn said, "I was just going to run some errands, so I'll ride down in the elevator with you."

"I'm glad to have the company," he said.

As they rode down, Tru was totally unaware that his attractive, fiftyish neighbor was "checking him out." He'd have been pleased, though, to know that she was guessing his age at fifty-five or -six, a good half dozen years younger than he actually was. Widowed for only a year, though, after over forty years of marriage, he was still very much unaware that women of varying ages found him attractive.

As they left the building, Evelyn asked, "Will Mrs. Lewis be joining you down here?"

"No," he said, "I'm a widower."

Having gleaned the information she wanted on the first try, Evelyn said, "Well, enjoy your walk on the beach, Tru. I'll see you later."

"It was very nice meeting you."

He headed for the beach without a backward look, and Evelyn, noticing this, started to worry that she needed to get her hair done again.

He was surprised at how much space there was on the beach. He'd thought that an illusion from his fourth-floor balcony, but it was the same up close. It wasn't that there were no people on the beach, it's just that there was so much sand.

Most of the people were scattered about, seated on lounges or folding chairs. Others—more intrepid, since it was chilly—were down by the water. He was surprised and pleased to notice that there was not a large number of small children. He found that, at his age, he had little tolerance for small children—even his own grandchildren, if he was around them long enough. Oh, he loved them, but in small doses.

He noticed there were quite a few men and women of his age on the beach. Most of them were in couples, but he noticed one man who had made himself comfortable on a lounger, tugged his cap down over his eyes, and gone to sleep. He thought that when he found a lounge chair available later in the week he might try that himself, after he had seen some of Sarasota first.

He checked out the snack bar, getting himself a Diet Coke—he thought he detected the hint of a New York accent in the speech patterns of the guy working there—and then the gift shop, picking up some postcards to send home to friends and family. After about an hour, he left the beach and went back to the condo to finish unpacking.

-2-

Several hours later, Truxton was unpacked and had made himself a cup of tea. He carried the cup around the place with him, familiarizing himself with it. It was much too big for one person to live in, with a large kitchen and living room, a small dining room, and two bedrooms. There was also a small room off the front door that could have been a family room or a small office. At the moment there was a wicker chair and desk set in there.

He found the master bedroom and decided to do what snooping he could do without opening any drawers or doors. He ended up simply studying some framed photographs on the dresser top. There were only shots of the same two people, a man and a woman, apparently middle-aged. There were pictures of each of them alone and then some of them together. He decided that while they made a handsome couple, they looked decidedly happier in the photos where they were pictured alone.

He finished the tea and carried the empty cup into the kitchen. He rinsed it out immediately rather than set it down in the sink. That done, he went back into the living room and looked out the window at the beach. The sun was going down and the beach was empty, except for someone walking here and there. On the beach where he had been that afternoon, he noticed that someone was still in a lounge chair. He thought it might be the man he'd seen with his cap pulled down over his eyes. Could he have fallen asleep and remained asleep this long?

While walking around familiarizing himself with the condo, he had seen a pair of binoculars. Where had it been? Oh, yes, on a shelf—there they were. Good ones too. High-powered. He took them to the sliding doors with him, stepped out onto the balcony, and trained them on the beach. Sure enough, he recognized the cap and jacket the man on the lounge chair had been wearing. It was windy now, and a flap of the man's jacket was blowing in the breeze. Wouldn't that be enough to wake him up?

Briefly, he considered calling 911, but what if he was wrong? He'd be some old, retired cop with an overactive imagination. Certainly a wrong impression to make on his first day.

He shook his head and went back inside. Better to just forget about it and not go looking for trouble where it didn't exist.

He tried to watch the TV, surfing the seventy or so cable channels that serviced the area, but half an hour later he was back at the balcony door, and the man was still on the lounge chair. Blowing air out of his mouth, he donned his jacket, left the Yankees cap behind, and left the condo to walk across to the beach and have a look for himself.

When he reached the beach, there was no one on it but the man on the lounge chair. No one within a hundred yards in either direction. The snack bar and gift shop were closed, and it was getting dark and cooler. If nothing else, maybe he'd just wake the man and keep him from getting cold and damp, maybe sick.

He approached the still figure and spoke.

"Hello?"

Nothing.

"Excuse me?"

No reply.

"Damn it," he said, aloud, "you better be a sound sleeper."

But he knew better, even as he approached. He'd seen enough dead bodies in his twenty-seven years with the department to have a sense about them.

He stopped at the chair, reached out, and removed the cap from the man's head. His eyes were closed, but he still could have been asleep.

"Yeah, yeah," Tru Lewis said, aloud. He reached out and pressed two fingers to the man's neck, but he could not locate a pulse. It was then that he saw the blood, inside the jacket, on the man's chest.

Somehow, in the middle of a populated beach, he'd managed to get himself shot to death with no one the wiser.

-3-

Tru had to deal first with the sheriff's department before he could get to the city detectives. He told his story to a deputy, then to the sheriff, then to a sheriff's detective, then to the city cops, then finally to a couple of Sarasota detectives. He told them all the same thing. He was a retired New York City cop vacationing here, and he had stumbled upon a dead body on the beach.

It was pitch dark out, with very little light from a sliver of a moon. Most of the light came from the police cars, whose headlights were trained on the body. They were still waiting for a coroner's wagon to come for the body, which remained on the lounger as if the man were simply asleep.

Tru was sitting in the back of the Sarasota detectives' unmarked car. The back door opened and one of them, holding two containers of coffee, got in with him.

"We sent somebody for these," he said to Tru. "One with milk, one without. I can take it either way, so you get your choice."

"Black," Tru said and accepted the container. "Thank you."

"Sugar?"

"I don't use it."

"Yeah," the man said, "I shouldn't either," but he proceeded to put three packets into the cup before stirring it with a red plastic stirrer.

This was Detective Bradley, middle-aged, with an open, pleasant face. His partner, about ten years younger, was Detective Simms, dark, glowering, not friendly looking at all. Who played good cop and bad cop was never an issue, Tru bet.

"Mr. Lewis," Bradley said, "we appreciate you sticking this out with us."

"My fault we're all here," Tru said. "After all, I found him."

"Excuse me, but it's the killer's fault we're here," Bradley said, "not yours."

"Good way to look at it, Detective."

Bradley studied Tru for a few moments in the light from the dome lamp and then said, "You were a boss, weren't you?"

Tru hesitated, then said, "I retired a captain of detectives."

"I knew it," Bradley said. "The way you talk to us, and hold yourself—"

"I mean no offense, Detective—" Tru said, hurriedly.

"No, no," Bradley said, "none taken. I'm just pleased with myself that I picked it up, is all."

"I see."

"Would you mind, Captain, telling me again how you figured out this man was dead?"

"I saw the blood—"

"I mean," Bradley said, cutting him off, "from your balcony."

Tru tried to be patient. After all, he'd been through this himself, asking the same questions over and over again during an investigation. However, he was finally getting to experience how it felt from the other end.

He explained again about arriving that day, interrupting his unpacking to walk on the beach, where he first noticed the man. Then explained about going back to the condo and spotting the man again from his balcony.

"It made me curious, is all," he said. "How somebody could just sit that way for so long."

"Did it occur to you he might just be asleep?"

"It did," he said. "His jacket was flapping in the wind, though. I thought that should have woken him."

"And how did you notice that?"

"With binoculars."

"Oh, right. Go ahead, please."

"After I used the binoculars and determined it was the same man, I decided to walk down here and check it out."

"Why not just call nine one one?"

"That would have been embarrassing if I was wrong," Tru said. "I didn't want to be the old geezer who jumped to conclusions."

"Not so old," Bradley said. "When did you retire?"

"Ten years ago."

Bradley looked surprised.

"After how many years?"

"Twenty-seven."

"If you don't mind me asking," Bradley said, "how old are you? I mean, you don't look old enough to have been in that long and retired that long."

"I'm sixty-one."

"God bless you," Bradley said. "I hope I look that good when I'm sixty-one."

Tru was aware he looked younger than he was but allowed himself to enjoy the comment nonetheless—heartfelt or not. He still didn't have a handle on Detective Bradley and didn't know if the man was buttering him up or not.

"Again, if you don't mind me asking," Bradley said, "you retired pretty young. . . ."

"Twenty-seven years seemed to be enough, Detective," he said, "and I wanted to spend some time with my wife, maybe travel a little."

"Did you travel?"

"As it happens, no," Tru said. "My wife's health began to fail. She wasn't up to travelling."

"And is she with you?"

"She died a little over a year ago, after a somewhat long and debilitating illness."

"Oh, I'm sorry. . . ."

"We never did get to travel," he repeated, "so I thought I'd do it myself."

"Which condos did you say you were in?"

"The place is called Key Waves."

"Expensive for a retired cop."

"I don't own it, Detective," Tru said, "I'm house-sitting."

"For free?"

"Actually," Tru said, "I'm paying something, but much less than it would normally rent out for."

"That's some deal," Bradley said. "How do you get a deal like that?"

"You advertise—"

The front passenger door was opened abruptly, and Bradley's partner stuck his head in.

"Coroner's here."

"About time," Bradley said. He looked at Tru. "You might actually get to go home tonight, Captain."

"Captain?" Detective Simms repeated.

Bradley opened the door on his side. "I'll explain later," he said, getting out.

-4-

They finally let Tru Lewis go home, with the understanding that they would come to the condo the next day to take a statement from him.

"I can come to your precinct—or whatever you call it down here—to do that," Tru had said.

"No, no," Bradley had said, "we'll come to you. Just call it professional courtesy."

"Well . . . ," Tru had said, ". . . I appreciate that. . . ."

"Besides," Simms chimed in, "we want to get a look at this balcony of yours."

So much for professional courtesy. . . .

They arrived the next morning after breakfast. Tru had a fresh pot of coffee going and offered them both some. They accepted, and all three carried cups out onto the balcony.

"Where are those binoculars you told us about?" Bradley asked.

"I'll get them."

Tru stepped back inside long enough to grab them, brought them out, and handed them to Bradley.

"Whoa!" he said when he held them to his eyes. "Is this how they were set when you used them?"

"Yes."

Bradley handed them to his partner.

"You can see every grain of sand," he said.

Simms nodded and held them to his eyes.

"You could only have seen the man's back, though," he said.

"And the part of his jacket that was flapping in the wind."

Simms turned and looked at him.

"And that was enough to tell you he was dead?"

"That was enough," Tru said, "to make me curious about why he was still out there."

"Let's go back inside," Bradley said.

They did, and Tru closed the door behind them.

"Don't do that," he said. He'd caught Simms starting to put his cup down on the expensive-looking coffee table in front of the sofa. "I don't live here. I'm just house-sitting."

"I'm finished with it," Simms said.

"Would you like some more?"

"No, thanks."

"Give it to me. I'll take it into the kitchen."

Simms handed Tru the cup.

"And you?"

"I don't drink mine as fast as my partner drinks his," Bradley said. "Thanks."

Tru took the empty cup and put it in the sink. He poured himself some more and went back to the living room. Bradley was sitting on the sofa. He noticed the detective was using a magazine as a coaster. Simms was sitting in one of the easy chairs. Tru sat in the other one.

"Captain, I told my partner your background," Bradley said. "I'm afraid he's not impressed."

"I don't like ex-cops who go private," Simms said frankly.

"Were you under the impression that I was a private eye or something?" Tru asked. "I'm here on vacation."

"And you found a body," Simms said.

"By accident."

"From up here."

"What are you implying, Detective Simms?" Tru asked. "That I arrived yesterday and decided to go down to the beach and kill a man?"

"Of course he's not implying that," Bradley said. "He's just being an asshole. Isn't that right, Hal?"

"Yeah," Simms said, "I'm bein' an asshole."

"Why don't you go down to the beach and talk to some people? The snack bar and gift shop should be open by now."

"I guess I'll do that," Simms said and left without another word to Tru.

"He's being an asshole," Bradley said. "He's like that."

Tru wasn't sure if they were trying to play good cop–bad cop with him or not.

"Tell me what you want, Detective Bradley," he said. "Without any games, just come out and ask me."

"I just want to know that you're telling us all there is to tell, Captain," Bradley said. "That's all."

"Everything I've told you is the truth."

"But have you told me everything?"

"Yes."

"I wrote down most of what you told me last night," Bradley said. "Enough to have it typed up." He took the typed statement from his pocket and handed it to Tru. "If it looks OK to you, you can sign it. If not, let me know."

Tru scanned the document and found it accurate.

"You either listen well or take good notes," he said, signing it and handing it back.

"A little of both, I think."

He put the statement away and then sat looking at Tru.

"Were you a good detective, Captain?"

Tru smiled.

"I'll bet you checked already."

Bradley smiled sheepishly, caught.

"You're right. I called New York and spoke to your chief of detectives. He said he'd take you back on the job right now if you'd go."

"That's nice of him."

"Said you were the best detective he ever saw."

"That's generous of him."

"Let me ask you this, Captain," Bradley said. "How does someone walk up to a man sitting on a lounge on a crowded beach, shoot him, and then get away without anyone hearing or seeing anything?"

"He doesn't," Tru said. "Can't be done."

"What about a gun with a silencer?"

"If he came from the water, he'd have to swim to shore from somewhere—a boat. Maybe he'd have to wear a wetsuit to swim that far. He'd have to keep the gun dry. After all that, he'd have to be able to shoot the man with no one noticing. Same thing with somebody just walking along the beach. They'd still have to stop by him and shoot him. I don't think it can be done. It's off-season and the beach is not that crowded. Somebody would have to have seen something."

"Well," Bradley said, standing up, "that's what my partner and I are going to try and find out today. Thanks for your time, Captain."

"Anything I can do to help."

Tru walked Bradley to the door.

"Did you identify the man?" he asked at the door.

"Yes," Bradley said. "His name was Philip Williams. He was retired, living in a condo across the bridge."

"What business was he in?"

"He was a stockbroker from New York."

Maybe that explained why the two detectives seemed so suspicious of him. He and the dead man were both from New York.

"The name ring a bell?"

"No," Tru said, "never heard of him. Did he have a wife?"

"A wife, and a mistress," Bradley said. "We're looking at both of them. One or both may have a boyfriend."

"I wish you luck."

"We've got to find out who did it in order to find out how," Bradley said. "That's what's driving me nuts. How?"

Tru let the detective out, then retrieved the detective's cup from the living room and put it in the sink. Again, he freshened his own cup, then took it out to the balcony with the binoculars.

He watched the two detectives for a while as they questioned people on the beach. No doubt they'd find some folks who had been there the day before and who'd be there again tomorrow. Regulars who might have noticed something out of the ordinary.

He went back out onto the balcony on and off over the next few hours. The detectives were gone when the sun started to set, and as the huge orange ball was slowly swallowed by the water, he watched the snack bar guy close up. Apparently, the gift shop had closed already. Except for the cars belonging to some couples who wanted to watch the sunset, the snack bar guy's car was the last one in the lot. Slowly, the couples drifted away as the sun disappeared, and then finally the guy come out of the snack bar, locked it, and walked to his car. After that the beach was empty. Anyone could have come and gone as they pleased. . . .

Anyone.

-5-

Under normal circumstances, Truxton Lewis was an early riser. On this morning, however, he was up before the sun, sitting on the balcony with a jacket on, the binoculars in his hands. As it started to get light, a car pulled into the parking lot of the public beach where he'd found the body. He trained the binoculars on the car and watched as the man who worked in the snack bar—and who probably owned it—got out. First to arrive in the morning, last to leave at night. . . .

He went inside and made a phone call. . . .

Later that day the doorbell rang. When he opened it, Detective Bradley was standing there.

"Where's your partner?"

"He didn't want to have to come here and tell you that you were right," Bradley said. "Can I come in?"

"Sure."

Tru closed the door and followed the detective into the living room.

"Maybe we should talk about this on the balcony," Bradley said. "Probably fitting."

They stepped out onto the balcony together. Tru didn't have the binoculars, but he could tell from where they were that the snack bar had closed early.

"You were right, Captain," Bradley said. "The owner of the snack bar is one Andrew Cranston. He's owned and operated it alone down here for about sixteen years. Everybody on that beach knows him as Andy."

Tru waited for the rest.

"Old Andy lived and worked in New York twenty years ago," Bradley went on. "You spotted what little was left of his New York accent. You've got a good ear."

"Thanks."

"When we approached him," Bradley said, "he denied it at first, but the more we pushed, the weaker his denial became until he finally spilled it."

"What's his story?"

"He and the dead man were partners on Wall Street years ago. They got into some trouble with the SEC—insider trading, I think. The dead man, Philip Williams, saved himself by rolling over on his partner. Cranston served two years in a country club, came out and spent two more years as an alcoholic. After he dried out, he came down here and he's been here ever since. The other day, who should walk up to his snack bar but his old partner. Retired and moved down here. Some coincidence, huh?"

"Lots of people retire and move down here," Tru said. "Lots of people come here from New York."

"Yeah, maybe," Bradley said, "but I still say it's a big coincidence."

"So how did he arrange to kill him?"

"Williams recognized him, greeted him like an old friend. And you know what? Cranston went along with it right away. He claims he had never had a thought of revenge in twenty years, but as soon as Philip Williams came up to his counter, he knew he was going to kill him. He went along with the old-friend act, eventually lured him down here early one morning and did what you said."

"He shot him," Tru said, "dragged him out to a lounger before anyone came to the beach, and left him there, looking like he was asleep."

"Right. Nobody noticed him all day. You called it, Captain. How did you do that? From up here with binoculars?"

"I didn't call it," Tru said. "I just happened to notice that he was the first to arrive and the last to leave, and I caught a hint of a New York accent. Also, I remembered that while Williams had been shot in the chest, there was no hole in his jacket. That meant that someone had shot him while the jacket was open, then zipped it to hide the wound from people on the beach. That was enough for me to call you and just suggest that you check his background."

"And we did," Bradley said, "but I don't know that we could have gotten him if he didn't confess."

"Well, you said he had no thought of revenge for twenty years," Tru said. "Maybe it was more than he could take."

"You might think that, except for one thing," Bradley said.

"What's that?" Tru asked.

"He left him out in the open, right on the beach where he owned the snack bar. You'd think he would have dumped him someplace out of the way, given his connection with the dead man."

"I was wondering about that myself," Tru said. "What possessed him to just lay him out there on the beach?"

"I asked him that," Bradley said. "You know what he said?"

"What?"

"He wanted to watch him out there all day, baking in the sun," the detective said. "He said he just wanted to enjoy it as long as he could before we found him."

"And you did."

"No," Bradley said, "you did, Captain. Another day in the sun and the body would have started to smell and bloat. We'd have had a panic on the beach on our hands."

Bradley put out his hand and Tru shook it.

"You've been here two days," Bradley said before he left. "Hate to see what's going to happen when you've been here two weeks."

Tahiti Junk Shop

LES STANDIFORD

I t's bad news, isn't it?"

Guerin didn't have to look up to see who was speaking. It was a favorite trick of Adele's, shadowing him down to the mail-boxes. He stood in a peeling little alcove off the shabby main lobby of their Hallandale building—a testament to the better intentions of another south Florida era. He studied the wall cracks that radiated out from the bank of brass boxes in the pattern of a giant spider web. In a moment, she'd deliver one of the incessant invitations to her apartment, for coffee, for cake, for a "little chat," as if they'd just happened to bump into one another.

He folded the letter and put it in the breast pocket of his coat, a smoking jacket he'd salvaged from the effects of his father decades ago. Adele watched him, practically gloating. Maybe she'd been reading over his shoulder.

"Investments," he said, affecting a philosophical tone. "One accepts the bad with the good." In truth, his heart had turned to lead.

"Sinking good money into a snow pea farm in the desert is not an investment," she said.

So she *had* been looking. He glanced about the tiny mailroom. Adele, no giant, nonetheless blocked his way to the door.

"You look a little gray," she said in a softened voice. "How about some chicken soup?"

"I have business," he said.

"There's always time to file bankruptcy," she sniffed. "Besides, I wanted to tell you. The Centurion Village representative is coming to talk today." She produced a colorful brochure from behind her back. He'd seen it before, littering the tables of the common rooms. It was full of pictures of oldsters biking, swimming, dancing, and shuffleboarding, cavorting in the Florida sun and enjoying the "golden years." Just looking at all the activity made him feel tired.

He took the brochure and pointed at the immense condominium building that was featured in almost every shot. "They ought to put some bars over all these windows," he told her. "Because none of these people will ever get out."

She snatched the brochure back. "That's ridiculous," she said. "This is a place where you could put what you've got left. It'll do you some good."

Guerin saw that her eyes were starting to water. He knew what she wanted. They should pledge all their assets, turn over everything to this coven of the dead and dying, and move in together. Wait hand in hand in a wallboard cave for the inevitable. He had to admit, they were clever, these Centurions. Just give up everything you have and they guarantee you peace of mind for as long as you live, and pray that it's not too long.

"That Centurion thing's a scam." It was a new voice echoing about the gloomy mailroom. Guerin and Adele spun around. A shambling man who might have been in his fifties—wearing a checked sport coat and white shoes and belt—had appeared in the doorway.

He indicated the brochure in Adele's hand. "You give 'em everything, including your Social Security, and sign a blanket power of attorney. They got you by the *cajones* for the rest of your life, which probably ain't too long given the quality of the food I hear they put out."

A white ring of fury had come to outline Adele's lips. "Who *are* you," she demanded. "How did you get in here?"

The man tipped an imaginary hat and smiled grandly. "Jack Squires, ma'am." He glanced at Guerin. "With Astral Investments." He broke off to consult a well-worn spiral notepad. "Came to see a Mister Gunderson who answered one of our ads: 'a little risk, a lotta return'. . . ."

"Oh, my God," Adele breathed.

Squires glanced up. "Something wrong?"

Guerin spoke up. "It's me," he said. "I'm Gunderson."

Squires grinned and snatched up Guerin's hand. "Imagine that," he said, pumping it vigorously. "Running into you right here."

"Not so strange," Guerin said, looking at Adele.

"Let go of his hand," Adele said.

"It took me a while to get back to you," Squires said, still pumping, "but now that I'm here, we're gonna roll."

"I'm calling the police," Adele said, making a tentative move for the door.

Guerin felt a warmth growing in the hand that Squires held. It was probably just the exercise. He couldn't remember a more vigorous handshake. Yet there seemed to be something more that coursed up his arm from Squires' big paw.

Guerin felt Adele's gaze burning upon him. "I'm a man of . . . some years," he said. "I need something solid."

Squires nodded, finally releasing his hand. "I couldn't agree more." He glanced at his notebook and shook his head. "Chinchillas, zoysia plantations, Mojave snow peas." He clucked his tongue in sympathy. "That's a tough run of luck."

"That's idiocy," Adele said.

"I need to be certain of my future. Take the down side into account for a change."

Squires nodded. "I know just what you mean. I've got a place for your cash."

"You don't give him a cent!" Adele's voice had risen to a shriek.

Squires put his hand on Guerin's shoulder. "Now, tell me. What kind of property is it you're most interested in? What is it you really want?"

Adele tried to jockey herself in front of Squires. "He wants some peace of mind. Not jackals trying to steal his money."

"Adele." Guerin tried to restrain her, but Squires was unfazed. He had not taken his eyes from Guerin.

"What is it that you really want, Mr. G?"

Guerin's eyes locked in on Squires'. He looked down the man's gaze until his head was swimming. He was on the staircase of their once-grand building, his legs limber, his flesh glowing, ascending the steps toward a glorious field of light. At every landing, well-wishers whooped and urged him on: 49ers with panning kits slung to their backs, men holding strange machines and hopeless patent applications, little girls in ballet dresses, a huge rabbit with a replica of a human foot hung around its neck for luck, thumping him with its paw . . .

Guerin pulled his glance away at last. Adele stared at him with concern. He nodded reassurance to her, then gathered himself to speak.

"Well, Mr. Jack, I'll tell you. Forty years I work, no union, no pension, but I put what I can aside, and I make investments . . ."

"*Investments?*" Adele cried.

". . . so that someday, I don't have to work for somebody anymore, and maybe, if things work out, I could retire," he looked sheepish, "in Tahiti, I think." He cleared his throat then and his face fell. "But, things, they don't work out so well." He threw up his hands.

Adele seemed relieved. She turned to Squires, vindicated.

"If you'll pardon us." Adele took Guerin's arm.

Guerin held back, looking at Squires in appeal. "So, to answer your question, if I had just one more chance to make it happen, I'd want a little carryout market, maybe. Nothing fancy, but on a good corner. Enough business so in a year or two, I sell out and go to Tahiti, unless you know someplace better."

Adele turned, astonished. Guerin avoided her and shrugged at Squires, who had, after all, asked.

Squires did not hesitate. "I can do it for you."

"Throw this crook out," Adele wailed.

"I don't need your money, Mr. G. This is one man of vision to another." Squires bent to jot a note on a slip of his pad. He stood and stuffed it into Guerin's pocket. "I'll be at this address at four. You think about it."

He slipped his pad into his pocket, nodded a good-bye to Adele, and clapped Guerin on the shoulder as he left. "You got a spirit I like."

Guerin pulled out the paper and took a look at the address. Adele stared up at him, anxious. Finally, Guerin turned to her.

"An honest face he had, don't you think?"

"Oh, my God," she wailed as she ran out the door. "Oh, my God."

As he moved further and further inland from his building and far from anyplace he knew, Guerin reassured himself that finding opportunity was, for one in his position, a matter of trusting one's intuitions over what others might call logic. There was the known path, and the other path. And he was destined to be an adventurer.

He was passing now through an area of ramshackle shops, including a laundry so filthy he wondered how anything could be cleaned there, then a liquor store with a row of swarthy men hunkered in a row beneath its front window. The proprietor stood near the barred doorway with a pistol in his hand and glared at Guerin as he passed.

In the next block, all the shops seemed closed, except for a balloon and message service from whose entry issued a blare of music he could not begin to identify. Outside, a van with gay balloons stenciled on its side sagged at the curb, its two right tires gone flat. Guerin peeked inside the shop and saw a young man with the made-up face of a woman standing bare-chested behind a counter. He was staring into a mirror and was sawing intently at his front teeth with a heavy file. Guerin staggered back into the street and hurried on, thinking that there were perhaps limits to adventure.

Soon he had passed into a district of warehouses and storage yards interspersed with vacant lots. It was there that he heard the first sound behind him. He spun about to check, but there was nothing but empty street to be seen. He paused, then forced himself onward. When he heard the sound again, he did not turn but walked more quickly to a corner ahead and ducked around the edge of a shuttered moving and storage building to wait.

As the footsteps neared, he thought of various assaults upon the unwary he might copy from his nights of television viewing, but then he thought of his dry and brittle bones snapping as he struck, and there was nothing to do but wait.

Shortly, his pursuer was upon him. He took a deep breath, stepped forward boldly . . . and caused Adele to shout her violent surprise into the calm of the deserted street.

They stood staring at each other for a moment, searching for words, two people met accidentally in hell. Finally, Adele surveyed their surroundings and sniffed, "This is not a neighborhood for decent people."

While Guerin considered what to say, a bag man pushing a grocery cart laden down with things that looked furry and once-alive jostled past them. Adele fell toward Guerin with a yelp. Shaken himself, he offered her his arm, and they hurried on.

The shadows had begun to lengthen when they reached the last possible block, another assemblage of broken buildings on a street that died against the high wall of an abandoned factory. At the corner, Guerin checked the address once more and shook his head. They stood in front of a grimy storefront where a sign dangled from a single bolt: ROGOVIN'S TRASH AND TREASURES, it read, rocking slightly in a breeze that skirted dust and yellowed newsprint pages at their feet. A wino snoozed in the shop's entryway.

Guerin turned glumly to Adele. "Let's go home," she said quietly and tugged at his arm.

Behind them came the tap of a car horn. They turned as a black limousine, its windows heavily smoked, purred up to the curb and Jack Squires danced nimbly out from the rear.

"You folks made the right decision," he said, extending his hand to Guerin. Adele huffed. Guerin studied the impressive car for a moment, then turned back to the junk shop, where the wino stirred, annoyed at this interruption of his nap.

"I thought we were talking a market," Guerin said.

Squires threw up his hands. "I'll be honest with you, Mr. G. The only market I had in your price range was in a bad neighborhood."

Ignoring Adele's gasp, Squires took Guerin by the arm and steered him toward the entrance of the shop, shooing the wino off with a wave of his hand.

"Market, *schmarket*. . . ." Squires said.

He unlocked the door and led the way into the place, flipping on a light switch. He turned, radiant with anticipation as Guerin and Adele followed him in, blinking in the dim light.

"*This*, Mr. G," he said, sweeping his arm about, "is the answer to your dreams."

Guerin stared. Instead of the vacant shop he expected, he found before him a rabbit warren of aisles toppling toward one another, jammed with junk store flotsam and jetsam. Here was a pile of Army helmets, there a stack of 78 records. One aisle was a tunnel through thick walls of magazines and newspapers. Nearby lay an ancient Coca-Cola tray atop a tumult of faded clothing. Adele glanced about distastefully, running her finger through a thick layer of dust on the front counter.

Guerin found himself drawn into the dim recesses of the shop, past banks of battered toasters, mixers, and blenders, beyond shelves full of cracked and mismatched china. At a twist in an aisle that seemed to dive off the face of the earth, he stumbled over a cobbler's anvil and found himself face to face with an Indian in war paint and headdress, a tomahawk raised to brain him. Guerin staggered backward, and a hand fell upon his shoulder.

"You're a very lucky man," Squires said. "The place has been tied up in probate for months. You get first crack."

Guerin stared, recovering from his fright. "But the price. Surely the three thousand I have is not sufficient."

Squires waved his concern away. "The old boy who ran the place croaked a while ago, and his heirs are back east. They don't know junk. I told 'em it'll cost two grand just to haul the stuff away, and they begged me, 'Sell. Sell the junk!'"

He patted the wooden Indian on the cheek and took Guerin back toward the front. "So you get all this," he continued, "and ten more years on the original lease.'"

They emerged into the light where Adele waited impatiently by the door. Squires ran his hand over an old brass cash register as he moved behind the counter to sweep aside a curtain there. He pointed in at a small room, where the corner of a single bed was visible. "There's even a living quarters here in the back."

Adele's mouth fell open. "What? Live in this rat's nest?" She hurried to Guerin's side. "You don't know what's going to crawl out of there in the night . . . and who's going to cook for you?"

Guerin patted her hand, then moved forward to peer into the tiny room which contained, besides the bed, a kitchenette, a small table, and a battered easy chair with a reading lamp beside it. He stepped inside and turned a knob on the stove. A jet of blue flame leaped up from a burner. He tried the sink faucet, and a stream of clear water gushed out. He turned to face Adele and Squires.

"This is a come-back neighborhood," Squires said. "It's a steal for a man of vision."

Guerin found himself nodding. "I used to have vision," he said softly.

"Guerin!" Adele cried.

Squires nodded, waving his note pad. "I know, Mr. G. We checked you out."

"This place has a nice feeling," Guerin said, warming.

"It's where you belong," Squires said.

Guerin nodded thoughtfully. "A market probably *is* a great deal of trouble."

Adele's eyes had begun to glaze. "He's lost his mind," she wailed.

"I took your best interest to heart," Squires said, stepping forward, his hand outstretched.

Guerin hesitated. His gaze went upward, to a shelf where a dusty candelabra stood, its cups cast in the shape of cherubs, which seemed to dance in the glint of the stove's blue flame.

"I'll take it," he said, and felt Squires' large hand envelop his. Adele stood weeping in the doorway.

Guerin stood outside his shop in the balmy air of a fine spring morning, nodding approval as the sign painter he had engaged leaned from his ladder for one last stroke. TAHITI JUNK SHOP, it read, with Guerin's name in script just to the side and the replica of a tiny island with a palm tree added for a logo.

Guerin motioned the man down and handed him some bills, then went back inside his shop. Caruso opera issued scratchily from an ancient Victrola placed beside the front counter. Behind the counter he had hung a thermometer-like sales chart with the legend "$10,000—Off for the Islands" scrawled at the top. He smiled and moved to lift the needle as the music stopped.

Behind him the doorbell of the shop tinkled, and he turned to greet his first customer . . . only to find Adele advancing upon him, her face gray and sunken.

"Adele," he said hopefully. "You've come for a little shopping."

She patted at her cheeks with a handkerchief. "I came to talk sense to you. Did you sign anything yet? Tell me it's not too late."

Though he felt impatience, her despair was disarming. He took her hand reassuringly. "Adele, a little less gloom, if you please. I am a *proprietor* now."

A thump sounded at the front window then, and they turned to see the wino glowering in at them. Adele banged her purse against the glass, and the man slunk away. She turned back.

"Wonderful. A room full of junk, in the middle of hell. That's what you've got."

Guerin took a deep breath, determined not to argue. While he understood the necessity of risk, he could not expect Adele to sympathize. He took her arm and drew her down the aisle.

"Let me show you something," he said, taking her around a dark turn and snapping on a light. They were now in a room larger than the first and even more crowded with aged merchandise.

"Look," he said, waving his arms. "Anything you want, you could find it here."

She stared about at piles of old coats, at paintings in bad colors in splintered frames, at shaky stacks of ancient saucers, and her lower lip began to quiver. "What are you talking about? These are things people threw out because they *didn't* want them."

She stared plaintively at him, but his attention had been drawn by a sled with wooden runners that leaned against the nearest wall. He shook his head—he had not noticed it before. Adele came to pull him back down the aisle.

"Listen, I had my nephew Myron, the attorney, do some checking. He found out the previous owner, God rest his soul, just disappeared last year without a trace."

Guerin looked over his shoulder toward the sled. "Maybe he had something better to do," he said, turning to her with a smile. "A trip to the islands maybe."

She huffed on toward the front, unamused. Guerin stopped to stare down at a wooden chest, another thing he had missed in all the clutter. A satin gown, glittering with sequins, trailed out of the partly opened lid. He found himself wondering if Adele had ever worn such a thing. Then she was back, pulling him impatiently along.

"I see these bums around here with their fires going and their cooking in the vacant lots. They probably took his money and his clothes and then they *ate* him."

At the counter, she turned to face him. She took a deep breath, her gaze faltering for a moment. "Guerin, come away from here. I want you to come with me to the Centurion place Myron found. I can cook for you. I'll take care of you. I have enough money for both of us."

She glanced away as she finished, and Guerin felt something knot in his throat. After a moment, he moved forward and took her shoulders gently.

"Adele, please. Try to understand. All my life I work for somebody else and try to get ahead and it never works out. Now I got this place that is mine. A market it isn't, but it's OK." He broke off and managed his broadest smile. "And God willing, I'll save my money, and someday I'll go off to Tahiti."

She opened her mouth to protest, but he held up his hand to stop her. "It's a nice dream, Adele, and I don't want you should give me such a hard time about it, OK?"

She stared at him, her face falling into inestimable sadness. "I knew you wouldn't listen," she said. "Oh, it's so awful to get old." Her eyes had begun to fill, and she turned quickly for the door. When he tried to follow, she pushed him away.

"Stay here, then. Stay with your junk."

The door slammed behind her, and Guerin stood staring uncertainly after her. Finally, he moved back behind the counter and sank glumly into the easy chair he had dragged out for better light, staring up at his bulletin board and his thermometer for success. He picked up an edition of Gauguin prints he'd found in the stacks and began to flip listlessly through the pages.

Shortly, his hands lay atop his favorite of the painter's illustrations, innocent natives awaiting a ship's arrival on their unspoiled beach. In this version, however, it was Guerin himself who stood at the prow of the vessel that was bound for the island port, the salt spray cool in his face and his eyes fixed upon a lovely maiden tying up her hair at the shore. Though it seemed impossible, and she was certainly younger and more carefree here, it was unmistakably Adele in the colorful sarong who awaited him. Even more astonishing than that was the happiness he felt as the ship moved inexorably toward the shore.

The doorbell of the shop sounded then, interrupting the snores of dreaming Guerin. He started awake, the book slipping to the floor, his gloom swooping back upon him as he stood to assume the role of proprietor.

It was a blonde woman wearing large-lensed sunglasses who came through the door, urging along her husband, a balding man in walking shorts and golf shirt, sporting around his neck a gold chain the thickness of Guerin's little finger.

"Oh, we're soooo glad to see you're open again, Mr. Rogovin. We just love your place," she cooed, already heading for the stacks.

The woman's husband came to clap him heartily on the shoulder. "Been out buying, have you? You must have scads of new things." He gave Guerin a wink and dove into the aisles after his wife, who had already begun squealing at some find.

As Guerin stared into the depths of the shop in befuddlement, there came the sounds of something heavy being dragged across the planked floor toward the front of the shop. Finally, the couple emerged, wrestling with a fortune-telling booth from a carnival arcade. The thing, the size of a phone booth, held a dummy gypsy wobbling over a cloudy crystal ball. Guerin clutched hold of the counter for support.

The wife motioned her husband forward with an unspoken command. The man affected unconcern as he approached Guerin. "Say, we've found something we *might* be interested in."

Guerin shook his head in wonder. "I've never seen that before. . . ."

The man turned to his wife, who frowned and lifted her chin in a commanding motion.

"So, we'd be willing to go . . . say, a hundred and a half."

"Charles!" his wife whispered. Charles shrugged.

"I meant to say two hundred."

"Two hundred dollars?" Guerin repeated, dumbfounded.

The woman drew her husband aside. "I *want* it," she hissed. Charles turned back to Guerin and slapped some bills into his palm. "Look, we'll go four hundred dollars and not a penny more."

Guerin stared at the hundred-dollar bills in his hand, wondering if he was still dreaming. The woman motioned to her husband, and they began wrestling the thing toward the door. "We just love it," she smiled, with a sidelong hateful glance at Charles. "You'd have to shoot us to stop us now."

"Shoot?" Guerin repeated. "Four hundred dollars?"

"Ciao!" she said, heaving the booth on out the door toward her husband.

He followed the pair outside and watched as they lifted the booth into the back of a Cadillac converted to a short-bed pickup, then returned the couple's wave as they sped off into the evening shadows.

He checked his watch and walked back into the shop, turning the window sign over and shooting the door bolt home. Through the glass he thought he saw the wino watching him from a storefront opposite, but when he blinked to clear his eyes, the vision was gone. He went quickly to the counter, certain that the cash too would have vanished, but it was still there, four crisp bills that marked the first notch upon his sales thermometer.

That night, though he did not dream, he awoke once with a start, certain he'd heard the sounds of thunderous surf about to crash down upon him. When he leaped from his small bed to investigate, he found that one of the paddle fans was rustling a grass skirt atop one of the stacks of papers. Guerin moved the skirt, then staggered back to bed and lay for hours, unable to sleep.

At eight the next morning, an insistent knocking roused him. He swung out of bed and drew on a satin dressing gown he'd scavenged from the stacks—it seemed like something his father would have fancied. If it *were* Adele come to pester him again, he'd offer her a gift, a gesture of peace, perhaps the sequined dress from the wooden chest.

When he opened up, he found instead two youths in ragged tennis shoes and jeans staring up at him warily. The taller youth stepped forward.

"We been looking for a basketball," he said, peering over Guerin's shoulder.

Guerin hesitated, doubtfully following the boy's glance. The shorter boy tried to pull his partner away. "I told you this ain't no place for a basketball."

The tall one restrained him and looked impatiently at Guerin. "Well, you got a basketball?"

"I don't think so." Guerin said, stepping back. "But you're welcome to look."

The tall boy nodded and started inside, pulling his reluctant partner along toward the stacks. Guerin rubbed his face and stared out into the brilliant morning. He was about to step out for a breath of air when he heard the unmistakable *thump, thump, thump* of a ball being dribbled along the wooden floor behind him.

They had found the ball atop a wooden chest, they said, and professed no knowledge of a big man named Squires who wore white shoes and rode in a limousine: "A *limo* in this neighborhood, man?"

Though they offered fifty cents, Guerin would take only a quarter. He watched the two leave, passing the battered basketball back and forth on the pavement, then turned back into the shop.

As he entered, he heard once more the unmistakable sounds of crashing surf. He hesitated, then drew his robe tightly around him and moved steadfastly into the shadows.

When he reached the wooden chest where Adele's dress had been, he froze. On the floor nearby lay a child's beach pail and shovel, and next to those, a battered beach chair with sailcloth seat and wooden frame. The sounds of the surf had died away. Uncertain, he extended his hand toward the chest. The lid was locked, or swelled shut, and the sequined dress was nowhere in sight. He grasped one of the heavy brass handles on the chest to pull it toward the front, but the thing would not budge. He straightened and looked warily about the darkened aisles. "Mr. Jack . . . ?" he called, but there was no answer. And then the doorbell began to ring in earnest.

It was nearly closing time when Adele did show up, her nephew Myron in tow. The pair had to stand aside at the doorway to let a stream of customers past. One man carried a huge moose head over his shoulder, followed by a couple toting an intricately molded brass bed. Next came a cigar-chewing man carrying a barber's pole, then a stylishly dressed couple pushing a jukebox out atop a dolly. The man winked at Adele, patting the jukebox with one hand: "Everything Ella ever did is right in here."

Guerin waved at Adele and Myron from his place in the canvas beach chair. He'd found an old-fashioned, knee-length bathing suit with a striped top and was basking in the glow of a battered sun lamp.

"I thought you said the place was belly up," Myron said. Adele bit her lip and turned upon Guerin.

"So this is how you wait on customers?"

Guerin rose amiably from his chair and snapped off the light. "I had an inspiration." He gestured at his trunks. "Goes with the name of the shop, don't you think?"

Myron nodded. "Business is looking up, I take it."

"Plenty of traffic. But I don't drive a very hard bargain, I'm afraid." Guerin swept his arm toward the dark aisles. "Have a look around. Maybe there's something you need."

Adele stepped impatiently between them. "Myron has come here to help you. He can get your money back."

Guerin looked at her in disbelief. Myron cleared his throat. "I put together a group looking for a public housing site; now I find out this whole block's available. You sign over your lease, I'll get you three thousand up front. Once the buildings go up, you get an override. In the long run you could clear some real coin."

"Clear some coin?" Guerin repeated. He gave Adele an exasperated look, then turned back to Myron. "I'm sorry you went to this trouble, Mr. . . ."

"Myron's fine."

Guerin nodded. "Well, Myron, do I look to you like a man concerned with the long run?"

Myron smiled tolerantly. "I heard you were tough. Tell you what. Being as you are a friend of the family, so to speak, I think we could go five thousand up front."

Guerin felt very tired. "I'm sorry. I don't want to sell."

Myron shot an inquiring glance at Adele, who silently urged him on. "Uh, yes," Myron continued, looking at the toe of one soft, leather loafer. "Well, my people have authorized me to offer ten thousand dollars."

Guerin took Adele by the arm and began to guide her sadly toward the door. "Take your nephew and go home," he said.

She stared at him, speechless.

"This is a rare opportunity," Myron protested.

"Take him home, Adele." Guerin ushered her out the door.

Myron hesitated at the threshold. "I don't get it. You could go to Tahiti the long way for ten thou."

Guerin stared at him steadily. Finally, Myron's gaze faltered. Guerin put a hand on his shoulder. "Come back someday on your own. We have nice things here." He smiled and closed the door.

It was dark and he was finishing a can of soup at his tiny kitchen table when he heard the tapping at the outer door.

"Please. I'm afraid out here." Adele's voice was muffled by the glass, but her fear kept its edge. He sighed and opened up.

"I thought you'd take the money," she said, sinking with exhaustion into the canvas beach chair.

Guerin turned over the beach pail and sat down stiffly on it. "You shouldn't have come here this late by yourself."

"You could have gone to Tahiti, if that's what you wanted." She shook her head sadly.

Guerin reached for her hand. "That was a very generous thing you did, Adele. A very kind and noble thing."

She looked at him tearfully. "Did you know it was my money Myron was talking about? Is that why you wouldn't take it?"

He shook his head. "Maybe I don't want to go anywhere after all."

She gave him an uncertain glance.

"You see, I am making some people very happy with the 'junk' they find here."

"But what about Tahiti?" Hope had entered her voice.

He paused, his gaze faltering for a moment. Finally, he rose and walked to the bulletin board. He turned to Adele with a wan smile and reached to take down the sales thermometer. Quickly, he tore it in half and dropped it into a trash bin.

"Tahiti was a dream, Adele. A dream like you need to get you through the days when other things are not the way you want them." He drifted off for a moment but caught himself and turned back to her, gesturing. "I'm very lucky to have found this place. I'm becoming important to my neighborhood."

She stared back at him, dumbfounded. "You really do want to stay here, don't you? I'd rather have you go off to that idiot island." She fumbled in her purse for a handkerchief and began to dab at her eyes.

Guerin came to take her by the shoulders. She stared up at him, uncertain. "Tell me, Adele, are you happy?"

She swallowed, drawing back from his touch. "Happy? I'm as happy as you can be at my age."

"And what does that mean?"

Her mouth drew grim. "It means that I'm old, and I'm going to die soon, and nobody is going to give a damn, that's what it means." She tried to meet his gaze defiantly but turned away suddenly. Her shoulders began to heave, and then she was sobbing.

Guerin stared down, gauging the depth of her despair. He put his hand on her shoulder. "It's that bad for you, isn't it?"

She nodded as she blew her nose into her hanky, and Guerin sat down beside her, brushing his hand at her tears. "You know, Adele, if you'd just learn to dream a little, maybe you and I . . ."

She looked up as he faltered. "Maybe you and I what?"

He felt his impatience growing and sighed. "Nothing. You don't understand. If a man can't go out and make something decent, what does he have to offer?"

"Is that it?" Her voice rose. "You think you have to be rich to make me happy?"

She reached for his hand. He drew back. "It's not rich I'm talking about, it's something else, it's . . ."

As he struggled for the right words, the door swung open behind her, and the wino from the streets entered, his hand shakily outstretched, waving something in the dim light. Guerin stood. "Can I help you. . . ?" His voice trailed off as he caught sight of the pistol that the man held, at the wild glint in his bloodshot eyes.

"Hit the register, old man. You had a great day. Now it's my turn."

Adele did not hesitate. "You march right out of here. . . ." She rose, swinging at him with her purse. The man ducked, then backhanded her into the beach chair.

Guerin made a dive for the pistol. The man stumbled back, clubbing Guerin to his knees, and the gun went off with a tremendous roar.

A mounted hawk above the counter exploded in a flurry of feathers and stuffing. The man trained his pistol on Guerin. "I won't ask again."

"For God's sake, give him the money." Adele wiped at her bloody lip and scrambled for the cash box that lay near the deck chair.

The man's eyes glittered as he snatched the box from her frightened grasp. He riffled through the thin stack of bills, then turned upon Guerin with menace. "I saw what walked out of here today. Where's the rest of the cash?"

Guerin shook his head helplessly. "It's all I asked for," he said.

The man didn't bother to argue. He swung his aim to Adele. "It's your last chance, Pops. I'll blow her away in a heartbeat."

Adele whimpered. Guerin scanned the shop, searching for a weapon, a miracle, a policeman . . . and froze when he beheld it.

Not ten feet away, at the mouth of an aisle, sat the chest he had tried to drag forward earlier. He could swear he heard the faint sounds of pounding surf, and if he were not mistaken, the heavy box swayed slightly with the rhythm of the waves.

As Guerin pulled his gaze away, he found the man smiling slyly at him. "So open it up, old man."

Guerin shook his head in protest. "You don't understand. There's no money in there."

He broke off as the man snatched Adele roughly by the hair, holding the pistol to her face.

Guerin, growing dizzy, found himself at the top of an endless staircase, winded, beaten, facing a doorway that opened upon an empty room. All the former well-wishers stood below on a vast landing, breathless, waiting for his move. Inside the room, a figure stirred in a darkened corner—a woman, he saw, as she came toward him, her hand outstretched, her face a mask of anguish. "Adele?" he said. . .

. . . and stepped forward to the chest. The top swung easily open at his touch, and Guerin stared down in disbelief at stacks and stacks of cash that neatly stuffed the box.

The man gave him a murderous smile and pushed Adele roughly aside.

"You old sonofabitch," he said, amazed.

He plunged his hand toward a stack of bills, keeping his pistol trained on Guerin. "You found a fortune." He riffled through a thick packet of cash and shrugged. "Too bad for you."

And indeed, Guerin thought, it was too bad, but then what good thing had he ever had that hadn't been taken away?

The man trained the pistol on Adele, who stirred groggily on the floor.

"Just take the box," Guerin cried. "It has everything you want."

The man sneered. "Nice of you to offer," he said and cocked the pistol.

As the cylinders of the gun fell into place, Guerin beheld the instantaneous, sorry history of his hopeful life: withered fields of once-grand snow peas, zoysia sod farms that had started out strong but had found the wilt, sullen cages full of molting chinchilla with no interest whatever in sex, a panorama of exotic failure, of promise gone wrong, capped by this last swell joke, a shop full of magic that would lead him to his death. And not, incidentally, lacking company for the trip.

He stole a glance at devastated Adele, felt his heart give, and, with nothing of his own to lose, took fate into his own hands for once. He ducked under the swiveling aim of the thief and drove him backward into the chest. The man's legs folded up as his knees caught the edge of the box, and he pitched over backward into the maw full of cash.

A great cloud of dust billowed up from the chest, driving Guerin away. The thief coughed wildly inside the pall and wilder still as the dust grew thicker, obliterating him finally from sight.

"What? Hey . . . HEY!" The disembodied screams lingered for a moment, and then there was a thud as the pistol fell to the floor and skittered to Guerin's feet, followed by another thump, which was the lid of the chest slamming down.

As quickly as it had sprung up, the cloud of dust drifted off, and Guerin and Adele were left to stare wonderingly at each other in a silent, vacant shop.

A muffled whining sound came from the chest, and Guerin edged cautiously toward it, the pistol wavering in his hand. Adele clutched his arm as he tried the lid. He gave her a look, then flipped the top all the way up. Inside, where a fortune had momentarily gathered and where there should have been a man, was now a skinny mongrel in an otherwise empty box. The thing cowered at their gaze, its tail curled through its legs in terror.

Still groggy, Adele stared down in surprise. "Why, the poor thing. How did he get in there? Do you suppose he scared that man away?"

Guerin stared into the depths of the shop. There were the far-off strains of Polynesian music sounding in his ears, but Adele seemed to hear none of it. "Something like that," he said. He ignored her perplexed stare to bend and pet the dog. The mutt whimpered and licked wildly at his hand.

"Do you think he's gone?" Adele peered anxiously into the dim recesses.

Guerin stared at the terrified animal. "Yes," he said finally, lifting the dog from the chest. "I'm sure of it."

She took his arm. "You saved my life," she began, and Guerin had started an embarrassed shuffling when there was a sudden crash of surf roaring at them out of the depths of the shop, and Adele screeched, clutching him in terror.

Guerin's mouth fell open as a wave of golden sunlight burst upon them, washing out of the aisle, and the glitter of light reflected from the water began to dance across their faces.

They stood transfixed as the shimmering landscape lay itself open before them, paradise where once aisles of stacked junk had lain.

Adele's lip trembled. "He shot us after all. This is how you die."

Guerin shook his head. "I don't think so. . . ." He stepped forward, feeling his foot sink into sand. He held his face up to the sun and felt the warmth soak his ancient cheeks. Though the brightness blinded him, he could sense that the beach stretched endlessly, and he could hear the rustle of the tall palms just above his head. He whistled, and the dog bounded in after him.

He smiled and turned back. "It's been here all this time, Adele."

He felt the old promise stirring within him, in the tang of the air that filled his lungs. And yet there was this one last, important thing, without which intuition and persistence and even dreams did not matter, without which he could not go forward. He held out his hand, which glowed with the beach's gleam.

"Come, Adele, don't be afraid," he said, warmed by the tropic sun. "Don't be afraid of your dreams."

She hesitated, glancing over her shoulder at the dark shop and the dark street that stretched beyond. She turned back. She met Guerin's hopeful eyes. Finally, she took his hand and stepped forward.

Outside the shop, Jack Squires stood, listening with satisfaction to the faint sounds of crashing surf and the shrieks and whoops and yaps of creatures frolicking somewhere on a happy beach.

He passed his hand before the entrance glass in greeting, perhaps, or was it bon voyage? CLOSED FOR VACATION read the sign that appeared there, just below the rendering of a little island and its palm tree that Guerin, in his perpetual hopefulness, had sketched beside his name.

Heart Throb

ROBERT W. WALKER

Police Headquarters, Daytona Beach, Florida

With her shadow falling across his desk, Detective Lieutenant Aaron Caul's black coffee grew darker before his eyes. His desk buttressed against his partner's, where the paperwork lay unruffled. By comparison, the paperwork Caul had been scanning lifted as if by a breeze. He wanted to analyze more closely the bloody Donald Simpson file. He wanted to understand clearly what they had on the murder and the crime scene, but she wanted his attention. He looked up, knowing it had to be Dr. Rena Stroud standing in his light.

"Having fun yet?" A grin curled her sumptuous lips where she sat, deflated, in Mike Eddy's chair across from Caul. "I know how you cops enjoy grim humor," she finished.

"Can I help you, Doctor?" He meant to give the so-called psychic nothing.

"Your suit betrays you as much as your voice, Aaron," she countered. "I'd say you haven't slept all night since you got the first call on this, right? Been out at the Sunshine Wharf alongside the Hilton since when? Three in the A.M.? Got another victim of the Heart Throb Killer, right?"

"Discovered by a party of sunrise worshippers—surfers—at ocean's edge."

"Just a kid, Donald, fourteen maybe, maybe fifteen? Runaway," she mused. "Streets here are full of 'em. Come to Daytona where it's warm year-round, but not for Donald, huh, Lieutenant?"

"Victim number five . . . all with corn-silk hair, washed up on a white sand beach. Fifth to fall prey to a vicious serial killer every detective in east central Florida would give his gold shield to put down."

"I hear the kid's chest was splayed open by some unknown weapon?"

"More likely a tool . . . according to the M.E.," he corrected. "Theorizes some ugly-assed tile cutter."

"Kid's heart ripped from his chest like the others?"

"Presumably the killer fed on it."

"Ugh!" She squirmed in response.

"Or worked some worse perversions on it." He thought he could make her squirm again; something sexy about it.

She didn't oblige him this time. Instead, Dr. Stroud's voice turned warm and conspiratorial, as if she felt his pain, he thought. "You know, Lieutenant Caul, you really shouldn't take each mutilation as if . . . well, so personally."

"Easier said than done."

"And you really ought not to take my being called in on the case so personally, either. I certainly don't want you to find me a . . . a threat."

"A *threat*? You hardly threaten me, Doctor. Man, you circus-show psychics are all alike."

"That remark might hurt if I were not a clinical psychiatrist as well as a psychic, Caul. And by the way, it's OK to call me doctor without making it sound like a four-letter word." The glint in her eye teased.

He frowned, thinking her beautiful. "What is it you want, Doctor?"

"I followed you from the debriefing to discuss—"

"Followed me? Really? You'll turn my head."

"—to discuss any fears you may harbor. . . ."

"Fears? Me? Really, Doctor, I have no fear of you."

"For your position then, with the Daytona Beach Police Department, perhaps?"

His laugh came out a sneer. "You people are really something. Some psychic. How do you square being a psychic with being such a poor judge of character?"

Dr. Stroud smiled and nodded. "All right, so you don't fear me, and you don't fear for your job, but you've made it perfectly clear you don't want me on the Heart Throb case. What is it, then, that you do fear, Lieutenant?"

He dug his fingers into both palms and made fists of them. "I'm not afraid of anything."

"No? Not even failure?"

He hesitated.

She parried, saying, "Come on, Lieutenant Caul. There's really not much separating the study of the criminal mind and *psi* powers." She pronounced *psi* as "sigh." "If you weren't so fearful, you and me together, we could make a powerful team."

Someone pushed through the front door, sending a shaft of brilliant Florida light between them, cutting like a mirrored knife. Again the Simpson file papers lifted as if possessed.

Caul opened his right hand and punctuated with it in meat-cleaver fashion. "No damn homicide investigation was ever solved by voodoo doctors, and no amount of symbolic wands you wave over the corpse is going to help us here. That clear enough?"

She slightly raised her shoulders and replied, "I understand, Caul. Understand your misgivings—concerns—at having me lay on hands, so to speak, talk to the M.E., see the body, read the protocol."

"Man, am I glad you understand."

"Buy me lunch, Detective."

"Me, buy you lunch? On what I make?"

"All right then . . .I'll buy."

"After all," he added, "you are on retainer from the city. Same goofy city that thinks you can perform magic."

"Yeah, good work if you can get it. So, are you *game*?"

"Game?"

"For lunch?"

"Yeah, sure I'm . . . game."

The Ocean Deck near the band shell on Atlantic Avenue exuded a party atmosphere at all times of the day: bright, cheery, open to the sea air, reggae music blasting. It attracted natives like Aaron Caul, the specialties being rock shrimp, buffalo shrimp, oysters, mahi-mahi, smoked mullet, Cajun crawfish, Florida gator tail, and a thing called barbecued grouper jaw. Rena Stroud found an odd elegance to the rustic, seashore café Caul had chosen for their first meal together. The waitresses wore cutoffs and T-shirts advertising the place. Rather than napkins, large Bounty paper towels sat perched at each table. The selection of music ranged from Bob Marley to Jimmy Buffet, nonstop, relenting for the occasional shout erupting from a nearby volleyball game on the beach. Rena stared out on a brilliant blue sky that had turned sunbathers and children into brown leather or red lobsters. Aside from the music and the frolic, the rhythmic roar of the surf created a hypnotic backdrop. Between sips of beer, detective and psychic looked out on people, young and old, strolling the promenade, running in the surf, enjoying the world's most famous beach.

After ordering, Rena Stroud said to Aaron Caul, "Isn't it just possible that you and your partner—Detective Eddy, right?—could benefit from a fresh perspective? Any fresh perspective?"

She felt his defenses rise like a thick door between them. "You mean someone not so emotionally involved, don't you?"

"You have to admit, you are pretty close to the case, emotionally."

He only breathed deeply and drank his imported dark beer. "Opted for the most expensive brew on the list," he replied, lifting the bottle in salute, "since you and the city're buying."

"You're quite good at that, aren't you?" she asked.

"At what?'

"Deflecting direct questions. I asked if a fresh perspective might not help, and you replied with an assumption about what my thoughts are."

"Well, being a cop, knowing interrogation techniques . . . all that," he replied with a slight shrug, "you take lessons from the past and apply them now."

"People, huh, Detective? How do you figure 'em? People lie, right?"

"Everybody lies about something, yeah. You got that right. In twenty-two years on the force—"

"You've seen it all, right?"

"Seen it all in the box."

"The interrogation sweatbox, yeah. But my guess, Caul, you learned the lessons of evasiveness much earlier in life."

"You questioning me *and* psychoanalyzing me, Doc? Guess there really is no such thing as a free lunch, now is there?"

"You got that right." Her eyes challenged his. "You do like to turn every question into a question of your own, don't you?"

"And you don't!" he nearly shouted. "Trust me, Doc, you don't want direct, not from me, you don't."

"Your father taught you control, didn't he?" *How's that for direct?* she thought.

"You don't know a damn thing about my father or me!"

"Taught you to avert your eyes?"

"That's enough."

"Ball your fists up?"

"Enough already with the third degree."

"To subvert your feelings?"

"I said—"

"I know, I know, Aaron, enough with the bull, I know." Frowning, relenting, she sat back, the booth seat groaning for her.

He opened his palms to her and smiled, saying, "Look, I don't have a problem with my father, and I didn't ask for any pseudo-psychobabble."

"I was told to do a profile."

"Profile? We have a killer profile and a victim profile in the murder book already. What could you possibly add to—"

"No, you misunderstand. Your superiors asked me in to do a profile on *you*."

"Me? Profile me? That's ridiculous."

"Is it? How is it ridiculous?"

"Profiles are for criminals, not cops . . . not the good guys."

"For psychos, and you're chasing a psycho, Detective, so it follows a psychic—a psychometrist, to be exact, and a psychiatrist to boot—can help you, Detective, detect a psycho's behavior. The department fears you may be too close to this case, so they want me to examine you to determine if—"

"Yeah, I see . . . to tell if I'm still working on all four burners, huh?"

"So your suspicions of me, your paranoia of me prove right, Caul. But remember, we all want the same thing, Caul. An end to the killing spree, to stop the person or persons who mutilated those boys, ripped their hearts out, and left their bodies for the crabs."

The subject of his own case made the man uneasy, she thought.

"Eddy and me, we've looked at all the similarities and cross-references of each victim. Been done. Eddy and me, we already—"

"I know. You know them intimately, every victim. Where they were minutes, hours before the murders, who they saw, spoke to, confronted, slept with—likes, dislikes, habits, jobs, sexual perversions," she rattled on.

"I know the drill," he replied, bored. "Profiles are to search for clues in a crime, so what're you talking about—this . . . profiling me? You profiling Eddy too? This something new? Profile the investigating cops?"

"Not Eddy . . . just you, Aaron Caul."

He stared deeply into her eyes now. "Just me?"

"Just need a little information, Lieutenant."

"Information?"

"Like why your father is such a sore point with you."

"Who said he was a sore point?"

"You did."

"The hell I did."

"Your body, then, tells me."

"My body?"

"Your heart rate increases when I ask about him, your sweat glands go into overdrive, your voice rises an octave or two."

"Eddy gave you this crap about my dad, didn't he?"

"No, you did, just now."

"You're no more psychic than my left toe."

"OK, Detective, you've unmasked me. Yes, I read your body language, and I do it well. I am a cunning woman. Fact is, Detective Eddy told me only that you would never *open up* about your father, but you have, in a sense."

He shook his head, grinned, laughed loudly, and said, "I get it. You're screwing with me, trying to get into my head."

"It's what profiles do, and if I do get inside, Caul, what will I find?"

The waitress interrupted them, asking after their comfort, her nails green with sparkles, the nose ring a match with the bellybutton ring. Caul didn't take notice, but Rena did, remarking on the glittering nails. "It must take you hours."

"No, not at all. . . ."

Caul turned to her once the waitress had left and bluntly said, "No doubt you've built quite a reputation for conjuring, Doctor, but we both know it's a sideshow parlor game you play, at best, so what can your so-called profile of me do to advance this case?"

"Why are you afraid of me, Aaron?"

"Damn it, I just don't want a circus atmosphere *contaminating* my case!"

"Are you worried about what your friends in the department, the press, and the public will think if you allow a psychic in on the case?"

He stared long at her. "We'll be viewed as a three-ring circus, clutching at straws, burning incense, and chanting."

Her probing, raven eyes set him off balance. "So appearances are important to you?"

"You know as well as I do that the mere suggestion of impropriety and some roving bastard working for the *News-Journal* would have our asses in a sling. One way or the other, they'll twist this into the department's mishandling and bungling. They always do."

"They'll say you're calling in ghost hunters and fortune-tellers from Cassadaga?"

"They'll say we're jacking off."

"First time I saw you in the briefing room, where all those pictures of all those dead boys are hanging, I'd have never taken you for camera-shy, Detective. Look, your partner, your captain, even the local FBI—they're all willing to give me a chance, but not you. Why is that? What are you really afraid of?"

"You tell me, if you won't accept my explanation." The bustle of people about them seemed to annoy Caul.

"Why haven't you been able to talk to your father about the case?"

"What?"

"He's a former cop, a detective, right?"

"Yeah, but . . . hey, how do you know I *haven't* discussed the case with him?"

"I'm psychic, remember? Good hit, huh?"

He clenched his teeth, realizing he had just given her evidence supporting her suspicion.

"So why not talk to the old man?" she pressed.

He squirmed in his seat, a bug under the scope. "Leave my dad out of this."

"Why?"

"I'm not in the market for psychoanalysis."

"How 'bout just a little understanding then? A little comfort, someone to confide in? Trust?"

He dropped his eyes, poked at his once-steaming clams that'd gone cold.

"Look," she continued, "my old man was a real bastard. Beat my mother and me senseless until one day something in me just snapped. I killed him with a butcher's knife, made it look like an intruder, and I got away with it. Mom and me, we lived with that lie until she died and I lived with it alone until . . . until just now, until I just told you, Aaron Caul. Feels good to tell somebody. Really does."

"We all got our . . . crosses to bear." Words remained his tool for keeping distance.

She further confessed, "I still know that my father, as mean and as vile as he was, is the reason I'm gifted, that this psychic gift is a by-product of the energies his anger and abuse unleashed. And, Aaron, I saw your cross when we met, were introduced, when I shook your hand. I saw it and I felt it. I know how utterly *alone* you are."

The look of fear grew like a cowl thrown over his features. He feared she knew . . . that she knew it all, everything . . . all that he ever was or ever would be. The thought terrified him.

"All got our crosses," he again muttered.

"I thought for a long time," she continued her confessional, "that I had overcome the pain, guilt, remorse, all the toxic stuff, you know? You can do that for a time, on a rational level—take charge."

"Yeah, maybe. . . ."

"You talk to yourself, talk yourself into things, into being the one in control, and by taking the power, you take away the hurt, the humiliation, suffering, grief, remorse, regret."

He shook his head slowly, saying, "I got no remorse, no regrets."

Ignoring this, she plowed on. "So, actually, we're all in it together, Aaron, and it's so easy to allow yourself to be a victim."

"A victim? I'm nobody's victim."

"But you are. We're all born victims in one fashion or another, Aaron. You may be a victim of yourself, your genes, even if what I'm reading is right."

"Victim of my green jeans, huh. That'd be my Levi's, right?" he joked and quickly swallowed the joke down with his beer.

"Your heredity, your lineage, your father, Aaron. And if it isn't genes, what is it? It's you and I as victims of our upbringing, our pasts, the world into which we fall at birth. Ante up, Aaron. You know it's true. You, me, all of us are *victims*."

He reached across the table and squeezed her hand, feeling a great sense of two-way warmth and energy igniting between them. She felt a release of pent-up anxieties in the same simple touch.

Allowing him to hold onto her hand, she continued. "But on an emotional level, Aaron, a strictly animalistic level of raw anxiety, no one is expected to cope with what we humans are capable of doing to one another. Sure, we might beat our feelings back for a time, hold them in check when we look at the brutalized body of a boy hardly in his teens, and we can anesthetize ourselves for the duration of a crime scene investigation, but our feelings will never be completely denied."

He pulled his hand away, a bit reluctantly, breaking contact. "You really ought to peddle your soft-soap psychic-detective act on Eddy, Doc. I don't need your brand of witchcraft, and neither does Daytona. We have enough weirdoes on A1A alone."

The insult she expected; he had fallen back.

"It's the little things that frighten you, Aaron. That much is clear now."

"So you read my file, so you think you can razzle-dazzle me with a choice piece of information here, a sleight of hand bit there. Sorry, Doc."

"Your file says nothing about a cramped, smelly crawl space below a stairwell where vermin and maggots resided, a place from which you can't seem to climb."

Hatred and fear darted from his cold, blue eyes. She saw the image she spoke of race through his mind, an image of a dirt-floor closet smelling of death and decay. "Bullshit," he muttered, "I don't crawl into any rabbit holes."

"Claustrophobic, I understand. But the rabbit hole I'm talking about is up here," she pointed to her head, "and it's one of your own making, Lieutenant."

He poked again at his food, smirked and shrugged. "Rabbit warrens of the mind, huh? Sorry to disappoint you, Doc, but again, you're way off. I go home from the job, I sleep like a baby."

"Yeah, like a baby smothering in a coffin."

The new image coming from her shocked him again. "Christ, guess you and my dad had a cozy little talk, huh?"

"Never met him, Aaron, only you."

"How did you know about my . . . my nightmares? I gotta know how you pulled that card outta your hat."

"I saw the cards—your nightmares—in here, in here." Again she pointed to her head. "When we *first* shook hands, in the debriefing room, remember? You could hardly look me in the eye."

"What else did you see?"

"Quite a lot, actually."

Again fear filled his eyes.

"I know it's unnerving to have someone know your inner thoughts, Aaron."

"Goddamn right."

"Look, I know you're surrounded by parasites in the department, on the street, in your dreams, all feeding on, or rather off, you."

"Maybe twelve years in Sex Crimes and ten in Homicide has an effect," he quietly agreed.

"Everybody siphoning off your energy, all feeding off a power you have."

"Yeah, yeah . . . I think I know what you mean."

"Sure you do. You've got a power that comes from within, a power the others can only hope to catch snatches of, maybe dream about. The street people you come into contact with, your colleagues, your partner, your captain, your father. They all want something from you, Aaron. Figure it out."

He smiled at the sentence formulating in his brain. "And what about you, Doc? You want a piece of me?" He didn't mask the sexual innuendo.

"Damned straight I do. We all want to reach out and touch the power residing so forcefully within you, Aaron. You're strong, virile, godly, and you wear a badge."

He toyed, childlike, with the salt cellar, blushing. "Whataya saying? That underneath this veneer of respectability, that you're just beating the bushes like any woman in search of a good man?"

She seductively licked her lips and stabbed at the air between them with a fork, saying, "You might say that I've set my sights for you, Lieutenant."

"Why me?" His smile had come full-blown now.

"People like you and me, Aaron, we're appealing because we're so sure of ourselves."

"Is that what your report, your profile, on me is going to say? Making me sound real modest here, Doc."

"People—especially young people—look at you, Aaron, and they see someone confident and self-assured, and they want some of that. You begin to represent some order amid the chaos of those tawdry streets out there."

"Flattery now."

"You can't deny that people gravitate to you, Aaron. To your power and charm. You use that charm like a lure."

"Like I lured you here? Come on, give me a break, Doc."

"And you have everyone around you buffaloed."

He sat up at this. "Buffaloed?"

"Into thinking you know more than they do."

"You trading compliments for insults and back again, Doctor?" His face had pinched now in confusion.

She brought her fist down on the table, making the forks dance and hop, her voice raised, saying, "Damn it, it has to do with perceptions. When others seek out people like you, like me, they're really looking for some part of that power—"

"What power?"

"The power they perceive us to have, Aaron."

"I have no such power or admirers. Ask anyone in the department."

"You've got it, I've got it . . . why deny it? So others come to drink from us, to fill their empty souls with us, and especially the helpless, the weak, the confused, the spiritually bereft, the homeless, the unloved, the lost. . . . They all come to us, Aaron, for . . . for some sort of *absolution*, which we may or may not wish to bestow."

For a moment, his eyes gave him away. Then it was gone, replaced by fear again, fear and anger exploding into words: "What's this absolution crap? Nobody's ever come to me for absolution. For that you gotta be a priest, not a murder cop."

His hands had tightened, but he held control, not allowing any fists. All the same, the effort alone told her something. She nearly whispered, "Every day, Aaron, people pull energy from me, just like you. But I gain from the experience. So did you, once. Before things changed." She reached across the table and took his hand in hers now. "For a moment, Aaron, *take from me.*"

He took the invitation further, reaching across to touch her breast. He allowed her warmth and the throbbing life within her to churn through his hand and into his being. A *throb, throb, throb* chorused from her and into him, her heartbeat like a mantra. There came a radiant heat between them, his passion stirring to a crescendo he could not fathom. Maybe she wasn't out to gain something from him when she said she liked his strength and power and charm. Maybe she really did like him for who he was.

"Just experience it," she whispered. "Don't analyze it, Detective."

"I'm . . . I'm doing just that."

Then he felt a strange, fuzzy, wormlike movement in his head, just to the left temple, followed by one at the right temple, and he saw how hard she was concentrating as she held firmly to his hand. He realized suddenly where she had gotten the details of his nightmares from. She'd been in his head the last time they had held hands, and here she was again—inside his head, roaming about in search of secrets he harbored there.

He tore his hand from her. "Damn you!" he cursed.

"What's wrong? There's no need for—"

"Whataya figure a little psychological blackmail is worth? You've got to know I'm feeling guilty about the deaths of all those . . . boys."

"I sensed as much, yes."

"Because I haven't been able to bring the monster to light, to *stop* him!"

She attempted to soothe him by nodding, agreeing with her eyes, and reaching out again for his hand, but he pulled away as if snake-bitten. "Cooperation on the case, Aaron, is all I've wanted from the start. That's all."

"That's hardly all that you want."

"My heart's an open book."

"And I read pretty damned well. And your heart's telling me that you think I'm too emotionally unstable to remain on this case, that maybe somewhere along the way I've lost sight . . . ahhh . . . direction, that I'm too involved."

"Now wasn't that good for you, Aaron?"

"Whataya talking about? Good? What's good?"

"Confession."

"What confession?"

"What confession? I'm saying what you think."

She smiled, rose to her feet, and winked. "I've got what I came for, Caul."

"What you came for?"

"Like you said, 'No such thing as a free lunch,' Detective. Certainly all those boys learned that. Funny thing, though, Aaron. . . ."

"What's that?"

"I really thought that having lunch with the notorious Heart Throb Killer would be more . . . I don't know . . . sexually *stimulating?*"

He stood now, reached out and grabbed hold of her wrist, squeezing hard. "You spread that lie and I'll sue your pretty ass for every penny it's worth, lady."

"Tell me, Aaron, why is it you always prefer seeing the parents of the dead boys? Why is it Mike Eddy is never put to that awful task? Can it be because you feel a sense of closure when you can see the pain and suffering you inflict?"

"That's a disgusting thing to say." His grip tightened with anger.

"Release me," she firmly ordered.

Gritting his teeth, his eyes boring into her, hatred pure and unleashed, he growled, "You could be the next body to wash up in Daytona, Doctor. You know that? You threaten me, I'll come after you." She clearly saw the eyes now of a madman.

Rena tore her arm from the demon's grip. "The M.E.'s waiting for me back at the Crime Lab, Aaron. Have a date to lay on hands over that last boy, Simpson. See what that turns up."

"Your mumbo-jumbo will never prove a thing."

"Maybe not, but now you know somebody walking this earth knows your secret, Aaron, knows your soul. Others know too. I'm wearing a wire, Aaron."

"Not a word we said here will hold up in a court of law, and I said nothing whatever to incriminate myself."

"You're sure of that? Fathers and sons, Aaron, that's what your rage is all about, fathers and sons, obedience and disobedience, good boys and bad boys. I talked Judge Steinberg into a warrant to wear this wire, and a lot of people are listening to us now, Aaron. Everyone knows but you!"

"You goddamn bitch! You seduced me!"

"What're you going to plead, entrapment?"

"You set me up, damn right, bitch, entrapment!"

"You damned fool. I'm a psychometrist, so you have to know that I gain psychic impressions through touch. *You* touched *me,* remember? And while you had your hands all over me, Caul, you in effect seduced yourself. And the last time I looked, this quasi-archaic state of ours still has some laws on the books protecting its women because—"

"You lousy bitch!" he repeated, clearing the table with his massive forearms, causing everyone in the Ocean Deck to gasp and stare.

"After all," she calmly continued, "we are, according to the sovereign State of Florida, the weaker sex, and for that reason, we still sit rather high upon a pedestal and find ourselves protected by men in power, like your captain, like Judge Steinberg, and I suspect a few of the men in your Internal Affairs Division."

"*Witch!*"

"I like the sound of that much better, Aaron, and I'll see you at your execution."

Hole in the Boat

ERIK WIKLUND

He was trolling for kings in the gulf off Sarasota on a brisk March morning and daydreaming about baseball. It was his every-day, every-night fantasy. He, John Roby, forty-one-year-old rookie pitching sensation. Ridiculously fast fastball. Knuckler his catcher simply couldn't handle. No hitters, one hitters every time out, and he could hit.

His only problem, as the author of this scenario, was that he could never get himself to make even one pitch, obsessed as he was about the details. What team did he play for? How often did he pitch? How did he and his catcher communicate? What was his salary situation? Were he and Karen still married? But John, the dreamer, didn't mind that John, the pitcher, stood frozen on the mound. He liked ironing out the details. That in itself was the challenge. The finer the weaving, the more real the feeling.

You could be living in a fugue state, a friend had told him, when John had mentioned his fantasy over drinks. His friend had read about fugues. The way he understood it, some people live halfway between the real world and an invented one. It's a psychological disorder, he said. John said he never mixed his fantasy with real life, so there wasn't any problem. As proof, he pointed out that Karen knew nothing about his being a major league pitcher. No, he told his friend, he was just doing Walter Mitty very thoroughly, in, say, a mature way.

Anyway, out on the gulf, John was working on whether or not he and Karen were still married when the bilge pump went on and expelled about a gallon of water, for about the fifth time since he'd left his dock. Something was wrong.

On his way back in, he anchored the twenty-footer over the huge sand flat bordering Big Pass, stripped to his shorts, grabbed his dive mask, and hopped into the waist-deep water. Chilly, but not too bad, there on the flat. He enjoyed swimming there in the winter anyway, ignoring the local heated pool a block from his house, to get his exercise a tougher, more natural way. A sportsman, he stayed tan year-round and kept his six-two, one-ninety frame fairly hard.

It took him only a couple of dives to find it. A small, clean hole, maybe an eighth of an inch in diameter, about six inches below the waterline, midway on the starboard side. Manmade—it had to be. Nothing eats fiberglass, and the hole was too perfect and free of any nearby shearing or crazing to have been caused by any impact. Someone had drilled a hole in his boat.

He seized on the run-in he'd had just the night before with the snook spearers. He'd noticed them from his kitchen window. Three beering twenty-somethings in a sparkling new twin-engine had cozied up to the halo of light surrounding the dock across the canal from his. One of them had a speargun and was on his belly on the bow. The others were crouching, watching. Sure enough, they got a snook and were damned tickled about it. John had then gone out onto his dock and shouted at them about it being illegal and so forth. The jerks had given it back to him real ugly and taken their sweet time leaving.

So it must have been them, John thought as he climbed back into his boat. The hole almost certainly wasn't there before the confrontation, he knew, because he'd taken the boat out briefly that afternoon and the pump hadn't gone on at all. But why not some easier form of vandalism? Maybe they thought he might have memorized their boat's number (he hadn't). A little hole, that was clever, sly. All right, but did they just happen to have a hand drill, a nearly extinct tool, onboard? The hole had to have been made with a hand drill because a battery-operated drill wouldn't work underwater, of course, and because that part of the hull was inaccessible from inside the boat, being below the deck and not close to any of the deck plates, the removable discs that let you reach certain areas down there. Or had they stayed hot enough to go home, maybe formulating their plan on the way, get a hand drill, and come back? One or the other, John figured, since he could think of no other possibilities.

John went home, found Karen in the kitchen and told her about the hole. "Bet it was those guys you argued with last night," she said. "The last word."

"That was my first thought."

"What are you going to do?"

"What can I do? Fix it."

There was just enough light left, after filleting the two kings he'd caught, for John to go to the boat supply store, find a patching compound you could apply underwater, and fill the hole. Then he sat on the boat, in the dark, smoking and waiting to see if the bilge would come on. "Phosphaditylserine, phosphaditylserine." The name of one of the brain pills he'd lately "prescribed" for himself to complement his fitness regimen kept running through his head, after a while like Chinese water torture, so he let his thoughts go where they wanted. Revenge. What he'd like to do, and what he would do, if he ran into the punks again. He was imagining shotgun blasts point blank to the face when Karen came out.

"Is it working?"

"I think so. Pump hasn't gone off."

"Mind if I sit with you?"

"I was just coming in."

John made his own nutritional dinner (he couldn't count on Karen to do it right) and after watching some TV with her, he told her he was going to the den to read. She shaded to sullen, icy, as if that helped John become more communicative, more intimate. A little later he heard her go to the bedroom and close the door. He moved his reading to the sunroom, where he could see the canal, and stayed up late.

The punks didn't come. He wasn't sure what he'd say or do if they did, outside of reporting them to the Marine Patrol for spearing game fish, if they came to do that. He determined to put the matter behind him and slipped into bed to begin considering the terms of his contract with either the Devil Rays or the Marlins. He preferred the National League, but the Devil Rays would be right next door in Tampa. He decided to develop different contract offers from each team before making his choice.

The next few days were typically uneventful, and that, as usual, surprised John, for he held the prestigious and potentially thrilling position of customer service representative for a paint manufacturer, a job he'd had to take a couple of years ago when he had come to terms with his dwindling success as an artist. Painter lately, that is, of insipid beach scenes, the only genre he could count on to make a hundred bucks every week or so, and only during tourist season. Of course, it was merely coincidence that each of his "careers" included paint. He shrugged off the irony and continued to do the paintings, without enthusiasm and without going to the beach, because it paid more by the hour than did the paint company. It paid for boat gas.

Karen kept to herself most of the week, doing her real estate deals, e-mailing friends and family, and watching satellite movies. She'd done a pretty good job of becoming more independent over the last couple of months, and for that John felt better for her. Her constant urging to work with her on their relationship was slackening, and John took that as a sign that she was beginning to understand he had to pull himself up first. If she didn't think he could, he'd understand if she left, he'd tell her. And he'd praise her for trying anything she could think of to help, even though he ignored her advice. It was all out on the table.

He went fishing Wednesday night in the bay and caught some snook and a black drum down in Snook Alley, and then again on Thursday night, closer to home, around Otter Key. That's when he saw the punks again, idling up to a dock on South Lido, a quarter mile or so from him. It was the dock lights that gave them away. A frisson of adrenaline rose through him. He watched them drop anchor. That's not where they live, he thought. Out came the speargun. John switched off his stern light, breaking the law in a small way himself in doing so, so there'd be no chance they'd recognize him or his boat. Now what? Radioing the Marine Patrol would be pointless, since he'd never seen them anywhere near this area at night. He'd call them tomorrow, though. Maybe they'd follow through on it. He got his binoculars out and wrote down the boat's number. Another confrontation? What would cursing and denials get him? No, he'd follow them, see where they came from, then decide what to do. He did want to do something.

They didn't spear anything at that dock or at the other two they visited afterwards. John tailed them at a discreet distance until they pulled up to a dock on a Bird Key canal, just a mile or so from his place. They tied up and went into the house on the property. No lift—it stays in the water. John drew close enough to see the driveway and anchored. A Cherokee, a pickup, and something like a Lexus. Twenty minutes later two of the punks left in the Cherokee. The pickup's the third one's, John figured. And the Lexus his daddy's, or mommy's, or grandfather's, or uncle's, and so is the boat. A few minutes later the third one left in the pickup, and John left too.

John didn't call the Marine Patrol the next day. On his lunch break, he coughed up seventy dollars for a hand drill and two dollars for an eighth-inch brad-point bit. The brad-point would get the hole started, keep the bit from sliding around on the slick, hard gel coat covering the fiberglass. He had a lot of tools at home but neither of these things.

OK, so the boat didn't belong to the punks. It was the message that mattered. If they want to come after my boat again, fine, John thought. Theirs cost ten times what I paid for mine, and I do most of my own repair and maintenance. If they come after me, that's fine too. I'll take a broken nose in exchange for what I'd get from the lawsuit. I could use the money, and there's plenty where that boat and house came from. And even if they didn't drill my boat, there's still the snook-spearing issue. But although he tried to ignore it—because recognizing it would strip the logic from his intentions—John knew he was acting largely out of boredom. Thinking about shotgunning them was fun. The adrenaline rush he got when he saw them the night before felt peculiarly good, and so would this.

Karen was out when John got home, so he immediately stowed the drill and his wetsuit on the boat. He hadn't told her he'd seen the punks, and he wouldn't tell her about this. He'd take her to an early movie—it was the weekend after all—then tell her he had to get out there, the fishing was supposed to be hot, hot, hot in spite of—no, because of—the low front that had pushed in earlier in the day, bringing rain and wind, which was good, John told himself, because the last thing he needed was a nice, quiet evening, seeing as how close together and near the water those Bird Key houses are. Karen would probably even give him a point or two for putting the movie before the fishing.

Sometime after midnight, he anchored along a stretch of seawall where densely growing sea grapes gave him some cover. The wind and rain had intensified. No one was out. And it all went very easily, both adrenaline and revenge factors high and satisfying. Rainsuit and moccasins off, wetsuit on. Water cold at first, then OK with the wetsuit. Slow breaststroke, with the drill, along the seawall to the side of the boat against the dock. Back against a dock piling, head above water, drill hole a little under the waterline, same place they drilled his. Swim back. No point waiting for the bilge pump to come on, he'd decided earlier. It would go on anyway to expel the rainwater. The little hole would add just a steady trickle, unless . . . Why hadn't he thought of this? Why hadn't he considered the possibility that the hull's foam core, there for flotation, might run behind the hole he'd drilled, keeping water from getting in? He wondered if they'd worried about the same thing when they'd drilled his boat, *if* they'd drilled his boat. He turned on his console light and looked at the bit. Some fiberglass shavings were stuck to it but no foam. Light off. If my boat took on water, theirs should too, he thought. But the question still nagged him as he sat there growing cold, the warmed, insulating water having drained from his wetsuit. Best to figure this out somewhere else, he decided, and he slipped away.

The lights were off at home. He quietly took everything, unused fishing tackle included, to the garage, where he hung his wetsuit out of sight in the water heater closet and stashed the drill, after rinsing it in the utility sink, in a box of old junk. Karen knew his tools pretty well. If she were to see a hand drill at his workbench, he'd have some explaining to do, since he'd told her the hole in his boat must have been drilled with one. On his way back, he'd decided he'd have to drill another hole, bigger this time and deep enough to penetrate any foam core, if his eighth-incher hadn't done the job. Sometime tomorrow he'd watch their boat from as far away as possible to see if the pump was coming on, or better, to find someone addressing the problem. If indeed his drill job had worked, he'd stay up the next two or three nights to keep an eye on his own boat, ready to face off against the punks. If it hadn't, he'd drill the bigger hole tomorrow night, bad weather or good. At his workbench, he opened his drill bit case to put the brad-point bit away with his regular bits and looked at the eighth-inch slot to see if it was occupied. It was, but something about the bit there looked funny. Unlike the others, it was rusty and. . . . He took it out and examined it. Rusty, and there were shavings on it, a couple of little curlicues of . . . fiberglass? Another adrenaline rush, this one not good. Karen?

He stayed there for a good while, sorting out the possibilities, eventually boiling it all down to there being a small chance that he'd forgotten he'd used that bit on the boat himself, gotten salt water on it, and put it away without cleaning it. Just a small to medium-small chance. But Karen going out and buying a hand drill?

In the morning he joined her in the sunroom, where she was reading the paper, and put the drill bit down in front of her. Nothing unusual about her expression, just raised eyebrows.

"Did you drill the hole in my boat?"

Still no sign. Same raised eyebrows, an angled stare.

"It's what I do, John. Drill holes in boats."

"Seriously."

And they got into it fairly deeply, John telling her he knew she hated the boat because she thought he used it to avoid her, Karen telling him he couldn't have found a better way to show her how little he cared for her than to accuse her of such a thing. They explored a few tangents of those themes, John atypically piloting the argument, before he tried a softer approach, asking her to understand how puzzling this was to him, disturbing even. Karen slumped in her chair. Gently:

"John, do you think you might have drilled the hole yourself?"

A strange sensation went through his head. An out-of-left-field question, that was why. A spin to try to match his seemingly ludicrous query. He shook his head pityingly and turned away.

"Think about it," she said. "Go take your dog saliva." And she went back to the paper.

He got his fishing tackle and took off in the boat. Dog saliva. Karen would pick at his brain supplements, whimsically taking one or another seemingly at random, despite his telling her again and again that you had to take them regularly to get any effect. Some of them were expensive, more than a dollar a pill. He wouldn't have minded the cost if she'd used them right, but picking at them was a waste of money, and it threw the relative quantities out of whack. So he'd relabeled them in a humorous way, he felt, with stickers he'd composed on the computer: dog saliva, buffered asbestos, and so on. He'd expected her to laugh with him about it, but she hadn't. "Dog saliva." "Think about it." But what, exactly, had she suggested? That he'd blacked out and unwittingly drilled his own boat? Amnesia? Or that he purposely staged the whole thing so he'd have a drama to enjoy? John laughed aloud and shook his head. He didn't have to think this through. He knew the only way she'd admit drilling the hole—if she had drilled it, damn it—was if he told her he understood that by drilling the hole she was simply, dramatically, illustrating the state of their relationship. He'd have to recognize the urgency of her last-resort method to prompt him to change, to promise to improve, to at least try. He'd have to tell her this time would be different from the hollow promises he'd made before. He'd have to sell the boat, and do this, that, and a bunch of other things to underscore his commitment. Well, he could easily understand those motives, he could tell her, but he couldn't just flick a switch and make the turnaround, because there wasn't such a switch. Still, she'd require all of this, and nothing short of it, before she'd admit it. If she'd done it.

It was cloudy and windy, but the rain had passed. He anchored a hundred and fifty yards from their boat and made like a Saturday-morning fisherman for an hour, by his watch, but their pump didn't go on. At one point he hooked a jack and laughed out loud at himself for the effort it took not to take his eyes from the boat while playing and releasing the little fireball.

After going out to buy a half-inch, foot-long paddle bit, he washed Karen's car, something he'd never done, seeing as she had it done professionally once or even twice a week as a function of her business. She rarely had it waxed, though, expensive as it was, so he did that for her too, to try to restore equilibrium and to buy another "fishing trip." She thanked him quietly and avoided him the rest of the day.

At one in the morning, under a cloudy sky, he put the tip of the paddle bit in the small hole he'd drilled the night before and cranked it through the fiberglass. There *was* some mild resistance behind it, transmitted noticeably now, he guessed, by the bigger, flat blade. He drove the bit all the way in. He was only halfway back to his boat when he heard splashing. He heard it again as he started his motor and turned to see a cylinder of water arcing from a bilge port near the stern, five seconds. Now we're talking, he thought.

Days passed and John lost a lot of sleep waiting for the punks to show, but they never did. He came home from work that Friday to a half-empty house and a short note. She'd left him. A phone number, for practical purposes, she said—no further explanation. John couldn't afford the rent by himself and couldn't imagine a roommate, so at the end of the month he moved to an apartment. He kept his boat on a trailer in the parking lot but didn't use it much because launching it was a pain. One day, out of idle curiosity, he looked up fugue states on the Internet and came away satisfied that he wasn't afflicted. But he did imagine himself in his later years babbling out loud about baseball, and thought he'd better keep taking his brain pills.

# Author Biographies

David Ash was born in Miami but now calls Longwood, Florida, home. He is a veteran, ex-cop, former painter, construction worker, and cargo handler. He has studied creative writing with James Lee Burke, Jim Hall, and Les Standiford.

E. C. (Gene) Ayres is an award-winning novelist, film, and animation writer/producer whose first mystery, *Hour of the Manatee*, won the St. Martin's Press/Private Eye Writers Association of America's Best First Novel contest. The second in the series featuring P.I. Tony Lowell was *Eye of the Gator*, followed by *Night of the Panther* and *Lair of the Lizard*. After graduating from Syracuse University and the Newhouse School of Communications, he worked in New York, producing short films for *Sesame Street*, ABC, and Time-Life Television as well as public television. In Los Angeles, he wrote for commercial television, particularly animation—the subject of his next book. He has been a feature development writer for Jack Arnold at Universal Pictures and won a Warner Brothers Writers' Fellowship in 1982. Ayres lives on Florida's Gulf Coast.

Wayne Barcomb served as president of a Boston-based college textbook publishing house before becoming a full-time professional writer. He was also chairman of the Executive Council for the Higher Education Division of the Association of American Publishers. Throughout his publishing career, he was a freelance writer, contributing to the *Boston Globe, Boston Herald, Boston Magazine*, and *Publishers Weekly*, among other publications. Additionally, he has written three novels and is at work on the fourth. He also recently completed a children's book and is a regular contributor to *Sarasota Magazine* and *City Tempo Magazine*. Barcomb and his wife, Susan, live in Sarasota, Florida.

Nancy Bartholomew is a psychotherapist in private practice who lives with her husband, two children, and a very large, very stupid dog named Bailey in Greensboro, North Carolina. Her first novel, *The Miracle Strip*, introduced tough girl/exotic dancer/ amateur sleuth, Sierra Lavotini. The second book in the Sierra Lavotini series, *Dragstrip*, was published in September 1999. The series grew out of "Sierra Reveals All," which won the 1996 Sleuthfest Short Story Contest. Bartholomew's first book in the Maggie Reid series, *Your Cheatin' Heart*, was also published in September 1999, and the author is also hard at work on her first police procedural.

David Beaty was born in Brazil of American parents. Raised in Miami, he worked in Greece, England, and Brazil before returning to Florida. A graduate of Columbia University, he earned an M.F.A. degree in creative writing from Florida International University in 1998, studying with Les Standiford and James W. Hall. Beaty currently lives in Coral Gables, Florida.

Edna Buchanan is the author of the Britt Montero series set in Miami. *Contents Under Pressure* began the series and was named one of the best works of crime fiction by the *Los Angeles Times Book*

Review and one of the best mysteries by the *San Francisco Chronicle*. The series continued in *Miami, It's Murder*, which was nominated for an Edgar Award. During her legendary career at the *Miami Herald*, Buchanan covered the police beat, garnering the Green Eyeshade Award for deadline reporting and the Pulitzer Prize. *The Corpse Had a Familiar Face*, an autobiographical account of covering Miami crime, was published in 1987. Touchstone Pictures' first made-for-television movie was based on *The Corpse Had a Familiar Face*, starring the late Elizabeth Montgomery as Edna. *Nobody Lives Forever* (1990) was nominated for an Edgar Award. Her latest novel, *Garden of Evil*, was published in 1999. Buchanan lives in Miami, Florida, with her two dogs and five cats.

Stanley Ellin (1916–1985) was the winner of three Edgar Awards as well as the Mystery Writers of America's prestigious Grand Master Award for lifetime achievement. He was the author of fourteen diverse novels and numerous award-winning and often anthologized short stories. Ellin lived in Brooklyn, New York, and Miami Beach, Florida, both of which were frequent settings for his fiction.

DeLoris Stanton Forbes is the author of more than forty books, beginning with *Annalisa*, followed by *If She Should Die, They're Not Home Yet*, and, most recently, *Graves, Worms and Epitaphs*. *Go to Thy Deathbed* was made into the film *Reflections of Fear*, and *Grieve for the Past* received the Mystery Writers of America Scroll Award for best mystery novel of the year. Forbes is currently writing short stories and published two manuscripts in 1999.

Carolina Garcia-Aguilera is the creator of a mystery series featuring private investigator Lupe Solano, including *Bloody Waters, Bloody Shame, Bloody Secrets*, and *A Miracle in Paradise*. After graduating from the University of South Florida with an M.B.A. in finance, Garcia-Aguilera became a licensed private investigator and started a detective agency in Miami, in order to gain the experience to authentically plot and write detective stories, in which she'd been interested all her life. Born in Cuba, Garcia-Aguilera has traveled extensively and lives in Miami Beach, Florida. She is currently working on the fifth book in the Lupe Solano series.

Jeremiah Healy, a graduate of Rutgers College and Harvard Law School, was a professor at the New England School of Law for eighteen years. He is the creator of John Francis Cuddy, a Boston-based private investigator. Healy's first book, *Blunt Darts*, was selected by *The New York Times* as one of the seven best mysteries of 1984. His second work, *The Staked Goat*, received the Shamus Award for Best Private Eye Novel of 1986. Twelve of Healy's books and short stories have been Shamus nominees, and his later novels include *So Like Sleep, Swan Dive, Yesterday's News, Right to Die, Shallow Graves, Foursome, Act of God, Rescue, Invasion of Privacy*, and *The Only Good Lawyer*. A legal thriller, *The Stalking of Sheilah Quinn*, and a collection of his short stories, *The Concise Cuddy*, were published in 1998. Healy lives in Boston's Back Bay most of the year, with three-month winter stints in Ft. Lauderdale, Florida.

Stuart Kaminsky is the author of forty novels, five biographies, four textbooks, and thirty-five short stories. He also has screen-writing credits for five films, including *Once Upon a Time in America, Enemy Territory*, and *Hidden Fears*. He is the immediate past president of the Mystery Writers of America and has been nominated for five Edgar Awards, a Shamus Award, and a McCavity Readers Choice Award. He won both an Edgar and the Prix De Roman D'Aventure of France for his novel *A Cold Red Sunrise*. Kaminsky earned a B.S. in journalism and an M.A. in English from the University of Illinois, as well as a Ph.D. in speech from Northwestern University. He taught at Northwestern for sixteen years and created a course called "Creative Writing for the Media" before becoming a professor at Florida State University. He lives with his wife and family in Sarasota, Florida.

David A. Kaufelt was born in New Jersey and earned a B.S.E. from the University of Pennsylvania's Wharton School of Finance and Commerce. He received an M.A. degree from New York University and spent two years in the Army. Not to be considered highlights of his life, these events nonetheless prepared him for seven years on Madison Avenue, writing such unforgettable ad campaigns as "Choosy mothers choose Jif," "Take Ex-Lax tonight— have a good day tomorrow," and "Get to the root of your dandruff problem—use Tegrin shampoo." He also wrote a novel, *Six Months with an Older Woman*, which was made into a film starring John Ritter. Fifteen more novels followed, including *Silver Rose, American Tropic*, and, most recently, *The Ruthless Realtor Murders*, third in the Wynn Lewis mystery series. Kaufelt and his wife, Lynn, live in Key West, Florida, with their son, Jackson.

Peter King has written over 40 stage plays and 30 radio plays, as well as 150 articles and short stories for leading magazines in the U.S. and England. He has written two travel books on France and one on Florida. His culinary mysteries series, featuring the Gourmet Detective, presents a new title each year; the fifth will appear in 2000.

John Lutz is the author of more than thirty novels and two hundred short stories and is a past president of Mystery Writers of America and Private Eye Writers of America. His novel *SWF Seeks Same* was made into the movie *Single White Female*, and he co-authored the screenplay for the movie *The Ex*, adapted from his novel of the same title. He has received the Edgar Award, the Shamus Award, and the Trophee 813 Award. Lutz is the author of two private eye series. His latest novel, *Final Seconds*, co-authored with David August, has been optioned for film. Lutz divides his time between St. Louis, Missouri, and Sarasota, Florida.

T. J. MacGregor is a former Spanish teacher and prison librarian. She is the author of nineteen suspense novels, most recently *The Seventh Sense*. She lives in Boynton Beach, Florida, with her husband, Rob, also an author.

Harold Q. Masur is the author of fourteen novels and several hundred short stories. A graduate of New York University's School of Law, he is a popular lecturer and occasionally teaches writing. The Pentagon has called him to Washington for imaginative thinking sessions on international tension areas. A past president of and General Counsel for the Mystery Writers of America, Masur lives in Boca Raton, Florida.

Stuart McIver, current president of the Florida Chapter of the Mystery Writers of America, is the author of over four hundred magazine stories and twelve books, including *Hemingway's Key West*, *Dreamers, Schemers, and Scalawags*, and *Murder in the Tropics*. He has also written nearly ninety scripts for documentary films, which have netted him two CINE Golden Eagle Awards and a Silver Medal at the Venice, Italy, film festival. A native of North Carolina and a graduate of the University of North Carolina, McIver has lived in south Florida since 1962. He lives in Lighthouse Point with his wife, Joan, also an author.

Billie Sue Mosiman is the author of *Night Cruise*, which was nominated by the Mystery Writers of America for an Edgar Award for the best paperback novel in 1993. In 1996 her book *Widow* was nominated for the Bram Stoker Award for superior novel. A native of Mobile, Alabama, Mosiman is a skillful practitioner of the South's story-telling tradition. She has published 8 novels and roughly 150 short stories in magazines and anthologies. In addition, she worked with Martin H. Greenberg as editor of *Death in Dixie*, an anthology of murder mysteries from the South. She lives in Texas and is currently working on two new novels. CNN recently gave Mosiman an "Author's Board" on its interactive website.

Robert J. Randisi has written close to three hundred books. He was born in Brooklyn, New York, where he lived for forty years before moving to St. Louis, Missouri. He founded the Private Eye Writers of America, created the Shamus Award, and co-founded *Mystery Scene Magazine* and the American Crime Writers League.

Les Standiford recently released *Presidential Deal,* sixth in his series featuring Miami building contractor John Deal. He wrote the screenplay adaptation of his first novel, *Spill,* and contributed to *Naked Came the Manatee,* which also included stories by James W. Hall, Carl Hiaasen, and Elmore Leonard. Standiford is a former recipient of the Frank O'Connor Award for Short Fiction and the National Endowment of the Arts Fellowship in Fiction and is a former screenwriting fellow and graduate of the American Film Institute in Los Angeles. He is currently a professor of English and director of the Creative Writing Program at Florida International University. His novel *Black Mountain* will be published early in 2000.

Robert W. Walker was born in Corinth, Mississippi, and grew up in Chicago, where he attended Northwestern University and earned a master's degree in English education. Walker began writing at age thirteen and has published thirty-five novels in a variety of categories. His most popular books have been his *Instinct* series, whose central character is medical examiner and FBI agent Jessica Coran. He also writes the popular *Edge* series with Cherokee Indian Detective Lucas Stonecoat. Walker's books have been published in Great Britain and Japan. He currently lives in Palm Coast, Florida, and teaches writing classes at Daytona Beach Community College.

Erik Wiklund has written and directed a wide variety of films and television programs. He won the 1986 Writers Guild of America annual award for excellence for his writing on ABC-TV's *Ryan's Hope*. A former professor of film and TV production at the University of Vermont and Florida State University, he now lives in Sarasota, Florida.